Dear R

Sequel
will reunite with Gwendolyn Taylor who made her first
appearance in 1994 in *Happily Ever After*.

Boston-bred newspaper journalist Gwen relocates to
Louisiana with the intention of restoring an antebellum
mansion left to her by a great-aunt. However, her plans
do not include solving a forty-year-old murder mystery,
learning about her late aunt's secret past or falling in love
with St. Martin Parish's sheriff, Shiloh Harper.

The untamed beauty of the bayou, Creole dialects and spicy
Cajun dishes are merely a backdrop to the heat served up
by Gwen and Shiloh in this passionate summer read that is
a continuation of stories linked by kinship and love.

Yours in romance,

Rochelle Alers

A
TIME to KEEP

ROCHELLE Alers

A TIME to KEEP

PRINTED IN U.S.A.

ARABESQUE®

If you purchased this book without a cover you should be aware
that this book is stolen property. It was reported as "unsold and
destroyed" to the publisher, and neither the author nor the
publisher has received any payment for this "stripped book."

ISBN: 1-58314-654-7

A TIME TO KEEP
Copyright © 2006 by Rochelle Alers

HAPPILY EVER AFTER
First published by Pinnacle Books in 1994
Copyright © 1994 by Rochelle Alers

All rights reserved. The reproduction, transmission or utilization
of this work in whole or in part in any form by any electronic, mechanical
or other means, now known or hereafter invented, including xerography,
photocopying and recording, or in any information storage or retrieval
system, is forbidden without written permission. For permission please
contact Kimani Press, Editorial Office, 233 Broadway, New York, NY
10279 U.S.A.

All characters in this book have no existence outside the imagination of
the author and have no relation whatsoever to anyone bearing the same
name or names. They are not even distantly inspired by any individual
known or unknown to the author, and all incidents are pure invention.
Any resemblance to actual persons, living or dead, is entirely coincidental.

® and TM are trademarks. Trademarks indicated with ® are registered in
the United States Patent and Trademark Office, the Canadian Trade Marks
Office and/or other countries.

www.kimanipress.com

Printed in U.S.A.

CONTENTS

CONTENTS

A TIME TO KEEP

Everything that happens in this world
happens at the time God chooses.
— *Ecclesiastes* 3:1

Chapter 1

The ring tone from Gwendolyn Taylor's cell phone playing Beethoven's Symphony no. 3 in E-flat major pulled her attention away from the panoramic landscape of Cajun country. She'd just passed a road sign that indicated she'd entered the town limits of Franklin, Louisiana.

Looking at the caller ID on her cell, she pushed a button on the hands-free receiver. "Yes, Lauren."

"Are we there yet?" Laughter followed the childish query.

Shaking her head and sucking her teeth, Gwen said loudly, "Girl, you need a job that takes you out of the house, because you're beginning to sound like your kids." Lauren, a literary researcher and her husband, bestselling author, Caleb Samuels, both worked from home.

"Are you there yet?" Lauren repeated.

She glanced at the GPS navigational screen. "Almost."

"How is Louisiana?"

"It's different from our neck of the woods."

Lauren's soft laughter came through the speaker. "Don't you mean *my* neck of the woods?"

Gwen smiled. "My driver's license still has a Boston address, my car a Massachusetts plate, and when I open my mouth and say *pawk* everyone will know that I will never be crowned Miss Sweet Tater Pone."

"You're right about that," Lauren agreed. "But you should know you're much too mature for an insipid beauty contest."

Gwen's delicate jaw dropped. "Mature? Speak for yourself, Mrs. Samuels. You're the one with three children, and a possible fourth on the way."

"I told you before that Royce is going to be my last baby."

"You said that after you had Kayla."

"He just happened, cuz."

"Getting pregnant doesn't just happen Lauren Taylor-Samuels. Didn't you tell me that you wind up pregnant whenever you and Caleb take afternoon naps together?"

"For your information, Miss Know-It-All, Cal and I no longer nap together in the afternoon."

"Are you saying you guys have given up knockin' boots?"

Lauren laughed again. "I refuse to answer that question on the grounds that it might incriminate me."

Gwen took another quick glance at the navigational screen. She was almost there. "You guys should have one more and make it an even four."

"I'll have one more if you have one."

"Can't, cuz. I don't have a man."

"You don't want a man, Gwen."

"Correction, Lauren. I don't need a man."

"You're going to need one to make a baby."

"Not if I go the test tube route."

"No! You can't, Gwendolyn."

Lauren only called her by her full name whenever she was upset with something Gwen said or did. "I can and I will if I'm not married by the time I'm thirty-eight."

"You better start looking for a man now because you'll be looking at thirty-eight in less than four years."

Slowing her late-model sedan, Gwen came to a complete stop at an intersection. Looking both ways she continued in a southwesterly direction. "So will you, Lauren Vernice Taylor-Samuels." She and Lauren were first cousins, born weeks apart.

"But, I'm the one with the husband and children."

"You don't have to rub it in, Lauren."

"I'm not rubbing it in. You would've married years before me if you hadn't broken off your engagement to Craig Hemming."

"Craig was wrong for me. He was too old and too posses-sive. I can't stand a man who won't allow me my space."

"Is that why you're running away, Gwen? Because you need space?"

"You know I'm not running away." She didn't want to argue with Lauren about why she'd sold her condominium and resigned her position as a lifestyle writer at the *Boston Gazette* to move fifteen hundred miles away and live in a house she'd inherited from a relative she hadn't seen in more than twenty years.

"I don't want you to think I'm giving you a hard time," Lauren continued in a tone she used when correcting her children. "It's just that I miss you already. You're more than a cousin. You are my sister."

"Stop it," Gwen chided softly, as her eyes filled with tears. "I can't drive and cry at the same time. I'll call you tomorrow after I see what Aunt Gwendolyn left me."

"You promise?"

She smiled, blinking back the tears shimmering in her

raven-colored eyes. "I promise. Kiss the children for me, and give Caleb my love."

"I will," Lauren said. "Later, cuz."

Pressing a button, Gwen ended the call, struggling to bring her emotions under control. She was frightened—no, petrified was a better word—to leave all that was familiar to her for something so removed from who or what she was. But she knew her life would not change unless she actively effected that change.

It had taken her four years to become the consummate minimalist; she'd streamlined her lifestyle eliminating what she considered excess as she purged her closet of clothes she hadn't worn more than twice in a given season, donated books to the local library and nursing homes that were collecting dust on her to-be-read pile, and gave up entertaining men who'd professed their undying love, but were unable to commit to something deeper.

Gwen was still trying to uncover what deeper meant. Did it translate to *I love you* instead of *I like you a lot?* Whatever it was, she wanted no part of their superficial games. At thirty-four she was ready to start anew in a different state and with property she'd inherited from her namesake—a reclusive, former actress—her great-aunt.

A smile slowly crept through her expression of uncertainty as she drove down Main Street. A wave of nostalgia swept over her; it was as if she'd stepped back in time. Old-fashioned street lamps lined the street, rolling out beneath an arbor of live oaks.

The lush setting had become a reality. Boston-born, reared, and educated, Gwendolyn Paulette Taylor was about to trade the cold, harsh New England winters for the lush, sultry heat of Bayou Teche, the largest of Louisiana's many bayous.

Her parents, her father in particular, were opposed to her

moving so far away. Millard and Paulette Taylor had lost one child, a son, to leukemia before he entered adolescence, and sought to hold onto their surviving child at all costs.

She took another quick look at the screen. She would be home within another two miles. Home—a house she'd only seen in photographs, a place that was hers to renovate or decorate to suit her tastes.

Gwen left Franklin's Main Street and maneuvered onto a narrow, winding road leading to the property known to the locals as *Bon Temps*. The setting sun turned the surrounding landscape into a swamp that she glimpsed through a shadowy veil. Cypress, pine and oak trees draped in Spanish moss stood like sentinels overlooking a body of slow-moving water teeming with various wildlife while providing perches for species of birds she'd never seen before.

She was so awed by the beauty of the scenery that she didn't see the three-legged dog hopping across the road. Swerving sharply to avoid hitting the dog, she veered to the right, skidded, and came to an abrupt end in a ditch.

"Damn!" she muttered between clenched teeth.

Taking a deep breath, she shifted into Reverse, then into Drive, stepped on the gas as the car went completely still. There was only the sound of spinning tires. She shifted again, this time into Park, and stared through the windshield. She was literally stuck in the mud.

Gwen saw something moving in the water less than a hundred feet from where she sat—stranded—a prisoner in her own vehicle. She didn't know what was gliding under the smooth surface, and didn't much want to know because she wasn't getting out of the car.

Reaching for her cell phone, she scrolled through the directory while she searched through her leather handbag on the passenger-side seat for her credit card case. Pressing a button, she listened to the ringing for a programmed number.

"Road assistance, Zack speaking."

Gwen gave Zack her name, membership number and her location. He took the information, telling her he would call her back as soon as he had located a nearby service station.

Drumming her fingers on the leather-wrapped steering wheel, she hummed a nameless tune while awaiting a call back. Ten minutes later, she grabbed the receiver after the first ring.

"Gwendolyn Taylor."

"Miss Taylor, this is Zack. I called two stations in your area, one doesn't have a tow truck, and the other is out on a call."

"What time will he be back?"

"It's going to be at least an hour."

"An hour!" she repeated, her voice rising slightly. There was no way she was going to sit in a car alone surrounded by who-knew-what type of wildlife creeping, crawling, or slithering around her.

"Do you want to wait, Miss Taylor?" Zack drawled.

Why, she wondered, did it take him more than thirty seconds to say seven words. The further south she'd driven, the more pronounced the drawl. "I'll call you back," she said, not knowing what else to say. She ended the call, then dialed nine-one-one.

"St. Martin Parish Police. Deputy Jameson speaking."

She took a deep breath. "Deputy Jameson, my name is Gwendolyn Taylor, and I'm stuck in a ditch on the road leading to *Bon Temps*. I called for road service, but was told they can't come for another hour."

"Are you alone, ma'am?"

"Yes."

"What type of *ve-hic-le* are you driving?"

Gwen shook her head. He'd drawled out *vehicle* into more than three syllables. "It's a dark blue BMW sedan."

"I'll radio one of our officers to assist you. Make certain you keep your cell phone on in case we have to call you."

"I will. Thank you, Deputy Jameson."

"No problem, ma'am."

Holding the tiny phone in a death grip, she sat back and waited for one of St. Martin Parish's finest to rescue her.

Sheriff Shiloh Harper glanced at the watch strapped to his left wrist for what seemed like the hundredth time in the past hour. He couldn't wait for his shift to end so he could go home, take a cool shower, and crawl into the hammock on the screened-in second-story veranda, where he could remind himself that he was one day closer to prosecuting criminals instead of arresting them.

He was covering for a vacationing deputy, and had spent the shift mediating petty incidents: a teenage boy had pumped two dollars more in gas than he had on him; a fifteen-year-old girl had tried to buy beer with a fake ID; and he'd issued a slew of tickets for drivers exceeding the speed limit in a school zone.

As he slowed the police-issued Suburban SUV, he maneuvered behind a copse of trees to wait for wannabe NASCAR drivers who used a stretch of roadway without a stop sign or traffic lights as their private racetrack. Leaning back in the leather seat, he stared at the radar device and waited for the sun to set. With the approach of nightfall, he was certain to catch at least a couple of speeders before his noon-to-eight-o'clock shift ended.

"Shiloh?"

He sat up, suddenly alert when his deputy's voice came through the small two-way radio clipped to his left shoulder. "Yes, Jimmie."

"I just got a call from a woman who's stranded along the

road to *Bon Temps*. I don't think she's from around here because she talks real funny. You want her number?"

"No. Call and let her know I'm on my way."

Shiloh ended the call, placed the red light on the dashboard and headed onto the roadway. Motorists, seeing the flashing red light, moved over to the shoulder to give the official vehicle the right of way. Within minutes of Jimmie Jameson's call, he had pulled up opposite a dark-colored, late-model sedan with Massachusetts license plates. A slight smile curved the corners of his mouth when he remembered what his deputy said about the stranded motorist talking funny. Pushing open the door, he reached for a flashlight before alighting from the SUV and approaching the car.

He switched on the flashlight and knocked softly on the driver's door. Large dark eyes stared at him through the glass; he gestured for her to lower the window. She complied and the smell of new leather mixed with the subtle scent of a sensual perfume wafted from the interior.

"I'm going to need you to step out of the vehicle, miss."

Gwen stared at the shadowy face of the man only inches from her own. "I can't," she said breathlessly. The eyes staring back at Gwen reminded of her a cat's. They were an odd shade of gold-green. What made them appear so unusual was that they were set in a brown face with hues ranging from sienna to alizarin.

His eyebrow lifted. "Are you injured?"

She shook her head like someone in a trance. The time she'd spent in the car waiting for assistance had traumatized her. She'd imagined the most macabre scenarios: an alligator climbing up on the hood of the car and smashing the wind-shield with his powerful tail; a venomous insect crawling in and biting her; or that the mud was quicksand.

"I can't get out," she said, unable to control the quiver in her voice.

Reaching into the car, Shiloh released the lock, and opened the door. Hunkering down, he directed the beam of light around the car's interior. He trained the flashlight on the woman's legs and feet, which were clad in a pair of cropped pants and sandals. His expressive eyebrows lifted again. She had nice legs and beautifully groomed feet. Her sandals screamed couture with a price tag that probably exceeded the weekly salary of many local residents.

"Can you walk?"

"Yes, but…" Her words trailed off as she stared at the tall man in a crisp tan uniform and western-style light-colored hat. A star on his chest identified him as the sheriff, and a name tag as Harper.

"But what?" Shiloh asked when she didn't complete her statement.

Sighing, Gwen closed her eyes. "I'm afraid."

"Afraid of what? Messing up your shoes?"

She opened her eyes and rolled them at the lawman. A slight frown marred her smooth forehead. How dare he believe she was so vain or insipid that she was more concerned about a pair of shoes than her personal safety.

"Alligators. Snakes."

A hint of a smile softened Shiloh's mouth. Jimmie was right about her talking funny. Her Boston accent was as thick as the haze blanketing the bayou before the heat of the sun pierced its shadowy veil.

"The snakes and gators are in the water, miss."

Her eyes narrowed. "Are you sure?" Smiling broadly, he nodded. "How do you know there isn't one under my car?"

"I don't know," he admitted. "But if there is, then I

wouldn't be here talking to you, because I definitely would've been dinner."

Gwen crossed her arms under her breasts over a white tank top, bringing his gaze to linger there. "Exactly. Now, unless you can assure me that there are no animals lurking next to my car I'm not getting out."

Shiloh was hard pressed not to bare his teeth at her. How was he going to get her car out of the ditch with her behind the wheel? If Miss Beantown refused to come to him, then he would have to take it to her.

After slipping the flashlight into a loop on his belt, he straightened up, reached into the car, and scooped her off the seat. The unexpected motion forced her to wrap her arms around his neck to maintain her balance. He shifted her slightly, molding her breasts to his chest.

"What the hell do you think you're doing?" Gwen shouted at him. Her right hand fisted. "Put me down."

Shiloh tightened his hold under her knees. "In the mud, miss?"

"No. Over there," she demanded, pointing to where he'd parked his sport utility vehicle.

He shifted her again, smiling. "What do you plan to do with that fist?"

Gwen looked at her hand as if it was something she'd never seen before. Heat suffused her face. There was no doubt she was ready to punch out the tall lawman holding her effortlessly as if she were a child. It was also apparent his diet wasn't made up of pizza and beer or coffee and greasy doughnuts like some of the cops she'd come to know during her years as a reporter for the *Boston Gazette*. She relaxed her fingers.

Shiloh smiled. "Good. Now I don't have to cuff you and haul you in for assaulting an officer. What's your name, miss?"

"Do you have to know my name?"

Crossing the road, Shiloh ignored her hostile query. "Yes. I'm going to have to file a report."

"Why?"

He met her questioning gaze in the waning daylight. "I don't know how you do things up north, but down here whenever someone places a call to our police department we follow up with a written report. Which means I'm going to need your license and registration."

Gwen frowned. "You think I stole the car?"

Not bothering to answer her question, Shiloh deposited her on the passenger seat of the Suburban. "Stay here until I come back."

Gwen registered the edge of authority in his slow drawling speech pattern. He'd told her to stay as if she were a dog. Where was she going in the backwoods, and in the dark?

Shiloh returned to her car. Not only did she talk funny, but she also had a quick tongue. What he didn't want to think about was how nice she smelled and how good she felt in his arms.

Slipping behind the wheel, he adjusted the lever under the front seat to accommodate his longer legs. Not bothering to close the driver-side door, he shifted into Reverse, turned the wheel slightly, then shifted into Drive, maneuvering out of the mud and onto the shoulder. He adjusted the air-conditioning, noting the gas gauge. It registered a half tank. At least she knew enough not to drive around on E, or even close to it.

He picked up her handbag off the passenger seat, recognizing the designer logo with a single glance. His ex-wife's closet overflowed with designer bags, shoes, sunglasses and clothes. If the item didn't have someone's name stitched or stamped on it, then she refused to buy it.

A knowing smile softened his mouth. Miss Beantown drove a six-figure car, wore very nice shoes and carried a very, very nice handbag. There was no doubt the lady from Massachusetts was top shelf. And he wondered, what was she doing driving around back roads at night in Cajun country?

Gwen could not stop the wave of heat washing over her face and upper body. All it took was a little maneuvering to get her car out of a ditch. How, she thought, was she able to drive through mounds of snow, not spin out on icy streets or highways, yet couldn't extricate herself from a mud bank?

She stared at the mud-covered boots rather than at the face of the man striding toward her, breathing in quick shallow breaths. Never had she been so embarrassed. She thought about slipping out of the SUV and making a run for her car, but quickly changed her mind. There were enough televised police chases, and she had no intention of adding to the footage.

The driver's side door opened and she stared, wide-eyed, at the man climbing into the vehicle beside her. Not only was he tall, but also big. Not fat big, but muscled big. His biceps bulged against the sleeves of his uniform, and she forced herself not to glance below his chest.

Tilting her chin, lowering her lashes, and affecting a smile that usually left men with their mouths gaping, Gwen sought to replace the scowl on Sheriff Harper's face with one that was more friendly. After all, he'd taken an oath to protect and serve, not berate and abuse.

Shiloh gave the woman sitting beside him a sidelong glance. "You can stop flirting with me because I'm not going to give you a citation." He dropped her handbag in her lap.

An audible gasp escaped Gwen's parted lips. Scorching

heat swept over her from head to toe. "I'm not flirting with you. Why would I? I've done nothing wrong."

"No, you haven't—not yet anyway." Shiloh gave her a direct stare. "May I have your license and registration?"

Gwen glanced at his long, well-groomed hands when he opened a leather binder, then removed a pen from a breast pocket. Searching through her handbag, she took out a small leather case and removed the documents he'd requested.

Shiloh took a quick glance at her license. "What's your name?"

"Gwendolyn Taylor."

"Address."

"Which one?"

Shiloh went completely still, his fingers tightening on the pen. "You have more than one?"

She smiled. "Yes. You have the one on my license and registration, but…"

"But what, Miss Taylor?" he asked when she didn't finish her statement.

"I have a new address."

He stared directly at her, liking what he saw. Gwendolyn Taylor wasn't as pretty as she was attractive—sensually attractive. Her round face made her look much younger than her actual age. Her large dark eyes sparkled like polished onyx in a flawless sable-brown face; her nose was short and cute, her mouth full and lush; and her hair was a profusion of dark flyaway curls that fell over her forehead and along the nape of her slender neck. He didn't want to think of her rounded body. It was a bouquet of lushness. He remembered the tagline about real women having curves. Gwendolyn Taylor had enough curves for two women.

"Where do you live now?"

"Here in St. Martin Parish. I'm moving into *Bon Temps*. Gwendolyn Pickering was my great-aunt."

Shiloh stared at Gwen. There had been a lot of talk after the owner of the house passed away earlier in the year. Developers swooped down on *Bon Temps* like scavengers on rotting carrion. The men had come, checkbooks in hand, to purchase the house and the six acres on which it sat, but Gwendolyn Pickering's attorney refused to meet with them. He'd turned them away because his client had willed her property to a relative—a Massachusetts relative.

"That should please a lot of folks around here," Shiloh said, after he'd recovered from his shock.

"Why's that?"

"Because a few fat cats came around asking about buying the property. You're not thinking of selling, are you?"

"Of course not."

Shiloh nodded and smiled at her. The expression transformed his handsome face and gave him a boyish look. "Good." Flipping the top to a computer, he entered the information from Gwendolyn Taylor's license.

She leaned to her left to view the screen. "I have no outstanding warrants or citations."

Shiloh inhaled the floral scent of the soft curls brushing his cheek. "Just procedure, Miss Taylor." He stared at the photograph on the screen. Gwendolyn's hair was much shorter, the style too severe for her face. She would turn thirty-five in November, and he'd just celebrated his thirty-ninth birthday the month before.

Gwen watched as he entered the information on her car's registration. The commonwealth of Massachusetts DMV had listed Gwendolyn P. Taylor as the owner of the car.

"What does the P stand for?"

"Paulette."

"Pretty," Shiloh said without any emotion in his voice.

"Can I go now?" she asked after he'd given her back her documents.

He noted the time on his watch and entered it into the computer. It was seven-forty-five. In fifteen minutes he would be officially off duty. "Yes, you can, Miss Taylor. I'll come around and help you down." Shiloh stepped out of the Suburban at the same time a police cruiser pulled up, lights flashing.

Frank Lincoln got out, right hand resting on his firearm. "You all right, boss?"

Shiloh stared at the overzealous young deputy. Frank's father was a special agent with the FBI, and his grandfather a retired Louisiana state trooper. He'd hired the new recruit because he was ambitious, honest and dedicated to his profession.

"I'm good, Frank."

There was just enough sunlight left to discern the flush creeping up his face, the bright color matching his orange hair. "I saw your flasher, then I noticed the perp sitting in the front seat, so I thought you were in trouble."

Now Shiloh knew why Frank had stopped. "Miss Taylor is not a perp. I stopped..."

His explanation died on his lips. He didn't have to explain to a subordinate what he was doing and why Gwendolyn Taylor was in the front seat instead of in the rear behind a heavy mesh partition where perpetrators were handcuffed when they were taken to the station house for questioning or locked up before they were arraigned at the courthouse.

"It's almost time for your shift, Lincoln." Whenever he addressed his deputies by their last name it was usually followed by a reprimand.

Frank saluted Shiloh. "Good night, sir."

He returned the salute. "Good night, Frank. Don't forget to turn off your lights."

"Yes, sir."

Waiting until the cruiser disappeared from view, Shiloh came around the SUV and scooped Gwen off the seat, then set her gently on her feet. Cupping her elbow, he led her back to her car. He released her arm and opened the door to the BMW.

"If you follow me, I'll show you how to get to *Bon Temps*."

Gwen studied his face, feature by feature, with a curious intensity as the gold-green eyes darkened with an unreadable expression. She liked his eyes and strong chin. There was just a hint of a cleft, as if nature hadn't quite made up its mind whether to give him one.

"Thank you, Sheriff Harper."

He touched the brim of the wide hat with a thumb and forefinger. "You're welcome, Miss Taylor."

Shiloh waited until she was seated before he returned to his SUV, turned off the flasher, executed a U-turn and headed southward. He glanced up at the rearview mirror. She was following him.

He decelerated and drove onto a paved road leading to a smaller version of the half-dozen restored antebellum mansions offering tours. Live oaks formed a natural canopy as he approached the house known as *Bon Temps*—meaning "good times" in French.

Shiloh wondered if Gwendolyn Taylor was aware of what had gone on behind the doors of the infamous mansion. He also wondered how well she'd known her namesake, Gwendolyn Pickering. A knowing smile parted his lips. If she didn't know, then she would once the gossips came to introduce themselves to the newcomer. His first instinct was to warn her, but he changed his mind. There was something about Gwendolyn Taylor that said she could hold her own with anything and anyone. She had with him.

He waited in his vehicle, watching Gwendolyn as she

parked her car, walked to the entrance of the house, and unlocked the front door. She disappeared inside and seconds later the first floor was flooded with soft light.

Shiloh smiled when she waved to him. He returned her wave, waiting until she closed the door. It wasn't until he'd left *Bon Temps* and headed in the direction of his own house that he chided himself for not checking to see if she was safe—that no intruder or squatter had taken up residence.

Flipping a signal, he drove back to *Bon Temps*.

Chapter 2

Gwen stood in the entryway, staring up at a cobweb-covered light fixture overhead. Muslin slipcovers were draped over all of the tables and chairs and a layer of dust coated the parquet floors bordered in a rosewood-inlay pattern.

Gwendolyn Pickering had passed away in late February, and it was now early May. It was that apparent no one had come to clean or air out the house. She pretended she didn't see the stained and peeling wallpaper. Walking across the living room, she saw a massive chandelier resting in a corner on a drop cloth, the sooty remains in the brick fireplace, and the threadbare carpeting on the staircase leading to the second floor. Despite the disrepair, she recognized the magnificence of the mansion, which dated back to the 1840s.

Bon Temps was home, and not the three-bedroom apartment on the top floor of a turn-of-the-century town house she'd occupied for the past decade.

Heading for the staircase, she flipped on the light switch on a wall panel and illuminated the landing and the hallway at the top of the staircase.

Her footsteps were slow and determined as she climbed the stairs to see what awaited her. Her late aunt's attorney had mailed her an envelope filled with photographs of the exterior and interior of *Bon Temps,* floor plans, copies of the original architectural drawings, and a description of the furnishings with authentication of every inventoried item.

The five-thousand-square-foot house contained four bedrooms, five-and-a-half bathrooms, a kitchen, a pantry, a laundry room, a formal living and dining room, and a small ballroom for entertaining. The floor plans also included a second-story veranda that overlooked an orchard and formal garden.

It took several hours after a lengthy conversation with Gwendolyn Pickering's attorney for Gwen to digest the information that she now owned a house that if restored, would be granted historic landmark status. Mr. Sykes said she could either turn *Bon Temps* into a museum or live in it, so she'd opted to claim it as her home.

Gwen stopped as she reached the last stair when the chiming of the doorbell echoed melodiously throughout the house. Had someone seen the lights and come to investigate? She tried to remember if she'd locked the door behind her. Turning, she descended the staircase and walked to the door. She breathed a sigh of relief. Unconsciously, she'd locked it. Living in a big city had honed her survival skills—never leave a door unlocked.

The bell chimed again. Peering through the security peephole, Gwen saw the distorted face of the man whom she'd left less than five minutes before.

"Yes?" she asked through the solid wood door.

"Miss Taylor, it's Shiloh. Please open the door."

Her eyebrows inched up. He hadn't identified himself as

Sheriff Harper. She disengaged the lock. The man who'd rescued her from the ditch looked different without his hat. His close-cropped black hair hugged his head like a cap. The soft yellow light from the porch lamps flattered the angles of his dark brown face. He looked like someone she'd seen before.

She affected a smile. "Yes, Sheriff?"

Shiloh's gold-flecked green eyes lingered on her lush mouth. "Please call me Shiloh."

Her smile faded. "Why?"

"Because I'm off duty. Your place has been vacant for several months although my men do check at least twice a week to make certain squatters or vandals haven't broken in. I just came back to make certain you were all right."

Gwen knew it was impolite to stare, but she couldn't take her gaze away from Shiloh's face. Who did he look like? She mentally ran through the faces of people she'd met and interviewed over the years, but came up blank.

She blinked as if coming out of a trance and opened the door wider. "You're off duty, yet you're still on the job?"

He angled his head, smiling. "I'm always on the job, Miss Taylor."

Shiloh liked listening to Gwendolyn Taylor's voice. It was a welcome change from the slow drawl and distinctive inflection of the Cajun dialect of most people in the parish. Not only did she talk different, but she also looked different from the women in the region. Despite her casual attire, there was something about her that silently screamed big city, and he wondered how long it would take for her to abandon *Bon Temps,* tire of the slower lifestyle, and return to Massachusetts.

Gwen gave him a warm smile and offered her right hand. "I'd like you to call me Gwen."

Shiloh took her smaller hand in his, enjoying its softness. It was with reluctance that he released it. He'd returned to *Bon*

Temps to make certain it was safe for Gwendolyn Taylor to enter, and he'd also returned to see her again. He didn't know what it was about the transplanted Bostonian, but something about her intrigued him. Not knowing whether there was a Mr. Taylor or a few little Taylors, but like a besotted teenager he'd come back for another glimpse of a woman whose voice drew him to her like a moth to a flame.

He nodded, smiling. "Then Gwen it is. Do you mind if I check around?"

She stepped aside. "Not at all."

Shiloh moved into the entryway, his sharp gaze cataloguing everything. Even to someone who lived his entire life in the South the heat inside the house was oppressive.

He walked into the living room, stopping short, and a soft body plowed into his back. Turning quickly, he reached out to steady Gwen as she swayed and struggled to keep her balance.

"Just where are you going?" he asked, glaring down at her stunned expression.

Gwen felt the unyielding strength in the fingers around her upper arms, inhaled the lingering scent of a provocative men's cologne, and shivered from the press of Shiloh's body against hers.

"I'm following you." She didn't recognize her own voice because it had come out in a breathless whisper.

Shiloh eased his grip on her arms, but didn't release her. A frown marred his smooth forehead. "No, you're not."

She bristled visibly. How dare he tell her what she could do in her own home? "And why not?"

"Because I'm the one with the big gun," he drawled. He hadn't bothered to hide his arrogance.

Gwen tried unsuccessfully to bite back a smile. "Oh, really, Mr. Lawman, sir."

Shiloh's hands fell away once he realized what he'd said.

There was no doubt she'd misconstrued his statement as a sexual taunt. Resting long, slender fingers on his waist, he smiled. "Would you like me to show it to you?" He got the reaction he sought when Gwen gasped and her eyes widened. "I personally prefer the Glock to the standard police-issue .38 revolver."

Gwen's gaze shifted from his Cheshire cat grin to the deadly looking firearm strapped to his waist. "I don't need to see it, Shiloh. What do you want me to do?"

"Stay here."

Recovering quickly, her eyes narrowed. "This is the second time you've told me to stay as if I were a dog."

It was Shiloh's turn to give a questioning look. One eyebrow lifted higher than the other and that was when Gwen knew who he reminded her of.

"Do you know that you look like The Rock?"

"The Rock?"

"Dwayne Johnson. The wrestler-turned-actor," she explained. "His complexion is lighter than yours, and your eyes aren't dark like his, but the two of you could pass for brothers."

Shiloh had lost count of the number of times people mentioned his resemblance to the wrestler, yet always claimed he'd never heard of the man.

"I suppose it's true about everyone having a double," he said glibly. "How about you, Gwen? Do you have someone who looks like you?"

"Yes, in fact I do. My first cousin Lauren and I look enough alike to be sisters. The only difference is that I'm about an inch taller and rounder than she is in certain places despite the fact that she's had three babies."

"Have many children do you have?" Shiloh asked, as his penetrating gaze moved slowly over her body.

"None."

"So, it's just going to be you and Mr. Taylor living here?"

She shook her head. "There is no Mr. Taylor, aside from my father and Uncle Roy. Will my marital status also go into your police report?"

Shiloh went completely still. Miss Gwendolyn Taylor was anything but shy, timid or submissive. "No, it won't."

Crossing her arms under her breasts, she took a step and looked directly into a pair of the most mesmerizing eyes she'd ever seen on a man. The gold was the perfect match for the undertones in his smooth-shaven jaw, the green dramatic and hypnotic.

"Good."

"Why good?"

"I always like to maintain a modicum of anonymity."

"That's not going to be an easy feat down here."

"Why not?" Gwen asked.

"We're in the bayou. That means everyone gets to know everyone else. The fact that you live out here may make it a little easier for you, but I wouldn't count on complete anonymity."

Shiloh wanted to tell Gwen that only Gwendolyn Pickering was able to keep her private life private. Those she'd invited to *Bon Temps* swore an oath never to reveal what went on behind the door once they crossed the threshold.

"What about yourself, Sheriff Harper? Does everyone know your business?"

"I'm a public servant and that means my life is an open book," he admitted.

"You don't have a private life?"

He hesitated, then said, "Right now I don't."

The journalist in Gwen wanted to know more about the sheriff, but she hadn't moved more than fifteen hundred miles to get involved, even if it was on a superficial level, with a man. Besides, she didn't know whether Shiloh was married, engaged or involved with a woman.

"I'll wait here for you to complete your search," she said, deftly dropping the topic and letting Shiloh know she wanted him gone.

Shiloh averted his gaze from the softly curved luscious mouth. "I'll try to be quick about it." He switched on a flashlight and headed for the staircase.

His footsteps were muffled by the pile of the well-worn carpet lining the winding staircase. He hadn't lied to Gwen about his private life. He hadn't had one in three years, not since his divorce, and not since he'd left the district attorney's office to serve out his father's term as sheriff after Virgil Harper was gunned down during a botched bank robbery.

Flipping on a light switch on the wall at the top of the stairs, he saw firsthand the fading beauty of *Bon Temps* concealed under dust and cobwebs. The last two years of Gwendolyn Pickering's life had been shrouded in mystery. She'd stopped receiving visitors and rarely ventured off the property.

Shiloh entered and exited bedrooms attached by adjoining sitting rooms and baths. He checked the locks on the wall-to-wall, floor-to-ceiling French doors in the bedrooms overlooking the rear.

It appeared as if no one, other than whoever had covered the furniture with dustcovers, had returned to the house since Gwendolyn Pickering passed away. One thing he knew was that the house was not fit for human habitation—at least not until it was aired out.

He returned to the first floor by a back stairway and found himself outside an expansive state-of-the-art, eat-in kitchen. A pantry and laundry room were set up in an alcove behind the kitchen. His booted feet left distinctive footprints on the tiled floor.

Turning the faucet on in one of the stainless steel twin sinks, Shiloh waited for the water to run clear. There were two things Gwen did not have to concern herself with: water and electricity. Both were in working order.

Returning to the front of the house, he found Gwen where he'd left her, in the living room. She stood next to the massive crystal chandelier resting on a drop cloth in a corner.

"You can't stay here tonight," he announced in a voice layered with an authoritative undertone.

Gwen turned, an expression of indecision freezing her delicate features. "What?"

Shiloh closed the distance between them. "The house is safe, but you can't stay," he repeated. "The air quality is unhealthy. This place has been closed up for months and should be dusted *and* aired out before you sleep here."

She groaned audibly. "It's that bad?"

He nodded. "Yes, it's that bad."

Gwen worried her lower lip between her teeth. "Is there a hotel or motel around here that I can check into?"

"The nearest motel is right off the interstate. But on the other hand, Jessup's boardinghouse is just up the road."

There was no need for her to agonize over where she would spend the night. After driving more than twelve hours Gwen loathed getting behind the wheel of her car again. Her eyelids fluttered. "I'll stay at the boardinghouse. How do I get there?"

"I'll show you." Shiloh extended his hand. "Give me your key and I'll lock up."

Delving her hand into the pocket of her slacks, Gwen handed him the key, then turned on her heels and walked out of the house, feeling the heat of Shiloh's gaze on her retreating back.

She got into her car and waited for Shiloh Harper to turn off the lights and lock up *Bon Temps*. And for the second time that night she found herself following his vehicle.

* * *

Gwen's eyelids drooped as she waited for the proprietor of Jessup's boardinghouse to swipe her credit card. She was past being tired; she was exhausted and hungry. She'd left Chattanooga, Tennessee earlier that morning, stopping only to refuel her car.

Forcing herself to stand upright, she gave Shiloh a half smile. He'd brought in her luggage and offered to wait until she had gotten a room in the family-owned establishment. "How can I thank you for all you've done for me?"

Crossing his arms over his chest, Shiloh angled his head. "You can buy a ticket to an upcoming fund-raising dinner-dance to benefit the bayou's needy families."

"How much are they?"

"Fifty."

"Put me down for two."

Shiloh lowered his arms. Gwen admitted to not being married, but she hadn't said anything about a boyfriend. Women who looked like Gwendolyn Taylor usually did not spend their weekends watching rented videos or reading novels that promised a happily-ever-after ending because it was missing in her life. He knew very little about the current owner of *Bon Temps,* but what he saw he definitely liked.

Willie Jessup placed a key and her card on the solid oak counter. "You're in room two-one-four. It's at the top of the stairs." He nodded to Shiloh. "I'll take her bags up," he said in French.

"It's all right, Willie. I'll do it," he replied in the same language. "Keep an eye on her, because she's not from around here," Shiloh said quietly.

"No problem," Willie replied.

Gwen's fatigue vanished quickly. She'd taken an accelerated course in French before her European vacation and had come away with only a rudimentary fluency in the language. During the two weeks she'd spent in France she was able to order food, ask street directions and negotiate with shopkeepers. The French were impressed because she'd at least tried to communicate with them in their language.

Shiloh picked up her bags and headed for the staircase, Gwen following. She was intrigued by the man named for a horrific Civil War battle; a man who as sheriff of St. Martin Parish had gone beyond the call of duty to make certain she was safe; a man who understood and spoke French fluently. The reporter in her wanted answers—a lot of answers, but they would have to wait until after she'd gotten some sleep.

Soft light coming from two table lamps revealed a room that was spacious and clean. A mahogany four-poster bed draped with mosquito netting, a matching highboy and rocker beckoned her to come and spend the night.

Shiloh placed her three bags on the floor next to a small, adjoining bathroom before he walked over to the French doors overlooking a balcony enclosed with decorative wrought-iron grillwork. He checked the lock, then flipped a wall switch and the blades of a ceiling fan stirred the air.

Turning around, he stared at Gwen who lay across the bed, eyes closed. Moving closer, he saw the gentle rise and fall of her breasts. She'd fallen asleep. Bending over, he removed her sandals. A knowing smile softened his firm mouth. He was right about her shoes costing more than some folks earned in a week. Gwen Taylor's size seven sandals were Jimmy Choos.

He couldn't pull his gaze away from her face and he noticed things that weren't apparent at first glance: the length of her lashes resting on a pair of high cheekbones, the narrowness of the bridge of her short nose, the incredibly smooth color of her sable-brown face, and the lush softness of her mouth.

An unbidden thought popped into and out of his head

quickly. Spinning on his heels he walked out of the room, closing the door softly. He checked the knob to make certain it was locked, then made his way down the staircase to the lobby.

"Bon soir," he said to Willie as he strolled across the lobby and out of the boardinghouse.

"A tout a l'heure, Shiloh," Willie called out at the same time the telephone rang.

Shiloh climbed behind the wheel of the black unmarked SUV and turned on the engine. The clock on the dashboard read 9:55. It wasn't often he worked overtime, but he didn't consider helping Gwendolyn Taylor work. It was one parish resident helping out another.

He drove away from Jessup's thinking about the woman asleep on the bed in a second-floor bedroom. She intrigued him, intrigued him enough to want to get to know her better. And like her namesake who'd occupied *Bon Temps* for half a century, he was certain this Gwendolyn would also get her share of male admirers.

What she didn't know was that she'd acquired her first one: Shiloh Harper.

Shiloh lay in the oversized hammock, his head resting on a down-filled pillow, his bare feet crossed at the ankles, arms crossed over an equally bared chest, listening to the nocturnal sounds of the bayou: the low growl of an alligator, the chirping of crickets, the croaking of frogs, and the occasional splash of a muskrat, opossum and other wildlife. The sounds had become a serenade, easing his frustration. And like those he'd tried and sent to prison he now counted the days, weeks, months, and it was now less than a year when he would eventually return to the D.A.'s office.

Four years of college, three in law school and countless hours studying to pass the Louisiana bar hadn't prepared him to become a sheriff. He loved preparing a case for trial, going to trial, and delivering opening and closing arguments. His mother called him a frustrated actor because there were times when his presentation was likened to a Hollywood A-list actor's performance.

Now, however, he wasn't a district attorney but Sheriff Shiloh Harper, and serving out his father's term had delayed his goal of becoming a judge by his fortieth birthday.

Shifting slightly in the hammock, he closed his eyes as the blades of one of the ceiling fans on the veranda moved the sultry air, caressing his scantily clad body. He was beginning to feel the effects of the two beers he'd drunk in lieu of eating his mother's jambalaya. After thirty-seven years of marriage his widowed mother still had not adjusted to cooking for one person. Any time he left the house where he'd grown up, it was with several containers of Moriah Harper's exquisitely prepared food.

The cell phone resting near his right hand rang a distinctive ring. Without glancing at the display he knew who'd dialed his number. He counted six rings before the voicemail feature activated. Then he picked up the telephone, deleted the message, and settled back to spend the night on the hammock.

There had been a time when he couldn't wait to talk to Deandrea Tate. But that was before he'd courted and married her. But everything changed eighteen months into their marriage when he came home and found another man in bed with his wife. They stopped talking and rage and acrimony surfaced as he filed for divorce. Now, there was nothing his ex-wife had to say that he wanted or needed to hear. He'd given Deandrea the monstrosity of a house she'd hounded him to buy and everything in it as a settlement—a house and furnishings she sold less than six months after their divorce.

She'd called because she probably needed money. Well, he'd given her all that he had, and then some.

Shiloh Harper wasn't the same man Deandrea married. She was now his past, and he had made it a practice not to dwell on what was, but prepare for what was to come.

Gwen opened her eyes, totally disoriented, her clothes pasted to her moist body. She stared up through the gauzy netting at the whirling blades of a ceiling fan. Within seconds she realized where she was, and recalled what had happened since she'd crossed the boundary into Bayou Teche.

She'd gotten stuck in a mud bank, was rescued by the police, surveyed the hot, musty, dusty interior of the house that was now her home, and instead of sleeping at *Bon Temps* was forced to spend the night at a local boardinghouse.

Sitting up and getting off the bed, Gwen made her way barefoot over to the smallest of her three pieces of luggage. Shiloh had carried all three bags in one trip while it had taken her two trips from her top floor apartment to bring them down to her car. Opening the bag, she withdrew a case with her cosmetics, and walked into the bathroom.

Half an hour later, she emerged from the bathroom, refreshed by a lukewarm shower. Turning off the table lamps, she parted the sheer netting, slipped under a crisp floral sheet, and within minutes went back to sleep.

Chapter 3

Gwen woke up ravenous. Rolling over, she reached for her watch on the bedside table. It was 11:20, and she did not want to do anything or make any decision until she'd eaten. Swinging her legs over the side of the bed, she stood up and headed for the bathroom.

Despite the growling sounds coming from her belly, Gwen lingered under the spray of the shower to wash and condition her hair. It was half past twelve when she descended the staircase and walked into the boardinghouse lobby. The expansive area was filled with wicker love seats and chairs cradling colorful floral cushions. An elderly woman with long, graying red hair stood behind the counter sorting mail.

Her head came up and she smiled at Gwen. "*Bonjour,* Miss Taylor. I'm Angelique Jessup. My nephew told me that Shiloh brought you in last night."

Clutching her purse to her middle, Gwen hoped to muffle

the sound of her growling belly. She wondered what else Shilòh had told Willie Jessup about her. Had he disclosed that she was now the new owner of *Bon Temps*? She also noticed that the older woman hadn't referred to Shiloh as Sheriff Harper.

"Good afternoon, Ms. Jessup. Perhaps you can tell me where I can get something to eat?"

"You missed breakfast, and we don't serve supper until six, so the only place open for lunch is the Outlaw."

Gwen groaned inwardly. "How far is it from here?"

Gesturing with a clawlike fingernail, Angelique said, "When you go out the door, turn to your right and walk toward the water. There you'll meet someone who'll take you across to the Outlaw."

She went completely still before her eyes widened. A *boat?* Gwen blinked once. "I have to take a boat across?"

Angelique nodded slowly. "You can't drive because after years of wrangling, the state finally gave us the money to repair the road on the east side of the parish. It will be closed for at least three months, so the only way to get to the Outlaw is by boat."

"How long will that take?"

"About ten minutes. As soon as you clear a sandbar you'll see the restaurant."

Gwen closed her eyes briefly as a spasm tightened her stomach muscles, leaving her light-headed. "Thank you."

"*Bon appetit,*" the older woman called out as Gwen headed toward the door.

"*Merci,*" she said, deciding it was time to begin practicing her limited French. She'd moved to southern Louisiana, the geographical heart of Acadiana, a region where she would hear the authentic dialect of the Acadian people.

The boardinghouse was situated along a block of attached two-story structures with decorative grillwork balconies representative of the region. The facades were shaded by rows of giant oak trees rising more than a hundred feet and trailing a yard of moss below their sweeping branches.

Everything about the bayou was so different from Boston: the architecture, topography, wildlife, flora, climate and people. Gwen felt as if she were being seduced, pulled into an atmosphere from which she did not want to escape. The cloying fragrance of flowering magnolia, honeysuckle and roses mingled with the distinctive smell of the water as she walked in the direction Angelique Jessup had indicated. The heat of the semitropical sun and humidity caressed her exposed skin under the lace-trimmed camisole she'd pulled on over a pair of worn jeans that she should've discarded when she emptied her closets.

What once had been a very active social life dwindled to an occasional encounter, most not going beyond the two-date limit. This suited her just fine because she preferred spending time alone, reading, seeing movies, and trying out new recipes to wasting her time with boorish, egotistical men who believed if they were treating her to dinner, then she should become their dessert at the end of the night.

She refused to become any man's dessert, possession, and definitely not his trophy. If they did not see or treat her as an equal, then she was prepared to spend the rest of her life—alone.

If she hadn't been so famished, she would've enjoyed her stroll. The fragrant odor of flowers growing wild faded as she approached the water. Her steps slowed as she saw *La Boule*, a boat painted a brilliant red and black, moored at the pier. She moved closer, the spongy earth giving way under the soles of her high-heel sandals.

"You want to cross the water with Etienne, missy?"

Gwen turned to find a wizened old man with a long beard that looked as if he'd glued a profusion of Spanish moss to his chin. He sat on a folding chair under a piece of tarpaulin supported by a quartet of rusting poles. Four late-model cars and six pickup trucks were parked nearby under a large tin shed open on two sides.

She assumed he was asking her whether she wanted him to take her across the bayou. "Yes, I do. How much is the fare to the Outlaw?"

"No pay if you go to the Outlaw," he mumbled. Etienne pushed off the wooden chair, adjusted the bib of his overalls, and shuffled down to the pier to the ferryboat. Gwen followed.

She made her way onto the ferryboat and sat down on a padded bench. As Etienne started up the engine and backed away from the shore, she stared at the passing landscape. Her breath caught in her chest as she entered an ethereal world that appeared primal and hostile. Moving at a speed less than three knots, *La Boule* provided her with a panoramic view of the bayou with its lush vegetation and ancient tree limbs before coming to a final rest in the muddy-water stream that meandered and twisted for a hundred and twenty-five miles.

Moving closer to the railing, she peered through a haze of muted gray and greens as a flock of snowy-white egrets settled down on the sandbar Angelique had mentioned. A loud splash garnered her attention; a large turtle swam just below the surface of the water.

She glimpsed the outline of a Greek Revival mansion through a copse of moss-draped oaks, the pristine white structure an exact replica of her home, but on a larger scale. She did not want to think about her ancestors who labored under the yoke of slavery to maintain the grandeur of the antebellum residences and the land from which the owners derived their wealth. The boat slowed, bumping against the wharf and Gwen leaned over the railing, peering up at a building erected on stilts.

Etienne turned the wheel until *La Boule* was parallel to the Outlaw's wharf. He cut the engine, left the wheelhouse and tossed a thick rope over a stanchion. He was waiting for Gwen as she disembarked. Cupping her elbow, he led her off the boat.

He smiled, displaying a mouth filled with worn yellow teeth. *"Bon appetit."*

She returned his smile, reaching into her cavernous leather bag. She pulled out several bills and pressed them into the ferryman's hand. *"Merci beaucoup."*

Etienne pocketed the money without glancing at what his passenger had given him. *"Merci,* missy."

Gwen climbed the wooden steps to the Outlaw as tantalizing smells wafted through the many screened-in windows. Right about now she was hungry enough to eat a critter: alligator, rattlesnake, squirrel, *or* possum.

Shiloh glanced up from the newspaper spread out on his left when the waitress placed his order on the table. "Thanks, Juleen."

Her dark eyes sparkled as she met Shiloh's gaze. "Do you want me to freshen up your coffee, Sheriff Harper?"

A frown replaced his forced smile. Most St. Martin Parish residents knew not to call him sheriff whenever he was out of uniform, but Juleen Aucoin persisted. The few times he'd spoken to his brother about it, Ian revealed that Juleen was looking to become the next Mrs. Shiloh Harper.

If Juleen believed she was flirting with him, then she'd just struck out—big time. Since his divorce he'd ignored every woman's attempt to tease, flirt or get him to either date her or share her bed. He wasn't exempt from making mistakes, but he was proud to admit that he'd never repeated one. He'd fallen in love and married, believing once he exchanged vows it would be happily ever after but it hadn't been and he'd sworn never to marry again.

"Please leave the pot, Juleen," he ordered in a soft voice.

Her pink lips parted at the same time a rush of color darkened her pretty face. "It's the only pot with coffee, Shiloh."

Shiloh exhaled audibly. "I'm certain my brother has another coffeepot somewhere in his kitchen."

"He does."

Raising his expressive eyebrows, he said, "Then I suggest you brew some more."

The waitress placed the half-filled carafe on the table and walked away, pouting. Short of stripping naked, she'd tried everything to get Shiloh Harper to notice her. The moment that rumors were confirmed that Shiloh had moved out of the restored mansion he'd shared with his wife and into a smaller house in a gated community, she along with every other eligible woman in the parish, regardless of their age flirted shamelessly with him. But to the women's consternation, the former district attorney ignored their overtures, leading most to believe that he hadn't gotten over Deandrea.

Rumors also circulated that if he wasn't seeing a woman, then he must be involved in a same-sex liaison, rumors Juleen refused to believe. One of her girlfriends who worked in the local Eckerd's where Shiloh bought his toiletries whispered that he never bought condoms, which led Juleen to believe that he was possibly celibate. And celibacy wasn't something she attributed to the acting sheriff. Men who looked like Shiloh Harper exuded too much sensuality to be asexual. She decided to give him one more try. The next time she would be subtler in her approach.

Shiloh picked up the carafe and refilled his coffee mug. He needed coffee to keep him alert—lots of it because he'd spent the night tossing and turning in the hammock until he was forced to abandon it in favor of his bed. He'd come to detest sleeping in the bed because it reminded him of how solitary his life had become. He had two days off—forty-eight hours in which he'd planned to read, watch a few movies, and do several loads of laundry.

He closed his eyes as he took a sip of the steaming black coffee liberally laced with chicory. Shiloh smiled. His younger brother Ian was known for brewing the best coffee in southern Louisiana.

A sudden and pregnant hush fell over the restaurant, and Shiloh opened his eyes to find Gwendolyn Taylor strolling into the Outlaw as if it was something she did every day. Coffee sloshed over the rim of the mug, burning his fingers, before he realized his hand was shaking. Setting down the cup, he shook his hand, then blotted up the liquid with a paper napkin.

Rising slowly to his feet, he watched her come closer, his penetrating gaze sweeping from her head to her feet within seconds. The flyway curly hairdo was missing, and in its place a chignon secured on the nape of her long, slender neck. She'd managed to tame the sensual curls with a style that was casual *and* chic at the same time.

She wore a silky, lace-trimmed, bright pink top over a pair of faded jeans that hugged her tight, compact body like a second skin. His gaze lingered on her feet. Today she wore a pair of high-heeled sandals in a rose-pink-and-navy print. Very pretty, but definitely not practical for a stroll.

He watched her looking around the restaurant for an empty table. It was lunchtime and the Outlaw was crowded with local fishermen who'd gone out in their boats before sunrise, returning hours later with their nets and traps filled with shrimp, oysters, crabs and crayfish.

Shiloh pushed back his chair at the same time François Broussard rose to his feet, heading toward Gwen. François, a direct descendant of the Acadian exiles who came from Canada to Louisiana in the mid 18th-century, had become the parish's wealthiest and most eligible bachelor. His much sought-after photographs and paintings were exhibited in museums and galleries throughout the country. Swarthy, silver-haired, urbane and jaded, he used his charm to seduce women as if it were his inalienable right.

Shiloh and François had grown up as friends, attended the same high school, dated some of the same girls, and François was one of several men Deandrea had slept with after she'd become Mrs. Shiloh Harper. To say there was bad blood between the two men was an understatement.

Shiloh made his way to Gwen seconds before François. Reaching for her hand, he held it firmly within his grasp, kissing the back of it. "I'd almost given up hope that you'd come," he said in a quiet voice, as she stared up at him. No doubt she was as shocked to see him, as he was she.

Gwen recognized Shiloh's voice before she realized he was out of uniform. Today he wore a light blue chambray shirt over a pair of jeans. His eyes were a deep moss green, the color contrasting his rich, sun-browned face. Her gaze shifted from the sheriff to the other man staring at her with an expectant expression. He had rakishly long silver hair that framed an unlined slender face with electric blue eyes and delicate features, which were better suited for a woman.

"Aren't you going to introduce me to the lady?" François asked Shiloh in a Creole dialect.

Tightening his hold on Gwen's fingers, he pulled her hand into the bend of his elbow. A slow smile softened his mouth. "Step off, Broussard, before I kick your ass," he threatened quietly in the same dialect. Turning his attention to Gwen, he gave her a wide grin. "Are you hungry, darling?"

"Starved," she answered truthfully, although completely

confused by the interaction between Shiloh and the man he'd called Broussard.

The conversations that had stopped when Gwen walked into the Outlaw started up again. Surreptitious stares were directed at François as he retreated to his table in a corner. Most of the men were silently applauding Shiloh's attempt to thwart another conquest for the arrogant, egotistical artist.

Shiloh led Gwen back to his table, pulled out a chair for her, then sat opposite her. His breathing deepened. The woman sitting only a few feet away was so ardently feminine that he found drawing a normal breath difficult.

Gwen forced herself not to stare at Shiloh's sandwich. Shredded lettuce, thinly sliced tomatoes, and a pile of golden fried oysters and shrimp were nestled between two slices of toasted French bread. A smaller plate held a cup of tartar sauce and lemon wedges.

Leaning over the small round table, she said, "Why did you call me darling?"

Ignoring her query, Shiloh picked up the plates and placed them in front of her. "You said you were starved, so please eat."

Her dark eyes widened. "I can't take your lunch."

"Yes, you can." Pushing back from the table, he stood up. "I'll order another one."

Gwen watched Shiloh's broad shoulders under the crisp shirt as he made his way toward the back of the restaurant and disappeared through a pair of swinging louvered doors. He looked equally good in or out of uniform, in dim or bright light, coming or going. Whoever claimed Shiloh Harper as boyfriend, fiancé or husband was one lucky woman. The word *darling* had rolled off his tongue as smoothly as watered silk. Some of the men she'd known thought calling her baby was the ultimate endearment. She'd permitted only one man to call her baby, and that man was Millard Taylor—her father, because he'd declared emphatically that she would always be his baby girl regardless of her age.

She squeezed a wedge of lemon over the mound of fried seafood, followed with a spoonful of tartar sauce, before topping it off with a small amount of hot pepper sauce. She picked up the sandwich and took a bite. A myriad of flavors tantalized her palate as she chewed slowly. Never had she eaten something so incredibly delectable. The lightly battered oysters and shrimp, the sweetness of the tartar sauce, and the sharp pungent bite of the hot sauce created a bouquet of flavors that literally exploded in her mouth. She'd eaten half of the sandwich before Shiloh returned with another one.

He sat down, smiling. "Do you like it?"

Dabbing the corners of her mouth with a napkin, Gwen sighed and closed her eyes. "I thought I'd died and gone to heaven when I took the first bite," she said when she opened her eyes to meet his amused stare.

"You've never eaten a po'boy?"

She went completely still. "A what?"

"Po'boy."

Gwen blinked once. "Don't you mean poor boy?"

Shiloh was hard pressed not to laugh. "It is not poor," he said, enunciating the *r*. "It's po' like in Edgar Allan Poe."

A hint of a smile crinkled her eyes at the corners. "But wouldn't it sound better to say poor rather than po'?"

Shiloh lathered tartar sauce over his po'boy, then added a liberal amount of pepper sauce. "It takes too long to say poor. Po' works for us down here."

Gwen reached for the coffee mug and took a swallow. It was strong and slightly bitter. She peered at Shiloh over the rim. "You all talk funny down here."

He eased the mug from her hand, smiling. "It's not you all, but y'all, Gwen."

"Hey, you're drinking my coffee," she said in protest.

Shiloh took a long swallow before refilling the mug. His eyes narrowed. "I offered you my po'boy, not my coffee."

Leaning back on her chair, she regarded him for a long moment. "Silly me for not remembering you're a cop."

"And what is that supposed to mean?"

Ignoring his defensive tone, Gwen reached over and patted the back of his hand. "Isn't drinking coffee and eating doughnuts a prerequisite for becoming a police officer?"

Shiloh's left eyebrow lifted slightly. "So, Miss Beantown, you've got cop jokes. For your information we don't eat doughnuts down here."

"What do you eat?"

"Beignets."

It was Gwen's turned to lift her eyebrows. "I've never eaten one."

"You po' deprived little thang," he teased. "There's nothing better for breakfast than café au lait and beignets."

Gwen wanted to laugh at his tortured expression. She hadn't known Shiloh Harper twenty-four hours, yet there was something about him that made her feel comfortable enough to verbally spar with him. There was something about him that said he was so very sure of himself and his rightful place in the universe.

"I'll make certain to sample one."

Shiloh rested his chin on a fisted hand. "I bet you won't be able to eat just one."

She assumed the same gesture, smiling. "That's one bet you're going to lose."

"Why would you say that?"

"Because I'm very, very disciplined."

"Don't you mean anal?"

Her dark eyes widened. "No!"

The beginnings of a smile touched Shiloh's mouth. "I think you protest too much."

"I'm not as anal as I am focused."

He lowered his hand without taking his gaze off the face of the woman sharing his table. He liked Gwen—her face, softly curving body, quick mind and witty repartee.

"What are you focused on now?"

"Fixing up my new home."

"And after that?"

"I don't know."

"You don't know?" he repeated. "What about a job?"

Gwen's body stiffened in shock that caused the words to wedge in her throat. "Are you interrogating me, Sheriff Harper?" she asked, recovering her voice.

"Of course not, Miss Gwendolyn Paulette Taylor."

A wave of heat swept up from her chest to her cheeks. "There's no need to call me by my government name," she said, frowning.

Shiloh threw back his head, laughing loudly, as everyone in the restaurant turned in his direction. Most couldn't remember the last time they'd heard Shiloh Harper laugh aloud. It was before his divorce and before Sheriff Virgil Harper died in the line of duty. Suddenly aware that he'd attracted attention, he glared at those staring at him and Gwen. One by one they turned away and went back to whatever it was they were discussing.

Gwen took another bite of her sandwich, chewing thoughtfully. Even if she didn't tell Shiloh of her plans, there was no doubt he would soon find out.

"I'm a journalist."

His sober expression did not change. "Radio, television, or print?"

"Print."

"Perhaps Nash McGraw could use you. He's the editor-in-chief of the *Teche Tribune,* and lately he's been putting out the paper using a skeleton staff."

"Is it a weekly?" she asked.

"Yes."

"If you run into him, please let him know that I'm interested in something part-time."

A hint of a smile crinkled the skin around Shiloh's eyes. "What else are you interested in?"

A shiver of annoyance raced up her spine and she had to admit that the man sitting across from her was good. He'd befriended her the night before and now had offered her his lunch while subtly interrogating her. She was a new resident, and he was probably intrigued that a single woman from Boston would relocate and take possession of a house sight unseen.

He'd retrieved all of her vital data when he entered her driver's license in a national DMV database, so if he wanted to check further into her background he could. Did he suspect she'd come to the Louisiana bayou to hide out, or establish a cover for a criminal operation? What the delicious-looking law enforcement officer didn't know was that she'd come to St. Martin Parish to start over. She wanted to restore *Bon Temps* to its original magnificence, work for a local newspaper, and if the latter did not materialize, then she would execute her Plan B. She would then apply for a teaching position at a local high school or college.

Shrugging a bare shoulder, she smiled at Shiloh through her lashes. "Not much else." She opened her handbag, took out a twenty and placed it on the table. "That should cover my lunch."

Shiloh's hand moved in a blur as he scooped up the bill and thrust it at her. "Keep your money. Lunch is on me."

Gwen glared at him glaring at her. "I'm sorry, Sheriff Harper, but I can't accept."

"Why not, Gwendolyn Paulette Taylor?"

A frown appeared between her eyes. "Stop calling me that."

"It's your name, isn't it?"

"Yes," she whispered loudly. "But there's no need to tell everyone who I am. I'm certain you're aware of identity theft nowadays. All someone needs is my social security number and I'm screwed."

Shiloh angled his head, and the sunlight coming in from a clerestory window slanted over his face, bathing him in a circle of light. The effect was so startling that Gwen didn't blink, swallow or breathe. The mesmerizing gold-green eyes were the colors of the swamp with slivers of sunlight piercing the towering cypress trees rising above the murky brown water.

"What are you running from?"

She blinked once. "Is that what you believe?"

He nodded. "Either you are running or hiding."

"Wrong, Shiloh. I'm doing neither. Four years ago I made a New Year's resolution to get rid of everything I didn't want or need. And when my aunt left me *Bon Temps* I decided it was time for a change of scenery. I'm here because I want to be here, not because I'm hiding or running from someone."

Standing, Shiloh came around the table, picked up the money and dropped it into her unzipped handbag. "Lunch is on me today. Once you're settled in you can repay the favor."

That said, he nodded and walked across the expansive restaurant. He knocked on a door with Office painted in large black letters. He opened it, walked in and closed the door, leaving Gwen staring at the space where he'd been.

She didn't know his connection with the owner of the Outlaw and didn't want to know. Gathering her handbag, she stood up and made her way to the entrance. The conversations stopped again as all eyes were trained on her. It was the first time in a very long time that she felt self-conscious. As a teenage girl she was always mindful whether her pants or tops were too tight whenever boys made ribald comments about her body. But as her body matured she'd learned to accept her looks and who she'd become.

Why, she asked herself as she stepped out into the bright sunlight, did she suddenly feel like an awkward teen who wanted to run home and change her clothes? It wasn't the first time men had stared at her in a pair of body-hugging jeans. However, it *was* the first time that a group of men had stopped talking to stare at her.

What made the men in southern Louisiana different from those in New England, other than they spoke a French dialect as well as English?

The questions bombarded Gwen's mind as she waited for the ferryboat. Was it because she was a stranger? Was it because the Outlaw was traditionally a male establishment? Or was it because Shiloh had called her darling in front of other patrons?

Moving over to a wooden bench positioned under a sun-bleached striped canvas awning, she sat and stared out at the slow-moving water. Instead of the uneasiness she'd experienced when seeing the murky swamp for the first time, she felt a wave of calm wash over her. It was as if she'd escaped into a world where the stress and craziness of what she was familiar with no longer existed.

Time moved on in a pace that could not be measured by seconds, minutes or hours. The sound of the approaching ferryboat shattered the stillness of the afternoon. Gwen stood up and walked down to the pier. It was time she returned to the boardinghouse, checked out and went home.

She knew that dust, grime and the musty smell associated with long-shuttered houses awaited her. But she welcomed the challenge. She couldn't wait to begin *Bon Temps'* makeover.

Chapter 4

Gwen worked nonstop around the clock, averaging five hours of sleep each night in order to make *Bon Temps* habitable. She knew she should've hired a cleaning company, but considered the housework she'd done therapy. She didn't have an office to go to, so airing, dusting, mopping floors and cleaning windows gave her a sense of purpose.

It took half a day to air out and clean the bedroom, sitting room and adjoining bath that she'd selected for herself. A search of the pantry yielded a large tin filled with exotic teas, and as dusk descended she'd sat on a cushioned love seat on the second-story veranda watching a cluster of fireflies illuminate the velvety darkness while listening to the unfamiliar nocturnal sounds.

The rest of the week was spent cleaning the other bedrooms, the kitchen and shopping in an upscale mall in Morgan City, twenty miles southeast of Franklin. It was the first time she chided herself for not having purchased a sport utility vehicle, considering how her trunk and the inside of her car now overflowed with grocery bags and other household items.

A moving company delivered cartons filled with her clothes, favorite books, electronic equipment, CDs, DVDs, her computer, photographs and family mementoes. And once a telephone technician installed the data lines she needed for a telephone, computer modem, and fax machine, she finally felt in control of her life. Aside from her cell phone she'd felt cut off from her family and friends.

Sitting at her computer, she opened a new document: Bon Temps Restorations. She wanted to replace the wallpaper throughout the house, reupholster sofas and chairs, repair and hang the magnificent living room and ballroom chandeliers, and repair the plasterwork on the ceilings. All of the wood floors and tables in the rooms on the first story were in need of refinishing. Bedroom closets overflowed with colorful dresses and costumes, suggesting that Gwendolyn Pickering had not led a reclusive lifestyle. The task of emptying the many closets still awaited her, a project she planned to tackle at her leisure.

The telephone rang, shattering her concentration. Peering at the display, she saw the name of her late aunt's attorney. She'd called his office in New Orleans, as he'd suggested during their last conversation, with her new number. Picking up the receiver, she introduced herself.

"Gwendolyn Taylor."

"Afternoon, Miss Taylor. Billy Sykes here."

She smiled. He'd referred to himself as Billy whereas stuffy Boston lawyers would've been Mr. Sykes. "Please call me Gwen."

A chuckle came through the earpiece. "I was hoping you'd allow me that honor. I suppose you're settlin' in all right."

"Yes, thank you."

"Good. I'd love to come down and sit a while with you, but right now I'm up to my eyeballs in a case that's sure to get a lot of media coverage. I just wanted to tell you that your aunt left a package with me about seven months before she passed away, and I'm going to send it to you by a bonded messenger."

"What's in it?"

He chuckled softly. "You'll see when you get it. He should get it to you by Thursday."

Her curiosity piqued, Gwen wondered how much Billy knew about Gwendolyn Pickering. She hadn't had much contact with her mother's favorite aunt. Gwendolyn, as she wanted to be called, traveled from Louisiana every five years to reconnect with relatives in Delaware, Pennsylvania and Massachusetts. She refused to vary her schedule, not even for a funeral. The year she celebrated her sixty-fifth birthday the visits, telephone calls, cards and letters—always without a return address—stopped. Everyone suspected she'd passed away until William Sykes called to inform Gwen that her great-aunt had left all of her worldly possessions to her namesake.

"How well did you know my aunt?"

"I didn't know her as well as my daddy did. But, he can't tell you anything because the Lord called him home last year. All I can tell you is that she didn't want me to contact you until after she'd been cremated."

"I'm glad she could trust you to follow her wishes, and I look forward to receiving the package."

"All I can say is Gwendolyn Pickering was quite a woman."

"Thank you, Billy, for everything, and if you're ever in the neighborhood, please come by."

"Why, thank you."

"Goodbye, Billy."

"'Bye, Gwen."

She hung up, wondering what else her aunt wanted her to

have. Her gaze shifted back to the blinking cursor on the computer screen. Her fingers touched the letters on the keyboard with lightning speed as the list lengthened. She'd just saved what she'd typed when the melodious chiming of the doorbell echoed throughout the house.

Walking out of the sun-filled room she'd set up as her office, she went to answer the door. It was probably the head of the landscaping crew who'd come earlier that morning to cut and weed the grass, and prune the fruit trees and flower beds. The aroma of freshly turned earth, cut grass and flowering blooms wafted through the many screened-in windows.

Peering through the security eye, she saw the face of a young man in a tan uniform. He wore the same hat she'd seen on Shiloh the night he'd answered her nine-one-one call.

She opened the door. The star on the man's shirt identified him as a deputy. "Good afternoon. Is there a problem, Deputy Lincoln?" she asked, reading his name badge.

Frank Lincoln removed his hat, cradling it to his chest. The sunlight glinted off his thick orange-red hair. "Good afternoon, Miss Taylor. I just came by to give you something from Sheriff Harper." He reached into the pocket of his shirt and handed her an envelope. "He said he'll come by later to talk to you about it."

Gwen took the envelope. She smiled at the deputy. "Please let Sheriff Harper I know I'll be expecting him."

Frank put back on his hat, grinning broadly. He'd recognized Gwendolyn Taylor as the woman who'd sat in the unmarked SUV with his boss. "You have a good day, Miss Taylor."

She returned his friendly smile. "Same to you, Deputy."

Gwen waited until he slipped behind the wheel of his cruiser and drove away before tapping the envelope against her palm and ripping off a corner. Opening the envelope she shook out two tickets. PAID, stamped in red, covered the face

of the tickets for a fund-raiser given by the Bayou Policemen's
Benevolent Association for Needy Families.

She closed the door to keep out the sultry heat, smiling.
She'd been so engrossed with cleaning *Bon Temps* that she'd
forgotten her commitment to purchase two tickets for the
fund-raiser.

Sitting on a formal high-back chair in the entryway, Gwen
placed the envelope and tickets on a mahogany table. Fatigue
washed over her and she closed her eyes. It wasn't until she
sat down that she became aware of how hard she'd worked,
pushing herself to the point of exhaustion.

A knowing smile softened her mouth. She'd told Shiloh she
was disciplined, focused, but he had countered, saying she
was anal. He was right, but that was something she wouldn't
readily admit.

What she did not want to acknowledge was that she was
an overachiever. From the first time she won a school-wide
spelling bee, made the high school honor roll and finally the
college's dean's list, Gwendolyn Paulette Taylor was moti-
vated to come out on top at all costs. And she hadn't needed
a psychologist to tell her she was overcompensating and
silently crying out for attention from her parents, who
obsessed about their terminally ill son. Langston was gone,
yet her drive for acceptance and approval continued until she
turned thirty.

With her New Year's resolution to streamline her life and
her decision to relocate to Louisiana, she'd finally accepted
that she hadn't needed anyone's approval except her own.

Shiloh slowed down as he maneuvered his sports car under
a live oak allée, coming to a stop at the end of a circular
driveway. He parked and turned off the engine. He'd called
himself king of fools for chasing after Gwen Taylor, but there
was something about her that wouldn't let him stay away.

He'd lost count of the number of times he'd driven past the road leading to her house and hadn't stopped to find out how she was settling in. What excuse would he use to explain his unannounced visit? He was certain Gwen would've recognized his deception if he told her that he was checking on residents in the area.

Shiloh reached for a decorative shopping bag on the passenger seat, opened the door to his Mustang convertible, stepped out, and glanced around him. The smell of grass and flowers hung in the air. It was a smell that had become an aphrodisiac, pulling him back to Teche even when he hadn't wanted to stay.

Soft gold light spilled from the floor-to-ceiling windows on the first story of the understated house with a full-height columned porch wrapping around the front and sides. He stepped onto the porch, rang the bell, waiting to come face-to-face with Gwen again. Less than a minute later he was met with the image of his ongoing musings bathed in light from an overhead fixture, and the sound of classical music.

His gaze moved over her features with the gentleness of an artist wielding a sable brush over a silk canvas. The unruly curls framed her face in sensual disarray, making her appear utterly wanton. The fitted halter dress displayed the fullness of her breasts and narrowness of her waist before flaring out around her hips and legs. His eyebrows lifted when he saw the color on her toes in a pair of black patent leather sandals was an exact match for her dress: vermilion red.

He smiled at Gwen as he handed her the shopping bag. "Good evening. Here's a little something to welcome you to the neighborhood."

Gwen stared up at the tall man in her doorway wearing an off-white, raw silk shirt, tailored black slacks, and Italian-made slip-ons, unable to ignore the tingling in the pit of her stomach. Despite her belief that she didn't have the time or inclination to indulge in a romantic entanglement, she knew she'd been waiting to see Shiloh again, even before his deputy came by to inform her that his boss would be stopping by. He'd come not as Sheriff Harper, but as Shiloh.

"Why, thank you. But you didn't have to. Besides, you've done enough." Her hand brushed his as she reached for the bag. A shiver raced up her arm with the slight contact. She knew Shiloh felt it, too, because he jerked his hand away as if he'd been burned.

He angled his head and smiled, wanting to tell Gwen that there were other things he'd wanted to do with her that he hadn't done with a woman in a long time. He wanted to take her to a place where they could eat, dance, and talk about any and everything.

"I don't know if you drink, but it's a bottle of French cognac."

"Thank you." Gwen grimaced. "I've forgotten my home training. Please come in."

He stepped into the entryway, noticing the obvious changes immediately. The scent of roses came from a burning pillar anchored in pink sand in a large glass chimney on the hand-kerchief table flanked by two hall chairs.

"Your place looks very nice. How long did it take the cleaning people to finish?"

Gwen left the shopping bag on the table, then felt the heat from Shiloh's gaze on her back as she led him into the living room. "I decided not to hire a cleaning company."

Reaching out, he caught her upper arm and turned her around to face him. "You cleaned this place by yourself?"

Tilting her chin, she gave him a direct stare. "Yes, I did. It's taken me a while, but I pretty much have everything under control. Right now I'm negotiating with the architectural firm that authenticated the furnishings to have them restore the moldings, ceilings, floors and walls."

Shiloh shook his head, unable to believe she'd taken on the Herculean project by herself. "What were you trying to do, kill yourself?"

Gwen stared at the fingers gripping her bare arm. "Please let me go, Shiloh." He complied and his hand fell to his side. "I'm sorry, sugah, but I'm not one of your hothouse Southern belles who wouldn't think of cleaning her own home because she just might chip a nail."

Her inflection was so unadulterated Deep South that Shiloh laughed. He wanted to tell Gwen that despite the backbreaking housework her nails were perfect. Cupping her elbow, he led her to a silk-covered sofa with a magnolia blossom print. He sat, and eased her gently down beside him.

"Let's not fight the Civil War again, Gwen."

She glared at him. "I would like to think that we would've been on the same side during *that* particular war."

"We *would*," he said, deadpan. "I didn't mean to imply that you were so helpless that you couldn't take care of yourself." He gave her a sidelong glance. "You strike me as a strong black woman who would be content to live your life with or without a man."

There was enough sarcasm in his statement to set Gwen's teeth on edge. "Men usually say that to me whenever I show them the door," she countered.

Shiloh turned to look at her. "How many have you shown the door?"

"Too many."

He lifted his left eyebrow. "It could be that you've been attracting the wrong kind of men."

Gwen rolled her eyes, shuddering. "Like a mega magnet."

He chuckled softly. "Perhaps your luck will change now that you've moved here."

She shook her head. "I'm really not looking for anyone.

Finding a partner is not at the top of my to-do list. In fact, it isn't even on my to-do list."

"How about an escort?"

Gwen sat up straighter. "What?"

"I'd like you to be my date for the fund-raiser."

Feeling strangely flattered by his interest in her, Gwen asked, "Wouldn't that pose a problem for Mrs. Harper?"

Shiloh shrugged a broad shoulder and flashed a smile. "Not in the least. My mother has her own escort for the affair, and I'm sure it wouldn't sit too well with my brother if my sister-in-law attended the fund-raiser with another man."

"Are you saying there are no Mrs. Harpers in St. Martin Parish other than your mother and sister-in-law?"

"They're the only two Mrs. Harpers," he confirmed.

Gwen hesitated, torn by conflicting emotions. The local hunk of the month had just asked her out, which should've flattered her, but she hadn't made time in her busy schedule for dating. She opened her mouth to decline his offer, then changed her mind. Shiloh had gone above and beyond his role as sheriff to make certain she was safe. What did she have to lose? The fund-raiser was only one date, not a commitment for something more.

"Excuse me, I'll be right back." She stood up, Shiloh also rising to his feet, and walked out of the living room. Two minutes later she returned and handed him an envelope.

Vertical lines appeared between his eyes. "What's this?"

She met his questioning gaze. "It's a check for the tickets."

Shiloh's frown vanished. "I already paid for the tickets."

"You paid for my ticket believing I would go with you?"

"I paid for your ticket with the hope that you *would* go with me."

She'd glimpsed an air of confidence in the man standing only inches away. She didn't know anything about Shiloh Harper, but liked what he'd shown her: confidence and truthfulness.

"I'll go with you, but on two conditions."

"Give it to me straight."

"I pay for my own ticket."

A hint of a smile softened his mouth. "Okay."

"And that you will not treat me as eye candy."

Lowering his head, Shiloh shook it slowly. "Now, that's going to pose a problem because—"

"Shiloh!" she chided, interrupting him.

He wagged a finger at her. "Gotcha!"

Gwen grabbed his finger. "I'd never figure you for a tease."

Shiloh sobered, his gaze betraying his thoughts. He wanted to tell Gwen that she was a tease. Everything about her face, body and intelligence teased and tantalized him.

"Only with you," he admitted. "Now if this knowledge goes beyond these walls, then my reputation as a tough lawman will be shattered completely."

"What goes on at *Bon Temps* stays at *Bon Temps.*"

Shiloh wondered if Gwen had knowledge of the gatherings that took place when her namesake owned the property. And for a quick moment he wondered if history would repeat itself. After all, the present-day Gwendolyn had admitted she wanted to remain anonymous.

"Promise?" he asked, lowering his head.

There was a beat of silence before Gwen whispered, "I promise." She wanted to tell Shiloh that he was too close, his virility too potent, and that she'd been without a man for too long, but the words were locked away in the back of her throat.

His head dipped and he breathed a kiss on one cheek, then the other. His free arm circled her waist. "I'll pick you up at six-thirty. This year's event will be a masquerade ball."

Gwen felt as if she were drowning in his gold-green flecked eyes. "Why a masquerade?"

Shiloh caught and held her entranced stare. "It depends on

which organization hosts the event. Last year the chamber of commerce's theme was Mardi Gras, and the year before, the fishermen association's theme was a hoedown." Releasing her waist, he took a backward step, leaving a modicum of space between them. "If you let go of my finger I'll let you get back to whatever it was you were doing."

Gwen released his finger as heat stole into her face. "I'm sorry."

Shiloh winked at her. "I'm not." He winked at her again. "I'll see you Friday."

"Friday," she repeated.

Shiloh hadn't kissed her, really kissed, yet the feel of his lips so close to hers made her want more—so much more. He was a tease—a tall, dark, devastatingly handsome man who made her forgo her promise not to date.

He pocketed the envelope with her check. "Your donation will be put to good use."

"I'm glad I have it to give."

Shiloh turned on his heel and strode for the door, Gwen watching his retreat. She stood in the same spot long after he'd gotten into his car and driven away. The soft ring of the telephone on a side table shattered her entrancement with a man who made her pulse race a little too quickly whenever she saw him, a man who was as different from the men she'd known in Boston as night was from day.

She reached for the cordless instrument. "Hello."

"How *y'all* doing?"

Gwen smiled. "Very funny, Lauren. Did you get my e-mail?"

"Yes. I'm sorry about not getting back to you sooner, but Cal and I just got back from New York. He was scheduled to meet with his publisher, so I went along and did some sight-seeing and shopping. We ate at a wonderful restaurant in your favorite neighborhood."

"How is Harlem?" Gwen asked as she settled down in a large club chair.

"Incredible. The changes are unbelievable with all of the gentrification. Enough talk about me. What's happening with you?"

Gwen gave her cousin a brief overview of her first week in the town, deliberately leaving out her encounters with Shiloh Harper. "The house is something out of *Gone With the Wind,* but on a smaller scale."

"Are you going to renovate it?"

"No," she answered truthfully. "I plan to restore it. The kitchen is the only room that doesn't conform to the original plans. It's the quintessential gourmet kitchen. As soon as I get the floors done I want you, Cal and the kids to come down for a visit."

"It'll have to be after the children are finished with summer camp and before school begins."

Cradling the phone between her chin and shoulder, Gwen ran a hand through her hair. "Good. I hope to have everything completed or near completion by that time, and hopefully will have perfected a few regional dishes by the time you guys get here."

"Don't forget to throw in a little social life along with your cooking and cleaning."

"I'm way ahead of you, cuz. I'm going to a masquerade ball Friday."

There was a pause on the other end of the wire. "Are you going alone?"

Gwen wanted to say yes, but had never lied to Lauren. "No."

"Who are you going with?"

"The local sheriff."

A soft gasp came through the earpiece. "Don't tell me you met him when he pulled you over for speeding? I shouldn't have to tell you that Louisiana isn't Boston where you were on a first-name basis with every traffic and beat cop."

As a reporter Gwen had what most in the newspaper business called a bloodhound's nose for a story, and early in her career she cultivated friendships with several high-ranking police officials, attending their fund-raisers and causes while reporting their acts of heroism in her column. She'd started at the *Gazette* as a crime reporter before she was reassigned to write the lifestyle column.

"No, Lauren." Gwen told her cousin how she came to meet Shiloh, leaving out the part where she wouldn't get out of her car and he had to carry her across the road.

"Does he at least look good in his uniform?" Lauren asked, giggling.

"Yes, but I think he looks better out of it." Shiloh wearing a shirt and jeans had the same impact on her as a man in formal attire; he carried himself with a commanding air of self-confidence that she hadn't encountered in any of the men she knew.

"You've seen him without his clothes?"

Gwen sucked her teeth while rolling her eyes. "Get your mind out of the gutter, Mrs. Samuels. I was talking about civilian clothes, not his birthday suit. And if you say anything else I'm going to hang up on you."

"There's no need to get *hos-tile*, Gwendolyn. I don't need to remind you that each sunrise brings you one day closer to thirty-eight."

"Hel-lo. Test tube," she countered in singsong.

"I'm hanging up," Lauren threatened.

"Good night, cuz," Gwen drawled, unable to stifle a laugh.

The distinctive sound of a dial tone reverberated in her ear before she pressed a button and placed the receiver in its cradle. She'd teased Lauren about artificial insemination even though she preferred getting pregnant naturally. Gwen doubted whether she would ever choose something so impersonal as going to a sperm bank. Adoption was her first choice, but that was an option that had remained secret.

Thinking of children reminded her of the upcoming fund-raiser to help needy families. Shiloh said the affair was a masquerade ball and she had to find something to wear.

"Aunt Gwendolyn," she whispered. Her aunt's closets overflowed with dresses and costumes from her days as an actress. She and her great-aunt were about the same height, and the last time she saw sixty-something Gwendolyn Pickering, the older woman had the figure of someone half her age.

It'd been years since she'd played dress-up; attending the fund-raiser would bring back memories of the Venetian masked balls during Carnival. There was something about the city built on water that reminded her of Bayou Teche. It was as if time stood still, leaving those trapped within in a spell that was far from reality.

She rose from the chair and headed for the staircase. The fund-raiser was only two days away.

Chapter 5

Sitting in a rocker on the porch of the Louisiana bayou plantation house where he'd grown up, Shiloh stared at his mother's delicate profile. "Are you sure you want to go with Augustine?"

Moriah Harper's hands tightened around the arms of a matching rocker as she stared at her bare feet resting on a cushioned footstool. "Yes, I'm sure, Shiloh." She turned her head and glared at her firstborn. "Do you have a problem with that?"

His jawline muscles clenched angrily to halt the flow of expletives poised on the tip of his tongue. He loved and respected his mother, but her decision to attend the fund-raiser with a man who'd pursued her relentlessly since she'd become a widow annoyed him. His father hadn't been buried a month when the man who owned the largest catfish farm in the region came calling.

"You're a grown woman, Mama, and—"

"Oh, so you've noticed," Moriah countered, interrupting him.

"Please don't be catty, Mama. It's not becoming," he chided softly.

Her green eyes sent off glints of anger and annoyance that her children—Shiloh in particular—were meddling in her life. She'd lost her husband, the love of her life, but she was still alive.

"What I find unbecoming is you trying to tell me how to live my life. Your daddy and I always talked about what we would do if one outlived the other. And we both decided that we wouldn't spend the rest of our lives mourning. I've gone to church every day since Virgil's funeral mass to light a candle for his soul. One morning last month Father Basil met me as I was leaving, asking whom I was lighting the candle for. When I told him that it was for Virgil, he said something to me that made me rethink my actions.

"I was lighting candles for someone who couldn't see the light, while my own light had gone out because I was mourning for what was, and would never be again. I'm saying this because Virgil's gone and he's not coming back. And in my heart of hearts, I know he doesn't want me to stop living, so that's why I accepted Augie's invitation to go with him to the fund-raiser." Her expression softened, making the elementary school nurse seem closer to fifty instead of sixty. "I'm sorry, but you're going to have to find your own date this year."

Shiloh smiled at the tall, slender woman with short curly salt-and-pepper hair. She'd inherited the large expressive green eyes from her Cajun father, and the richness of her chestnut-brown complexion from her African-American mother. "I already have a date."

The lashes shadowing Moriah's eyes fluttered as she sat up straighter. Her heart pounding a runaway rhythm, she prayed Shiloh hadn't reconciled with his ex-wife.

"Who is she?"

Crossing his arms over his chest, Shiloh leaned back on the chair, smiling. "You don't know her."

"Does she have a name?"

"Miss Taylor."

"Does Miss Taylor have a first name?"

"Gwendolyn."

It was Moriah's turn to smile. "Where did you meet her?"

"I picked her up along the road."

"Along the road as in hitchhiking?"

Reaching over and patting his mother's hand, Shiloh winked at her. "No more questions, Mama. You'll get to meet her Friday." Rising from his rocker, he leaned over, and kissed Moriah's scented cheek. "Good night, beautiful."

Moriah smiled, patting his back over the bulge of the firearm concealed under his shirt. "You be careful, son."

"I will."

She stared through the screen as he walked off the porch, got into his car and drove away. She'd always warned Virgil to be careful each time he left the house, and it was no different with her son.

"You'll get to meet her Friday." Shiloh's words stayed with her long after he'd left. While she'd lit candles for her dead husband, she'd also prayed for her son, prayed that he would meet someone who would make him laugh again.

She hoped this Gwendolyn Taylor would be the one who would help soften his heart.

It was six-twenty, and Gwen still hadn't slipped into the burgundy Renaissance-inspired ball gown. She was partial to the gown because it was in keeping with a black lace mask adorned with burgundy silk ties. She'd found the mask in a box stacked in a walk-in closet in one of the guest bedrooms.

Gwendolyn Pickering's closets were a treasure trove of

clothes and costumes spanning decades. Her aunt had made her theatrical debut at the age of six in a church musical, and as she matured, went on to starring and supporting roles in dozens of independent black films until her unexpected retirement in the early '50s. She left California for Louisiana, moving into *Bon Temps*.

Sitting on a padded bench in front of a vanity mirror, the bulbs surrounding the mirror set for nighttime illumination, Gwen outlined her mouth with a shade of wine-colored lipstick. She wondered how many times her aunt had sat on the stool making up her face before putting on her evening finery to descend the curving staircase and greet her guests who'd gathered in the ballroom.

Her aunt's life had always been shrouded in mystery, but some of that mystery was about to be stripped away. Gwen had found a large corrugated box filled with letters addressed to Miss Gwendolyn Pickering at *Bon Temps*. None of the envelopes bore a return address, but a postmark indicated they'd been mailed from New Orleans.

She applied a second coat of lipstick, pleased with the result. The upper half of her face would be hidden under the mask, so attention would be drawn to her mouth. A light coat of loose powder, a few brushstrokes over her hair pulled off her face and secured on the nape of her neck with ruby-jeweled hairpins that were in the package Billy Sykes had sent to her completed her exotic look. Her aunt had entrusted her lawyer with a small rosewood box filled with pieces of estate jewelry and an accompanying appraisal that listed the contents at half a million dollars. A teardrop-shaped ruby pendant suspended on an ornate filigree gold chain resting between the valley of her breasts matched the earrings dangling from Gwen's pierced lobes.

She left the dressing room for the bedroom. Picking the ball gown off the bed, she stepped into it and eased it up her hose-covered legs and over the bodice of a strapless black bustier. Narrow bands to billowy gauzy silk sleeves with gold-threaded embroidered cuffs were attached to the beaded off-the-shoulder straps. The revealing décolletage that flowed into a full skirt was not a garment for a lady invited to the de Medici court, but of a Venetian courtesan.

The doorbell chimed, and she went completely still. Turning, she stared at the clock on the fireplace mantel. It was 6:30. Shiloh was on time. Clutching the back of her dress with her left hand, she used her right to lift the sweeping skirt, and raced out of her bedroom and down the long hallway to the staircase.

"I'm coming!" she shouted as she descended the staircase in her stocking feet. She made it to the door before it rang again, opened it, and went completely still.

Shiloh stood under the beam of twin porch lamps in sartorial splendor. Light slanted over his deeply tanned brown face, making his eyes appear lighter than they actually were. Her gaze moved slowly from his stunned expression to a white tie under a matching spread collar shirt and dinner jacket with shawl lapels. Black dress trousers and slip-ons pulled together his winning formal dress.

"I'm still dressing," she said breathlessly.

"So I see," Shiloh confirmed, staring at the swell of flawless brown flesh rising and falling above the incredibly beautiful gown draping the body of the woman who'd occupied his every waking moment. He'd given up trying to identify why he'd found himself drawn to Gwendolyn Taylor and decided to give in to whatever it was that made him want to know her—every way possible.

Gwen moved behind the door. "Please come in. As soon as I hook myself up and get my shoes I'll be ready."

Stepping into the entryway, he eased the door from her grip

and closed it. His gaze never wavered as he stared down at the woman who'd caught him in a web of seduction with her lovely face, curvaceous body and sassy tongue.

"Let me hook you up."

Gwen shook her head. "No. I can do it."

"It'll go faster if I do it."

"No, Shiloh."

"Hush, darling," he crooned, ignoring her protest. Moving behind her, he began slipping the many hooks into the corresponding eyes, silently admiring the flawless skin on her back and curbing an urge to press his mouth to the velvety perfumed flesh.

Gwen suffered his closeness, his fingers brushing her bare skin. "I'm not your darling," she said in a strained voice she didn't recognize as her own.

Shiloh leaned closer, his mouth inches from her ear. "It's just a figure of speech down these parts, darling."

"Up where I come from it has a different connotation."

"You're no longer up North, darling, but in the good ole South. We may not be as liberal or freethinking as the people you're used to, but what we are is honest and for the most part God-fearing folks who'd go out of their way for a neighbor in need. You hang around here long enough and you'll see that."

She drew in a breath. "Are you chastising me, Shiloh Harper?"

He pressed a kiss to the side of her neck, smiling. "No, darling, I'm not. And I think you have the hang of it already."

"Hang of what?"

"Calling someone by their full name when you're pissed off."

Gwen could not stop the smile curving the corners of her mouth upward. "I believe that is a black thing."

"Black *and* southern."

"How did you get the name Shiloh?"

"I'll tell you in the car," he promised, fastening the last hook. "You're done."

Resting his hands on her shoulders, he turned her around to face him. A swath of heat raced through him and settled in his groin as he swallowed an expletive. Gwen Taylor wasn't beautiful. She was magnificent! The swell of breasts rising above the revealing décolletage spelled trouble—trouble for him.

"What's the matter?" Gwen asked when she saw his expression.

"Nothing," he answered truthfully. But if Gwen asked him the same question after the men attending the fund-raiser at the restored mansion near Shadows-on-the-Teche caught sight of her bosom, the response would have been another matter indeed.

She smiled at him. "Thanks for hooking me up. Give me five minutes and I'll be right back."

Shiloh watched her retreating figure, then sat down on one of the hall chairs and waited. He crossed one leg over the opposite knee, smiling. He knew attending the fund-raiser with Gwen would shock more than a few people because he hadn't been seen with a woman since his divorce.

He'd heard the rumors about his sexual preference, but hadn't bothered to refute them. He still preferred women, just not the ones who threw themselves at him. When he met Deandrea she'd come on to him like a voracious piranha. Her insatiable sex drive appealed to his ego because she claimed he was the first man who could satisfy her. They'd spent their entire honeymoon in bed, leaving only to eat and bathe.

However, the honeymoon ended a year later with him filing for divorce. He cited irreconcilable differences rather than adultery. Not outing Deandrea and François salvaged their reputations and his pride; he hadn't wanted anyone to know that he'd been cuckolded by his best friend.

Shiloh caught movement out of the corner of his eye and

rose slowly to his feet. Gwen came toward him, the toes of a pair of black silk-covered high heels peeking out from under the sweeping skirt of her gown. She handed him a lace mask with dark-red ties, as a small evening pouch suspended from her wrist by a silk cord bumped against her side.

"Can you help me with this?" Presenting him with her back, Gwen felt the warmth and inhaled the scent of the tall, muscular body.

Leaning closer, his chest pressed to her back, Shiloh placed the mask over her eyes and nose and tied the ribbons in a neat bow. "I'm going to have to renege on a promise."

Gwen shivered from the moist breath whispering over the nape of her neck. "Which one?" Her voice was low, throaty as she found the act of breathing difficult.

Shiloh smiled when he detected the slight shiver of her body. "Not to see you as eye candy tonight. You are beyond beautiful, Gwen. You look incredible," he said, unable to conceal his awe.

Gwen closed her eyes, swaying slightly as she felt the sexual magnetism that made Shiloh so attractive, so confident. A secret smile parted her glossy lips. She hadn't given him a hard time, but she also hadn't been that accommodating either.

She'd been forthcoming when she told Shiloh that finding a boyfriend, partner or husband wasn't at the top of her wish list. She wanted to meet someone, fall in love, marry and have a baby or two, but hadn't felt compelled to do so now. When many of her girlfriends were either getting engaged or marrying, she felt as if she were missing out on something—so she had agreed to become Mrs. Craig Hemming.

But it wasn't Craig paying her a compliment, but Shiloh—a man to whom she didn't want to be attracted, a man who reminded her that as a woman she had needs, a man who would introduce her to Louisiana's social scene.

"I'm going to allow you a reprieve, but only for tonight," she said quietly.

Shiloh's smile widened. "What's that, darling?"

Gwen shifted slightly, grinning at him over her shoulder. "I'll be your eye candy if you'll be my beefcake."

"Wh-wha-t!"

Staring at Shiloh's shocked expression through the openings in the mask, she cupped a hand behind an ear. "I can't hear you, darling."

Shiloh sobered up, then threw back his head and howled. "Okay. I accept." Winding an arm around her waist, he pulled Gwen flush against his length. She was unlike any other woman he'd met. He liked her, liked her a lot.

"How do you like your beef?"

There was a tingling in the pit of Gwen's stomach. He was so disturbing to her in every way that she was ready to throw caution to the wind.

"Well-done."

Shiloh's penetrating gaze moved from her mouth to her chest. "You like your beef well-done and I'm partial to dark chocolate." He leaned closer. "Especially when it's soft and extra sweet."

Gwen went completely still as a throbbing sensation beat wildly in her throat. Three inches of heels put the top of her head at Shiloh's chin, and she tilted her head to meet his mesmerizing gaze. She knew each time she saw him her feelings intensified, and this frightened her. She had to slow it down, take control of her emotions or she would find herself in too deep.

"I'm ready to leave now." Easing out of his grip, she reached for her keys on the entryway table.

Shiloh opened the door and waited for Gwen to lock up the house. He took her hand and led her to where he'd parked his

car. It had rained earlier that afternoon and the smell of rich
damp earth and flowers in bloom lingered. He helped her
into the Mustang, removed his jacket, placing it over the rear
seats, then slipped behind the wheel. Turning the key in the
ignition, he shifted into gear and the sports car shot forward
in a powerful burst of speed. The sound of a guitar and a tinny
piano playing a soulful Delta blues number came through the
speakers, the composition filled with anguish, hopelessness
and suffering.

Gwen relaxed against the leather seat, eyes closed, cooling
air from the dashboard's vent feathering over her masked
face. This was to become her second masquerade ball. The
first time had been ten years before in Venice, Italy for
Carnival. Craig had asked her where she wanted to celebrate
Valentine's Day, and she'd said Italy. He'd waited until they'd
boarded a gondola to attend a ball to propose marriage. Amid
a city inundated with tourists desperate to show off their
finery, and under a snowy sky with a biting wind she accepted
his ring and promise to marry. Four months later she'd
returned his ring and refused to accept his telephone calls. The
break was swift and without regret—at least for her.

"Were you named for the Civil War battle?" Her soft voice
shattered the comfortable silence.

Shiloh, content to drive, listen to music and enjoy the scent
and closeness of a woman whose presence made him feel and
say things he could've never imagined, gave Gwen a quick
glance before returning his gaze to the winding road. He liked
everything about her: her curly hair whether pulled off her
face as it was now or in a tousled style that made him want
to run his fingers through it, her rounded curvy body, her
femininity and confidence that let her wear a dress like the
one she wore, which ardently displayed her breasts in an

homage to womanhood. What confounded and kept him off-kilter was that he normally did not find himself attracted to women who looked like Gwendolyn Taylor.

"Nope. My folks named me after a church."

Shifting on her seat, Gwen turned and stared at his distinctive profile. "A church?"

"Weird, isn't it?"

She hesitated, a smile stealing its way across her face. "Not as weird as it is interesting."

"It's hardly headline news."

"Let me be the judge of that. I've written stories in my old column at the *Boston Gazette* that garnered more attention than the regular headlines."

"What type of stories did you write?"

"People stories, home and style features about ordinary people leading extraordinary lives. My home and style articles highlighted living space makeovers, or people who had unusual and sometimes very bizarre collections."

"Tell me about someone who really impressed you."

"I featured an elderly, childless widow who'd crocheted more than five thousand sets of baby booties and hats for teenage mothers living in group homes over a twenty-year period. I spent more than five hours with her, and during that time she'd crocheted a complete set, with matching ribbons. She used a portion of her Social Security check to purchase the yarn, but once the article was published a major yarn company pledged to send her whatever supplies she needed. I'd referred to Agnes Mueller as the 'angel of hope,' and the name stuck.

"Two years ago she was forced to give up needlework because a crippling form of arthritis made it impossible for her to hold the hook. I contacted the directors of the group homes, who in turn got in touch with all of the young women whose babies were lucky enough to receive Miss Mueller's gifts. All but three attended a special event where she was presented with a quilt stitched with the names of every baby who'd received her handmade hats and booties. The mayor made an appearance, along with a few other local officials, who gave her a proclamation in honor of her selfless work."

There were only the sounds of the music coming from the satellite radio station and the slip-slap of rubber on the roadway. Gwen turned to stare out the side window. The event honoring Miss Mueller was the highlight of her journalism career, and the man to whom she'd found herself drawn, the man who for some reason she couldn't explain she wanted to care about what she'd accomplished stared straight ahead, silently.

"You did good, Gwendolyn Taylor," Shiloh whispered in a reverent tone. He turned and smiled at her. "You did real good, darling."

She closed her eyes, swallowing the lump forming in her throat. "Please don't call me that, Shiloh."

"What? Gwendolyn?"

"No. Darling."

"And why not, darling?"

"Because where I come from men don't call women darling unless there's something between them. It's a word of endearment. A term of affection."

Shiloh bit back a smug grin. "I happen to know what an endearment means, Miss Wordsmith Newspaper Lady."

Gwen rested a hand on her hip. "Do you have something against journalists?"

Downshifting, he slowed as he negotiated a sharp curve. "Are you getting an attitude?"

"No way," she crooned. There was no way she wanted him

to believe he'd gotten to her. But, he had gotten to her. There was something about the sexy lawman that made her forget her promise not to get involved, because there were too many other things she wanted and needed to accomplish before she considered a relationship.

Shiloh drove another quarter of a mile before he spoke again. "You still want to know how I got my name?"

"Yes."

"It's a simple tale."

Gwen stared at him. "I still would like to hear it."

He gave her a quick glance. "My folks were on their way to New Orleans to visit with my daddy's people when Mama went into labor. She panicked because I was three weeks early. It was Sunday morning and Daddy stopped at a small church, hoping they had a telephone he could use to call a hospital. Before the pastor could make the call I was ready to make my grand entrance.

"The pastor's wife, who was a nurse, delivered me, so once the ambulance arrived there was nothing for the emergency medical personnel to do except take Mama and me to the hospital. Mama and Daddy had already selected names for their first child, but scrapped them in lieu of Shiloh in honor of Bayou Cane's Mount Shiloh Baptist Church."

Gwen smiled. "That's the kind of story that I would've written for my people column."

"Did you always write feel-good stories?"

"Yes. It was a breath of fresh air after four years as a crime reporter."

Shiloh wanted to ask her about some of the cases she'd covered, but they'd run out of time. He turned onto a paved road under an arbor of oak trees. Chauvin Hall stood at the end of the road, rising like a wedding cake sitting on a dark-green tablecloth. Towering ancient cypress framed wing pavilions, a Greek Revival facade, a Regency-style entrance and an octagonal cupola.

Red-jacketed valets jumped into and out of cars, maneuvering them into a designated parking area. A teenage girl sat on a stool holding a sign printed with large black letters: LAW ENFORCEMENT PERSONNEL PARKING ONLY.

Shiloh slowed, shifted into neutral and applied the emergency brake. "This is as far as we go."

A valet opened his door, handing him a ticket and a tuberose boutonniere. He smiled, his white teeth a startling contrast to his dark brown face. "Evening, Sheriff Harper."

Shiloh stepped out of the car, returning the smile, and patted the young man's shoulder. "How are you doing, Xavier?"

"Fine, sir."

Reaching for his jacket, Shiloh slipped his arms into it as he rounded the Mustang. He opened the passenger-side door, offered a hand to Gwen, and pulled her gently to her feet.

He showed her the boutonniere. "Can you please help me with this?"

Gwen took the fragrant, delicate flower and pinned it on his left lapel, then straightened his tie. "Where's your mask?"

Shiloh stared at his date under lowered lids, wondering if she was aware of the effect she had on him. She was the first woman, since he was introduced to Deandrea, that made him want to bed her without getting to know her first. There was something so wanton in Gwendolyn Taylor that evoked an emotion that bordered on recklessness more frightening than his facing down someone with a loaded gun.

His physical attraction to Gwen was undeniable, however, he wanted more than a quick romp in the bed. That he'd done with Deandrea and the act only served as a precursor to failure.

Reaching for her hand, Shiloh held it firmly. "None of the

hosts wear masks. However, at the strike of midnight all masks come off."

Gwen flashed an attractive moue. "I neglected to tell you that I have a midnight curfew."

He released her hand, wrapped an arm around her waist, and led her toward the entrance of the brightly lit mansion. "What happens if you break curfew?"

Leaning against his side, Gwen smiled up at her date. I don't know," she teased. "I've never broken curfew."

His eyebrows lifted. "Are you warning me that you're a good girl?"

She nodded. "A very, very good girl."

His fingers tightened against her ribs. "You don't have to worry about your virtue tonight."

"Why not?"

Shiloh stopped and winked at her. "If you can't trust your local law enforcement, then who can you trust?"

Gwen gave him a direct stare through the openings in her mask. "That would depend on whether you're Shiloh or Sheriff Harper tonight."

Lowering his head, he pressed his mouth to her temple. "That decision will rest with you."

"Why me?" she whispered.

"At the strike of midnight you'll have to let me know who you want me to be."

For the first time in a very long time Gwen had no comeback. Shiloh had absolved himself of all responsibility as to where their relationship would take them. He'd thrown down the gauntlet, and she would accept his challenge—but only if she could set the rules.

Chapter 6

Gwen made her way into the entryway of Chauvin Hall on Shiloh's arm, her gaze widening when she saw the expanse of skin. *And I thought my dress was risqué,* she mused.

Period evening gowns from the Italian Renaissance to the nineteenth-century bared backs, arms and ample bosoms, and the precious gems encircling necks, wrists, fingers and dangling from earlobes verified those in attendance were not members of needy families. Some of the men preened like peacocks in their formal and semiformal attire as they gazed adoringly into the eyes of their women. A frown furrowed her forehead when she spotted an elderly man in a Confederate military uniform.

She leaned into Shiloh, her frown in place. "I thought the war ended at Appomattox," she whispered under her breath.

Shiloh covered the small hand resting on his sleeve, lowering his head and his voice. "Retired Army Colonel Dean Staunton is a military expert. Last year he came as a German Hessian."

"Interesting."

He gave her fingers a gentle squeeze. "Do I detect a hint of cynicism, darling?"

Her frown fading, Gwen affected a saucy grin. "Of course not, dah-ling."

Shiloh stared at Gwen, momentarily speechless in his surprise. She'd chided him for calling her darling because she viewed it as a term of endearment. "Be careful how you use that word, because I just might think you like me a little."

"Of course I like you a little, Shiloh," she admitted. "If I didn't, then I wouldn't have come here with you."

"I thought—"

"Please, Shiloh. Let's try to get through this evening together without debating whether we like each other."

Shiloh's gaze lingered on the black lace mask concealing the upper half of her face. He wanted to tell Gwen that what he was beginning to feel for her went beyond mere liking, that the more time they spent together the more his liking intensified. She was right. He didn't want to spend the night arguing or debating issues, but enjoying her witty conversation and sensual femininity. The crowd in the entryway thinned out and he gave his name to one of two masked women in powdered pompadour wigs.

"Sheriff Harper, you're on the dais. Your lady will be at table number two."

Gwen compressed her lips tightly, wondering why Shiloh had asked her to accompany him if they weren't going to be seated together.

"I'll only be on the dais until we dispense with the speeches," he whispered close to her ear, answering her unspoken query. "Then I'll be yours for the rest of the night."

She was glad that her darker coloring and the mask hid the flush suffusing her face. "I'd like to apologize."

"For what?"

"For referring to you as a piece of meat."

Shiloh pressed a gentle kiss across her forehead. "Apology graciously accepted." Pulling back, he angled his head. "We'll hang out together until I'm called to the dais."

She nodded, smiling. "Okay."

He smiled at the woman with whom he'd found himself utterly enthralled. She was highly intelligent, a trait he admired in women, and she appeared very secure, an even more admirable trait. She was opinionated, which meant they would never have a boring conversation, and most of all Gwen was sexy as hell without even trying.

Gwen followed Shiloh into a ballroom the length of a football field. Prisms of light from a dozen chandeliers sparkled like diamonds on table centerpieces of full-leaded crystal vases that overflowed with white flowers in every variety. The scent of flowers and perfumed bodies would've been overpowering if not for the climate-controlled air. A classical composition performed by an orchestra made entirely of string instruments provided the perfect backdrop for the elegantly attired people filing into the historic mansion.

Shiloh wrapped his left arm around Gwen's waist. "I'd like you to meet someone."

"Who?"

The skin around his eyes crinkled when he smiled. "You'll see," he answered cryptically.

He rested a hand in the small of Gwen's back, steering her over to a tall slender woman in black, wielding a black lace fan, who looked as if she'd stepped out of the pages of a Jane Austen novel. A swarthy-skinned man with steel-gray hair dressed as a nineteenth-century gentleman farmer hung onto her every word.

"Mama?"

Moriah Harper turned at the sound of the familiar voice,

her green eyes widening behind her mask. "Shiloh, darling," she said, smiling.

He cradled her to his chest and kissed her cheek. "You look beautiful." Acknowledging her date for the evening, Shiloh extended his right hand. "Augustine."

The older man shook his hand, his lips twisting into a cynical smile. "Shiloh."

Augustine Leblanc, aware that Shiloh didn't approve of his intentions toward his widowed mother, had decided incurring the younger man's wrath was worth the risk to convince Moriah to attend the fund-raiser with him.

Shiloh released Augustine's hand, but did not drop his hostile glare. *The son of a bitch is taunting me,* he thought. His other arm tightened around Gwen's waist, the warmth of her body burning his fingers through her dress. Within seconds Shiloh had dismissed Augustine in his mind.

"Mama, I'd like for you to meet Miss Gwendolyn Taylor. Gwen, my mother, Moriah Harper."

Gwen moved away from Shiloh before she did something she would regret later. She wanted to kick him for putting her on the spot, because this was the first time she'd ever met a man's mother on their first date.

Recovering quickly, she offered her hand. "It's nice meeting you, Mrs. Harper."

Moriah shook the hand of the petite woman with a lush curvy body. She'd tried imagining what Gwendolyn Taylor would look like, and had failed miserably.

"It's my pleasure, Gwendolyn. And please call me Moriah."

Gwen liked Moriah immediately. She was friendly and unpretentious. "I'll call you Moriah only if you call me Gwen."

Moriah's rose-colored lips parted in a warm smile. "Then Gwen it is." She looped an arm through Augustine's. "This is my friend, Augustine Leblanc."

The older man nodded to Gwen. "Miss Taylor, you don't sound as if you're from down here."

The instant she opened her mouth everyone knew she was an outsider. "That's because I'm not from down here."

Moriah fanned her moist face. "Where are you from, Gwen?"

"Boston."

"Are you here on holiday?" Augustine asked.

Gwen noticed Augustine had said holiday instead of vacation. Shiloh had mentioned the region's isolation, so she assumed some European customs and vernacular still persisted more than two hundred and fifty years later.

"No, I'm not. I've just moved here."

Moriah's expressive eyebrows lifted as she stared at Shiloh. "Where are you living now?"

"St. Martin Parish."

"Where in the parish?" Augustine asked.

"Bon Temps."

The masks covering the faces of Moriah and Augustine wouldn't permit Gwen to see their shocked expressions. Moriah recovered first. Her smile was dazzling. "Have you sampled any of our Cajun cuisine?" she asked, deftly changing the topic.

"I've had a poor boy—I mean a po'boy at the Outlaw." The three shared a smile.

Moriah tapped her fan against her palm. "What about red beans and rice, peppers and grits or Creole shrimp and egg-plant?"

"No, ma'am."

Moriah flicked open the fan with a quick snap of her wrist. "That settles it. You must come for dinner next Sunday. You will bring Gwen when you come, won't you, Shiloh?"

He glared at his mother. "Why don't you wait for her to either accept or decline your invitation, Mama?"

Moriah ignored her son's reprimand, and smiled sweetly at Gwen. "Should I expect you, my dear?"

Gwen struggled to hide her confusion. What did Moriah expect her to say? No, I can't come? No, because her attempt at matchmaking is anything but subtle. No, because I don't need to spend any more time with your son than necessary. And no, no, no because Shiloh Harper wasn't a man she could date and relate to as a friend. Three pairs of eyes stared at her, the silence lengthening between them and making her uneasy.

"Yes," she said after a pregnant pause.

Exhaling audibly, Moriah pressed her palms together. "Good. You will bring her, Shiloh, won't you?"

He rolled his eyes at Moriah. "Yes, Mother, I'll bring Gwen with me," he said through clenched teeth. "Please excuse us, but we must circulate."

Shiloh shouldered his way through the crowd filling up the ballroom. He reached for a glass of champagne from the tray of a passing waiter and handed it to Gwen before he took one for himself.

She rested a hand on his sleeve. "You don't have to take me to your mother's."

He frowned at her. "Why not?"

"I can go alone."

His frown vanished. "You think my mother coerced me into agreeing to bring you?"

"Well, she did put you on the spot."

"No, she didn't."

"She's playing matchmaker, Shiloh."

"Moriah's being Moriah."

"What's that suppose to mean?"

"You'll find out after spending a couple of hours with her." He touched his flute to Gwen's and took a sip. The champagne was excellent.

Gwen moved closer to Shiloh. "Why are you being so evasive?"

A sensual smile softened his mouth. "Why are you so suspicious, darling? What you see is what you get."

"And I happen to like what I see, darling," crooned a sultry feminine voice.

Gwen turned to find a masked woman cradled in an embrace with a man who, although masked, reminded her of Shiloh. They shared the same hair texture, jawline and chin. He was an inch or two taller, his body larger, bulkier.

"Your woman is shameless, little brother."

Ian Harper dropped a kiss on his wife's braided head. "I wouldn't have her any other way. Well, big brother, have you forgotten your manners? Aren't you going to introduce us to your lady?"

Shiloh glanced down at Gwen and found her staring up at him. "Gwen, this masked man is my younger brother Ian, who also happens to own the Outlaw. And the beautiful woman with him is my sister-in-law Natalee. Ian, Natalee, Gwendolyn Taylor."

Gwen shook hands with Ian, then Natalee Harper. When she'd asked Shiloh about a Mrs. Harper, he'd confirmed there were only two. Moriah was the first, and she'd just met the second one. Natalee, a statuesque beauty with flawless mahogany-brown skin, was stunning in a black-and-red silk cheongsam. Her neatly braided hair was secured in a chignon on the nape of her long, slender neck.

"Your jewelry is exquisite, Gwen."

Gwen rested a hand over the blood-red stone resting in the valley of her breasts. "Thank you."

Shiloh listened to the exchange between Natalee and his date. Gwen's jewelry was exquisite, but he'd found her more ravishing than the world's most expensive bauble.

She claimed a natural lush beauty that literally took his breath away.

Natalee's gaze narrowed. "Do I detect a slight New England accent?"

"Boston," Gwen confirmed.

Natalee's vermilion-colored lips parted as she displayed her perfectly aligned white teeth. "I'm from Worcester. How long will you be staying in Acadiana?"

"I hope for a long time," she answered, smiling. "I'm now living at *Bon Temps*."

Natalee shook her finger at Shiloh. "I've got a bone to pick with you, brother love. You didn't tell me you had a girl-friend, and one who happens to be a homegirl."

Gwen's attempt to explain she wasn't Shiloh's girlfriend was preempted by a deep voice coming through speakers. "Gentlemen, please seat yo' ladies. And will the officers of the Bayou Policemen's Benevolent Association please take their seats on the dais."

"If you're not doing anything tomorrow, I'd love for us to have a girls' night out," Natalee said as Ian took her hand.

"What time do you want to get together?" Gwen asked, not seeing Shiloh's frown.

"I'll come and pick you up around eight," Natalee offered.

Gwen smiled at her. "Okay."

Shiloh curved an arm around Gwen's waist, directing her to a table positioned directly in front of the dais. His fast-talking sister-in-law had thwarted his plan to introduce Gwen to Cajun and zydeco music. He pulled out a chair and seated her. Leaning over, he splayed his fingers over her back. "Don't run away, Cinderella."

She stared at the luminous eyes that had darkened to a mossy green. Her eyelids fluttered as she inhaled the intoxicating fragrance of his cologne warmed by his body's natural scent.

Gwen felt a vaguely sensuous light pass between them that filled her whole being with a wanting so foreign it frightened her. She wasn't a novice when it came to men, but there was something about Shiloh Harper that made her feel like a virgin about to embark on a journey that would transport her from innocent to wanton within seconds if she were to lie with him.

"I can't run," she whispered.

His eyes widened. "And I don't want you to."

"Sheriff Harper, we all waitin' for ya," the voice boomed again.

Heads turned in their direction, while hundreds of pairs of eyes watched St. Martin Parish's sheriff straighten slowly and make his way to the dais. He sat, staring boldly and longingly at the woman whose beauty and vitality drew her to him like a powerful magnet.

Gwen hadn't realized she'd been holding her breath until she pulled her gaze away from the man who'd come out of the night to calm her fear of the unknown.

She, Gwendolyn Taylor, purportedly a strong, independent black woman, found herself falling for a lawman in a region of the United States where counties were parishes, where the number and differing species of wildlife outnumbered the residents, and where the racial and ethnic mix was as varied as the cuisine imbued with a distinctive flavor summed up in the phrase, *Laissez les bon temps rouler!*

Was she, or could she let go of her inflexible rules and regulations to let her good times roll?

She stole another glance at Shiloh who'd leaned closer to the man on his left to listen to what he was saying. Without warning, his gaze shifted and he stared at her. A knowing smile softened his mouth, and she returned his smile.

Yes, you can, the silent voice in her head taunted seductively. Within seconds, conservative, sensible and levelheaded

Gwendolyn Paulette Taylor decided to discard the resolutions she'd set down for herself four years before.

She was ready for Shiloh Harper, and ready to let *her* own good times roll!

A gangling man with a drooping white mustache stepped in front of the podium and a minute later silence descended over the ballroom. He cleared his throat before leaning closer to the microphone.

"For those who don't recognize me, I'm Rene Vacherie, sheriff of Lafayette Parish. As president of the Bayou Policemen's Benevolent Association for Needy Families, I would like to welcome everyone to what has become a yearly event wherein we all give a little more of ourselves to help the less fortunate.

"I've been threatened with bodily harm from my brethren sitting behind me that if my speech runs more than ten minutes, they're going to resort to an extreme type of punishment that will change me from a baritone to a soprano in zero to twenty seconds."

Everyone laughed while the seven officers hung their heads in what could be interpreted as a gesture of shame and remorse. A female officer, waiting for the laughter to subside, held up her hand.

"I keep telling the guys that I don't want to be the only woman sitting up here." Her statement elicited another round of laughter.

Rene placed a hand on his hip, and rolled his eyes. "Do they make pumps in a size fourteen?"

"I've got a pair in my closet," a very masculine voice called out from the back of the ballroom.

Yvette Vacherie, who sat across the table from Gwen, shook her fist at her husband. "If I find you wearing women's shoes, then you can kiss thirty-two years of marriage *adieu*, Rene Valjean Vacherie."

Gwen laughed so hard she had to put her hand over her mouth. And she wasn't the only one who found herself with tears in her eyes.

Rene sobered long enough to introduce the members of his board, each of whom came to the podium to say a few words. Gwen's heart turned over when it was Shiloh's turn to speak. A secret smile stole across her face when she heard gasps from a table behind her.

"I'm willing to bet I could gobble him up in six bites or less," came a muffled feminine voice.

"I'm not selfish, Mindy. Mama only wants a little piece," another voice whispered.

He's hot and mine for the night. The thought had popped into Gwen's head, unbidden.

Shiloh adjusted the microphone. "I'm Shiloh Harper, sheriff of St. Martin, and I'm proud to announce that our parish's fund-raising efforts have far exceeded this year's goal. Several of our families have been hit particularly hard because of hurricanes Katrina and Rita and many of our military reservists have been deployed to the Middle East. Last night we received a check from an anonymous donor who earmarked the funds to cover four years of college for Xavier Jefferson, Jr. who'd recently lost his father, Captain Jefferson, in Afghanistan."

Shiloh's penetrating gaze swept over the room as everyone rose to their feet, applauding. He stared at Augustine, who was gazing longingly at Moriah. He froze, realization dawning. His mother, who was Xavier's godmother, had gotten Augustine Leblanc to write a check for the pre-med student's college tuition.

Augustine turned from Moriah and stared at Shiloh. Raising his right hand, he touched his forehead in a mock salute, smiling when Shiloh returned the barely perceptible gesture. The two men had called a truce—at least temporarily.

Shiloh relinquished the podium to Rene who asked Father Raymond to offer the benediction as the wait staff stood ready to serve the two hundred gathered at the damask-covered tables.

He left the dais as soon as the speeches ended, taking his seat beside Gwen. Reaching for her hand under the table-cloth he gently squeezed her fingers. Her hand was freezing. The mansion was cool, but not so cool that she would require a wrap.

"Are you cold?"

She shook her head. "No."

"Then why are your hands so chilled?"

Gwen leaned against his shoulder. "Cold hands, warm heart."

Shiloh let go of her hand, removed a stud on his dress shirt, then reached for her left hand. He didn't give her time to react as the heat of his body warmed her icy fingers.

"How's that, darling?"

"Shiloh, no!" she gasped, as he tightened his grip on her delicate wrist. Shifting slightly on her chair, she met his gaze. Her breath caught in her throat as she slumped against the tufted back, her eyelids fluttering. What she saw in the gold-green eyes spoke volumes. He didn't have to breathe a word because the deep-set luminous orbs communicated what she was feeling, had felt since the first night he'd come to *Bon Temps* to check on her.

His lids came down, hiding his innermost feelings as a sly smile parted his lips. "Better, darling?"

"Yes, Dr. Feelgood," she whispered after an interminable pause.

Chuckling under his breath, Shiloh let go of her hand and replaced the shirt stud as waiters set out plates of broiled and fried fish fritters with accompanying sauces, carafes of wine and crystal pitchers filled with iced tea, water and soft drinks.

Gwen leaned closer to Shiloh, her bare shoulder pressing against his muscled one. "You're going to have to identify a few of the items on my plate."

Picking up a fork at his place setting, Shiloh identified the corresponding varieties of shellfish on his plate. "Scallops, fried clams, shrimp tempura, soft-shell crabs, oysters, conch, and frogs' legs."

She wrinkled her nose, grimacing. "Frog legs."

"They're delicious with *beurre noisette.*"

"Lemon butter sauce or not, I'm not eating them."

"I didn't know you understood French."

"Actually, I don't," she admitted. Gwen told him about her trip to Paris. "Yours truly loves to eat, so the first thing I learn when traveling to a foreign country is how to order food."

Angling his head, Shiloh stared at Gwen's enchanting profile. Even with the mask concealing most of her face he was still enthralled with her. She was the complete opposite of the women he'd found himself drawn to in the past. The women he'd dated before were very tall and thin, though he had no preference as to their complexion.

However, Gwen Taylor wasn't tall and she wasn't thin. And she wasn't a type. She was an enigma, a mystery woman who lived by her own rules. He viewed her as an independent career woman in her mid-thirties, unmarried, childless, who did not appear to be remotely interested in hooking up with a man. And if he had to sum up her motto, it would be: *I can do it myself.*

"Careful with that," he said softly when he saw her dip a broiled shrimp into a spicy hot sauce.

Gwen cut her eyes at him. "I can handle this." Her burgundy-colored lips parted in a smile when Shiloh reached for a water goblet. "Are you thirsty, darling?"

He shook his head. "No, sweetheart. I'm just standing by

in case you're going to need to put out the fire that's about to start in your mouth."

She grunted softly. "Keep waiting." Their gazes met and fused as she popped the shrimp into her mouth. It took her more than a minute to chew and swallow the flavorful morsel. She was hard pressed not to laugh at Shiloh's stunned expression. "What's the matter, darling?"

He blinked once. "I…I just thought you couldn't…well wouldn't be able to eat something that spicy."

"Why not?"

He took a deep swallow from his water goblet, then set it down on the table. "Because you're from Massachusetts I assumed your taste in food would lean more toward bland dishes."

"Oh, really? You've got Bay State jokes. And just what is it you think I eat?"

"Corn pudding, chowders and kidney pie."

Gwen wrinkled her nose in revulsion. "Why kidney pie?"

"I tried it once at a Boston restaurant. I took a trip up to Massachusetts a week before Ian and Natalee's wedding to see the city and take in some of the sights. After the third night I'm ashamed to admit that I went to every fast food place I could find for breakfast, lunch and dinner."

She affected a moue. "I'm sorry about that, but if I'd known you then I would've either taken you to several wonderful restaurants or invited you to my place for a home-cooked dinner."

He leaned closer. "Can you really cook?"

Tilting her chin, Gwen said haughtily. "All I'm going to say is that this sister's got mad game in the kitchen." As teenagers she and Lauren spent their summers with their paternal grandmother, who'd taught them to how to prepare everything from soups and salads to desserts.

"When are you going to cook for me?" he whispered close to her ear.

"It's your call," she countered.

"I'm off next Tuesday and Wednesday."

"Make it Wednesday. Is there anything you can't eat?"

He gave her a lingering stare. "Nope."

"Then I'll expect you Wednesday."

"What time should I come?"

"Seven."

Shiloh nodded, then turned his attention to the woman on his right who'd placed a hand on his jacket just as the first course was removed. The next of the seven-course dinner appeared as if out of nowhere. Most of the fish entrées were as exquisitely pleasing to the eye as they were to the palate.

"Aren't you going to have dessert?" Shiloh asked Gwen three hours later when coffee and platters of miniature cakes, pastries and seasonal fruits were set out on the table.

"No. I'm too full."

His eyes widened. "But you hardly ate anything." She'd left food on her plate with each course.

"I ate more than I would usually consume in one sitting."

Shiloh wanted to ask her if she was dieting, but realized it might be inappropriate. This was only his first date with Gwen, and he didn't want to do anything to jeopardize their fragile friendship.

When he'd asked her to accompany him to the fund-raiser and she'd accepted he'd thought himself lucky. But luck was as fickle as the turn of a card or a roll of the dice—it was there one second, then gone the next.

The lights dimmed twice. "Dancing will begin in fifteen minutes," Shiloh said to Gwen.

"I'm going to the powder room to freshen up." Shiloh

stood up and pulled back her chair. "Don't run away, Prince Charming," she teased, referring to what he'd said to her before he was called to the dais.

He laughed, the rumbling sound coming from deep within his broad chest. Those familiar with Shiloh turned and stared at the sheriff with incredulous expressions. It was obvious to many of them that the woman in the revealing dark-red dress was special, special enough to remind them how much their homegrown son had changed once his fairy-tale marriage ended.

At the stroke of midnight Gwen reached up and removed her mask. Shiloh's impassive expression did not change, his gaze fixed on her mouth. He took a step, lowered his head, and brushed his mouth over hers. She gasped in surprise, her lips parting and permitting him to deepen the kiss as desire arced through her like a jolt of electricity.

"Why did you do that?" she asked in a breathless whisper.

Shiloh winked at her. "It's a tradition." He waved a hand. "Look around you."

Shifting, she saw couples sans masks embracing and kissing. "You could've warned me, Shiloh."

Anchoring a finger under her chin, he kissed her again. "Don't you know how be spontaneous?"

"Not here and not now."

Wrapping his arms around her waist, Shiloh pulled Gwen against his chest. "Did I embarrass you?"

She rested her hands on his lapels. "No. You just caught me off guard."

He chuckled. "I'm sorry if I don't come with a warning label."

Gwen wanted to tell Shiloh that he needed to come with warning and rating labels. Her hands moved up over his shoulders until her arms circled his neck. Rising on tiptoes, her mouth only inches from his, she winked at him.

"Let's dance."

Shiloh complied, pulling her closer. A jazz band had replaced the orchestra, playing a popular love song that had everyone up and dancing. She danced every number with Shiloh until Ian broke in. Without his mask, his resemblance to his brother was uncanny. Even though they looked alike, their personalities were completely opposite. She found him witty and easygoing.

An elderly man poked Ian's back. "May I cut in?"

Ian lifted his eyebrows, and stared down at a diminutive man with an ill-fitting toupee.

Gwen stared at Ian, silently imploring him to refuse the request after she saw the man gawking at her chest. He was practically salivating. Her silent plea went unanswered as Ian released her. She suffered through the slow number with the scratchy hairpiece grazing her bosom.

The selection ended and she wended her way through the crowd, left the ballroom, and stepped out onto a gallery with old-fashioned lampposts that cast soft yellow light over a formal garden. The humid night air wrapped around Gwen like a diaphanous veil as the tangy smell of the Gulf wafted in her nostrils. The sounds of voices and muted laughter came from the garden.

"Miss Taylor?"

Turning around, she stared at a formally dressed, middle-aged man with neatly brushed silver hair and a deeply tanned face. It wasn't until he moved closer that she was able to discern his delicate features. His eyes, a brilliant bluish-gray, were mesmerizing.

"Who's asking?"

He inclined his head politely. "Nash McGraw, ma'am. I'm publisher and editor-in-chief of the *Teche Tribune*. Sheriff Harper told me that you were interested in a part-time position with the newspaper."

"I am, but—"

"You don't have to give me an answer now, Miss Taylor," Nash interrupted in a quiet drawling cadence. He reached into the breast pocket of his tuxedo jacket and handed her a business card. "Give me a call and we'll talk about when you can start."

Vertical lines appeared between her eyes. "Won't you need references?"

He gave her a boyish smile that transformed his face, making him appear years younger. "No. I've checked out your column on the Web." He inclined his head again. "I'm sorry to have bothered you."

He turned and walked back into Chauvin Hall. Gwen was still standing in the same spot when Shiloh found her.

Wrapping his arms around her waist, he pulled her gently to his chest. "Are you ready to go home, princess?"

Leaning back in his embrace, she nodded. "Yes, prince."

Shiloh held onto Gwen's hand as he walked her to the door. It was after two in the morning and he still hadn't wanted their date to end. He eased her key from her loose grip and opened the door. Stepping into the entryway, he placed the key on the table, then turned and cradled her face between his hands.

"I'll see you Wednesday." He kissed the end of her nose. "Thank you for a wonderful evening."

Gwen smiled. "Thank you for making it wonderful." Rising on tiptoe, she touched her lips to his. "Good night, Sheriff Harper."

Chuckling softly, he pressed a kiss along the column of her scented neck. "Good night, Gwen."

Ten minutes later he unlocked the door to his house, undressed, showered, and for the first time in a long time he sought out his bed instead of the hammock.

Chapter 7

Gwen woke to the hypnotic sound of rain tapping against the French doors. Rolling over and sitting up, she peered at the clock on the bedside table. She'd overslept—again.

As she swung her legs over the side of the bed and slipped her feet into her fuzzy slippers, reality dawned. She wasn't in Boston, didn't have to get out of bed, didn't have a job, and she didn't have to do anything she didn't want to do.

Her life had changed—dramatically. Minutes, hours, meetings, daily calendars and deadlines no longer measured her life.

Within a month of listing her condominium with a Realtor she had a buyer. A husband-and-wife artist team made an offer she would've been a fool to refuse.

Upon the recommendation of her financial advisor, Gwen invested the proceeds of the sale and donated the apartment's furnishings to a local church and her favorite charity.

Rising from the bed she made her way into the bathroom. After an evening of eating, drinking and dancing she looked forward to a more leisurely day. What she did not want to think about were the hours she'd spent with Shiloh. He'd been the perfect date: charming and attentive. She knew many of the parish's longtime residents were curious about her, and she truly felt like Cinderella when she overheard curious whispers speculating about her identity. But unlike Cinderella, she did not flee the ball at the stroke of midnight. She did find herself in the arms of her prince when Shiloh gave her a kiss that heated her blood and left her wanting more—much more.

After breakfast she planned to call Nash McGraw, the *Tribune*'s editor. She also wanted to go through at least one of the guest bedroom closets, and read some of her late aunt's letters before she prepared to go out with Shiloh's sister-in-law.

Gwen picked up the carafe to refill her coffee cup when the doorbell rang, startling her. She didn't think she would ever get used to the sound that reminded her of pealing church bells.

"That doorbell has got to go," she mumbled under her breath as she walked out of the kitchen to answer the door.

Peering through the peephole, she saw a woman with a small child. She opened the door to discover that the rain had stopped and the rays of a watery sun pierced an overcast sky. A top-of-the-line Jaguar was parked in the driveway.

She smiled at a tall, thin woman with raven-black hair, alabaster skin, and cornflower-blue eyes. She reminded Gwen of a Ralph Lauren model in a white linen sheath dress and matching pearl necklace.

"Good afternoon, Miss Taylor. I'm Holly Turner, and this is my son, Kyle. I saw you at the dance last night with Sheriff Harper." She handed Gwen a pale blue wicker basket wrapped in gold cellophane. *Turner Treats* was imprinted on a profusion of matching streamers. "I wanted to give you time to settle in before welcoming you to town."

"My mama makes the best chocolate chip cookies in the whole wide world," Kyle said proudly.

Gwen smiled at the child, whom she assumed to be about four years old. A spray of freckles over his nose and cheeks was the only color in what would've otherwise been a very pale face. Kyle Turner was a small male version of his mother.

Her smile widened. "Yum-yum. My favorite." She redirected her attention to Holly. "Won't you come in? And please call me Gwen."

Holly shook her head. "I'm sorry, but I can't stay." She ruffled her son's hair. "Kyle has a long overdue appointment with his barber. If you're free tomorrow evening, I'd like you to join a few of your neighbors for an early Sunday evening get-together."

Gwen knew she'd become an object of curiosity after she'd attended the fund-raiser with Teche's sheriff. She hadn't planned anything for the next day, but wanted to remain an enigma for as long as she could.

"I'm sorry, but I won't be able to make it."

"How about next Sunday?"

She wouldn't be available the following Sunday because she'd committed to share dinner with Moriah. "If the invitation is still open in two weeks, then I'll join you."

Holly gave her a triumphant grin. "Of course it is, Gwen. The other ladies are just dying to meet you." She'd drawn out the word *dying* into three syllables.

What they're dying to know is my business, Gwen mused, returning Holly's smile. She'd admitted to Shiloh that she wanted to maintain a measure of anonymity, but that would be difficult once she was introduced to Holly's social circle.

"Do you want a puppy, Miss Taylor?"

Holly gave Kyle a warning look. "Mind your manners, darling."

"But you said we have to give them away, Mama."

Gwen smiled at the interchange between mother and son that reminded her of Lauren and her children. "What kind of puppies are you giving away?"

Kyle scrunched up his face. "What kind are they, Mama?"

Holly met Gwen's amused gaze. "They're purebred toy poodles. I have AKA papers on them."

"How old?"

"Three months."

"Color and sex?" Gwen asked Holly. She'd grown up with cats and dogs as pets.

"I have two. Both female. One is like a sandy-beige and the other a chocolate brown. They're already paper-trained and a vet has given them their shots."

Gwen decided having a little dog would be fun. "I'll take the brown one."

A flush suffused Holly's face. "I don't want you to think I'm here because I want to give away a puppy."

"Of course not," Gwen said softly, hoping to put the obviously flustered woman at ease. "It's been a long time since I've had a pet and I have more than enough room for a tiny dog to have the run of the place."

Holly's blush deepened. "If it's all right with you, I'll drop her off later this afternoon."

Gwen nodded. "I'll be here." She waited until Holly and Kyle returned to their car before she closed the door.

She had the house and now a dog. All she needed was a husband and children. As soon as the thought popped into her head, she dismissed it. Lauren's teasing was getting to her.

She didn't need a husband or children. Not now, not when her sole mission was restoring her new home.

* * *

Shiloh looked up with a knock at the door. He closed the cover on the report compiled by the Louisiana Bureau of Investigation. Deputy Jameson's stocky body filled the doorway.

"Yes, Jimmie?"

"A Marvin Oliver wants to see you."

Shiloh stared at the man who was certain to become sheriff once his term expired. "What does he want, Jimmie?"

James Jameson shook his shaved head. The Dillard University graduate stepped into the office, closing the door behind him. "I don't know, Shiloh."

"Didn't you ask him?"

Jimmie nodded. "Yeah. But he wouldn't tell me," he said in a hushed whisper. "The suit smells like the law."

Shiloh smiled at his deputy. He was the brightest police officer Shiloh had ever encountered. The FBI had recruited Jimmie within weeks of his graduation because they were actively seeking African-American agents.

Jimmie's tenure with the bureau was ten years, after which he returned to Louisiana to help his father with his younger siblings after his mother died of a massive stroke.

"Which one, deputy?"

Jimmie flashed a smug grin. "U.S. Marshal or DEA."

Pushing back his chair, Shiloh came to his feet. "We'll find out soon enough. Send him in."

He was still standing when a slender man entered his office. He was the quintessential bureaucrat—short, conservative haircut and dark suit.

Shiloh extended a hand. "Special Agent Oliver, or is it Marshal Oliver?"

Marvin Oliver went completely still as he stared at Sheriff Harper. "Who told you?"

"Which one is it?"

Recovering quickly, he shook the proffered hand. "It's Special Agent Oliver. DEA. How did you know?"

"Deputy Jameson, the man you just blew off like a gnat, made you the instant you walked in here. Please sit down, Agent Oliver." He motioned to a leather love seat. He waited for the drug enforcement agent to sit before he took a matching chair. Shiloh turned the chair around to face him.

"You're here because you either need my assistance, or you are going to tell me something I already know," he said, not bothering to conceal his irritation.

"Look, Harper—"

"No, Oliver," Shiloh countered, interrupting him. "I'm more than happy to cooperate with your agency, but I'm going to demand one thing from you."

There was a moment of tense silence before the agent asked, "What's that?"

"Respect. You will respect *my* office *and* the people who work here. When Deputy Jameson asked you to identify yourself, then you should've done so."

Marvin Oliver's gaze narrowed; he was smarting from the reprimand. His supervisor had briefed him about Sheriff Shiloh Harper. The arrogant former district attorney had been on a fast track for a judgeship before he was appointed to serve out his father's term. It was apparent he wasn't too happy in his present position.

"I didn't come down to this *swamp* to mix it up with you, Sheriff Harper. I'd like to believe we're on the same side."

Shiloh schooled his facial expression not to react to the remark. Crossing his knee over the opposite leg, he stared at the toe of his polished boot. His head came up slowly as he gave the DEA agent a long look.

"Are you here on an undercover assignment?"

"No. Why?"

"Because I'm willing to bet that you'll end up as gator bait before the end of the week."

The agent's back stiffened as he leaned forward. "Is that a threat, Sheriff?"

Shiloh's expression was impassive. "As a former officer of the court I know enough not to threaten a federal officer. I'm just cautioning you that if you don't change your attitude, then you're going nowhere—fast. Folks around here don't take kindly to outsiders looking down their noses at them."

Agent Oliver shifted uncomfortably. He hadn't wanted to come to the bayou because of the heat, humidity, mosquitoes, snakes and alligators. Layers of sunscreen and insect repellant provided little or no protection for his fair skin.

"I'm here to brief you on an operation that has been approved by your Police Jury Association." When Shiloh's expression did not change, he continued. "Last year we busted up a major meth operation outside Natchitoches. Informants tell us that several meth production sites have moved into southern Louisiana, which makes it more difficult for undercover agents unfamiliar with this part of the state. Once we got your report about the hijacking of a truck carrying anhydrous ammonia, we were certain that they had set up something around here."

Shiloh lowered his leg, placing his feet firmly on the carpeted floor. "Do you have enough agents to cover the twenty-two parishes that make up southern Louisiana?"

Marvin shook his head. "We don't have enough agents who are able to blend in in this part of the country."

"Who do you have?"

"Inez Leroux. She lived in Lake Charles for sixteen years before her family moved to Shreveport. What's good is that she speaks the Cajun dialect."

Shiloh listened intently to Agent Oliver as he related the

background information on the special agent assigned to his jurisdiction. "My field director believes your brother's restaurant is the best place for Inez because it's a hangout during the week, and most of the locals gather there on the weekend. We're certain she'll overhear something that just might give us a lead."

Ninety minutes after the DEA agent walked out of his office, Shiloh read the fax signed by the executive director of the Police Jury Association. The directive confirmed the co-operation of local law enforcement with the U.S. Drug Enforcement Administration's fight against the manufacture and sale of methamphetamine. Reaching for his telephone, he dialed his brother's private number.

"Ian here."

"How long are you going to be there?"

"Until closing time. What's up, brother?"

Shiloh stared at the Baton Rogue address on the fax. "I'll tell you when I see you."

"Is it about Mama and Augustine?"

He exhaled, running a hand over his face. "No, Ian. Mama can see whoever she wants."

"Is it because of a beautiful young woman in a red dress that you changed your mind?"

"Don't bring Gwen into this."

"We'll talk about her once you get here," Ian said, chuckling softly.

"No, we *won't*. I'll see you later." Shiloh replaced the receiver, ending the call. He didn't want to discuss Gwen Taylor with his brother, because he didn't want to lie to Ian about what he was beginning to feel for her.

He stared at the daily roll call schedule tacked to a corkboard, then pressed a button on an intercom. When Jimmie answered, Shiloh said, "Have Rossier cover the front desk for you."

He had to inform his highest-ranking deputy that a special undercover agent from the DEA was scheduled to go undercover in their parish before the end of the month.

Gwen answered the doorbell, a ball of fur nipping at her heels. She smiled at the puppy. "It's not for you, Cocoa."

Holly, as promised, had dropped off the poodle along with a large sack of food, a collar, a leash, a supply of wee-wee pads, a record of the dog's vaccinations, and a natural wicker bed with a blue-and-white gingham cushion.

She'd named the puppy, small enough to fit in the palm of her hand, Cocoa because her coloring reminded her of dark milk chocolate, and within an hour of their meeting, master and dog had bonded.

Natalee Harper stood on the porch dressed all in black— pants, halter top and sandals. Braids from her ponytail cascaded over one shoulder. Cocoa yipped and nipped at her toes seconds before Gwen scooped her up.

"If you're going to live here, then you can't go after company," she said softly, scolding the puppy. She smiled at Natalee. "I'm sorry about Cocoa. It's going to be a while before I can train her. Please come in."

"Girl, I love your shoes," Natalee crooned.

"Thanks." Gwen's animal print fabric pumps matched the silk camisole she'd pulled on over a pair of cuffed linen capri slacks.

Natalee touched the handkerchief table in the entryway. "My word. How old is this table?"

Gwen glanced over her shoulder. "I think that piece is eighteenth century."

"Incredible." There was no mistaking the awe in Natalee's voice as she followed Gwen into the living room. Red tags were attached to tables and chairs. "Are you having a tag sale?"

"No. The tagged pieces have to be refinished. I have a decorator coming in next week to give me an estimate. Would you like a quick tour before we leave?"

"Why sure, honey," Natalee drawled in a thick Southern accent.

The two transplanted New Englanders laughed hysterically, as if sharing a secret. Gwen left Cocoa in the laundry room, closing the door behind the whining puppy before leading Natalee in and out of rooms, lingering to give her an overview on a few priceless antiques.

"How long did your aunt live here?" Natalee asked.

"At least fifty years."

"Did she decorate the house?"

"I don't know," Gwen answered. "All my family knew was that Gwendolyn Pickering lived in Louisiana, but not once did she ever say, 'Y'all come on down.' My mother called her the 'black Greta Garbo.'"

Natalee tossed her braided hair over her shoulder. "I've lived here for two years, and in all of that time I'd never caught a glimpse of Gwendolyn Pickering. There's always been a lot of talk about her, but Ian claims it was just hearsay."

Gwen's curiosity was piqued. "What kind of talk?"

"She was a kept woman."

"By whom?"

Natalee paused. "I don't know. But it was said she had a secret lover."

"That sounds like a soap opera storyline."

"From what I've heard it was more like 'Desperate Housewives.'"

Gwen grimaced. "That scandalous?"

"That's the rumor."

She'd begun reading her aunt's letters, but hadn't come across anything that indicated that she was having an affair with the man who'd signed the letters with the initials—A.C.

He was a musician who lived in New Orleans, and was obviously an obsessed fan. She had tried researching information about her aunt online, but the search yielded little.

"Gossip is always more attention-grabbing than truth," she told Natalee.

Nodding in agreement, Natalee pressed a hand to her flat middle, affecting a dramatic pose. "I don't know about you, girlfriend, but right about now I have to get my eat on."

Gwen smiled. "I was trying to be polite and not say anything, but I'm so hungry I could eat an alligator."

Staring at each other for a split second, Natalee and Gwen shook their heads. "Not!" they chimed in unison.

Gwen discovered that Natalee drove as fast as she talked. During the ride Natalee told her that she'd been a jewelry appraiser for Sotheby's for five years. She had left the auction house to become a jewelry designer to a select group of clients that included athletes and entertainers. What surprised Gwen was that despite her profession, Natalee wore a narrow, unadorned yellow gold wedding band.

"How did you meet Ian?"

The jewelry designer smiled. "I'd come to New Orleans to see a client who'd commissioned me to design a necklace for his wife's fiftieth birthday. He invited me to attend a Saints pre-season game, and Ian was in an adjoining box with a number of chefs who'd gotten together for a food magazine layout. I'm not ashamed to say I flirted shamelessly with him, and at halftime we exchanged telephone numbers. What saved my pride was that he contacted me first. We dated long-distance for three months, then had a Christmas Eve wedding two years ago."

Gwen waited for Natalee to talk about Shiloh. She still had another four days before she would see him again, and whenever she remembered how she felt every time he'd held her in his arms, her heart did a flip-flop.

She'd told herself that she did not want to get involved with a man—especially one as sexy as Shiloh Harper. But the voice in her head screamed LIAR!

Natalee downshifted, maneuvering along the road leading to the ferryboat landing. *La Boule* was filled to capacity, and Gwen managed to find an empty seat at the railing, while Natalee sat near the pilothouse.

Leaning over the railing, she saw the shiny red eyes of the alligators as they glided just below the surface of the brackish water. She knew she never would've moved into *Bon Temps* if it had been built close to the water.

Three blasts of the horn echoed over the countryside as the ferryboat pulled slowly away from the landing. The setting sun turned the landscape into a surreal world that reminded Gwen of a Hollywood version of Armageddon. She sat motionless, stunned by the panorama that held her captive until bright lights, loud music and the sounds of laughter coming from the Outlaw broke the spell.

"The place is really jumping," she said to Natalee as they disembarked.

"Friday and Saturdays nights are always a little more raucous. It's the end of the week and folks look forward to letting off some steam. The Outlaw is always closed on Sunday, but during June, July, and August it closes on Sunday and Monday."

They made their way to the entrance, Gwen stopped short as she came face-to-face with Shiloh. He was in uniform.

Touching the brim of his hat, Shiloh stared at Gwen. "Good evening, Gwen, Nattie."

Gwen's expression matched his impassive one. "Hello, Shiloh."

Natalee patted his shoulder. "Gwen and I are going to be here a while. We'd love for you to join us after you're off duty."

"I'm off duty now," he said, his gaze not straying from the soft cloud of dark hair framing Gwen's face.

Natalee leaned in and kissed his cheek. "Then get out of that do-do brown outfit, brother love, and come hang out with us."

He touched the brim of his hat again. "I'll see you later."

"How much later?" Natalee asked as he turned to make his way down to the landing.

"As soon as I can get out of this doo-doo brown get up," he called out, not turning around.

Natalee looped her arm through Gwen's, smiling. "You know he likes you," she whispered.

"And I like him."

"You don't understand, Gwen."

"What's there not to understand?"

Natalee sobered, her dark eyes serious. She steered Gwen away from the couples going into the restaurant. "Shiloh never hangs out here at night. He'll stop by for lunch, but that's the extent of his socializing."

"Why are you telling me this, Natalee?"

"You're the first woman Shiloh has been seen with since his divorce."

Gwen stared at Natalee with a look of complete surprise on her face. She'd questioned Shiloh about being married, unaware there *had* been an ex-Mrs. Shiloh Harper.

"Oh, so you don't know about Deandrea?"

"No."

She didn't know about Deandrea, and did not care to know anything about the woman, because she had no intention of becoming *that* involved with Shiloh Harper.

"You're dating him, yet he hasn't told you?"

Gwen shook her head. "We're not dating."

"Come again."

"Shiloh asked me to accompany him to the fund-raiser and I accepted."

Natalee's jaw dropped. "I thought you two were..." Her words trailed off.

"Sleeping together?" Gwen said, completing her assumption. "Yes."

"We're not," she confirmed. "Shiloh and I are friends."

"Is that what you want from him? Friendship?"

It was a loaded question. She could tell Natalee no because it'd been years since she'd slept with a man. And she could truthfully say yes because every woman needs a male friend. She decided on the latter.

"Yes."

"Good luck with that," Natalee mumbled under her breath.

An expression of confusion stole across her face. "What did you say?"

She knew she sounded defensive, but didn't much care. She wanted to set the record straight that she and the sheriff were not involved with each other, that because they were seen publicly at a fund-raising event it didn't translate into their sharing a bed.

Natalee knew she'd crossed the line of propriety when she heard Gwen's tone. "Sorry about that." Her mood changed, brightening. "Let's go in before they run out of food."

Needing no further prompting, Gwen followed her new friend into the restaurant.

Chapter 8

Shiloh shouldered his way through the crowd, oblivious to the driving rhythms coming from several large speakers set up on a raised stage. The band, made up of local musicians, had most of the crowd up and on their feet dancing to an infectious dance beat.

The Outlaw came alive on Friday and Saturday nights. Fridays catered to the over-forty crowd with a buffet dinner, two-for-one drinks and music that spanned several decades. Saturdays accommodated the twenty to thirtysomething set with live music, and a buffet featuring regional cuisine, along with raw clam and sushi bars.

A Saturday-night visit to his brother's restaurant was a rare outing for Shiloh. He came whenever he was called in an official capacity as sheriff, or when he needed to talk to Ian about something that couldn't wait until the following day. Tonight, however, was the exception. He'd come because of a woman.

He scanned the throng, his gaze sweeping over the dance floor. Tables were positioned for maximum seating. The length of one wall was set up for a hot and cold buffet, and at the end was the bar. His eyes widened. Gwen sat at the bar, a rapt expression on her face as she listened to one of his former colleagues.

Ignoring curious stares from those who rarely saw him in the restaurant out of uniform, he headed toward the bar. As he neared Gwen, he noticed things about her he hadn't before: the play of light on her flawless skin, the wealth of unbound curls that seemingly took on a life of their own whenever she moved her head, and the perfection of her delicate profile.

He stopped, visually drinking in the startling dark beauty of the woman who'd ensnared him in an invisible web of seduction. Shiloh held his breath when she tilted her head, baring her throat, and laughed softly. At that moment he wanted to press his mouth to her pulse at the base of her throat, feeling the soft flutters keeping time with his own runaway heartbeat.

"Gwen."

Her head came around as she swiveled on the bar stool. He hadn't realized he'd called her name. Her smile vanished as if in slow motion. Her stunned expression lasted seconds, replaced by a sensual smile that indicated she *was* as glad to see him as he her.

Gwen felt a warm glow flow through her as she stared at Shiloh. His damp spiky hair, loose-fitting blue-gray silk shirt, well-washed jeans and running shoes gave him a rugged, disheveled appearance.

"You came back." She didn't recognize her own voice, which had lowered an octave as her rapidly beating heart slammed against her ribs.

Shiloh lowered his voice and his gaze. "I told you I would."

Keith Nichols nodded to the acting sheriff who'd been his boss at the D.A.'s office. He reached into the pocket of his slacks and left a bill on the bar, and waved at the bartender. "Keep the change."

Keith smiled at Gwen. "It was nice meeting you, Gwendolyn," he said before offering his hand to Shiloh. "We're counting down the days, boss."

Shiloh tightened his grip on the blond, preppy-looking A.D.A.'s hand. "Thanks."

Keith's hazel eyes crinkled behind the lenses of his round, wire-rimmed glasses. "See you around."

"You bet," Shiloh said as he took the stool the young lawyer had vacated. He stared at the glass of clear liquid with a wedge of lime in Gwen's glass. "What are you drinking?"

"Club soda."

Resting an elbow on the mahogany bar, he signaled for the bartender. "Are you designated driver tonight?"

Gwen stared at him through her lashes, a mysterious smile parting her lips. Shiloh Harper looked and smelled good enough to eat. She wrapped both hands around her glass so as not to touch him.

"No. Natalee drove."

"Where is she?"

"She said she had to take care of some business in Ian's office. Why?"

"Give me three kings on the rocks," Shiloh said to the bartender who came over to take his beverage order. Rising to his feet, he winked at Gwen. "I'll be right back."

She placed a hand over his. "Where are you going?"

The smile in his eyes contained a sensuous flame. "To tell Nattie that I'll take you home."

Her fingers tightened. "I'm not ready to leave. I like the

band." She liked the food, music, and the friendly, outgoing people who'd come to the Outlaw with the intent of having a good time.

Shiloh leaned closer. "Whenever you're ready to go home I'll make certain you get there...safely," he added.

Gwen removed her hand, her breathing in concert with Shiloh's, their chests rising and falling in a measured syncopated rhythm. "Are you *that* certain I'll be safe with you?"

He moved and stood behind her, inhaling the warmth of her perfumed flesh. A shudder eddied down his body, and he resisted the urge to pull her into his arms and kiss her with a passion that had eluded him for longer than he was willing to admit.

"No," he whispered, pressing a kiss to the nape of her neck.

He was there, then he was gone, Gwen watching his retreat and unaware she'd been holding her breath.

Picking up her glass, she took a long swallow, and welcomed the iciness bathing her constricted throat. She'd asked, and Shiloh had answered. But it wasn't the answer she expected.

The fluttering in her chest eased as satisfaction pursed her mouth. A feeling of calm swept over her, and she knew she was ready to let her good times roll. Three minutes later he was back.

"That was quick." She scooped up the small purse she'd placed on the stool next to her.

He tugged gently at the curls falling over her ear. "Thanks for saving me a seat."

She gave him a sassy smile. "You don't know what I had to go through to make certain nobody sat here."

"What did you do, darling?"

"I'm not telling," she whispered, staring up at Shiloh through her lashes.

His gaze lingered on her parted lips. "I never thought you'd be a tease."

Her expression changed. "Tease how?"

Shiloh hesitated, wondering how to explain to Gwen how being in her presence affected him. Would she believe he was coming on too strong if he told her that he wanted to see her every day, that there was something about her that made him want to know her—in and out of bed.

"There's something about the way you stare at a man that makes me believe you're flirting when I know that isn't your intent."

"You've got that right, Shiloh Harper. I've never had to flirt with a man to get his attention," she said without bravado.

His gaze moved slowly from her face to her breasts, then down to her feet before reversing itself. A knowing smile creased the skin around his luminous eyes and curved his strong mouth upward.

"I can see why," he crooned.

A swath of heat burned Gwen's face when she registered his blatant suggestion. She picked up her glass and drained it at the same time the bartender placed Shiloh's drink in front of him.

"First one is on the house tonight."

Shifting on the stool, Shiloh reached into his pocket and pressed a bill into the bartender's hand. "Thanks, Z. That's from me and the lady."

A dreadlocked, tattooed Zachary Howard palmed the bill, grinning. "Thanks, man."

Shiloh looped an arm around Gwen's waist. "Have you eaten?" She nodded. His arm tightened. "Then come with me."

He helped her off the stool. Balancing his drink in his free hand, he led her through the restaurant to a side door with an Employees Only sign. "What are you doing?" Gwen asked as he punched in a code on a keypad.

"I want a quiet place where we can talk."

Her eyes widened when she found herself in a room overlooking the water. A daybed and rocker with a footstool covered with matching floral cushions, two round tables with pull-up chairs, and a quartet of flickering candles under chimneys set the scene.

"Talk about what?"

"Us."

"I didn't know there was an us," she said softly.

Shiloh eased Gwen down to the daybed, then sat next to her. He rested his arm over her shoulders as he took a big gulp of his drink, grimacing as the bite from the liquor exploded in his chest.

He sighed, closed his eyes, and smiled. "I want to know if there can be an us?"

Caught off-guard by the question and the seriousness in Shiloh's voice, Gwen was barely able to swallow her gasp of surprise. It wasn't often that she was at a loss for words, and it was a full minute before she was able to form a reply.

"Us how?"

"Getting to know one another better."

Reaching for his glass, she placed it on the table before she turned and gave Shiloh a long, penetrating stare. The flickering candlelight flattered the ridges and angles of his handsome face.

"Are you asking me to sleep with you?" His eyes widened until she saw their jade-green depths.

"Did I ask you to sleep with me?"

"No. But—"

"But nothing," Shiloh said, cutting her off. "I've never had a problem making myself understood, Gwen. If I'd wanted you to sleep with me I would've said that." He ignored her soft exhalation. "I want to know if we can keep company?"

Her eyebrows lifted. "Company?"

"Date, go out, be seen with, court."

Her eyes narrowed. "You don't have to be so sarcastic, Shiloh. I don't think it's an admirable trait in a man."

"Oh, so you think it's better in a woman?"

"I didn't come in here to debate."

"Point taken." A sly smile softened his firm mouth. "If that's the case, then I suggest we get back to the subject of us dating each other. I'd like you to go out with me."

Everything that made Shiloh Harper who he was wrapped itself around her, and held her hostage to emotions she did not want to feel. It'd been four years since a man had reminded her why she'd been born a woman, and she had no intention of allowing herself to fall under the sensual, erotic spell that told her to throw caution and common sense to the wind.

"Why me and not some other woman, Shiloh?" she asked, sidestepping his question. "You're young, intelligent, single and attractive. I'm certain there're a lot of women who would go out with you if you asked them."

Shiloh crossed his arms over his chest while stretching out his long legs. "I'm not talking about other women. I'm talking about you."

"Why me?"

"I'm not interested in women who do the chasing."

Gwen sat up straighter. "Most men would find that a turn-on."

"I don't."

Virgil Harper had always cautioned his sons not to kiss and tell, but Shiloh wanted to open up to Gwen about his ex-wife, who pursued him until he married her. And she continued to chase any man who gave him the slightest glance.

Gwen didn't know whether to be insulted or flattered by his assessment of her. What Shiloh wasn't aware of was that she *was* interested in him, but had become quite adept in hiding her feelings behind a facade of indifference.

But she was anything but indifferent about Shiloh Harper, because she'd known there was something special about him the first time she found herself in his arms. She liked everything about him: his face, soft, drawling voice, his smell, the protective warmth of his embrace and his masculinity. The more she saw him, the longer she remained in his presence, the more her pledge not to get involved with another man shattered into millions of pieces.

The harder she tried to ignore the truth the more it nagged at her. She wanted the man out of bed, and she needed him in bed. Her lids slipped down over her eyes, hiding her innermost feelings.

"If I'm not involved with something, then yes I will go out with you." She kept all emotion out of her face and voice, determined to show Shiloh how unconcerned she was about his invitation.

Placing two fingers against the column of her neck, Shiloh shook his head slowly. Her pulse pounded a runaway rhythm. "You'll never be as accomplished as your actress aunt."

"You..." Her words trailed off when Shiloh covered her mouth with his, permitting her to taste the liquor on his tongue. Her arms came up of their own volition, tightening around his strong neck as he fell back on the daybed, bringing her down with him.

"Don't talk, darling. Please don't say anything," he murmured in between soft, nibbling kisses at the corners of her mouth.

She lay atop Shiloh, her breasts against the solid wall of his chest, legs cradled between his, and his hardness reminding her of where she was, and what could possibly happen.

Shiloh heard the sound before Gwen. Within seconds he eased her off his body. "Someone's coming," he whispered harshly.

The door opened, and Juleen walked in. She stopped when she saw Shiloh sitting on the daybed with a woman.

"I'm...I'm sorry, Shiloh," she stammered.

He beckoned to the waitress. "Come on in, Juleen. Gwen and I are just talking."

Gwen forced herself not to glance at Shiloh. They were doing a lot more than talking. If they hadn't been interrupted, then she wasn't certain how far they would've gone.

Juleen shook her head. "It's all right, Shiloh. I'll find someplace else to take my break."

Reaching for Gwen's hand, he stood, pulling her gently up with him. "Stay. We're leaving."

Gwen wasn't given the opportunity to protest as Shiloh opened the screen door and led her down a back staircase to the landing where *La Boule*'s engines were revving for a return trip. They boarded the ferryboat, sat together holding hands, both lost in their private thoughts.

It wasn't until Shiloh maneuvered his car along a road in the opposite direction from her house that she broke the comfortable silence.

"Where are you taking me?"

"To my place."

"To do what?"

"Talk, listen to music, and hopefully you'll let me dance with you." They were all the things he'd missed sharing with a woman.

"We can do that at my place."

Shiloh gave Gwen a quick glance. It was apparent that she was apprehensive about going home with him. "You're going to have to learn to trust me. Nothing's going to happen that you don't want to happen."

Gwen closed her eyes and pressed her head against the headrest. She trusted Shiloh. It was herself that she didn't trust. When she opened her eyes she realized the landscape had changed. The paved road ended, and trees and underbrush crowded what had become a narrow, winding gravel path.

Gwen, her gaze fixed on the bright beam of light from the car's headlights, said quietly, "You live in the country."

Shiloh chuckled, but did not take his gaze off the road. "Southern Louisiana *is* the country."

"You know what I mean."

"I suppose to a city girl any place with trees and a one-lane road is the country."

"Correction, darling. Dirt road."

He liked when she called him darling. Did he want to become her darling? Yes. Did he want her to become his darling? A knowing smile found its way over his face. Yes, he did.

Reaching for a device attached to the windshield visor, Shiloh pressed a button and a wooden barrier lifted. He drove past the manned gatehouse, passing several newly erected homes before driving the Mustang around to the back of his house and parking alongside the Suburban. He helped Gwen out of the car, then led her up the double stairway of a two-story Louisiana Cajun country house. Soft lighting illuminated the first story within seconds of his unlocking the door and deactivating a security alarm.

Gwen didn't know what to expect, but it wasn't the cookie-cutter kitchen she'd expected. Recessed lighting, Tiffany-style ceiling fixtures, and white Euro-style cabinetry, devoid of any detail, gave the open space a clean look. A countertop divided the kitchen from a living/dining room and flowed into another area that doubled as a family room. The inside of the house had a new smell.

"How long have you lived here?"

"Not long," Shiloh said, removing his holstered automatic and concealing it in the top drawer under the countertop.

"How long is not long?" Gwen asked, as she braced her arms on the partition separating the kitchen from the dining area.

"I moved in at the beginning of the year. Why?"

"It doesn't look lived in."

Shiloh closed the distance between them and propped his elbows on the partition. "The only thing I haven't used is the stove."

She met his amused gaze. "Do you at least know how to turn it on?"

Pressing his forehead to her hers, he kissed the end of her nose. "You got jokes, Miss Taylor?"

Gwen affected a sensual moue, bringing his gaze to linger on her mouth. "No. I just want to know whether you're domestically challenged."

"On a scale of one to ten I'm about a six. I know how to use the microwave, do laundry, iron and make a bed."

She smiled. "Do you cook?"

"Nope. One chef in the family is enough."

"How long has the Outlaw been in business?"

Straightening up, Shiloh held out his hand. "Come with me. I'll give you a quick tour while I bring you up-to-date on a few colorful characters in my family."

He led Gwen up a staircase to the second story and regaled her with stories of his bootlegger maternal grandfather who'd earned the sobriquet, the Outlaw, because as a teenage boy, he had successfully evaded revenue agents during Prohibition.

The three-bedroom house was designed with sitting rooms and adjoining baths, and the master bedroom was the only one of the three furnished and decorated. The bedroom had a king-size bed with a wrought-iron frame, a massive bleached pine armoire, with matching nightstands complementing the soft café-au-lait-colored walls.

The living-dining room, and family areas were defined by the positioning of furniture, and not walls. A drop-leaf table was filled with photographs of several generations of Shiloh's family.

Shiloh pointed to one of a couple in their wedding finery. "These were my mama's people."

Gwen peered closer at a tall bearded man with a petite black woman. "So, he was the infamous Outlaw."

He pointed to another wedding photo. "Those were my daddy's folks, and this one was taken the day Dad was sworn in as the parish's first black sheriff." He ran a finger around one with an oval silver frame. "This is the last picture my parents took together."

Gwen heard the pain in Shiloh's voice before she glanced at his face. A muscle twitched in his jaw. "What happened, Shiloh?" Her voice was low, soothing. When he didn't answer her, she turned and curved her arms under his shoulders, holding him as if she were offering comfort to a child. Resting her cheek on his chest, she listened to the strong pumping of his heart. They stood motionless, heart to heart, offering and accepting comfort and trust.

Shiloh's hands moved up and cradled Gwen's head. Lowering his head, he pressed his mouth to her hair. "That photograph was taken the day Virgil and Moriah Harper celebrated their thirty-seventh wedding anniversary. It was also the day Dad announced that he was going to retire once his term expired. A week later he was gunned down when he walked in on a bank robbery in progress. I..." His words trailed off as he recalled the telephone call from his mother telling him that his father had been shot.

"What happened to the bank robber, darling?" The endearment had slipped unbidden from Gwen's lips.

Inhaling, Shiloh continued, "He took his own life right there in the bank. He was a fifteen-year-old kid who'd acted on a dare because he'd wanted to fit in with a group of older boys who were always getting into trouble. The whole damn thing was so useless because the lives of two good people ended because of a stupid-ass prank. All of Teche turned out for the funerals when my mother buried her husband and Clovis Ward buried her only child within days of each other."

Easing back, Gwen stared up at Shiloh staring down at her. "What happened to the other boys?"

"My last act as district attorney before I was appointed to serve out my father's term was to bring conspiracy indictments against three of the six boys. One was sent to a juvenile detention facility. He'll be there until his nineteenth birthday. The other two were given probation."

Shiloh's disclosure that he was a lawyer explained A.D.A. Keith Nichols's cryptic parting remark: *We're counting down the days, boss.* "Locking someone up won't bring back your father or that other kid, but at least it sends a message that you can't throw the rock, then hide your hand."

Shiloh nodded. "You're right. The case served to broaden the state's conspiracy laws."

"How does Moriah feel about you being sheriff?"

"It is a subject we don't discuss."

Gwen tightened her grip around his shoulders. "Once you serve out your father's term, are you going to run for the office?"

"No," he said smoothly, with no expression on his face. "I like prosecuting the bad guys and sending them away where they can't hurt law-abiding citizens."

Gwen sighed. "Good."

Shiloh stared down at her. "Why would you say that?"

"Prosecuting criminals is safer than arresting them."

His eyebrows lifted as he bit back a smile. "Don't tell me you're concerned about my well-being."

"Yeah, I am," she teased. "I think I like you, Shiloh Harper, and because I do, I don't want anything to happen to you."

His fingers tightened on her scalp. "You like me?"

She nodded, wrinkling her short nose. "Just a little."

"Why only a little?"

"I don't know you."

"Do you want to get to know me?"

Gwen was certain he could feel her heart beating against his chest. "Yes, I do."

His head came down slowly. "And so do I." He nuzzled the side of her neck. "I want to know everything about you. What makes you laugh, cry, happy or sad. And I want to know what I have to do to make you feel good."

Her trembling limbs clung to him as she inhaled his masculine scent, luxuriated in his body's heat, and gloried in the strength of his embrace. She shivered when his warm breath feathered over an ear.

Men had held her before, but this was the first time she felt protected *and* fulfilled. Shiloh hadn't made love to her, yet the sensations coursing throughout her body were similar to those she experienced in the aftermath of a climax.

She closed her eyes and smiled. "We can begin with honesty and respect."

"You've got it. What else, darling?"

"Trust. I have to be able to trust you, Shiloh."

"I promise never to give you a reason not to trust me."

Gwen opened her eyes. "Don't promise. Just do it."

Shiloh's hands fell away from her head, coming to rest on her shoulders. His stare drilled into her with a gentle but firm warning. "Please don't lecture me about trust, Gwen. I married a woman, believing I could trust her, but I was wrong. I know firsthand what it feels like to be deceived, not only in my own bed but also with my best friend."

His revelation stunned Gwen. His coming home and finding a man in bed with his woman was like a TV melodrama. "What did you do?" she whispered.

Shiloh did not want to relive the scene that was imprinted

on his mind, but he'd promised Gwen that he would be truthful with her. "I told them that I was going out, and when I returned, I hoped not to see them. I drove around for a couple of hours with a loaded gun on the passenger seat while asking myself if I wanted to stand trial for two counts of murder.

"I spent the night sitting by my father's grave. I suppose I was looking for answers from a dead man because I missed our father-son talks. Then I thought about Mama. She'd just lost her husband, and it would've destroyed her to lose her son, too. I returned home, packed my clothes, and moved back with my mother until my divorce was final. I gave Deandrea everything she wanted just to be rid of her. Everything I had with her up to that point ended when she moved back to New Orleans."

Rising on tiptoe, Gwen brushed her lips against Shiloh's. "I'm glad you didn't shoot them."

"So am I," he said as his lips left hers to sear a path down her neck, and further to her bare, scented shoulders.

Gwen opened her mouth and gave in to the dizzying sensations pulling her into an erotic undertow from which there was no escape. She swallowed a moan as the pulsing between her thighs thrummed in concert with the tingling sensation in her breasts. She didn't know Shiloh Harper, but none of that mattered. Touching him, tasting him, smelling him was a dreamy intimacy that hinted of more—so much more than she was ready for at the moment.

Reluctantly, she pulled back, her chest rising and falling as if she'd run a grueling race. "Take me home, Shiloh."

He cradled her face between his hands, his gaze racing over her strained features. "What's the matter, darling?"

Her eyelids fluttered wildly. "Take me home before I ask you to do something I know I'll regret later."

"What do you want?"

Gwen closed her eyes against his penetrating stare. "Please, don't ask me."

"Did we not promise to be truthful with each other?"

She opened her eyes. "That's doesn't mean I have to tell you my innermost secrets."

Shiloh refused to relent. "I'm not going to take you home until you tell me what's bothering you."

"You can't do that."

"Why not? After all, I am the law."

"That constitutes an abuse of power."

"You can file a complaint."

She stomped her foot. "Shiloh!"

He laughed, the sound low, throaty. "Tell me what it is you want, Gwendolyn."

Gwen knew she had to tell Shiloh or their impasse would never be resolved. She'd met someone who was as stubborn as she was. "It's been a long time since I've been involved with a man."

"How long?"

"Four years."

"Go on," he urged gently.

She stared at a spot over his shoulder. "Being here with you, kissing you just reminded me of what I haven't had in four years."

"Look at me, Gwen. Look at me," Shiloh repeated when she hesitated. He caught and held her gaze. "This is just not about you or me. It's about us. I know what you're feeling because I have the same feelings. If we're going to have any type of relationship I don't want it to be based on sex. That I can get from any woman."

"Or me from any man," Gwen added.

Shiloh nodded. "If and when we share a bed, it will be at the right time and for the right reason."

"What would constitute the right reason?"

The gold-green eyes smoldered with passion and tenderness. "A commitment to see each other exclusively."

Gwen blinked once. Shiloh Harper offered her what she'd sought from a man the first time she'd thought that she was in love. A smile softened her mouth. She would enjoy her time with Shiloh, and if or when it ended she would be left with her memories.

"You can take me home now."

Without verbalizing it, Gwen had let Shiloh know that he could look forward to reviving a part of his life that had ended with his marriage—a social life.

He'd brought her home to talk, listen to music and dance.

They'd talked.

Dancing and listening to music would have to come later.

Chapter 9

I want to know everything about you.

What makes you laugh, cry, happy or sad.

And I want to know what I have to do to make you feel good.

Gwen smothered a yawn behind her hand as the interior decorator removed an instrument with a flat blade from her leather satchel. She was exhausted.

She'd spent the past few nights tossing and turning as she agonized over whether she'd made a mistake in agreeing to date Shiloh. The physical attraction was evident—for both—but she had to ask herself whether she needed Shiloh as much as she wanted him. Everything about him was a constant reminder of how long it'd been since she'd decided not to become involved with a man.

Tuesday morning she'd spent three hours in the *Tribune*'s office. Nash McGraw had talked nonstop, giving her an historical overview of the parish. The newspaper's part-time staff of four included two contributing editors from the neighboring parishes of St. Mary and the northern portion of Terrebonne, and because she'd begun her tenure with the *Gazette* covering the crime desk, Nash wanted her to write the Blotter.

She now wondered if the editor's decision to hire her as a crime reporter was based on her prior experience or because she'd attended the fund-raiser with the local sheriff.

Gwen, aware that she would be the liaison between the *Tribune* and the St. Martin Parish Police Department, had to keep in mind that her position with the newspaper could possibly impact her attempt to have a personal relationship with Shiloh.

"There's another pattern under this one."

The interior decorator's voice pulled her out of her reverie. "What did you say?" She looked at the woman as she peeled an inch-wide strip of paper off the wall in the master bedroom.

The auburn-haired woman with sparkling emerald-green eyes removed a second layer of paper from the wall. "It looks as if there are several more layers here." Turning, she stared at Gwen. "What do you want to do?"

"What are my alternatives?" she asked, answering Lina Davidson's question with one of her own.

"I can have all of the paper removed, repair whatever damage there is to the walls and paint them."

Resting a hand against her cheek, Gwen shook her head. "No." Within seconds she reached a decision. "I want all of the bedrooms papered."

"What about the sitting rooms?"

"I want them painted in pastels that correspond to the wall-paper's dominant color."

"What colors do you want for this room?"

Gwen stared at the fading blue and peach-colored pat-terned paper. "Pale yellow, lime-green and ecru. The walls in the sitting room can be painted yellow or a pale green. Will you be able to get fabric in the same pattern as the paper?"

Lina smiled as she entered notes into her Blackberry. "Yes. The textile manufacturer I work with does happen to make matching paper and fabric. What do you want the fabric for?"

"The window seats." Many of the window seat cushions in the sitting rooms showed signs of wear and tear. "And I want a more masculine look in one bedroom."

"How masculine?"

"Pinstriped paper. I'd like a soft dove gray background with a barely discernible white-striped pattern."

"Do you want the same pattern on the window seat?" Lina asked, her thumbs moving over the handheld computer with amazing speed.

Pulling her lower lip between her teeth, Gwen closed her eyes. "No," she said as she opened her eyes. "I'd like to go with a herringbone, glen plaid, or perhaps a tweed."

Lina flashed a wide grin. "Very formal and somewhat British."

Gwen was certain her father, uncle and brother-in-law would prefer sleeping in an English-inspired bedroom to one decorated with flowers and frills.

Lina made a call to a moving company to arrange to pick up the pieces to be refurbished by a team of renowned cabinetmakers. "They'll be here tomorrow to pick up all of the tagged items. A team of workmen will come Thursday to begin all of the outdoor work before the tropical storm season begins. They'll start with the replacement of window sashes and shutters. Then they'll move indoors. I project a couple of weeks for them to complete the walls before they strip the floors. You should consider finding somewhere else to stay while the floors are being scraped. The dust and the odor of the polyurethane can be irritating."

Gwen nodded. If she had to be out of the house while work was being done, then she would stay at Jessup's boardinghouse.

Lina dropped the Blackberry into her bag. "I'm going to need keys for the workmen. All of them are bonded, which means you can leave them here even if you're not."

Reaching for a set of keys hanging from a hook under a cabinet, Gwen handed them to Lina. She took a quick glance at the clock over the stove. It was almost four-thirty. She had less than three hours before Shiloh's arrival.

"I'll be here when they come tomorrow morning," she told Lina as she walked her to her car.

Within minutes of the decorator's departure, she returned to the house to prepare for her date.

Gwen positioned a crystal vase of fresh-cut flowers between a matching pair of five-shell-base Georgian silver candlesticks. Taking a step backwards, she surveyed the table in the kitchen's dining area. It would just be she and Shiloh for dinner, but she'd decided on a formal table setting.

Something soft brushed against her ankle, and she glanced down to find Cocoa. She'd had to lock the dog in the laundry room to keep her from biting Lina's sandal-shod toes.

Bending over, she wagged a finger at the frisky puppy. "I won't lock you up again under one condition," she crooned softly. Cocoa jumped up at the wagging finger. "Don't bite my boyfriend." Gwen swallowed a groan. "No, I didn't call him that." The words were barely off her tongue when the doorbell chimed.

Gwen opened the door, her breath catching momentarily in her throat when she saw Shiloh smiling down at her. He wore a wheat-colored linen suit, sky-blue shirt, and tan and navy-blue patterned tie.

She smiled at him. "Please come in."

Wiping his feet on a thick straw mat, Shiloh moved into the entryway, leaned over, brushed a kiss on her cheek, before handing her a blue-and-white checkered bag from Turner Treats. "I brought pralines for dessert."

Gwen took his hand, leading him across the living room and into the kitchen. "I made dessert." She'd baked a jellyroll cake.

He sniffed the air, smiling. "I smell it. What do you have there?" he asked when he spied a flurry of brown scooting across the kitchen floor.

Gwen let go of Shiloh's hand and placed the bag on the cooking island. "Cocoa Taylor."

He clapped his hands, and the dog came over to investigate the sound. He scooped up Cocoa. "Hey, pretty girl. She looks like one of Holly Turner's prize-winning poodles."

Gwen met his gaze, nodding. "She is."

"Lucky you."

Gwen opened the refrigerator and removed plastic covered dishes with marinated vegetables and lamb chops. "She gave me Cocoa and a batch of delicious chocolate chip cookies as a welcome to the neighborhood gift."

Shiloh rubbed a forefinger over the puppy's head. "Did she invite you to her Sunday afternoon soiree?"

"Yes, she did. How did you know?"

"A couple of years back Mrs. Turner and her genteel Southern ladies were accused of racism after they'd rejected a woman of color who'd showed up at one of their gatherings uninvited. Since that time they've embarked on an ongoing campaign to integrate the parish's Genteel Magnolia Society."

"How long have they been meeting?"

Shiloh angled his head. "They go back to the late 1890s. Membership is based on family name, and passed down from great-grandmother, grandmother, daughter and granddaughter."

Gwen turned on the stovetop grill, her thoughts tumbling over themselves. There was no doubt that the Magnolia Society ladies could become an inexhaustible source of information about the comings and goings on in the parish. Yes, she decided. She would join Holly and her friends for their Sunday-afternoon tea party.

"Be careful Cocoa doesn't nip your ankles," she warned Shiloh as he set the puppy on its feet. The tiny dog turned over on her back, her tiny tail twitching. Gwen clapped her hands. "What do you think you're doing, Cocoa Taylor? Stop showing your business!"

Shaking his head, Shiloh laughed. "You sound like a mother with a fast daughter."

"I'd say the same if *she* were male." She clapped again. Cocoa did not move. "Now, roll over, you shameless little hussy."

Cocoa lay on the tiled floor, her underside exposed until Shiloh hunkered down and tickled her belly. He picked her up again. "Come to daddy, baby girl. Mama just doesn't want you to have any fun."

Resting her hands on her hips, Gwen glared at the man who was a constant reminder of what she'd sacrificed for longer than she wanted to acknowledge. If she'd met Shiloh Harper four years ago she knew she would not be the woman she was now.

"I can see what kind of father you're going to be."

"And that is?"

"A punk."

Shiloh lifted an eyebrow, struggling not to laugh. "I think not."

"I think yes," she argued softly.

He moved closer to Gwen, his gaze lingering on the tempting curve of her full lower lip. "And you think you'd be less of a punk than I?"

She gave him a saucy grin. "I know I would. My cousin's

children know that when Auntie Gwennie says no, then it's no. Now, please stop spoiling my dog."

A slow smile parted Shiloh's lips as he set Cocoa on her feet. "You're tough until they hug you and tell you that you're the best auntie in the whole wide world."

Her smile matched his. "No lie," she agreed.

Shiloh's gaze never strayed from her upturned face. Everything about Gwendolyn Taylor was hypnotic: the hair floating around her flawless face in sensual disarray, the sparkle in her fathomless dark eyes, the scent of her perfume, the delicate fabric of a classic white silk blouse she'd tucked into the waistband of a pair of coffee-colored linen slacks. Her feet were covered with a pair of high-heeled leopard-print pumps. There was no doubt that she was addicted to shoes.

He leaned a hip against the edge of a countertop, arms crossed over his chest. "Do you think you would be a good mother?"

Gwen felt as if her emotions were under attack. Her knees shook, her heart raced a little too quickly, and she chided herself for broaching the subject of parenting. She wondered whether Shiloh was challenging or just teasing her.

"I pray I'd be a good mother. I know I'd love my children, and most importantly establish boundaries."

His expressive left eyebrow lifted. "Do you want children?"

"How did we get onto this topic?"

"You started it, Gwen." Leaning closer, Shiloh pressed his mouth to her forehead. "Do you want children?" he asked again.

"Eventually."

"When?"

"I've given myself until I'm thirty-eight."

He pulled back, vertical lines appearing between his eyes. "Do you always run your life by a timetable?"

"Yes, because it works for me, Shiloh."

"What about marriage? At what age would that work for you?"

Gwen forced all expression from her face. Shiloh wanted an answer to a question she wasn't prepared to answer. Changing her marital status was something she hadn't given any consideration since ending her short-lived engagement ten years before.

"Nemo tenetur seipsum accusare."

Shiloh lowered his arms, his eyes widening, momentarily speechless in his surprise. Gwen Taylor was unlike any woman he'd ever met or interacted with. She wasn't beautiful in the classical sense of the word, but there was something about her that was so ardently feminine, sensual, that whenever they occupied the same space he'd found himself at a loss for words. She was smart, very, very smart, outspoken, and secure enough not to downplay her intelligence in order to impress a man.

Gwen represented a total package—everything he'd looked for *and* wanted in a woman.

"No man is bound to accuse himself," he translated. "Where did you learn to speak Latin?"

She adjusted the grill's thermostat. "I went to a parochial high school, and took Latin for three years in college."

"We have something in common. I also had a parochial school education before I attended a Catholic college."

"Which one?"

"Notre Dame." Shiloh met her gaze. "Which college did you go to?"

"Mount Holyoke."

"You stayed in Massachusetts." Her jaw tightened, and he knew Gwen wasn't going to elaborate about her decision not to attend an out-of-state college.

His gaze moved to the beautifully set table in a spacious alcove. He felt he had to do something—anything but stand and watch the woman to whom he'd found himself drawn when she hadn't given him any indication that she wanted more from him other than friendship.

"Can I help with something?"

Gwen nodded, not meeting his gaze. "You can open a bottle of red wine. It's in the fridge on the lower shelf."

Shrugging out of his jacket, Shiloh left it on the back of a high stool at the cooking island. Reaching behind his back, he left his holstered handgun on the stool's rush-covered seat, and made his way to the half bath to wash his hands. He returned to the kitchen and was met with the tantalizing aroma of grilling meat and vegetables.

Shiloh closed his eyes and smiled. The whirring sound of the blades from the back porch ceiling fan joined the cacophony of nocturnal sounds sweeping over the countryside. The air was thick with perfume from blooming night flowers as streaks of lightning crisscrossed the nighttime sky.

He lay on a cushioned recliner, a barefoot Gwen resting between his outstretched legs and Cocoa, who had fallen asleep, on her lap. Light from antique wrought-iron lanterns positioned between tall windows framed by sea-foam-green shutters cast a soft golden light on the worn, uneven porch floor. Her warmth, the curves of her body merged with the peace that made him want to stay where he lay until the dawn of a new day.

Dining had become a comfortable and relaxed three-hour interlude. Gwen had loaded a CD carousel with discs from her aunt's jazz collection, and over an appetizer of crab-stuffed shrimp with a basil sauce, a mixed green salad with a Thai-peanut dressing, grilled asparagus with lemon and garlic, grilled mint-flavored lamb chops, fluffy white rice and a dessert of jellyroll cake topped with fresh whipped cream they discussed everything from sports to politics.

She talked about growing up in Boston, the summers she'd spent with her grandmother learning to swim and cook, her brother's illness, and the devastating effects of his death on her family. It was after this disclosure that he understood her reason not to attend an out-of-state college. She revealed that her parents hadn't wanted her to move from Massachusetts to Louisiana, but in the end they were forced to accept and respect her decision.

"You were right." His drawling voice broke the comfortable silence.

Shifting slightly, Gwen glanced over her shoulder at Shiloh. "About what?"

He opened his eyes. "You're wicked in the kitchen."

"Is that wicked good or bad?"

Twisting several strands of her fragrant hair around his forefinger, Shiloh chuckled, the velvet sound rumbling deep in his chest. "Wicked good."

She moved again, disturbing Cocoa who whined and yawned before settling back to sleep. "You're spoiling my pet."

"How so?"

"She usually sleeps in her own bed and not with me."

Shiloh wanted to tell Gwen that he wanted to sleep with her. He wanted to share her bed *and* make love to her. "I don't think this one time is going to spoil her."

"If Cocoa becomes a doggie gone bad, then she's going home with you."

Lines fanned out around his eyes with his smile. "I'll take her, but not without her mama."

Gwen froze, only the rise and fall of her chest revealing that she was still alive. Her temporary shock was short-lived as she recovered. Her attempt to move off the recliner was thwarted by the arm under her breasts.

"No," she whispered.

"Why not?" Shiloh whispered back.

"Because we barely know each other. It hasn't been two weeks since—"

"There you go with your annoying timetable, Gwen," Shiloh interrupted, his warm breath sweeping over an ear. "Stop living your life by minutes and seconds."

She wiggled, trying to escape his hold but the motion only served to arouse a part of his body that had remained undisturbed since he'd kissed her on the daybed in the Outlaw's employee break room; however, her impromptu lap dance had his self-control fleeing and a rush of desire taking its place; he was helpless and unable to get his body in sync with his brain.

"Don't move," he gasped.

"Let me go."

"Not until you stop wiggling."

Gwen was too incensed to notice the solid bulge pressing against her hips. "I'm not your prisoner, so don't give me orders."

"Gwendolyn!" His shouting her name startled her and Cocoa. "Baby, please," he pleaded, his tone softening. "You're going to make me embarrass myself."

Within seconds she acknowledged the throbbing hardness, and her own body reacted violently. She ignored Shiloh's directive not to move when he loosened his grip, as she lay half-on and half-off his body. Cocoa scooted to a more comfortable spot on Shiloh's shoulder.

Eyes wide, her heart beating uncontrollably, Gwen felt what Shiloh was feeling and more. The area between her thighs thrummed with long forgotten sensations that melted the resistance she'd erected to protect her heart from disappointment and the anguish of another failed relationship.

Her breasts swelled, the nipples tightening and aching with a need that had been denied for far too long. She lay atop a man, a man she'd aroused, and she was unable to tell him what lay in her heart, what she wanted him to do with her because the words were locked in the back of her throat.

She wanted Shiloh to make love to her yet the fact that she'd just met him, hadn't known him a month, nagged at her conscience. "I think you better leave before I ask you to do something I'm not ready for."

Shiloh held her gaze with his. "What's that?"

"Make love to me." The words tumbled over each other.

"Don't you remember me telling you that if and when we make love to each other it will be at the right time and for the right reason? Even though I want you, I know it's not the right time—at least not for you."

"It may never be the right time because of my position with the *Tribune*."

Anchoring his hands under her arms, Shiloh lifted Gwen to straddle his thighs. "What are you talking about?"

"Nash assigned me to cover the Blotter."

"You think because we're seeing each other that becoming the crime reporter would compromise your ethics?"

Gwen nodded. "Yes."

"That won't happen if your SMPD contact is Deputy Sheriff James Jameson. I'll let Jimmie know you'll be in touch with him, and that he's to cooperate fully with you."

Looping an arm around his neck, Gwen pressed a kiss to the side of his strong neck. "Thank you, darling."

Cradling her head between his hands, he gently massaged her scalp. "You're welcome," he crooned, as he dropped tiny kisses at the corners of her mouth.

Gwen lowered her head to his shoulder and smiled at the puppy curled up on the opposite shoulder. There was no doubt the Taylor women were quite taken with the sheriff of St. Martin Parish.

A rumble of thunder joined the intermittent flashes of lightning, disturbing the tranquility of the mood and the night. Cocoa woke up, whining and cowering. Shiloh grabbed her before she tumbled off the recliner.

Gwen took the puppy from him. "I'd better take her inside before she's traumatized."

Raising his arm, Shiloh glanced at his watch. It was after eleven. "And it's time I head home." He waited until Gwen swung her legs over the side of the recliner before he stood up. The top of her head came to his shoulder. Wrapping an arm around her waist, he led her into the house, closing and locking the door behind them.

Rising on tiptoe, Gwen kissed his cheek. "Thank you for coming."

"Thank you for inviting me. I'd like to do this again."

"When?" she asked.

"Saturday night."

A flash of humor crossed Gwen's face. "Are you going to cook for me?"

"No. You know I can't cook. I want to take you to Breaux Bridge for a crawfish festival."

"Aren't they tiny lobster-looking shellfish that you bite off the heads and suck the meat from their tails?"

Shiloh's expressive eyebrows lifted in surprise. He hadn't expected Gwen to know about the caviar of Louisiana Cajun cuisine. "You've eaten them?"

"No," Gwen admitted, "but I've always wanted to try them."

He pulled her closer. "And you will, princess. I'll pick you up around six."

She smiled up at him. "I'll be ready."

Lowering his head, Shiloh brushed a kiss over her lips. "I'll see you Saturday."

Gwen stood on the front porch with Cocoa, staring through a curtain of softly falling rain, long after the taillights from Shiloh's car disappeared from view. She'd verbalized to him that she wanted him to make love to her although the timing wasn't right.

She'd lied.

The time was right.

It was right the first time she'd permitted him to cross her threshold.

It was right because Shiloh Harper reminded her that she was a woman—a normal woman who had known of the strong passion within her; a woman who had begun to recognize her own needs; a woman who had found herself wanting a man she did not want to want; a man she had found herself falling in love with against her better judgment; and she knew what she'd shared and felt for Shiloh would have to be resolved.

Gwen closed and locked the front door and then mounted the staircase to her bedroom. She placed Cocoa in her wicker bed in a corner of the bathroom. Twenty minutes later she slipped into her own bed, and her last waking thought before she drifted into sleep was her body's reaction to Shiloh's arousal.

Chapter 10

After the furniture earmarked for refurbishing was removed from *Bon Temps,* Gwen retreated to her study, sat down on a rocker and picked up a letter from the stack on a side table.

She'd read more than sixty letters from the New Orleans-based musician to her late aunt, and discovered their relationship wasn't a relationship but one of adoring fan to an artist. That was what she believed until she read one dated June 14, 1972:

> My Dearest Angel,
> You could not imagine my surprise when the house lights came up last night and I saw you sitting in the audience. At that moment I wanted to leap off the stage and kiss you until I stopped breathing. I know how difficult it was for you to come see me. I love you even more for risking everything you have to make the trip.
> I heard from Buddy Deblieux about your party at

Bon Temps. I also read about it in The Times-Picayune.
The next time you have a party I could come as one of
the horn players.
My undying love,
AC

Gwen placed the letter in the corresponding envelope. She
pushed off the rocker and picked up the telephone on her
desk. Punching in the number for the *Tribune,* she identified
herself and asked to speak to Nash.

"Please don't tell me that you're quitting even before
you begin."

"Not at all," she said, hoping to put the newspaperman at
ease. "I want to know if you have any available back issues
of the *Tribune.*"

"How far back, Gwendolyn?"

"Fifty years." It was the first number that came to mind
because her aunt had lived at *Bon Temps* for half a century.

"I know I have bound copies that go back at least forty years."

"May I come in and take a look at them?"

Nash cleared his throat. "You don't have to make the trip.
I'm leaving the office within the next hour. I'll drop them by
on my way home."

Gwen smiled. "Thanks, Nash."

"Don't mention it, Gwendolyn."

She'd told her boss to call her Gwen, but Nash admitted
he was old-fashioned and never shortened anyone's name. She
ended the call, replacing the telephone on its cradle. She went
back to the rocker, sat down and removed another letter from
its envelope.

Eyes wide, she felt like a voyeur when she read the words
written by a man who had fallen inexorably in love with a
woman unable to return his affection.

* * *

I've been stood up! The enormity of what had occurred had Gwen's moods vacillating between rage and humiliation.

Since she'd begun dating at seventeen, she'd had some exceptional, and not-so-good, and downright horrible dates, but she'd never been stood up!

"Why can't I trust a man, Cocoa?" The puppy sat on its haunches staring up at Gwen as she paced back and forth. "I can't believe I fell for his smack about making me feel good. 'Oh, darling, I need to know what I have to do to make you happy,'" she drawled, sneering. "Well, Mister Five-O, the only thing that will make me happy right about now is if I never see you again!"

Shiloh called around three to tell her he would pick her up at six, but six had come and gone and it was now after ten and still no Shiloh Harper. If he'd called her once, then he could've called her a second time to let her know he'd be late or even to cancel. He could've also sent one of his deputies as he'd done before. After all, she considered herself a reasonable individual. While she was no stranger to rejection, what she couldn't abide was poor home training, she continued in her silent rant.

Gwen stopped pacing, going completely still as a feeling of dread swept over her. But…but what if he couldn't send word to her because he wasn't able to.

What if…what if something had happened to him?

What if he'd been injured or…

Her thoughts trailed off as her eyes filled with tears. She was so busy berating Shiloh that she hadn't thought maybe something had gone wrong.

Her knees were shaking when she walked through her bedroom and into the sitting room. She sat down on the cushioned window seat and clasped her hands together to stop their trembling.

How had she become so self-absorbed that she only thought of herself? Just because she existed in a cocoon of relative safety she'd dismissed the reality that each time Shiloh went on duty to uphold the oath he had sworn to protect the citizens of St. Martin Parish he put his life in jeopardy.

Closing her eyes, she whispered a prayer. Even if he had blown off their date, she still wanted him safe because she'd denied what had been so obvious from their first encounter. She liked Shiloh Harper more than she was able to openly acknowledge.

And what she did not want to do was fall in love. It was something she'd done far too often. Excitement, euphoria, an indescribable soaring feeling of love and being loved usually preceded heartbreak, heartache and disappointment. She'd once thought she'd set her standards too high, but that notion lasted all of five seconds. Her demands—trust, openness, honesty, intelligence, respect and passion—were not negotiable.

Gwen willed the tears behind her eyelids not to fall, but they did. They flowed as she cried without making a sound. She did not move to Louisiana to become involved with a man, but she had. And she did not want to fall in love again, but she had.

She lost track of time as she sat, staring into space. Cocoa ambled into the sitting room and sniffed her feet. She leaned over and settled the puppy on her lap. Half an hour later, she placed the dog in its bed, and made her way into the bathroom.

"Are you sure you don't want me to wait for you?"

Shiloh shook his head as he stared through the windshield of the police cruiser. "I'm sure, Jimmie."

"Look, man, it's almost three o'clock and either she's asleep or she's not home."

Shiloh shook his head again. "She's here. That's her car."

He pointed at the dark sedan parked alongside the north side of *Bon Temps*.

"Come home with me, Shiloh. You can bed down in one of the spare rooms in the attic. I've soundproofed it and you won't hear the kids when they start acting up."

James Jameson had known Shiloh for most of his life, and tonight was the first time he'd witnessed another side of the sensitive, compassionate man. If he hadn't come upon the horrific automobile accident, Jimmie knew he would've been the one to arrest Sheriff Shiloh Harper for murder instead of the former St. Martin High School all-star athlete who'd crashed his car head-on into a van, killing the driver along with three other passengers.

Shiloh had handcuffed the driver to his car's steering wheel to keep him from fleeing the scene. However, as Shiloh struggled to free the four people trapped inside the burning van, the young man, in a rampage fueled by alcohol and methamphetamine, kicked out the windshield, ripped the wheel from the steering column, and crawled over the hood of his Porsche only to face Shiloh, who'd drawn his handgun. Jimmie recalled Shiloh's statement that if he was ever in the position where he had to draw his gun, then he was prepared to use deadly force.

"Thanks for the offer, Jimmie, but I'm going to be all right." He unfastened the seat belt. "I'm going to take a few days off to get my head together."

Jimmie stared at his superior's strained expression, then shifted his gaze to the bandages covering Shiloh's left arm. "It's going to be more than a few days, Shiloh. You know you can't come back until you get medical clearance. Meanwhile, I'll handle everything."

A tired smile twisted Shiloh's mouth. "I know you will. Thanks, Jimmie."

"Don't worry about the Suburban. Frank said he'll drive it back to your place."

Shiloh nodded, opened the door, stepped out of the car, and made his way up the porch steps. Waiting until the taillights from the cruiser disappeared into the night, he rang the bell to Gwen Taylor's house. He rang it again a minute later, listening for movement behind the door.

He walked off the porch and around to the back of the house. Bending down, he picked up pebbles around a flower bed and pitched them at the French doors to her bedroom. There were times when he'd shimmied up porch columns or climbed tree limbs to see a girl he liked, but that time had passed. He was no longer daring, reckless or agile enough to risk falling and injuring himself. Besides, his arm hurt like hell.

He pitched another pebble, then another. A smile eased the lines of tension around his mouth when a light came on.

Gwen opened her eyes when she heard the tapping sound against the glass. Silvered light from a near-full moon came through the delicate fabric spanning the length and width of the French doors. The sound wasn't rain.

She glanced at the clock on a small round table with a vase of fragrant white peonies and sunny-yellow freesia. The glowing green numbers read 2:50 a.m.

Switching on a bedside lamp, she swung her legs over the side of the bed and walked to the French doors. Pulling back a panel of ivory-white silk drapes, she peered through the glass. A large figure moved from the shadows and into light from a motion detector. A wave of relief rippled through her body as she unlocked the floor-to-ceiling doors and stepped out onto the veranda.

Now that she saw for herself that Shiloh was in one piece,

her anger returned like a volcanic eruption. "What the hell are you doing here?" she shouted at him.

Shiloh motioned to her. "Come down and open the door and I'll tell you."

"No!"

He knew Gwen had every reason in the world to be angry with him, but he had to tell her why he hadn't been able to contact her.

"Please open the door and let me explain, darling."

Her temper flared. "Don't you dare darling me, Shiloh Harper. You stand me up, then show up in the middle of the night and expect me to open the door. I don't think so, playa."

Shiloh took a deep breath. "It's not what you think."

"Don't presume to tell me what I think, Shiloh. Please go home and leave me alone." Her tone had softened considerably.

"I can't do that, Gwen."

Resting her forearms on the railing, Gwen stared down at the shadowy figure of the man with whom she had fallen in love. "And why not?"

"I've seen too much death tonight and I need to hold on to someone warm, alive."

Time stood still, Gwen's heart beating a double-time rhythm. He had come to her not because he wanted her, but because he needed her.

She backed off the veranda, closed the doors, and unmindful of her revealing eyelet-laced cotton nightgown and bare feet, raced out of the bedroom, down the hallway and staircase to the front door. It took two attempts before she was able to unlock it. Within seconds she found herself in Shiloh's arms, her body pressed intimately to his.

"My baby. My sweet, sweet darling," he crooned, brushing feathery kisses over her parted lips.

Anchoring her arms under his shoulders, Gwen leaned into

the contours of his hard, solid body. He was stiff, brittle enough to break into thousands of tiny pieces.

"I'm here, Shiloh. I am here, darling."

Shiloh tightened his hold on Gwen's waist, lifting her off her feet, and taking possession of her mouth like a man under a spell. Touching her, tasting her, replaced the horrific images of burned and broken bodies and a newborn's weak cry; he'd delivered the premature infant as its mother lay dying from the burns that had covered most of her body. It had taken only minutes for a teenage driver to wipe out a family of four.

Gwen, ensnared in her own spell of drugging desire pulling her into a netherworld of strange and disturbing sensations, knew she was in love with the man whose arms held her. During moments of reality and complete lucidity she was forced to accept what she wanted to deny.

She'd told herself that she didn't want or need a man to make her a complete woman, that she had other projects to see to their conclusion before she sought out a life partner, and that she could continue to sleep alone while ignoring the strong urges within her.

Her hands moved down his back. The fingers of her right hand touched his forearm, and she went completely still. A gauze dressing covered Shiloh's left arm from elbow to wrist.

"What happened to you?" She was unable to keep the panic from her voice.

Shiloh glanced at his arm. "It's just a little burn."

He'd lied. It was more than a little burn. He'd suffered second-degree burns to his arm when he attempted to get the pregnant woman out of the burning van before it exploded.

Reaching up, Gwen touched his cheek. The stubble of an emerging beard grazed her fingertips. It was the first time she'd found him other than clean-shaven.

He swayed, and she clasped both arms around his waist to

steady him. He was in uniform, but he wasn't carrying his gun. "Come to bed, Shiloh." There was no doubt he was exhausted.

She closed and locked the door, then supporting his sagging body, led him up the staircase to the first bedroom at the top of the stairs. She touched a wall switch, and the room was flooded with soft light from two bedside lamps. His eyelids were drooping when Gwen steered Shiloh to a large brass bed. He sat down heavily, fell back to a mound of pillows, and closed his eyes.

"I just need to sleep."

The lamps highlighted what Gwen did not see when they'd stood in the entryway. There were abrasions on Shiloh's forehead, left cheek, and his chin. She hadn't realized how much her hands were shaking until she tried to unbutton his shirt. She worked carefully, undoing all of the buttons and easing it gently off his shoulders and down his injured arm.

The antiseptic smell associated with hospitals clung to his hair and skin. Her touch was as impersonal as a medical professional as she removed his shoes, socks, slacks, and covered him with a sheet. What puzzled Gwen was that the official police uniform didn't fit Shiloh. The shirt was a size too small, and the matching pants too big in the waist.

"Don't leave me," Shiloh slurred, not opening his eyes. "Please stay with me until I fall asleep. Just five minutes," he said when she didn't move or answer. He opened his eyes and a smile tilted the corners of his mouth. "Five minutes, baby." The injection he'd been given at the hospital was beginning to take effect.

Smiling, Gwen leaned over and pressed a kiss on his forehead. "Five minutes," she repeated. She turned off the lamps, pulled back the sheet, and got into bed with Shiloh. And with a pull as strong as the moon on the tide, she turned to face him.

Five minutes went by, ten, then fifteen, and she still hadn't moved. Pinpoints of light pierced the night sky with the rising sun, and Gwen lay motionless. She had fallen asleep, her breathing coming in concert with the man pressed intimately to her side.

Gwen walked into the kitchen with Cocoa at her heels. Picking up a remote device, she turned on a small television anchored under a cabinet. It wasn't until she woke to find the hard body in bed with her and glimpsed the scrapes on Shiloh's face and the startling white bandage on his arm that she remembered vividly what had happened only hours before.

She went through the laundry room and opened the rear door. "Outside, Miss Cocoa," she said cheerfully. The puppy usually frolicked and rolled around in the grass until she tired. She then came back looking for food and water.

Gwen filled the puppy's water bowl from the sink in the laundry room, then spooned a small amount of food into another bowl. She returned to the kitchen and sat down on a tall stool. A newscaster mentioning Shiloh's name captured her rapt attention.

She stared at the small television screen, transfixed as a reporter recounted the details of an automobile accident that had claimed the lives of a man, his pregnant wife, and their four-year-old twin daughters. A split screen showed the grim face of a St. Martin Parish deputy sheriff and the chief of neonatal medicine at a Baton Rogue hospital.

Deputy James Jameson reported that Sheriff Harper, who was off-duty at the time, was the first officer on the scene. He'd risked his life to pull all of the occupants from the burning wreckage before the vehicle exploded.

The force of impact triggered an onset of labor for the mother who was expected to deliver her baby in seven weeks.

Sheriff Harper delivered a three-pound baby boy. EMTs had worked feverishly to save her life, but she succumbed to burns and massive head trauma. Mercifully her husband and daughters were killed instantly. The camera angle changed, focusing on the doctor who reported the baby's prognosis for survival was upgraded from grave to good. Pressing the power button on the remote, Gwen turned off the television.

I've seen too much death tonight, and I need to hold on to someone warm, alive. His plea would be branded into her brain for an eternity.

The chiming of the doorbell broke into her thoughts. Who, she wondered as she slipped off the stool, had come to see her at seven in the morning? Gwen did not have long to ponder the question when she opened the door to find Moriah Harper pacing back and forth on the porch. Her short curly hair looked as if she'd combed it with her fingers.

The dark green eyes were filled with fear. "Jimmie Jameson called and told me that he dropped Shiloh off here. How is he?" The words tumbled from her trembling lips.

Gwen smiled, hoping to alleviate the older woman's anxiety. "He's upstairs sleeping. Why don't you go up and see him."

Moriah curbed the urge to hug the woman who had bewitched her son. "Thank you."

"I'm going to put up some coffee. Would you like a cup?" she asked Shiloh's mother.

Smiling for the first time since she'd gotten the call from the deputy sheriff, Moriah managed a smile. "Yes, thank you."

Moriah took the staircase to the second floor. It had been years since she'd been inside *Bon Temps*. Gwendolyn Pickering had invited her and Virgil to celebrate his becoming the parish's first black sheriff. It was her first invitation, and over the next twenty years she and her husband were invited to many other soirees at Miss Pickering's home.

She found Shiloh asleep, his injured left arm resting on a pillow. Jimmie told her that he'd been sedated. Moving closer, Moriah saw the bruises on his face. Crossing her chest, she mumbled a silent prayer of thanks. Her son was safe.

She'd thought it odd that Shiloh would seek out Gwen Taylor instead of coming to her house. Moriah didn't know anything about Gwen Taylor, and hadn't sought to find out anything about her because she'd never been a mother who meddled in her grown sons' lives. All she ever wanted for Shiloh and Ian was for them to find happiness with a woman whom they'd chosen to share their lives and future.

But, on the other hand, she'd detected something in her former daughter-in-law Shiloh either did not or chose not to see: deceit. She walked out of the bedroom and made her way down the staircase to the kitchen. The tantalizing smell of brewing coffee filled the large space.

"Now, that smells wonderful."

Gwen turned and smiled at Moriah. "Nothing smells better than breakfast."

Moriah nodded. "I agree."

"Will you stay and share breakfast with me?"

Attractive lines fanned out around Moriah's emerald-green eyes. "Of course."

"I'll—" Whatever Gwen was going to say was preempted by the doorbell.

Gwen excused herself and went to answer the door. It had become a very busy Sunday morning at *Bon Temps*. Ian and Natalee Harper were her second visitors of the day.

"Where is he?" Ian asked without preamble.

Natalee rolled her eyes at her husband. "Good morning, Gwen. We're sorry to come without calling, but Moriah called and said that we would find Shiloh here."

Gwen waved a hand, opening the door wider. "No need to

apologize. Come on in. Shiloh's in the first bedroom at the top of the stairs."

Leaning over, Ian pressed a kiss to her cheek. "Sorry about that."

Gwen offered him a shy smile. "Go see your brother."

Ian raced across the living room, taking the stairs two at a time, while Natalee quickened her pace to catch up with him.

Gwen stood in the middle of the near-empty living room. Her home was filled with Harpers. Once they'd received the news that Shiloh was at *Bon Temps* they'd come. She returned to the kitchen to find Moriah opening overhead cabinets.

"What do you need?"

Flashing a smile that reminded Gwen of Shiloh's, Moriah said, "I wanted to set the table. I feel so useless standing around doing nothing. I tend to eat whenever I'm upset."

Gwen wanted to tell Moriah that it was apparent she didn't get upset too often. Her slender body was remarkable for a woman her age. "The dishes are in the cabinet to your left. By the way, that was Ian and Natalee."

"I'm surprised I made it here before Ian. He drives like a maniac."

Moriah set the table while Gwen searched her refrigerator for breakfast foods. Ian and Natalee walked into the kitchen, holding hands.

"Brother love is awake and wants to see you, Gwen," Natalee announced loudly.

"Go see him," Moriah urged in a quiet voice. "Ian and I will take care of breakfast."

Gwen smiled and shook her head. The Harpers had commandeered her kitchen. She winked at Ian. "I like my bacon well-done."

"How about your eggs?" he asked.

"Any kind will do."

"Hot damn, Yankee girl has Tabasco," Ian drawled when he opened a cabinet filled with spices. "I can't get Natalee to touch the stuff." He ignored his wife when she stuck out her tongue at him.

Gwen walked into the bedroom and smiled. Shiloh sat up, his back supported by several pillows. The bandage on his arm was a stark reminder of how close he'd come to losing his own life. Her gaze moved slowly over his stubbly jaw before dropping to his smooth, dark-brown chest. The power in his upper body was blatantly displayed with muscled shoulders, solid pectorals, and rock-hard abs.

Shiloh smiled and patted the mattress. "Please come sit next to me."

She sat down and was swallowed up in a longing that made drawing a normal breath difficult. She leaned against his shoulder. "How are you?"

"Good," he lied smoothly. He pressed his mouth to her hair. "I'd like to apologize."

"For what?"

"For the Harpers descending on you like a swarm of locusts."

Tilting her chin, Gwen smiled at him. "They just needed to see for themselves that you're still in one piece."

He closed his eyes. "I'm all right," he lied again. His arm would heal, but it would take a lot longer to rid himself of the images he would probably carry to his grave.

Shiloh didn't know why he'd ordered Jimmie to take him to *Bon Temps*—not until now. Under another set of circumstances he would've gone to his mother's house. That may have been before he'd found himself enthralled by a woman who made him do things he didn't want to do, a woman who made him want her when he'd told himself he didn't need any woman. And not when he'd sworn an oath never to trust another woman. But there was something about Gwendolyn Taylor that made him break every promise he'd made to himself. Something unspoken whispered to him that not only could he trust her, but he also wanted her to become a part of his life.

"Does it hurt much?"

He sighed softly. "It's bearable."

"You didn't answer my question, Shiloh Harper."

He glared at her, but she didn't drop her gaze. The curls framing her face gave her a doll-like appearance. Her large dark eyes, button nose, and lush curved mouth reminded him of the delicate dolls on display in store windows during the Christmas season.

"Yes, Gwendolyn Paulette Taylor, it hurts."

Her eyes narrowed. "You're lucky you're injured or I'd give you a knuckle sandwich." She pushed her fist close to his nose. "I've warned you about using my government name."

He lifted his eyebrow. "And, I've told you about threatening a peace officer."

She shuddered noticeably. "Ooo-wee. I'm scared. You're not going anywhere or arresting anyone with that well-done wing."

Shiloh stared numbly at Gwen before he threw back his head and howled. Seconds later, her laughter joined his, and they laughed until tears rolled down their faces.

Gwen sobered first. "Do you think you can make it downstairs for breakfast or would you prefer eating in bed?"

His gaze softened, his eyes devouring her whole. "I'll eat in bed if you'll join me."

A wave of heat swept over her face. "I can't. Not with your family downstairs," she whispered.

"Maybe after they leave."

It took a moment for Gwen to interpret his double meaning. "I don't think you're up to doing too much with that arm. Once the doctor says you're okay to return to duty I'll take you up on your offer."

Smiling, Shiloh leaned closer to her. "Does that mean you're going to become my roommate?"

"No," she whispered. "It means I won't feel guilty for taking advantage of you."

His expressive eyebrows shot up. "I don't mind if you take advantage of me as long as it feels good." He pressed a kiss to her forehead. "If I'm going downstairs, then I'm going to need my clothes, darling."

Gwen left the bed and went over to the closet. When she returned she found Shiloh with his eyes closed, cradling his left arm in his right hand. He'd lied to her. He was in pain— lots of pain.

"Where are the pills, Shiloh?"

He opened his eyes. "What are you talking about?"

"Jimmie told your mother that the doctor at the hospital gave you something for pain."

He closed his eyes again. "Jimmie shouldn't be running off at the mouth."

Resting her hands on her hips, Gwen moved closer. "Where are you hiding them?"

Shifting slightly, he reached for his slacks and pulled a small white envelope from the pocket. She took the envelope, reading the printed instructions: take one tablet by mouth every four hours as needed. She was certain it had been more than four hours since he had the last one.

"I'll be back with some water," she said over her shoulder as she headed to the bathroom. A minute later she handed him a cup. "Open your mouth."

Shiloh frowned. "Damn, darling. You could've said please."

She thrust her face close to his. "I'm not feeling too dip-lomatic right about now, because I'm not impressed with acts of machismo. There's nothing wrong with admitting that you're in pain."

Shiloh took the pill from her hand and placed it on the tip of his tongue. He swallowed it and washed it down with the water. "Better?" he drawled sarcastically.

Gwen flashed a facetious grin. "Yes, darling. Should I send your mother up to help you wash?"

He rolled his eyes at her. "I believe I can manage without her assistance."

Gwen touched his shoulder. "I'll wait until you're finished. Then I'll help you downstairs."

Not waiting for Shiloh to accept or reject her offer, she sat on the side of the bed to wait.

Gwen sat across the table from Shiloh, watching as he became less and less animated.

"When do you have to go back to the doctor?" Moriah asked him.

"Tuesday morning."

"I'll take you."

He shook his head as he tried focusing on Gwen's face. The drugging effects of the narcotic had kicked in. "I don't want you to take off from work."

"School ends next week, and I don't believe I'm going to lose my job if I take a day off to accompany my son to the doctor."

"Let it go, Mama," Ian warned softly in French, as he picked up a forkful of poached eggs with hollandaise sauce.

Moriah's gaze shifted from Shiloh to Gwen, then back to Shiloh. She'd missed what should've been so obvious. Even though he'd spoken to her he couldn't take his eyes off Gwen. She was familiar with Shiloh's expression because she'd been the recipient of the same adoring look from her late husband.

There was no doubt that her son had fallen in love with Gwendolyn Taylor.

Shiloh's head bobbed up and down before he pushed back his chair. "You good folks are going to have to excuse me, but I'm going to hang out on the back porch. Please give me an hour, then I'll be ready to go home."

Ian rose with him, wrapping an arm around his shoulders. "Steady there, big brother." Three pairs of eyes were fixed on the tall, broad-shouldered brothers as they made their way out of the kitchen.

Gwen pulled her gaze from Shiloh's retreating figure to find Moriah watching her. She lowered her head and pretended interest in the food on her plate. What, she wondered, had Shiloh's mother read into his recuperating under her roof? Did she believe they were a couple when they weren't?

She and Shiloh were friends, and friends were expected to look out for each other in their time of need.

Chapter 11

Gwen walked into the building housing the offices of the *Teche Tribune* half an hour before she was scheduled to begin work. As agreed upon with Nash McGraw, she would work Tuesday and Wednesday. She planned to do her interviewing on Tuesday, and revise and submit her copy to Nash before four o'clock Wednesday. Ads and copy for the weekly were submitted to a local printer Thursday for Friday publication. Nash said the residents of St. Martin and the surrounding parishes looked forward to the *Tribune* for their weekend reading. The weekly, with its distinctive hometown flavor, was a refreshing alternative to the New Orleans-based *Times-Picayune*.

She wanted to talk to Nash about an unsolved murder that had captured her interest once she began going through the back issues. Her need to uncover information on Gwendolyn Pickering was overshadowed by the 1964 murder of a high school prom queen.

Nash's gleaming silver head came up when she rapped lightly on his open door. "Good morning," she said cheerfully.

The editor's blue eyes widened as if he hadn't expected to see her. "Good morning, Gwendolyn. I'm glad you're here early because I want to talk to you about that car accident that everyone in the parish has been talking about." He beckoned her closer. "Come in and sit down."

Nash watched Gwendolyn Taylor as she walked into his office. He'd thought himself blessed when Shiloh had come to him with her name and mentioned that she was looking for part-time employment. Within minutes of searching her name through the Internet, he knew he'd struck the mother lode. Gwendolyn had written hundreds of articles, many of them syndicated in other papers throughout the country.

During her interview, he felt she'd presented herself well. She was confident without being pretentious. She'd come to the interview wearing a business suit that would've been appropriate for a board meeting or an after-work dinner encounter. Today she wore a pair of black linen slacks and a delicate sky-blue linen shirt over a matching tank top, and despite her big-city sophistication she exuded a down-home style, which was certain to put those she interviewed completely at ease.

"I'd like you to get as much information as you can regarding this horrific incident." *Horrific* had come out in three distinctive syllables. "First I want you to interview Jimmie Jameson, who's now filling in for Shiloh. Get what information you can from Shiloh, who was the first one on the scene, and the arresting officer. Then I need you to talk to anyone at the D.A.'s office to find out what they're charging that boy with.

"And, if you're lucky I want you to talk to the boy's folks." Nash handed Gwen a piece of paper with the names and address of Willis Benton's parents. "It might be a little difficult because Mr. Benton's lawyer has cautioned him against speaking directly to the press."

"Why?"

"Abraham Benton is a Washington lobbyist who prefers keeping a low profile."

Gwen opened her purse and removed a pad and pencil. "What's his lawyer's name?" She wrote down the information Nash gave her. "Let me see what I can uncover before we put out this week's edition."

Nash rose to his feet at the same time she stood up. "Did you see your desk when you came in?"

She went still, momentarily surprised with this disclosure because she thought she would be working from home. "No, I didn't."

Rounding his cluttered desk, Nash cupped her elbow. "Come, let me show you where you'll be working."

He led her down a hallway and opened the door to an office next to the advertising manager. The space was small and overlooked the front of the two-story building. French doors opened out to a grillwork-enclosed balcony.

A desk, desk lamp, workstation with a computer, printer and fax machine, two two-drawer file cabinets and a well-worn cordovan-brown love seat completed what would become her home away from home for the two days she spent at the paper's offices.

Nash turned a small wood plaque over on the desk. "Welcome aboard."

Gwen's smile was dazzling. The plaque read: Gwendolyn Taylor, Editor, Crime Desk. "I suppose it's too late to back out now."

"If you try I'll sue you for breach of a verbal contract."

She shook her head slowly. "Shame on you, Nash. I can't

believe a respected journalist of your caliber would have to resort to threats and intimidation to maintain his staff."

The editor flushed beneath his deep tan. "People resort to desperate measures during desperate times." Nash's eyes were cold despite the smile curving his mouth.

Gwen looped the strap of her handbag over her shoulder. "That sounds like my cue to hit the bricks and get my story."

"Thank you, Deputy Jameson, for agreeing to meet with me. I promise not to take up too much of your time."

Jimmie Jameson's expression did not change when Gwendolyn Taylor was shown into his office. Now he knew why Shiloh was so taken with her. The profusion of black curls falling around her flawless face, large sparkling eyes, and her warm, inviting smile were captivating.

He extended his hand. "I hope I can be of some assistance to you."

Gwen shook the acting sheriff's hand. She'd done her homework on James Jameson. It was rumored that the former FBI special agent was certain to be elected sheriff in the next election.

"Please sit down, Miss Taylor."

"Thank you."

Gwen placed a pocket-sized recorder on Acting Sheriff James Jameson's desk before she sat down and pulled out a small notebook with the questions she wanted to ask regarding the accident that placed Shiloh on medical leave. She'd come to the station house as Gwendolyn Taylor, crime reporter for the *Teche Tribune*.

Her head came up and she met the stare of the stocky man with a shaved head. His full, unlined face made it difficult to pinpoint his exact age.

"What can you tell me about the automobile accident that

occurred late Saturday afternoon that resulted in the loss of life for a family of four?"

Jimmie focused on a photograph on a facing wall to bring his emotions under control. He was a husband, father and son and his heart ached when he had to inform the deceased's next-of-kin of the tragedy.

"Willis Raymond Benton has been charged with vehicular homicide and reckless endangerment in the deaths of Barry Edmondson, thirty-six, his wife, Selma, thirty-two, and their four-year-old twin daughters, Naomi and Ruth."

"Why reckless endangerment?" Gwen asked.

"Mr. Benton's blood alcohol was twice the state's legal limit, and a subsequent toxicology report indicated a substantial amount of crystal meth. He became a suicide bomber the moment he got behind the wheel of his car."

"Has he been arraigned?"

Jimmie nodded. "Yes."

"Has he been denied bail?" she asked.

A look of hardness glittered in the deputy's eyes. "No. The district attorney's office asked he be remanded without bail, but Benton's attorney argued that this is his first offense, and that he isn't a flight risk."

"He's out on bail?"

Jimmie nodded. "His daddy posted a two-million-dollar bond. If Willis had been other than some fat cat lobbyist kid he would never see the light of day."

Gwen leaned forward. "Are you telling me that you expect him to beat the charge?"

"Charges," Jimmie said, correcting her.

"Okay," she conceded. "Charges."

Jimmie gave Gwen a long, penetrating look. The tape recorder was running, and he didn't want to say anything to compromise himself or the sheriff's office. "We arrest, not prosecute, Miss Taylor. I suggest you ask Keith Nichols that question."

She remembered the A.D.A. she'd met at the Outlaw. "Has Mr. Nichols been assigned the case?"

"I believe he has."

Gwen checked off her next question. "Can you give me any details of the accident?"

"I can only tell you what I witnessed once I arrived on the scene. If you want a more detailed eyewitness account, then you're going to have to talk to Sheriff Harper."

She closed her pad and stopped the tape recorder, putting both in her handbag. "Thank you, Deputy Jameson. You've been very helpful."

Jimmie stared at the profusion of curls that reminded him of a cluster of black grapes. "What I'm going to say to you is off the record."

Unconsciously, Gwen's brown furrowed. When she'd covered the crime desk for the *Gazette* she'd gotten more information from police personnel off the record than on. She wasn't certain what it was but apparently they sensed they could trust her with facts they hadn't made known to other reporters. And they were right to trust her because she never leaked information or revealed her sources.

"Okay," she said in a quiet voice.

"Willie Ray Benton will never step foot inside a prison."

Her lips parting in surprise, Gwen stared at the deputy. "Why would you say that? After all, he's responsible for killing four people. And if Sheriff Harper hadn't delivered Mrs. Edmondson's baby, the count would be five. Didn't you say he tested positive for alcohol and meth?"

"The facts are inconclusive as to whether he was drinking and using drugs, but Bram Benton wields a lot of political power in Louisiana. Last year he was responsible for pork barrel appropriations totaling more than a billion dollars. There aren't too many folk willing to incur Abraham Benton's wrath or the loss of funds he throws their way if they send his boy to prison."

Jury tampering. The two words jarred Gwen with the same intensity as a sharp instrument colliding with the soft tissue under her fingernail. If Jimmie Jameson suspected what she thought, then it would be up to the district attorney's office to request a change of venue to a district where most of the citizens weren't aware of Benton's political influence. But where, she wondered.

Gathering her large leather handbag, she stood up. "I'll think about what you've just told me off the record."

Jimmie pushed back his chair, his expression tight, solemn. "I'll walk you out."

Gwen offered him her hand. "Thank you, Deputy Jameson."

A hint of a smile softened his firm mouth. "You're welcome, Miss Taylor."

He walked her through the station house, ignoring the curious stares from those who made up the SMPD and several civilian employees. Gwendolyn Taylor was new to the parish, but after her byline appeared in the *Tribune* everyone would come to know her as the paper's crime reporter and the current owner of *Bon Temps*.

Gwen walked to her car in the parking lot adjacent to the building housing the SMPD, and using a remote device unlocked the doors. She slipped behind the wheel, but did not turn on the ignition. She had to make two calls and two visits before returning to the newspaper office.

Retrieving her cell phone, she scrolled through the directory for the number she'd programmed before leaving the *Tribune*. She pushed the talk button, then waited.

"St. Martin Parish District Attorney's office."

She smiled when she heard the slight inflection peculiar to the region. Even though it had been more than two hundred years since the Acadians were exiled to southern Louisiana, when they said *about* it sounded like *a boot*.

"I'm Gwendolyn Taylor, and I'd like to speak to A.D.A. Nichols."

"I'm sorry, Miss Taylor, but Mr. Nichols is in court."

"May I leave a message for him?"

"Yes. I'll put you through to his voice mail."

Gwen left her name, cell phone number and the reason for her call. She pressed the End button, then dialed Shiloh's cell phone. She smiled as she waited for him to answer.

He'd left *Bon Temps* Sunday afternoon then called her from his brother's house that evening. He said he preferred staying with Ian and Natalee because Moriah tended to treat his injury as if he were an ICU patient.

Monday was the official observation of Memorial Day, and Natalee invited her to celebrate the holiday with the Harpers, but she'd declined. It was the first time since relocating that she felt like an alien in her own country. She was fifteen hundred miles away from her family and she missed her mother, father and her cousins. It took her a while to diagnose the feeling of abandonment and isolation as homesickness.

A telephone call from her mother had become the highlight of the day. They'd talked for hours, Gwen disclosing what she'd uncovered about her mother's favorite aunt. Paulette Taylor confessed that she'd wanted to become an actress like her aunt. However, Gwendolyn Pickering had strongly cautioned her niece about the pitfalls of the profession, and suggested the young girl consider a career in education. Now, at sixty-three, Paulette Taylor had two more years before she retired as a high school principal.

Shiloh's drawling voice coming through the tiny earpiece captured her attention. "Harper. Leave a message."

Gwen lifted her eyebrows. His voice mail message was so impersonal. "Sheriff Harper, this is Gwendolyn Taylor, from the *Tribune*. Please call me when you get this message. I'd like to interview you for this week's Blotter. Thank you."

Shiloh left the doctor's office and activated his cell phone. The nurse had applied a soothing salve and covered his forearm with a breathable bandage. His prognosis was good: he could expect to return to full duty in two to three weeks.

The dermatologist had offered to write another prescription for pain because the one he'd been taking elicited hallucinations despite not being a hallucinogenic. The opiate-derivative induced dreams filled with images of Gwen and babies. He didn't want another prescription; he just didn't want to experience the disturbing images.

He had two voice-mail messages. The first was from Jimmie who informed him that the DEA agent was in place at the Outlaw, and that he could expect a call from a very pretty reporter from the *Tribune*.

Shiloh smiled when he recognized the number of the second caller. His smile vanished quickly when he heard her voice with the distinctive Bostonian intonation. She'd identified herself as Gwendolyn Taylor. She'd reverted to being Miss Taylor, the haughty young woman who'd refused to get out of her car because she feared becoming gator bait.

He planned to return Miss Taylor's call, but only after he filed the prescription for the soothing salve that would speed the burn's healing process.

It was apparent she wanted to talk business, and what he wanted to talk to her about was anything but business.

* * *

Gwen slowed and stopped at the gatehouse to the private community. A uniformed guard slid back the window to his air-cooled space. She smiled. "Gwendolyn Taylor. Mr. Harper is expecting me."

The guard typed her name into an electronic device, waiting until her name appeared on a monitor. He pressed a button, and a wooden arm lifted. "Stay to your right, Miss Taylor. Mr. Harper's residence is the last on the right."

She nodded. "Thank you."

Gwen wanted to tell the man that she knew where she was going. It hadn't been two weeks since Shiloh brought her to his home yet it seemed more time had passed. So much had happened since the fateful night he'd come to her rescue when she'd driven into the ditch.

She wanted Shiloh not only to want her, but also to need her for more than a slacking of sexual frustration. He'd promised her honesty, respect and trust. What he hadn't promised was love. At thirty-four she'd been engaged, had more than her share of blind dates, and the two physical liaisons she preferred to forget. However, none of the men in her past elicited the physical longing she felt whenever she and Shiloh Harper occupied the same space.

Although gentle and soft-spoken, he oozed the coiled menace of a panther, and she'd come to believe she was attracted to him because of the latent danger. Why was it that most good girls found themselves drawn to bad boys?

The very object of her erotic musings stood on the porch waiting for her. He wore a black tank top and pair of faded, tattered jeans that rode low on his slim hips, jeans that should've been discarded a long time ago. The dressing on his left arm was clearly visible as he crossed his arms over his chest.

Gwen forced a smile as her pulse quickened. He

appeared taller, more muscled, and virile, and the stubble on his jaw made her breath catch in her chest. Had she made a mistake, she asked herself, coming to his house to interview him when she should've asked him to come to the newspaper's office?

Pull it together, girl, she told herself as she parked behind Shiloh's Mustang and cut off the engine. She couldn't afford to fall apart because he looked good enough to eat. By the time she removed the key he'd moved off the porch and come over to open her door.

Wrapping his uninjured arm around her waist, Shiloh pulled Gwen close to his chest. "Hey, you."

She smiled up at him. "Hey, yourself."

Lowering his head, he kissed her. He increased the pressure until her lips parted under his tender onslaught. "I've missed you."

A warming snaked through Gwen, settling in her middle. "Don't be silly, Shiloh. It's only been two days."

His gold-green eyes searched her face. "That's two days too long." His fingers tightened at her waist. "Come in out of the heat." It wasn't officially summer, but the heat, coupled with the humidity was oppressive.

Gwen followed Shiloh up the back twin staircase and into the kitchen. The air coming from strategically placed vents quickly cooled her fevered body. He led her down the two steps into the dining area and through the open space to the family room. A tray on a beveled glass-topped rattan table held a glass pitcher filled with iced tea and lemon slices, and a plate with twisted dough sprinkled with chopped nuts.

"Oh, my goodness. You cooked."

"Very funny," Shiloh drawled, as he seated Gwen on a love seat covered in an off-white Haitian cotton fabric. "I asked Ian to make them for the Memorial Day gathering." He sat down next to her. "I was disappointed when you didn't come."

"I couldn't because I was expecting telephone calls from home." She hadn't known her mother was going to call, so what she'd told Shiloh wasn't entirely untrue.

He studied her delicate profile. Soft black curls framed her face and grazed the nape of her neck. "I was under the impression that St. Martin Parish was home."

Shifting slightly, Gwen stared at Shiloh. She'd committed the slant of his luminous eyes, shape of his strong mouth, sweeping curve of his black eyebrows, and the slightly flaring nostrils of his nose to memory, but each time she came face-to-face with him she never failed to marvel at how much he affected her.

"It is," she said in a quiet tone, "but it's going to take me a while to think of it as home."

"How long, darling?"

Gwen held his gaze. "How long what?"

He leaned closer. "Will it take you to think of…to…" His words halted as he placed light kisses along the column of her neck.

Closing her eyes, she slumped weakly against him. "Don't, Shiloh," she pleaded without conviction. "I came here to interview you."

"You want to know about the accident?"

"Yes-s-s." She'd slurred the word. She couldn't think straight with his mouth mapping the nape of her neck.

Easing back, Shiloh smiled. "Do you have a tape recorder?"

Gwen opened her eyes. "Yes. Why?"

He extended his hand. "Give it to me, Miss Taylor, and I'll tell you what you want to know."

Reaching for her handbag, she took out the palm-sized instrument and handed it to him. Shiloh pushed the record button. "Hey," Gwen said, trying to take the recorder from him. "I need to ask you some pertinent questions," she said when he cleared his voice.

He held it out of her reach. "Let me interview myself. If there's anything else you need to know, then I'll answer your pertinent questions."

He was the sheriff of St. Martin Parish and she was the crime reporter for the *Teche Tribune*. And because she needed his eyewitness account of the traffic accident that was on the lips of every parish resident, she decided to capitulate.

Gwen's head went up and down like a bobble head doll. His unwillingness to let her direct the interview told her more about Shiloh Harper than he'd disclosed during their prior encounters. He was used to being in control.

Just this one time, darling, she mused, flashing a wry smile.

Settling back against the plump pillow, she listened as Shiloh spoke into the tiny microphone. It took less than five minutes for him to answer all of her questions and those she hadn't thought of asking.

She closed her eyes, listening to the hoarse quality of his voice when he told of pulling the tiny burned bodies of the little girls from the van, then their father, and finally the pregnant woman. It changed to a tremulous whisper when he recounted how he'd delivered the tiny baby boy and wrapped it in his soot-covered shirt. It changed again, hardening ruthlessly once he retold how Willie Ray Benton, in a drug-crazed rampage, tried to escape.

Shiloh paused. "Jimmie arrived along with three other deputies and the EMTs. I rode along in the ambulance with the baby, who was later airlifted to a neonatal unit of a Baton Rouge children's hospital. Willie Ray was read his rights and hauled off to jail." His gaze widened as it fused with Gwen's, and the beginning of a smile tipped the corners of his mouth.

"That's it, Miss Taylor. The truth, the whole truth, and nothing but the truth."

Gwen held out her hand for the recorder, and she wasn't disappointed when he turned it off and placed it on her outstretched palm. "Thank you, Sheriff Harper."

Bracing his left arm over the back of the love seat, Shiloh smiled at her. "You're welcome. Now, can I stop being Sheriff Harper, Miss Gwendolyn Taylor?"

She lifted an eyebrow. "Is there a difference?"

He leaned closer. "Of course. As Sheriff Harper I wouldn't be able to do this." Placing his right hand against her waist, he drew her to him, lowered his head, and slanted his mouth over hers.

Gwen jumped, as if she'd been jolted with a bolt of electricity. The mere touch of his hand burned her flesh through the fabric of her blouse. The heat spread, moving lower and even lower, until the area between her legs ignited in a throbbing that craved to be assuaged.

Her fingers unclenched, the recorder falling between the seat cushions, as she reached up and cradled Shiloh's bearded face. She felt his warmth, inhaled his scent, and luxuriated in the strength of his solid body. One hand moved up to his shoulder, and higher still where her fingertips grazed the soft strands on the nape of his strong neck.

Shiloh, who prided himself on his rigid self-control since his divorce, yielded to the rush of desire that made him unable to stop the blood pooling in his groin. "Please, darling." His plea was a tortured groan.

Gwen locked herself into his embrace, wanting him, needing him like she'd never wanted or needed any man. She knew Shiloh was asking to make love to her, and she wanted him to.

"Yes." The word was barely off her tongue when she found

herself in his arms as he rose to his feet. "Your arm," she whispered against his ear.

Smiling, he adjusted her weight. "It's okay."

"I don't want you to hurt yourself."

A knowing smile parted his lips. "Right about now, it's not my arm that's aching."

Tightening her grip around his neck, Gwen moistened her lips. She knew what was about to happen yet was helpless to stop it because she didn't want to. She wanted the man, needed the man holding her to his heart.

"I need you to protect me, Shiloh. I can't get pregnant now."

Jaw clenched and eyes narrowing, Shiloh glared at the woman in his arms. Annoyance temporarily overrode the throbbing desire threatening to tear him asunder. "I know. You don't want a baby."

Gwen opened her mouth to refute him, but the retort died on her lips. She hadn't said she didn't *want* a baby, but that she couldn't afford to get pregnant. Not when she'd hadn't done all she'd planned to do.

Relaxing in the strong embrace, she closed her eyes as Shiloh mounted the staircase to the second floor. Fear, need and desire merged to leave her heart pounding wildly under her breasts. Strange and foreign questions surfaced, shattering her resolve. It had taken four years to open up enough to sleep with a man, and only a month to find herself in love with that man.

"It's going to be all good, darling."

She opened her eyes and smiled. There was something in the way Shiloh looked at her that said he was right, the time was right, and she was ready for what was to come.

Chapter 12

Shiloh placed Gwen on his bed, his body following hers down. He put pressure on his left elbow rather than his forearm, and cradled her face between his hands. The large dark eyes staring back at him were filled with fear and another emotion he was unable to identify.

"It's been longer for you than it has for me," he said softly, "so why don't we do this together. I'll undress you and you can undress me."

A tender smile broke through the expression of uncertainty freezing Gwen's features. "Thank you," she whispered before she closed her eyes and let her senses take over.

She felt the gossamer touch of her soon-to-be lover's fingers as he reached down and removed her shoes, undid the buttons on her blouse, then her slacks, instinctively raising her hips to aid him in removing them. Her breath quickened when he eased the tank top up her chest, baring her breasts to his heated gaze.

Shiloh expelled a lungful of breath. Gwen's clothes had artfully concealed a pair of full breasts, hips and a flat belly. Lowering his head, he pulled a nipple into his mouth, sucking gently. It swelled and hardened at the same time she arched off the mattress, gasping. He released it with a soft pop before giving the other breast equal attention. Her moans, his groans mingled as rising passions spun out of control.

Gwen did not remember when Shiloh divested her of her tank top or bikini panties. Navigating through a sensual haze bordering on hysteria, she removed his top, unsnapped his jeans, and pushed them and his briefs down around his hips and legs. Tears welled in her eyes, her hands shook, and she bit down on her lower lip to keep from crying out how much she wanted and loved Shiloh Harper. Straddling him, she wrapped her arms around his neck.

Shiloh combed his fingers through her curls, holding them off her face, and pressed a kiss to her forehead. "I feel you, baby." He could feel and smell the rising scent of her desire, an aphrodisiac that shattered the vestiges of the iron-will control he'd erected to protect his emotional stability. He'd loved and lost, and since meeting Gwen he hadn't wanted to risk losing his heart to another woman. But something told him that he could love and trust her completely.

Gwen couldn't stop the shudders rippling through her body. She was close enough to Shiloh to feel his heartbeat. She was in his bedroom, naked, her body pressed to his, and she was scared witless.

Shiloh's hand moved up and down her spine in a soothing motion. "Relax, darling. That's it. Take a deep breath. Now exhale."

She followed his instruction, slowing down her heartbeat. A soft moan escaped her when he cupped her buttocks, pulling her closer as she anchored her arms under his shoulders.

Smiling, Shiloh buried his face in her fragrant hair. "We don't have to do anything."

Gwen froze. "What do you mean?"

"We can just sit and hold each other."

Easing back, she stared up at him staring down at her. "Are you a voyeur?"

Vertical lines furrowed his forehead. "No. Why would you ask me that?"

"If I'm going to take off my clothes and let you see my business, then I expect you to do something."

Shiloh chuckled softly, the sound rumbling in his chest. "I just want to know if you're ready for what we're about to share."

Gwen gave him a long, penetrating stare. She was more than ready. What she hadn't known was that she was ready for Shiloh the night he'd come to answer her nine-eleven call.

"Yes, darling," she crooned. "I'm ready. Are you?"

A sensual smile softened his mouth. "You can't imagine how ready I am for you." His hands moved from her hips to cradle her face between his large hands. "I adore you, Gwendolyn Paulette Taylor."

Gwen pressed her mouth to the fading bruise on his cheekbone. "This is one time I'm going to forgive you for using my government name."

He chuckled again. "Thank you."

Her kisses became bolder, moving from his jaw to his chin, the column of his strong neck, collarbone, and lower to his chest. He gasped loudly when the tip of her tongue swept over his chest.

There was a time when Shiloh pleaded with Gwen not to move, but not now. The pressure of her hips and the soft crush of her breasts against his chest was his undoing.

The stirring flesh between his thighs hardened quickly, and he told himself that he needed to go slowly—for Gwen and himself. Both had been denied sexual gratification for a long time. He'd promised himself that whenever he shared a bed with a woman again it would be because of unspoken emotions that couldn't be translated into words, and not to slake his sexual frustration. For that he didn't need a woman.

He kissed her mouth, softly, tenderly. His tongue outlined the shape of her mouth before he eased it between her parted lips. His tongue touched the roof of her mouth, grazed the ridge of her even bite, the smoothness of her inner cheek before it touched hers, tentatively testing her response.

Gwen literally inhaled Shiloh—his unique body scent mingling with a clean, citrusy cologne. Her mouth was everywhere: the pulse at the base of his throat, shoulders, and chest. It was as if she couldn't get enough of his smell, the firm muscle and sinew under her fingertips, and the unyielding strength of his large, solid body.

She tried ignoring the throbbing under her hips, but failed. Her hips began their own dance of desire as she rocked back and forth on Shiloh's powerful thighs. A rush of moisture preceded the scorching heat taking over her mind and body.

"Please," she gasped, quickening her movements. Gwen knew she was close to climaxing as the flaming heat inside of her became more intense with every passing second.

Shiloh reached over and opened the drawer to the nightstand and grasped a condom. Using his teeth, he tore it open, unaware that his hands were shaking. He eased Gwen down to the mattress, looming above her while slipping the latex sheath over his erection.

Time stood still, the world stopped spinning on its axis, when his gaze met the woman, who within mere seconds would become his and he hers. He'd thought her magnificent when dressed in the revealing burgundy gown and adorned with precious jewels, but that image paled in comparison to what he now gazed upon. Gwen transfixed him with her pouting mouth, heaving bosom, and the sensual way she stared up at him through her lashes.

They shared a smile, he easing his swollen flesh into her waiting body. His eyes darkened in passion as Gwen closed her eyes, sighing softly as he penetrated her inch by slow, erotic inch. Once joined, they sighed in unison.

Waves of ecstasy throbbed through Gwen as she welcomed the slow, deliberate cadence that elicited a pleasure that was pure and explosive. Her body melted with the heat flowing through her like warmed honey. Shiloh anchored his hands under her bottom, lifting her hips off the mattress and angling her body for maximum pleasure.

She couldn't disguise her body's reaction to a lovemaking that had awakened a dormant sensuality she'd forgotten existed. The tremors inside her thighs and groin quickened, and she surrendered to the raw act of possession that bound her to the man who freed her from an existence filled with doubt about whether she would ever love again.

Gwen opened her eyes at the exact moment Shiloh's passions erupted in a fireball of erotic pleasure. He closed his eyes, going completely still, and growled out his satisfaction as her pulsing flesh pulled him in, making them one.

He collapsed facedown on the bed, struggling to slow down his runaway heart. Shifting slightly, he wrapped an arm around Gwen's waist, pulled her closer, and dropped a kiss on the end of her nose.

"You are incredible," he whispered reverently.

Satisfaction pursed Gwen's mouth as she closed her eyes. Shiloh wanted to talk when all she wanted to do was sleep. Snuggling closer, she rested her head on his shoulder and fell asleep.

* * *

Gwen woke to find herself in total darkness. She sat up, glancing around her. It wasn't until she moved her legs and felt the tightness in her thigh muscles that she remembered where she was and whom she was with. Easing away from the prone figure and bringing her left arm close to her face, she peered at the glowing hands on the watch strapped to her wrist. It was after nine o'clock. She went completely still. Cocoa! She had to go home, feed the puppy and let her out.

Moving quietly off the bed, she crawled around on the floor, hoping to retrieve her shoes and clothes without waking Shiloh. She gritted her teeth in frustration. She'd found everything except her panties.

Clutching her discarded clothes to her chest, she tiptoed on bare feet down the staircase. The only illumination was baseboard lighting. She pulled on her clothes, ran her fingers through her mussed hair, and literally felt her way to the family room to get her handbag. As she reached the compartment for her car key, she froze. Her tape recorder was missing!

Standing in the middle of Shiloh's family room, Gwen tried remembering if she'd put it back in her handbag. Biting down on her lower lip, she mentally replayed the interview with Shiloh. He'd taken the recorder, given it back to her, and she'd dropped it. Going to her knees, she felt under the table. A raw expletive had formed on her lips, then she remembered. Lifting a cushion on the love seat, she found it.

She didn't know whether Shiloh had reset his house alarm, but she would soon find out as she made her way to the rear door. Turning the knob, she eased it open, sighing. Unless there was a silent alarm, she had made it out undetected.

Gwen got into her car, started up the engine, and drove away from the private development and the man she loved beyond description.

* * *

Shiloh turned over on his left side, and woke immediately. "Damn!" he gasped. He'd put too much pressure on his blistered forearm.

He quickly dismissed the pain when he detected the floral fragrance on the pillow next to his. Smiling, he reached out, but his smile vanished within seconds when he grabbed a handful of linen.

Turning on a bedside lamp, Shiloh glanced around the bedroom, looking for Gwen. He swung his legs over the side of the bed, and looked down: her clothes were gone. The only thing that remained was a scrap of silk in a soft powder blue that lay on the floor next to his shirt and jeans.

He picked up her panties, left the bedroom, and made his way down the staircase, wondering where she could've gone without her underwear. It wasn't until he stared at the space where her car had been that he realized she'd left sometime during the night.

Shiloh tightened his grip on the silk fabric, his expression a mask of stone. He didn't know what had sent Gwen fleeing his bed but he intended to find out.

"What the—" Gwen didn't complete her sentence when Cocoa's barking joined the chiming of the doorbell. Putting the puppy in her bed, she went downstairs to answer the door. Peering through the security eye she recognized the distorted face of Shiloh scowling at her.

"Open the damn door, Gwendolyn Paulette Taylor!"

"I will if you lay off the damn bell, Shiloh Harper!" she shouted back, unlocking the door.

She'd left his house, and returned home to find that Cocoa had piddled on the laundry room's cement floor. She fed her pet before cleaning up the urine. Cocoa shadowed her relentlessly, wherever she went. Usually the tiny dog fled the bathroom whenever she turned on the shower, but not tonight. It was as if the canine feared being left alone again.

Gwen took a step backwards as Shiloh moved into the entryway. She stared silently as he closed and locked the door. She did not have time to react when he scooped her up in his arms and headed for the staircase.

"What are you doing, Shiloh?"

The scene from *Gone With the Wind* when Rhett Butler swept Scarlett O'Hara up in his arms and carried her up the staircase sprang to mind. But in that scene Rhett was drunk, jealous that his wife continued to lust after another woman's husband. The reality was that Gwendolyn Taylor wasn't Scarlett, Shiloh no Rhett, and there was certainly no Ashley Wilkes to come between them. And Shiloh wasn't drunk. His warm breath smelled of mint and his body of soap. He'd showered before coming to her.

She barely had time to catch her breath when he stalked into her bedroom and placed her on the bed. There was a look in his eyes that unnerved her. Galvanized into action, she came to her knees at the same time he reached behind his back. Without warning she felt a band of metal around her left wrist. The distinctive sound echoed a second time when the remaining cuff circled his right wrist.

"Oh, no!" she wailed when she realized he'd handcuffed them together.

Towering above Gwen like an avenging angel, Shiloh intoned in a voice totally void of emotion, "You're under arrest for unlawful flight. You have the right to remain silent and refuse to answer questions." He was hard pressed not to laugh when he saw her shocked expression. "Do you understand? Anything you say may be used against you in a court of law. Do you understand? You have the right to consult an attorney before speaking to the police and to have an attorney present during questioning now or in the future. Do you understand?"

Gwen stared at the man whose passionate, tender lovemaking took her to heights of sensuality she'd only glimpsed in the past. "You're kidding, aren't you?" Her query was a breathless whisper.

Lifting his expressive eyebrow, Shiloh continued with the Miranda warning, "If you cannot afford an attorney, one will be appointed for you before questioning if you wish. Do you understand?" A hint of a smile deepened the lines around his eyes when her breath came in shuddering gasps. "If you decide to answer questions now without an attorney present you will still have the right to stop answering at any time until you talk to an attorney. Do you understand me, darling? Knowing and understanding your rights as I have explained them to you, are you willing to answer my questions without an attorney present?"

Her shock fading and the beginnings of a smile parting her lips, Gwen asked, "What is it again that you're charging me with, Sheriff Harper?"

He sat down and moved over her body. "Unlawful flight, Miss Taylor. I never would've imagined you to be a flight risk."

"I had to—"

His head swooped down and he stopped her explanation, his mouth smothering hers in an act that had become total possession.

"Don't say anything, darling. Not without your attorney."

Gwen closed her eyes. "Can't you be my attorney?"

Shiloh nibbled her lower lip. "No, baby. That would be unethical." He kissed her again as the fingers of his right hand touched her damp hair.

"What you're doing to me is not only unethical but can also be interpreted as police brutality."

"Have I brutalized you, baby?"

She nodded. "Yes. You break into my—"

"Wrong," he said, nuzzling the side of her neck. "You let me in."

Gwen closed her eyes. "Point taken. I let you in. But, once inside you decide to take me captive."

Shiloh's soft laugh caressed her ear. "Wrong again, darling. I'm not holding you captive, because both of us are cuffed."

"You're using that as a technicality," she countered.

"Wrong again, beautiful. I came here to visit my girlfriend, and ended up engaging in a little sexual bondage."

Anchoring her free hand on Shiloh's shoulder, Gwen tried to push him off her and failed. "I don't do bondage or S and M."

He sobered quickly. "They usually aren't in my sexual repertoire either, but if I go to bed with you at night, then I'd like to wake up with you in the morning."

"I had to come home and take care of Cocoa."

Shiloh exhaled an audible breath. "I thought I'd become a one-night stand."

Gwen stared wordlessly up at Shiloh, her heart pounding, before her gaze narrowed. "You believe I'm the type of woman who would hit it, then run?"

He shook his head. "No, baby."

Her temper flared. "Don't you dare *no baby* me, Shiloh Harper. You came here because your inflated ego couldn't deal with a woman sleeping with you, then not staying for seconds."

A rush of blood darkened his face. "Wrong, Gwen. I was raised not to kiss and tell, but I've slept with women who opted out of a repeat performance. I've also slept with women where we both knew after the first sexual encounter that we'd never be compatible."

Her gaze searched his expression. "Would it matter that much if I opted out, Shiloh?"

Studying Gwen thoughtfully for a moment, Shiloh knew he had to be truthful with her. "Yes, it would."

The seconds ticked off as they stared at each other. "Why?" she asked after what appeared to be an interminable span of silence.

Shiloh looked at Gwen as if he were photographing her with his eyes. His gaze lingered on the swell of her breasts in a pale pink camisole before it moved down to a pair of striped pajama pants. He wanted her, not just the little pieces of herself she parceled out like sips of water to a man dying of thirst, but all of her.

But, if that weren't possible then he would have to be content with mental images of a woman with a lush body, sassy mouth, and a face that haunted his dreams and his waking hours. Gwendolyn Taylor had become his drug of choice, an addictive drug he did not want to rid himself of.

"Because I love you."

A quiver surged through Gwen's veins. Had she heard correctly? Had he confessed to loving her? "No, Shiloh," she whispered hoarsely.

He lowered his head and pressed his mouth to the column of her neck. "Yes, baby. You don't have to say anything. I'd promised myself that I would never give my heart to another woman because I never wanted to be that vulnerable again. Yet you came along and made a liar out of me. It's nothing you've done or said, except be Gwendolyn Taylor. You're smart, beautiful, talented and wicked in the kitchen and in the bedroom."

Gwen's left hand inched under his T-shirt. The heat of his bare flesh burned her palm. She didn't think she would ever tire of touching him. He was in love with her, and she'd fallen in love with him. Where, she thought, do they go from there.

"You love me and I find myself in love with you," she confessed softly. "What happens next?"

A smile of triumph curved Shiloh's mouth. They'd promised each other honesty, and it had manifested itself in a shared declaration of love. "What do you want to happen?"

It was the first time that he could remember that Gwen didn't have a comeback. She, who'd been called "Motor Mouth," and "Mouth Almighty," was rendered mute by a simple query as to where she wanted her relationship with Shiloh Harper to go.

"I don't know," she answered honestly. "Where do you want it to go?"

Raising his head, he caught and held her steady gaze. The light from the lamp on the bedside table flattered her delicate features. "I want to court you, have an engagement of short duration, marry you, and make some babies."

Gwen's heart slammed against her ribs as a knot rose in her throat. She'd waited a decade to hear what Shiloh had just offered her, and meanwhile she thought she'd imagined it.

"When do you plan to do all of this?"

Reaching into the back pocket of his jeans, Shiloh withdrew the key for the handcuffs and unlocked them. "You're the planner, sweetheart. I'll let you set the timetable."

Rubbing her wrist although the cuffs weren't tight enough to impede her circulation, Gwen pushed herself into a sitting position. She pushed out her lower lip. "That's not fair."

Wrapping an arm around her waist, Shiloh settled her over his thighs and pressed his forehead to hers. "What wouldn't be fair is my making all of the decisions for us. I don't ever want you to accuse me of pressuring you to do something you don't want to do."

She closed her eyes. Shiloh was offering her what Craig Hemming hadn't offered: independence. Twelve years her senior, Craig had become more of a father figure than a fiancé. If it hadn't been his way, then it was no way. The only decision the investment banker permitted her to make was their trip to Venice, Italy.

Gwen opened her eyes. "When will your term as sheriff expire?"

"December thirty-first."

Resting her palms over his pectorals, she kissed the end of Shiloh's nose. "Would you mind if we got married on that day?"

His hands slipped down the length of her back, under the drawstring waistband of her cotton pajama pants, and whispered a silent prayer of thanks.

"No, I don't mind. I would've preferred if you'd said next week, but I'll wait."

"You're damn skippy you'll wait. Am I not worth it?"

His fingers tightened on her buttocks. "Yes, you are. I hadn't realized that I'd been waiting all of my life for someone like you."

Hot tears pricked the backs of Gwen's eyes. "And I you," she whispered. She lay motionless as he undressed her, then himself. Reaching over, he turned off the lamp, and she went into his warm, protective embrace.

She listened as Shiloh's breathing deepened, the enormity of what she'd agreed to sweeping over her and shaking her sensibilities. She'd just agreed to marry a man she'd known a month! Had she gone and lost what was left of her mind?

Never had she ever been that impulsive. She, who planned what she'd wear a week ahead, what she wanted to eat days in advance, Gwendolyn Taylor who as journalist checked with her sources over and over to make certain the information they'd given her was accurate.

She closed her eyes, chewing her lower lip in consternation while contemplating what she would tell her parents when she spoke to them again. Her eyes opened. She would wait, wait until she and Shiloh officially announced their engagement before informing her family that her marital status would change before the year ended.

Shifting on her side, Gwen rested her arm over Shiloh's belly, and minutes later she joined him in sleep.

Chapter 13

Gwen woke to find light coming through the panels on the French doors. Shiloh lay beside her, on his back, injured arm above his head. She shifted her position. He turned and rested his arm over her waist.

"Hey, you," she whispered.

"Hey, yourself."

Shiloh stared at Gwen. *Damn, she's beautiful in the morning.* The thought had come to his mind unbidden. Even with her mussed up hair and bare face Gwen Taylor made his breath catch in his throat. His gaze dropped from her eyes to her mouth. He smiled, the gesture as warm and inviting as the sun. Without warning, he swept back the sheet covering her nude body.

"Is this what I can look forward to waking up to for the next fifty years?"

"What you see now will not look the same in another fifty years."

"It will look even better," he crooned.

"You're wonderful for a woman's ego."

Shiloh hadn't shaved in days, and the short beard merely added to his blatantly sensual virility. Smiling, she ran her hand over his jaw. At first she'd thought Shiloh confessing his love for her was because in the heat of passion men tended to say things they never would've said given another set of circumstances. Yet hours later, and not in the heat of passion, he still professed that he loved her.

A well of emotion made it impossible for her to confess to Shiloh that what she felt for him frightened her. It frightened her because it'd happened too quickly, so fast that it may have been infatuation—their hormones calling out to one another.

Uncertainty filled her eyes when she asked herself if she loved Shiloh, if she was actually capable of loving a man. All of the signs were there, but something wouldn't permit her to let go and trust him completely because men had confessed to loving her, then went on to do things that negated everything they'd said. They'd lied, and there wasn't anything she detested more than a liar.

A familiar whining caught her attention. Cocoa was up. "Please, let me up, Shiloh," she pleaded softly.

"Why? So you can run off again."

"No. I have to get up and let Cocoa out."

"I'll do it." Swinging his legs over the side of the bed, Shiloh reached for his jeans at the foot of the large bed.

Gwen stared at the muscles in his back, rippling under his brown skin. "Will you stay for breakfast?"

Smiling over his shoulder, he winked. "Does a dog love to chase its tail?"

"I'll take that as a yes."

He nodded as he stood up. "It is. Will you share dinner with me tonight?"

Vertical lines appeared between Gwen's eyes as she pulled the sheet over her bare breasts. "I can't." She had an appointment to interview Keith Nichols.

Shiloh lifted a questioning eyebrow. "Are you free tomorrow night?"

"I'm free tonight, but not for dinner."

He caught her meaning immediately, a slight smile softening the brackets around his mouth. "Should I expect a sleepover?"

Gwen gave him a saucy smile. "Yes."

His eyes deepening to a mossy green, Shiloh thought about what he wanted to do make the night a memorable event. Walking on bare feet, he picked up Cocoa and cradled her to his chest. "Hey there, baby girl. Daddy's going to take care of you today. You're coming home with me and we'll hang out together."

A soft gasp escaped Gwen before she blurted out, "I told you about spoiling my dog. If she goes home with you, then she stays with you."

"Don't matter none now," he drawled, "because we'll all be living together by the end of the year." He kissed the puppy's head as he made his way across the bedroom. "There's a little guy who belongs to my next-door neighbor who I'm certain would flip over you, Miss Cocoa Taylor, soon-to-be Harper. And you don't have to worry about your virtue because he's been fixed."

Gwen fell back to the pillows, laughing at Shiloh's monologue with her pet. She stared up at the plasterwork on the ceiling until pressure in her lower belly forced her out of bed and into the bathroom.

Gwen placed the final revised copy of her column in the wire basket on Nash's desk. She'd transcribed her interviews with

Jimmie Jameson and Shiloh, edited her first draft, then using a blue pencil tightened phrases, then read it aloud for clarity.

"How is it?" Nash McGraw asked as he entered his office. Gwen turned and smiled at him. "Good." Her smile faded quickly. "It would've been better if I'd been able to talk to A.D.A. Nichols before this week's deadline." It was four in the afternoon and there wasn't a wrinkle in his custom-made shirt. She suspected that he'd gone home and changed.

He gestured to the chair next to his desk. "Please sit." He waited for Gwen to sit before he sat. "Even if you'd gotten a statement from him I wouldn't have run it until next week."

A slight frown creased her smooth forehead. "Why?"

"It's been a long time since a crime of this magnitude has affected the residents of this parish. And the fact that the defendant is the son of a political power broker is what sells papers because of the controversy."

A scowl crossed Gwen's face. "There shouldn't be any controversy. The boy was pumped up on drugs and alcohol, and then got behind the wheel of a car, which in his hands became a dangerous weapon."

Nash went completely still, his laser blue-gray eyes boring into her. "What happened to impartiality? We're journalists, Miss Taylor, and that means we don't take sides."

Annoyance gripped Gwen as she schooled her expression not to reveal what she was feeling at that moment. Choosing her words carefully, she said in a quiet tone, "I'm more than aware of not permitting my personal feelings to come into play when reporting the facts. However, I'm going to say off the record that I hope Willis Raymond Benton gets the maximum sentence for what he did."

A hint of a smile touched Nash's mouth. "You and more than half the parish feel the same way. But, the fact remains that the boy is entitled to a fair trial."

Gwen wanted to scream at Nash about fairness. Did Bram Benton's son think of that before he started drinking and drugging? Didn't someone or something tell him it was wrong to try to drive while under the influence?

Not wanting to engage in a verbal confrontation with her boss, she decided to change the subject. "I've been going over some back issues, and there is an unsolved murder case that intrigues me."

Nash angled his head as he laced his fingers together. "Which one?"

"The 1964 prom queen murder." The editor's only reaction was the whitening of his knuckles when he tightened his grip. "I can't believe," Gwen continued, "that the police closed the case two months after she went missing." The extremely popular coed's badly decomposed nude body had been found in a shallow grave with a single gunshot to the back of her head. There were no suspects and the gun used in the murder was never recovered.

Swiveling on his chair, Nash stared out the window. "They couldn't find any evidence linking anyone to Shelby Carruthers' murder."

"I'd like to research the case."

"Let it go, Miss Taylor."

Gwen watched her boss. There was no expression on his face. "Are you saying don't or I shouldn't?"

Nash turned back to glare at her, meeting her implacable challenging stare. "I have no say in what you do when you're not working on *Tribune* business, but I suggest that you let sleeping dogs lie."

Her nerves tensed immediately. What she hadn't expected was for Nash to warn her. If she were still the crime reporter at the *Gazette* the editor would've jumped at the opportunity to make headline news by solving a cold case.

Irritated by his critical tone, she said, "I'll take your warning under advisement." She glanced at her watch. "If you don't need me for anything else, I'm going to leave now or I'll be late for my appointment with Keith Nichols."

"Go," Nash said, waving a manicured hand in dismissal.

Gwen walked out of the editor's office and into her own. She shut down her computer, turned off the desk lamp, and closed the door.

She waved to Nash's niece, Lisa McGraw. "I'll see you Tuesday."

The high school junior glanced up. She came to the paper's office after classes to proofread for her uncle's paper. It was apparent the journalistic bug had bitten another generation of McGraws. Lisa had been elected to take over the position of editor-in-chief of the *Bayou Sentinel,* the high school newspaper, a position Nash had held forty years ago.

The redhead smiled. "Later, Miss Taylor."

Gwen returned her friendly smile, when at that moment it was the last thing she felt like doing. Nash had chastised her as if she were an intern, and his warning to *let sleeping dogs lie* set her teeth on edge. Something unknown told her that the man had issued a veiled warning not to get involved. But why? she wondered. Questions fell over themselves in her head, and she hoped someone at the D.A.'s office would be able to provide her with a few answers.

She left her car in the parking space behind the newspaper's office and walked the two blocks to the historic square where the parish courthouse was erected in a quadrangle with the police station and a two-story municipal building.

Gwen saw the blue-and-white-striped awning shading the entrance to Turner Treats. She'd promised Holly Turner she would come to her Sunday social. It was apparent the Genteel Magnolia Society ladies wanted to get into her business, and she wanted to get into theirs. And because most of them were direct descendants of the original European inhabitants of the parish there was no doubt they would be able to answer many of her questions with regard to Gwendolyn Pickering and Shelby Carruthers.

She opened the door to the melodious chiming of a bell. Turner Treats was small, but elegantly furnished. Its signature striped wallpaper, a white-and-blue-veined marble floor, and pale blue ceiling fans added to the charm of the patisserie. Holly sat at an antique table, taking an order from an elderly woman. Mouthwatering smells permeated the artificially-cooled air as Gwen stared at showcases filled with delicate confections that looked too pretty to eat.

"May I help you?"

Gwen pulled her gaze away from a tray of petit fours to find a young woman in a blue-and-white shirtwaist dress smiling at her. Her complexion matched the rich color of the chocolate covering the many desserts lining the showcase shelves.

A minute on my lips and forever on my hips. The mantra reminded Gwen that her weakness for chocolate spelled disaster for her full figure. Common sense told her to say no, but she'd found out the hard way that common sense wasn't that common.

The petit fours were labeled: raspberry brandy, orange almond paste, crystallized ginger, coffee and cognac, nougat and amaretto, black forest and rum.

Without regard to the consequences, she said, "Give me one of each in two boxes." She would give one box to Shiloh and the other to Keith Nichols.

"Gwendolyn, how nice of you to drop in," said Holly Turner. She'd recognized Gwendolyn Taylor as soon as she'd walked in, but wanted to conclude her business with Lucinda Wentworth before approaching her.

Gwen offered Holly a friendly smile. "Actually I came in to see you," she said candidly, "but I couldn't resist your petit fours."

"The coffee and cognac is Shiloh's favorite." Holly's arched eyebrows lifted slightly when Gwen stared at her as if she'd spoken a foreign language. "Aren't you going out with him?"

"Who told you?"

Holly waved a slender hand. "Nothing is sacred in St. Martin Parish. I heard someone say that they saw you leaving his house last night."

"I—" Gwen's explanation died on her lips. She'd gone to Shiloh's house to interview him. What had begun as business had ended not so businesslike, but as a grown woman she had no intention of explaining her comings and goings to others.

"I came by to tell you that I intend to join you and your friends this Sunday." She'd managed to direct the conversation away from herself.

"Wonderful," Holly said pressing her palms together. "You can get to my house by going north on Michel Road. As soon as you reach Benoit Lane, make a right. My house is at the end of Benoit. You can't pass it because we look out onto the bayou."

"What time?"

"Six. We usually conclude by eight-thirty, because the ladies want to be home in time for *Desperate Housewives*."

Gwen wanted to tell Holly that her genteel ladies were probably more desperate and frustrated than the television characters.

"Should I bring anything?"

"Please no. Just bring yourself."

"I'd like to place an order for next Saturday." Gwen had promised Moriah that she would make up their aborted Sunday dinner get-together. She stared at the showcase filled with cakes. "I'd like sweet chestnut and cream squares."

Holly nodded. "Do you want to pick it up, or have it delivered?"

"I'll pick it up before you close," she said quickly. There was enough talk about her and Shiloh, and she didn't want to grease the gossip mill by having the chocolate patisserie delivered to Moriah Harper's house.

The salesgirl rang up her purchases, putting the boxes in separate bags with corresponding ribbons. Gwen paid for the petit fours, confirmed her order for the following week, and left Turner Treats for the courthouse.

A uniformed court officer was stationed in the lobby of the century-old building. Gwen placed her oversize satchel with the bags of petit fours on the magnetometer and walked through a security gate without setting off the sensors. She followed the signs directing her to the district attorney's office. Her steps slowed, halting when she saw a series of black-and-white photographs behind a wall of glass. Her gaze raced over the pictures of district attorneys dating back to the mid-nineteenth century. A nameplate identified each by name and the date of their terms. Among the dozens of photographs, there wasn't one woman and only one African-American, Shiloh Harper.

Her pulse quickened when she stared at the enigmatic expression on the face of the man with whom she had fallen in love. The date under Shiloh's tenure read 2004 with a blank space. He was on official leave, and it was apparent he would return at the beginning of the following year.

Gwen opened a door, stepping into a large room separated by a counter; there was a flurry of activity as employees readied themselves to leave for the day.

An elderly woman with champagne-pink hair squinted at her. "Are you Miss Taylor?"

"Yes, I am," Gwen confirmed.

She pressed a button under the counter, disengaging the lock on a gate. "Mr. Nichols said to send you in when you got here. He's in office number two."

Gwen walked through the gate and made her way down a hallway to Keith's office. She knocked lightly on the door.

"Come in."

She opened the door as Keith came to his feet. A wine-colored tie hung loosely from his unbuttoned collar. His short blond hair looked as if he'd combed it with his fingers. Smiling broadly, he adjusted his glasses.

"I got caught up with something that took up most of my afternoon, so I hope you don't mind that I ordered takeout for dinner." Keith had wanted to take Gwen to a restaurant where they could relax and talk without being interrupted by the telephone or someone walking into his office.

Gwen shook her head. "Of course I don't mind."

"I ordered a cold antipasto, Caesar salad with grilled Gulf shrimp and marinated asparagus."

"It sounds delicious. I brought dessert from Turner Treats." She knew the prosecutor had set aside time in his extremely busy schedule to meet with her.

Keith flashed a set of straight white teeth. "Now, you're talking." He came around the desk and pulled out a chair at a round table in a corner. "We'll eat, then we'll talk."

Two hours after she'd entered the courthouse, Gwen walked back to pick up her car. The prosecutor's office had decided to try Willis Raymond Benton in St. Martin Parish. When she asked Keith about the elder Benton's political influence when it came to selecting an impartial jury, the prosecutor said he was willing to err on the side of public sentiment. Most parish residents were outraged with Willie

Ray because he had yet to issue a public apology, expressing remorse for his actions.

After turning off her tape recorder she'd asked Keith about Shelby Carruthers' unsolved murder, and he promised he would direct a clerk to pull the records of the forty-two-year-old case.

Her pulse quickened when she thought of her sleepover with Shiloh, a sleepover that would extend to more than one night. Retrieving her cell phone, she punched in his number. He answered after the third ring.

"Hello."

Gwen smiled when his drawling voice came through the tiny earpiece. "Hello back to you."

"Are you calling to cancel?"

"No. I'm calling to tell you that I'll see you in a couple of hours. I'm going home to change and pack a bag."

"Good."

"How's Cocoa?"

"Impossible."

"What do you mean?"

"She's spoiled rotten."

"I leave my dog with you for less than a day, and now you tell me that she's spoiled rotten."

"You can't expect her to adjust to a new environment that quickly."

Gwen gritted her teeth. "Don't tell me you've been carrying her around. Shiloh Harper," she practically shouted when encountering silence.

"I can't hear you so well. I think we're breaking up, darling."

"There's nothing wrong with my cell phone. The only breaking that's going to go on is when I break your neck."

"You can't threaten a peace officer without reprisals, Miss Taylor."

"Consider yourself threatened, Sheriff Harper." That said, she ended the call, fuming.

A sixth sense had told her not to let Shiloh take Cocoa home with him. The puppy had become Shiloh's shadow, she following him everywhere, he picking her up whenever she whined. Now, she was forced to undo the damage.

Gwen lay in the oversize hammock, her body curving into Shiloh's as dusk settled over St. Martin Parish. The lighted candles under glass chimneys flickered in the encroaching darkness like fireflies.

Shiloh had tempered her annoyance when he opened the front door and she was met with a trail of flower petals that led across the living room floor, up the winding staircase, down the hallway leading into the bedroom, and out to the veranda. Half a dozen lighted pillars, a bottle of chilled champagne and softly playing music beckoned her to come and stay awhile. And she'd stayed, sipping champagne and dancing with him. After her second glass of the dry, bubbly wine she sought out the hammock, content to listen to the music from a satellite radio station coming through a small but powerful speaker.

Cocoa whined softly before settling down to a more comfortable position on Shiloh's shoulder. "Just because you conspired to get me drunk so that you can seduce me, don't think I've forgiven you about spoiling my pet."

Shiloh pressed his mouth to Gwen's slightly damp hair. "It's too late for that," he murmured.

"And it's not too late to send her to obedience school."

"You're not going to take my dog anywhere."

Pulling out of his loose embrace, Gwen sat up. "Who said Cocoa is yours?"

A hint of a smile curved the corners of Shiloh's mouth upward. "You did."

"No, I didn't!"

"Sure you did. When you agreed to marry me I interpreted that to mean that whatever we have we would share and share alike."

"You're interpreting all of this without thinking that perhaps I didn't want to share my pet with you."

Shiloh wrapped an arm around her shoulders, easing her down beside him. "We shouldn't be arguing about a dog."

"I'm not arguing, Shiloh. I'm just stating a fact. And the fact remains that Cocoa is *my* dog."

"Is it going to be your children, my children or our children?"

"Don't you dare try and equate a dog with—"

Shiloh stopped her tirade with a kiss that stole the breath from her lungs. Shifting on the hammock, he covered her body with his, and permitted her to feel the surge of passion straining for escape.

"You've just been overruled, Miss Taylor."

Breathing heavily, Gwen sought to evade his marauding mouth. "Stop, Shiloh," she pleaded.

"Stop what?" he asked as his hand slipped between her thighs. A pair of cotton shorts and a tank top did little to conceal her lush curves. "Stop loving you? Or stop wanting to make love to you?"

Gwen gasped when his hand covered her mound. "O-o-o-h," she moaned in protest, as her body betrayed her.

Shiloh hardened quickly, and he knew he had to take Gwen to bed before they wound up copulating in the hammock. He scooped up Cocoa, opened the screen door to the bedroom, and placed the puppy on the floor. Reaching for Gwen, he carried her into the room, closing the door behind them.

One moment his body was pressing hers down to the hammock, and moments later Gwen found herself in the bedroom, on the bed, Shiloh straddling her, and stripping her naked within minutes.

He hadn't turned on a light, and the flickering flames from the candles on the veranda provided enough illumination for her to make out the outline of his large body as he stripped off his shirt, jeans, and underwear.

She was on fire. Shiloh Harper had ignited a flame that only he could assuage. She gasped, her nerve endings screaming when his fingertips began a sensual trail that began at the hollow of her neck and ended along the soles of her feet.

His mouth replaced his fingers, kissing the rapidly beating pulse in her throat, his tongue tracing the areolae of her breasts; he teased and tasted her fragrant flesh until she screamed and pleaded for him to stop his sexual assault on her body, heart and mind.

"Please don't!" she sobbed as he inhaled the heady scent between her thighs. Her protests were ignored when he buried his face between her legs. Shiloh was doing to her what she'd never permitted *any* man to do, but she was helpless to stop him. It was as if he'd brainwashed her, controlled her. She was as helpless as a newborn. She cried, pounded his head and shoulders, but to no avail.

Shiloh was relentless as he luxuriated in the sexual bouquet that made him want to gorge on Gwen's curvy, scented body. Everything about her face and body turned him on until he couldn't think straight, couldn't get a restful night's sleep.

His tongue searched her moist folds, plunging deeper, deep enough for him to register the strong pulsing that indicated the woman between whose legs he lay, the woman with whom he'd fallen in love and given his heart to, was poised to climax.

He loathed withdrawing, but wanted to experience that oneness with her again. Reaching for the condom on the bedside table, he slipped it on, entered her slowly, reviving their passions.

Gwen knew what she shared with Shiloh filled a physical need she'd denied for far too long; but what he also offered her was much more. His lovemaking stripped away her defenses, forced her to see herself as someone who could love him without rules, restrictions, game plan or timetable. Not only had she welcomed him into her body but also her life.

Waves of ecstasy throbbed through her body like a runaway freight train. Skin to skin, heart to heart, she became one with Shiloh, and she couldn't control the outcry of delight when she arched as convulsions shook her from head to toe.

Rising to meet Shiloh's strong thrusts, her fingernails scoring his back, Gwen threw back her head and screamed as she soared freely to a place where she'd never been. A flood tide of uncontrollable joy made it impossible for her to breathe, speak or move.

Shiloh couldn't believe the pleasure Gwen offered him. The tremors and heat wrapped around his engorged flesh, the passion radiating from the soft core of her body was akin to an ache, a sensual, excoriating ache that only she could relieve. Electricity arced through his lower body, and within seconds he surrendered all he had and who he was to the woman to whom he'd pledged his life and future.

He waited until his respiration slowed, then he moved off Gwen and lay facedown on the bed. What they'd just shared wasn't lovemaking but a raw act of possession, a mating.

After what seemed an interminable amount of time, he reached down and pulled a sheet up over their moist bodies. He'd slept alone for years, but it had only taken twenty-four hours for that to change. Even if he and Gwen didn't make love he still wanted her in his bed.

Seconds before he succumbed to the comforting embrace of Morpheus, Shiloh knew inexorably that Gwendolyn Paulette Taylor was to become the last woman in his life.

Chapter 14

Gwen placed an embroidered linen napkin over her knees before picking up a cup of mint tea as she settled down to interact with the ladies of the Genteel Magnolia Society. Holly Turner, who was serving the second year of her two-year term as president, was responsible for hosting the Sunday-afternoon soirees. The current members had gathered in the screened-in back porch of a meticulously restored antebellum mansion.

Without looking for the stamp under the saucer Gwen recognized the Sèvres pattern. She'd inherited a set of the incredibly beautiful porcelain from her aunt.

"Would you like a tart, Gwendolyn?" Holly asked, extending a matching plate filled with an assortment of miniature cookies and cakes.

Smiling, Gwen shook her head. "No, thank you."

"I hope you're not dieting because you have a wonderful figure," said an elderly woman with snow-white hair as she peered at Gwen over her half glasses. The size of the double strand of pearls circling her neck was as large as jawbreakers. "I can't believe the lengths you young women go through to look as if you're starving. All that dieting and liposuction business is simply preposterous, if you ask me."

Gwen smiled as she sipped her tea. She wasn't going to comment on dieting because there were occasions when she'd embarked on several weight-loss regimens. In the end she'd come to the realization that as an adult she would never be a size six, and had come to accept her full hips and her intelligence as her best assets. She'd been told more than once by men that they liked the "junk in her trunk."

She'd come to the Genteel Magnolia Society get-together only to discover she was the youngest of the twelve and the only woman of color. The members ranged in age from late thirties to eighties and claimed names associated with the earth, flora and fauna: Beryl, Rose, Hyacinth, Lily, Violet, Fern, Dahlia, Iris, Olive, Laurel and Holly. They were educated, wore classic clothes, conservative hairstyles, vintage jewelry, and were the descendants of the Revolutionary War and Civil War families.

She'd decided to forego her favored capris in favor of a sky-blue linen sheath dress. Her accessories were a pair of pale blue-and-white high-heel leather pumps, a single strand of perfectly matched pearls, a gift from her mother for her sixteenth birthday, and pearl studs. She'd secured her hair in a twist on the nape of her neck.

Shiloh had teased her relentlessly as she dressed for the occasion, declaring she was a perfect candidate to integrate the centuries-old snobby group. Unknowingly, she'd become a Genteel Magnolia Society lady who just happened to be a darker hue.

"I just adore your accent, Gwendolyn," said Fern, a natural redhead with sparkling green eyes and a friendly smile.

Picking up her napkin and dabbing the corners of her mouth, Gwen lifted her eyebrows. She'd hoped the woman meant regional inflection instead of an accent. She stared at Fern until the woman lowered her gaze.

"I know I don't sound like *you all*, but no one has ever accused me of having an accent," she said defensively.

Olive placed a wrinkled hand over her pearls. "You sound like those Kennedys. I think the way they speak is simply charming."

The tension left Gwen's body. Unconsciously she was ready to go to the mat to defend her home state. And what she intended to say wouldn't have been very genteel.

"Why, thank you, Miss Olive," she drawled in her best southern imitation. Everyone laughed, and so did Gwen. The tense moment had passed.

"I read your article in the *Tribune,* Gwendolyn," Holly said as she sat down at the head of the table. "I must congratulate you on your wonderful talent. How you managed to write what you did without pointing a finger is amazing."

"It's a skill I learned in journalism school."

Gwen was bombarded with questions as to her background and education, and she was candid and forthcoming in telling them she'd gone to college with the intent of becoming an English teacher. She'd taught high school English for two years before opting for a career in journalism.

"Do you think you'd ever go back to teaching?" Dahlia Townsend asked.

Gwen smiled at the tall, slender woman with ash-blond hair who bore a striking resemblance to Grace Kelly, the late princess of Monaco.

"I've thought about it."

"If you're serious, then please send me your résumé. I'm

the principal at the high school. Several teachers are retiring and we need to fill their positions before the new school year."

Not willing to commit, Gwen said, "I'll have to update my résumé."

"You can drop it off or mail it to the high school." Dahlia's cool looks were a deceptive foil for a dynamic personality that made her a highly respected and effective administrator.

Holly dropped a cube of sugar into her teacup. "Have you adjusted to living at *Bon Temps*?"

Gwen was hard pressed not to smile. Holly had just presented her with an opportunity to talk about her aunt. "Yes, I have."

Olive crossed her arms. "I met my Gilbert, God rest his soul, at *Bon Temps*."

Leaning forward, her pulse quickening, Gwen flashed a smile. She'd finally met someone, she hoped, who could possibly clear up some of the mystery surrounding Gwendolyn Pickering. "How well did you know my aunt?"

"Not too well. Gwendolyn never let people get too close to her. She kept to herself except when she hosted her balls at *Bon Temps*."

Teacups were refilled and pastries passed around as Olive Peyton revealed the details about a liaison that crossed color lines and spanned decades. Gwendolyn Pickering had become a "kept woman." She'd caught the eye of Robert LeRoque, a married bank president who set her up at *Bon Temps* while showering her with expensive gifts.

Olivia paused for effect. It wasn't often she was able to garner the rapt attention of the women, and she intended to savor the moment. "Robert was generous *and* controlling. He bought *Bon Temps* for her, but poor Gwendolyn had to get his permission to do anything, even visit her family. She was a beautiful caged bird whose wings were clipped so she wouldn't be able to fly away."

Gwen slumped back on her chair. *I know how difficult it was for you to come see me. I love you even more for risking everything you have to make the trip.* The words written by the New Orleans musician came rushing back in vivid clarity. Gwendolyn Pickering loved A.C., not Robert LeRoque, yet she wasn't willing to risk forfeiting a glamorous lifestyle for love.

"Where is Robert LeRoque now?" Gwen asked Olivia.

"He died about twenty years ago. And it seemed as if Gwendolyn died with him. She stopped giving balls, and whenever she left *Bon Temps* she was dressed in black with a veil concealing her face. We all but forgot about her until she passed away earlier in the year."

Gwen managed a tentative smile. "Thank you, Miss Olive, for clearing up a lot of questions about my great-aunt." Olive Peyton puffed up her chest like a hen settling on her nest. "Do you ladies have a historian for your group?" Eleven pairs of eyes were trained on Gwen.

"No...no, we don't," Holly said tentatively.

Dahlia pressed her palms together. "And we should. We've been meeting for more than a hundred years and no one has ever chronicled our meetings or our causes."

Holly's blue eyes danced with excitement. "Will you do it, Gwen? Will you become our historian?"

"I can't."

Bright red spots appeared on Holly's pale cheeks. "Why not?"

"Firstly, I'm not a member of your august group. And, secondly I know nothing about the Genteel Magnolia Society."

"But you could become a member," Holly said quickly.

Gwen successfully hid a smile as she brought her napkin to her mouth. "Don't you have criteria for membership?"

"Yes, we do," Dahlia concurred, "but we can always amend that."

There was a swollen silence as Gwen gave each of the women sitting at the table a look. "I'm aware of the incident wherein a woman of color sought membership but was denied not because of who she was but what she was. And while you've tried to make amends by inviting me to join you for your Sunday-afternoon soirees I applaud you for trying to right your wrong."

Faces flushed or blanched with Gwen's soft chastisement. "Times change and people change," she continued. "And even though I don't know the woman you snubbed, I'll accept your apology on her behalf. I won't be your historian, but what I will agree to do is write your history. I'd like each of you to record your experiences into a tape recorder and send them to me. You can talk about anything you want. Miss Olive, since you're the eldest one here I expect you to become the definitive voice for the other ladies.

"I don't want a literary account, but a blend of eloquence and down-home. Miss Olive, you can talk about the balls at *Bon Temps,* and the fact that you met your husband there. Please, ladies, do not gloss over history or paint a picture that St. Martin Parish was exempt from racial bigotry and the evils of Jim Crow. If you give me what I want, then I'm certain I can put together something worthy of a bestseller."

A flush suffused Dahlia's face to her pale hairline. "It sounds so incredible. Have you thought of a title?"

Gwen smiled. *"Sunday Tea with the Genteel Magnolia Society."*

Olive shook her snow-white head. "You are extraordinary!"

"No, Miss Olive, you ladies are extraordinary that you've maintained a cohesiveness that has survived for more than a century. I urge you to contact a professional photographer so that you can take a group picture which can be used for the back cover."

"Will you join us for the photo shoot?" Holly asked.

"I'll let you know," Gwen said, unwilling to commit to becoming a Genteel Magnolia. She placed her napkin on the table and pushed back her chair. "I'm sorry, ladies, but I'm going to have to take my leave now." She stood up. "Thank you so much for inviting me. It's been charming."

Amid a chorus of "thank you" and "nice meeting you," Holly escorted Gwen to where she'd parked her car among the other luxury vehicles.

She reached out and grasped Gwen's hand. "I can't thank you enough for coming. I'm going to submit your name for membership and I hope you'll accept. We do champion many important local issues. The past two years we've supported Tabasco's cause to preserve Louisiana's wetland for future generations. We've raised more than fifty thousand dollars to increase efforts to save one of America's ecological treasures."

"I'll give it some serious thought."

Pulling her hand from Holly's loose grip, Gwen pressed her car's remote device, unlocking the doors. The smile curving her mouth as she drove away was still in place when she turned in to the driveway to Shiloh's house.

Shiloh sat on a padded bench in the expansive bathroom, watching Gwen as she removed the pins from her hair and fluffed up her curls. He'd picked up her shoes to keep Cocoa from gnawing on them.

He lifted his eyebrow when he saw the name of the shoe designer. "You really like shoes, don't you?"

Gwen caught his reflection in the mirrored wall. "Don't

start in about my shoes, Shiloh. Heels are the best way to connect to one's soul."

"Soul or sole?" he quipped.

She patted her chest. "This soul. When I'm stressed out I buy shoes instead of food."

"You must get stressed a lot," he drawled, "because I've never seen you wear the same pair twice."

Turning slowly, she held his gaze. "Let's settle something before we move forward in this relationship. I won't put up with you monitoring what I wear or buy. And if you feel you can't afford me, then I suggest we cut it off now."

A slow building anger paled Shiloh's eyes until they were a brilliant gold, all traces of green missing. "Don't ever tell me what I can or cannot pay for, Gwendolyn. I can afford to house you, feed you, provide for our children, and buy you Ferragamo, Weitzman, Choo, Blahnik, Chanel or Cole Haan.

"What's the matter?" he spat out when her jaw dropped. "You didn't think I knew the names? I know them all," he continued, not giving her a chance to reply. "My ex-wife had closets filled with labels from every well-known and up-and-coming designer in the business."

Gwen's eyes widened before she went completely still. "Don't ever compare me with your ex-wife, Shiloh. I don't know anything about her, and I don't want to know. But, let me know now if the label in my shoes is a problem, because I'll save both us the cost of a wedding and a subsequent divorce. I can walk away from you and forget that you ever existed."

Shiloh closed the distance between them, his hands going to her bare shoulders and pulling her close to his chest. "You're not going anywhere."

He'd said it so softly that Gwen thought she'd imagined his threat. "You can't stop me."

There was a pregnant pause before he whispered, "I know

I can't. But, if you do, then I want you to know that I will love you until my last breath."

Gwen felt her heart turn over with his passionate confession. Tears filled her eyes and trickled down her cheeks. He loved her and she loved him—more than she'd ever loved any man. Why, she asked herself, was she fighting with Shiloh? Was it because she had to keep him at a distance because she feared being hurt again? Was it because although she loved him she still wasn't able to trust a man without reservation?

Rising on tiptoes, she wound her arms under his shoulders. "Show me how much you love me, Shiloh."

Reaching around her back, Shiloh unhooked her bra, letting it fall to the floor. He cradled her breasts, squeezing them gently. Gwen expelled a lungful of breath. Vertical lines appeared between his eyes. "What's the matter, baby?"

She buried her face against the column of his strong neck. "They're tender because I'm ovulating."

His hands moved from her chest to cradle her face. The smile in his eyes contained a sensuous flame. "Do you want to make a baby?"

The heavy lashes that shadowed Gwen's eyes flew up. "You're kidding, aren't you?"

He shook his head slowly. "I've never been more serious in my life."

"What happened to a period of courtship, then a short engagement before we marry and have children?"

"I still want those, but I want you to have my baby now."

"Before we get married?"

Shiloh's eyes darkened with an unnamed emotion. "We can get married next week. Don't most women want to be June brides?"

Gwen wanted so much to say yes, but couldn't. "I can't,

Shiloh. Not when you still have to carry a gun for your job. I know you believe I have this tough big-city attitude, but I'm not so tough that I'm willing to risk marrying you, then have to deal with one of your deputies knocking on the door to tell me that my husband died heroically in the line of duty. My answer to becoming a June bride is hell to the no."

Chuckling, Shiloh nuzzled her ear. "Nothing's going to happen to me."

"Can you guarantee that?" she asked.

"Nothing is guaranteed. Not even the next minute."

Gwen studied his stoic expression for a moment. "You're right. The only thing I'll agree to change is a shorter courtship."

"If that's what you want, then we'll announce our engagement tonight."

Grinning broadly, Shiloh swung Gwen up into his arms, carried her from the bathroom and into the bedroom. He placed on her bed and sat down beside her. Picking up the telephone, he handed it to her.

"Call your folks and let them know. I'll use my cell phone to call my mother." He got up, rounded the bed, and reached for the cell phone on the matching bedside table.

They sat, back to back, and informed their respective family members of their upcoming nuptials. Gwen told her parents to call Lauren and let her know that she wanted her to become her matron of honor, and that she would call her tomorrow to bring her up-to-date on what had been going in her life since they last spoke.

Shiloh made two calls: one to Moriah, and the other to his jewelry designer sister-in-law. He wanted Natalee to confer with Gwen so that she could design an engagement ring that was unique to her personality.

They ended their calls, smiling at each other. Gwen went into Shiloh's embrace as he finished undressing her before he undressed himself. They lay in bed, fused. There was no need to say anything because they let their bodies speak for them.

It wasn't until after Shiloh withdrew from her that Gwen felt a sense of loss and regret. Loss of the warmth and hardness of his body, and regret that he'd used protection.

Despite her fears that she could possibly lose Shiloh while he remained sheriff of St. Martin Parish she wanted a baby—Shiloh's baby.

Chapter 15

Gwen felt as if she were on a nonstop roller coaster, going faster and faster along a winding track that had no beginning and no end.

She'd become the first woman of color to become a member of the St. Martin Parish Genteel Magnolia Society, updated her résumé and mailed it off to Dahlia Townsend at the high school, met with Deputy Sheriff Jameson on Tuesday mornings for updates on DUI and DWIs, burglaries, armed robberies, assaults and felonious mischief, or domestic disputes and had begun her own independent investigation into Shelby Carruthers' unsolved murder.

It was July 15, and her parents' flight that was scheduled to arrive at the Baton Rouge airport at eleven was more than an hour late. Millard and Paulette Taylor were traveling to Louisiana to reunite with their daughter and meet the family of the man who was to become their son-in-law.

She'd wanted her parents to wait until the interior repairs to *Bon Temps* were completed, but Paulette huffed and puffed, declaring she could always stay in a hotel. However, when Gwen disclosed her mother's plan to Shiloh, he said Paulette and Millard could stay at his house. Moriah overruled him saying the elder Taylors would stay with her.

Gwen alternated pacing with staring at the electronic screen for arriving flights. Shiloh, who'd just spent three days in Baton Rouge attending a conference of the state's Police Jury Association, had promised to meet her at the airport.

Shiloh walked into the terminal, looking for Gwen. He saw her staring up at a monitor. His gaze softened as he approached her. It'd been six weeks since they'd officially announced their engagement, and each sunrise brought him closer to the time when they would become husband and wife.

His disability leave had become a delightfully memorable three weeks. He went to bed and woke up with Gwen, she taught him to make his favorite breakfast food—buttermilk pancakes from scratch, and they'd begun decorating the house that was to become their home when she admitted that she'd changed her mind about making *Bon Temps* her permanent residence.

She told him what she'd discovered about Gwendolyn Pickering's unconventional thirty-year relationship with Robert LeRoque, and also the former actress's love for Arthur Connelly, a New Orleans trumpeter. LeRoque's death from a ruptured appendix preceded Connelly's by three days, and it was Arthur Connelly's and not Robert LeRoque's passing that Gwendolyn had mourned for the last twenty years of her life.

Once the contractors completed their restoration work, she planned to list *Bon Temps* with the National Trust for Historic Preservation. The antebellum mansion would be added to the six others in the region open for tours.

* * *

"Waiting for someone, beautiful?"

Gwen spun around, fists in front of her in a fighting stance. The flawless emerald-cut diamond and princess-cut baguettes on her left hand gave off blue-white sparks. It had taken her less than an hour to select the design from the unique sketches in Natalee Harper's portfolio.

"Shiloh," she hissed angrily as she lowered her hands. "What are you doing sneaking up on me? I was ready to drop you."

His gaze moved slowly over her face, committing it to memory. He loved her flawless skin, curly hair, the way light slanted over the rich dark skin shimmering with the glow of good health, and the curves of her lush body that never failed to send his libido into overdrive.

Taking off his hat, he leaned over and pressed a kiss on her cheek. "Take your best shot, baby."

"Not here," she whispered.

Shiloh kissed her again. "Hey, you," he drawled.

"Hey, yourself."

Gwen flashed a sensual smile. It didn't matter whether he wore his regulation uniform, street clothes, or no clothes, the man she planned to marry in another five months was so heart-stoppingly virile that she found it difficult to draw a normal breath.

"How was your conference?"

"It went okay."

Shiloh reluctantly pulled his gaze away from Gwen and glanced up at the monitor. Keith Nichols would inform her that Willis Raymond Benton's attorney was going to base his client's defense on someone dropping crystal meth into his drink when he and a group of his friends got together to celebrate their college graduation.

Jury selection for Benton's trial that was scheduled to begin in late July had been postponed indefinitely, pending the defendant's full recovery from surgery to repair a ruptured aorta. Willie Ray had survived a horrific automobile accident only to face death from a lethal mix of drugs and alcohol.

Thirty-year-old undercover DEA agent Inez Leroux, who looked young enough to be a college student, had reported to the regional DEA field director that she'd befriended one of Willie Ray's friends, hoping to gather evidence to locate the meth lab.

The information on the arrival and departure monitors changed. "They're on the ground," Shiloh said in a quiet voice.

He thought about the time he'd met Deandrea's parents for the first time, then quickly dismissed it. He and Deandrea had married for the wrong reason: lust. He wanted to marry Gwen because not only did he love her, but he was also in love with her.

Gwen flashed a dazzling smile when she spied her mother and father. Paulette Taylor, carrying a garment bag over her arm, walked several paces ahead of her husband who was towing a large Pullman. They were the poster couple for middle age: salt-and-pepper hair, smooth, glowing skin, slender, conservatively dressed.

Gwen met her mother, wrapping her arms around her neck and kissing her soft, scented cheek. Paulette Taylor had always turned heads whenever she entered a room. She was petite, and had affected a short fashionable haircut that flattered her round face and delicate features. The silver in her hair was the perfect foil for her nut-brown complexion.

"Hi, Mama. You look beautiful, as usual."

Paulette pulled back, smiling. Her daughter looked different. She radiated a glow that hadn't been apparent when she was engaged to Craig Hemming.

"Thank you, sweetheart." She kissed Gwen's forehead, then reached for her left hand. The ring on Gwen's finger was magnificent. "It's beautiful." Her voice was soft, reverent. "Does he make you happy?"

"I'm delirious, Mama." Turning, Gwen motioned to her fiancé standing a distance away watching the interchange. "I want you to meet Shiloh."

He took three long strides, smiling at the woman who'd given birth to the woman he knew he would love forever. Leaning down from his impressive height, he kissed Paulette's cheek.

"Welcome to Louisiana."

Paulette's delicate jaw dropped, dark eyes widening as she stared numbly at the star pinned to the tan blouse before her gaze swept over his uniform.

"You're a cop," she whispered once she'd recovered her voice.

Shiloh's gaze shifted from his future mother-in-law to his fiancée. "Only until the end of the year."

"But...but Gwendolyn told me that you were a lawyer."

"I am an attorney, Mrs. Taylor."

"Stop interrogating the man, Paul," Millard Taylor chastised softly, calling his wife of more than three decades by her pet name. His clear brown eyes crinkled in a smile as he extended his hand to Shiloh. "Mills Taylor."

Shiloh grasped Gwen's father's hand; he liked the friendly, spontaneous man. "Shiloh Harper, sir."

Millard shook his head. "None of that sir business. It's Mills."

"Okay, Mills." Shiloh reached for the Taylors' luggage, his free hand going to the small of Paulette's back, leaving Gwen to follow with her father.

He would give the Taylors a personal police escort back to St. Martin Parish.

Gwen sat next to her father on a cushioned rattan love seat on Moriah's porch, her head resting on his shoulder. "I've never known Mama to go to bed this early."

Moriah had spent all day cooking Creole and Cajun dishes in a celebration of the state's cuisine: shrimp Creole and étouffée, dirty rice, pan-fried catfish, red beans and sausages, and a spicy jambalaya.

Gwen had made *maquechoux*, a Cajun dish of mixed vegetables that Moriah had taught her to make, and a pan of rich, buttery cornbread.

Millard smiled. "She didn't get much sleep last night. You know she comes undone whenever she has to fly."

Nodding, Gwen closed her eyes. Her mother did not like flying, and had to swallow her protests once Shiloh informed the elder Taylors that they would not spend a week in a hotel, but at his mother's house. Paulette pouted during the drive southward but her attitude changed as the topography changed. The untamed beauty of Southern Louisiana's bayou had left her awestruck.

She opened her eyes and stared through the mesh of the screened-in porch. There was a solid wall of black beyond the beams of the porch lamps. It had only taken three months for her to get used to living in the country.

"Why don't you go inside where it's cool, Daddy?" The intense summer heat and humidity lingered for hours after the setting sun.

"I'm good, princess. I can't lie down on a full stomach." He patted his flat belly. "Moriah is an incredible cook."

Gwen nodded. "That she is." Ian had planned a special dinner for her parents the following evening at the Outlaw.

Millard sighed. "I can't believe I ate so much."

"You weren't the only one who overate."

He angled his head, staring at Gwen. "I've never seen you eat so much. Are you sure you're not…" His words trailed off when he realized what he wanted to ask his daughter was too personal in nature.

Gwen smiled and snuggled closer to her father's side. She'd caught his meaning immediately. "No, Daddy. I'm not pregnant."

There was a pause before he asked, "Do you and Shiloh plan on starting a family?"

Do you want to make a baby? Shiloh's query was imprinted on her brain.

A smile softened her mouth. "Yes."

"When?"

"As soon as we're married."

"Why wait?"

Gwen's forehead furrowed with her father's query. She straightened. "Are you saying I shouldn't wait to get married before becoming pregnant?"

"No, princess, I'd never presume to tell you how to live your life. But, why are you waiting until the end of the year to get married? Your mother and I coming down here should've been for your wedding, not just to meet your future in-laws."

She wavered, trying to comprehend what she was hearing. Why was her father pressuring her to change her plans? "Shiloh has less than six months to finish out his father's term as sheriff before he goes back to the district attorney's office."

Millard lifted his eyebrows in a questioning expression. "And?"

"And what, Daddy?"

"What does that have to do with you marrying him before the end of the year?"

"He carries a gun, Daddy."

"Most law enforcement officers do."

"I know that."

"So, what's the problem, Gwendolyn?"

Whenever her father called her Gwendolyn it usually preceded a heated verbal exchange. Her jaw hardened. "I don't want to become a cop's widow."

Reaching up, Millard tugged gently on the curls covering her ear. "Nothing is guaranteed, princess. Look what happened to your brother. When Langston was born your mother and I never ever would've believed that we would bury him. You've been obsessed with calendars, planners, and to-do lists from the time you learned to read and write. Langston wasn't that privileged once he was diagnosed with leukemia. He had to live every day as if it were his last.

"You have something Langston didn't have—your health and the chance to become an adult. You're blessed to have found someone like Shiloh. He told me that he loves you and wants to spend the rest of his life taking care of you. Don't blow it because you can't let go of your New Year's resolutions and wish lists. You're so busy planning your future that you're forgetting how to enjoy life. Marry the man and give your mother a grandchild so she can stop nagging the hell out of me because of some silly argument she had with Odessa."

Gwen frowned. "What does Lauren's mother have to do with my having a baby?"

Millard shook his head. "Don't start me lying, Gwendolyn," he drawled. "I love my brother's wife, but I don't know how he's put up with Odessa all these years. She's the most opinionated woman on the planet."

"What did Aunt Dessa say to Mama?"

"The rumor is that she said something insensitive about not being totally fulfilled until you've had grandchildren."

"But that's only Aunt Dessa's opinion, Daddy."

"That's what I told your mother, but she wouldn't listen to me. She claims Odessa has always been jealous of her."

Gwen stared at her father, complete surprise freezing her features. This was the first time she'd heard that the two women who'd married brothers were less than amicable toward each other.

"That's so juvenile," she whispered, recovering her voice. "That's why I stay out of it."

Gwen settled back against her father again. "I am going to marry Shiloh and make you a grandfather." She'd said it with so much conviction, as if certain she were carrying Shiloh's child beneath her heart.

The night before Shiloh was scheduled to leave for his conference in Baton Rouge they'd made love without using protection. In a moment of madness, Shiloh was unable to stop and she hadn't asked him to, and it was only after they lay together after a shared flight of free-fall that they were cognizant of the consequences of unprotected sex.

Shiloh was effusive in his apology while she hadn't been as upset as he. Unknowingly, she had let go some of the rigid rules for running her life. Falling in love had changed her.

"Mama and Aunt Dessa better settle their mess before my wedding. I'm not going to put up with them getting into it on my big day."

Millard patted her cheek. "Don't worry. I'll tell my brother to talk to his wife."

Gwen sucked her teeth. "You know Uncle Roy is a pussycat whenever it comes to Odessa."

"She will not spoil your wedding. I promise you that."

"Thanks, Daddy."

There was a long, comfortable silence with only the nocturnal sounds of bayou wildlife serenading the countryside. It had been a long time, too long, since Gwen had sat with her father, his arms holding her protectively.

"I like your young man, princess."

Gwen couldn't help the smile stealing its way across her face. "So do I."

"If that's so, then why aren't you with him?"

Heat flooded her face. She'd told Shiloh that she would

sleep at Moriah's during her parents' visit. "I can't sleep with him while you and Mama are here."

"Why can't you?" Millard asked. "Your mother and I slept together two years before we got married." Leaning over, he dropped a kiss on her hair. "Get out of here before it gets too late. And tell my future son-in-law that I'm ready to go fishing whenever he is."

Gwen kissed her father's cheek. "I will. And thank you, Daddy."

He angled his head. "What for, princess?"

She slipped off the love seat. "I thank you for helping me to see life from another angle."

She was alive, in love, and looked forward to sharing her life with a man who made her want to have his babies. She'd made lists all of her life, crossing and adding items to suit the situation.

However, when she made the decision to relocate to Louisiana she hadn't planned on meeting a man or falling in love with him. But it all had happened so quickly that she hadn't had time to formulate a game plan.

Shiloh Harper had come into her life like a sirocco, sweeping her emotions up in a maelstrom of uncertainty. But, on the other hand, there was one thing she was certain of—that she intended to hold onto him for an eternity. This was a time to keep.

Millard stood up and pulled Gwen to his chest. He knew he'd neglected his daughter emotionally when she needed him most. He may have lost his son, but he still had his daughter. She was his firstborn *and* his only child.

"I know I don't say it enough, but I so love you, baby girl."

Tears quickly filled Gwen's eyes as she sagged weakly against her father. For years she'd cried out silently for attention from her father. As her brother lay dying she was in the full throes of puberty with erratic and fluctuating hormone levels, her inability to accept her rapidly changing body, and her belief that her parents no longer loved her.

"And I love you, too, Daddy." She sobbed, tears flowing unchecked.

They stood together, offering love and comfort, unaware of a pair of dark green eyes watching the interchange. Moriah turned and retreated to her bedroom. Picking up a telephone, she spoke softly into the receiver before replacing it on the cradle. She then sat down in her favorite armchair and waited.

Gwen's sobs had subsided to soft hiccups when she felt her father stiffen. Pulling back, she glanced up at the stunned expression on his face. "What's the matter, Daddy?"

"There's someone here for you."

"What are you talking about?"

Millard dropped his arms. "Turn around, princess, and see for yourself."

Gwen turned to find Shiloh standing on the top step leading to the enclosed porch. He'd eaten with them, but didn't linger because he was scheduled to work a midnight to 8:00 a.m. shift.

But he was back, dressed in a white T-shirt and a pair of cutoffs. She watched, as if in slow motion, as he opened the porch door and walked in.

Shiloh had driven like a maniac to get to his mother's house after her cryptic call. Once he heard Moriah say, *Gwen's crying* he'd abruptly ended the call and raced over. Normally what would've been a ten-minute drive was accomplished in under five.

His gaze lingered on her moist cheeks. What had happened to make her cry? He'd found her to be independent, feisty, spirited and not prone to tears.

He nodded, acknowledging the older man. "Good evening, Mills."

Millard stared at Shiloh as if he were an apparition. "Good evening, Shiloh. I thought you'd gone home."

"I did, but I came back because I forgot something."

"What?" Gwen asked as she wiped her moist cheeks with her fingertips.

He lifted his expressive eyebrow in a perfect Rock imitation. "Not what, darling."

Her eyes widened. "I don't understand, Shiloh."

He took a step, bringing them inches apart. "What's not to understand? I came back to take you home." Ignoring her soft gasp, Shiloh nodded to Millard. "If you're finished with Gwen I'd like her to come with me."

Millard forced back a smile. "We're finished." He patted Gwen's shoulder. "Go home, princess."

Gwen stared at Shiloh, then her father, wondering if the two men had planned this beforehand. Turning, she kissed Millard's smooth jaw. "I'll see you tomorrow morning."

Smiling, he patted her cheek. "Don't come too early. I plan to sleep in late." He winked conspiratorially. "And if I'm lucky I'll get your mother to stay in bed with me."

Her smile was dazzling. "Have fun."

"You, too," he said.

She glanced at Shiloh, unable to interpret his closed expression. It was the first time since meeting him that he seemed more stranger than lover. He extended his hand, his expression softening when she placed her palm on his. He tightened his grip, tucking her hand into the bend of his elbow. He led her off the porch to where he'd parked his car.

Gwen, waiting until she was seated and belted in Shiloh's car, asked, "Why did you come for me?"

Shiloh wanted to tell her he'd come because he'd missed

her, that sleeping alone for the past three nights had been pure torture, that he he'd stayed up most nights watching movies in his hotel room, but decided to be truthful. There was no way he wanted his relationship with her to be based on lies.

"My mother called and told me you were upset about something, and before you say anything about her meddling in our business I'm going to defend her. She sees you as a daughter, as she does with Nattie, and all she wants is for her children to be happy."

Reaching over, Gwen rested her left hand on his right thigh. "I'm not angry with your mother, Shiloh. Her calling you just hastened what my father wanted me to do."

"What's that?"

"Go home with you."

Shiloh took his eyes off the unlit road for several seconds. "I thought you were concerned what your folks would say if they found out we were living together."

"I'm sure they know we've been sleeping together, but what I don't want to do is flaunt it in their faces."

Shiloh smiled. "I'm glad I'm marrying an old-fashioned girl."

She squeezed his knee. "Old-fashioned girls don't live and sleep with their future husbands."

A low chuckle rumbled in his chest. "Think of me as a pair of shoes. Would you buy me without trying me on? Here's another scenario. What if you entered a contest and one of the prizes was a pair of Manolo Blahniks in your size. Would you accept the shoes because you like the designer, or would you accept the lesser prize of a year's supply of Spam?"

"If I took the shoes and they didn't fit, then I'd give them away."

He lifted an eyebrow. "Are you saying that if we didn't make love until our wedding night and *if* I turned out to be a dud spud, then you'd trade me in for another man?"

"No, darling," she said softly. "If you were a dud spud, which you aren't, I'd just have to teach you how to please me."

"Do I please you, Gwen?"

"You have no idea how much you please me, in and out of bed."

Shiloh gave her another quick glance. "I think I do because I feel what you feel whenever we're together. You complete me, darling."

There came another period of silence before Gwen said, "Daddy doesn't want us to wait until the end of the year to marry."

"Why?"

Gwen told Shiloh about her conversation with her father, how he helped make her see things differently, that there was no need for her to be so rigid when it came to following what she'd planned for her life.

Shiloh slowed down as he neared the gatehouse. He pressed a button on the device under the visor, and the wooden arm swung up. Minutes later, he maneuvered into the driveway at the rear of his house and parked behind the Suburban. He turned off the headlights, but not the engine.

"You want to change the date." His query was a statement. She nodded.

The cool air sweeping over his face and upper body failed to ease Shiloh's anxiety. Gwen had become an enigma, her moods vacillating, and she was seemingly changing before his eyes. If he hadn't seen her tears for himself he never would've believed his mother.

He expelled an audible breath as he stared out the windshield. "When, darling?"

"Next month."

"Next month," he repeated. Shifting on his seat, he stared at her as if she'd taken leave of her senses. "Why?"

Gwen glared at him. "You have the audacity to ask me why, Shiloh Harper."

"I need to know what's up with you," he spat out. "I told you that I wanted to marry you in June, but you wanted to wait until the end of the year. Now, you tell me you want us to get married next month."

"Do you or don't you want to get married, Shiloh?"

"Yes, baby, I do want to marry you." His voice had softened considerably. Resting his right hand over her headrest, he leaned closer and pressed his mouth to her temple. "We can marry, but we won't be able to take a honeymoon until later in the year. The vacation schedule at the station house is already in place, and I wouldn't think of asking anyone to switch with me."

Gwen unbuckled her seat belt and wrapped her arms around Shiloh's neck. "I don't need a honeymoon as much as I want to be married to you," she whispered close to his ear.

"Okay. You pick the date, and I'll show up."

Easing back, she stared at him staring back at her. "You think I'm losing it, don't you?"

A smile ruffled the corners of his mouth. "I have to admit I kind of like seeing you this way."

"You like me crazy?"

"You're not crazy, darling. This is the first since I've known you that you're acting on what you feel in here." He rested a hand over her heart. "Whenever we make love you let yourself go, and it's only during that act I come to know who the real Gwendolyn is. It hasn't always been that way out of bed. So, do I like what you're showing me now? If it's not you being in control, then yes. If it means spontaneity, then yes. And if it means we get to have each other for the rest of our lives, then it's yes, yes, yes!"

Gwen's smile reminded him of the rising sun. "Let's go inside before I jump your bones right here."

His left hand searched under the hem of her blouse, feathering up her rib cage. "Use me, abuse me, and I promise not to complain," he whispered in singsong.

She giggled like a little girl. "You may come to regret those words when I sop you up like a biscuit and molasses."

"I don't think so, darling. And I'm willing to bet that you won't be so smug when I drink you up like fine wine."

"Are you threatening me, darling?"

"*Oui, Mademoiselle.*" Shiloh turned off the engine, then came around the car to assist Gwen, his arm looping protectively around her waist.

"Will you teach our children to speak French?" she asked as he punched in the code to deactivate the security system.

"No. Moriah can teach them French, because I don't speak the language as well as I should."

"But, I heard you speak it."

"What you heard me speak is a French Creole dialect."

"Is there a difference?"

Shiloh closed the door, resetting the alarm. "Not much. The primary pronunciation influence of Creole comes from the French spoken by slaves brought to Louisiana from Haiti. The result is that the Creole spoken today is a mix of seventeenth-century French and African tribal dialects. The Creole word for to buy is *ashte,* from the French word *acheter. Coun* in Creole means to go, which is very similar to the word *courir* in French."

Cradling Gwen's face between his hands, Shiloh kissed the end of her nose at the same time Cocoa raced across the living room floor, her feet going out under her in her haste to greet them. Shiloh hunkered down and scratched the puppy behind her ears. "You're going to have to sleep down here tonight because Mama and Daddy are going to be very busy, and we don't want any interruptions." Whenever he brought Cocoa upstairs, she had the habit of whining and scratching on the bedroom door until he opened it to let her in.

Gwen rolled her eyes at Shiloh as she headed for the staircase. "I told you what was going to happen if you spoiled her. And if she scratches on the door tonight you get *nada, nulla.*" She paused on a stair. "How do you say nothing in French?"

"*Rien.*"

"Yeah, and that too," she drawled, continuing up the staircase.

Throwing back his head, Shiloh laughed as Cocoa yipped along with him.

Chapter 16

Gwen stole a surreptitious glance at her watch. If she didn't leave within the next fifteen minutes she was going to be late for dinner at the Outlaw. She'd spent the past three hours with Shelby Carruthers' mother, listening to the still-grieving woman extol the brains and beauty of her slain daughter, while revealing facts and details Gwen hadn't been able to glean from the sheriff's department and medical examiner transcripts.

Janet Carruthers was eighty, a very old eighty. Her lank white hair was pulled into a single braid that reached her hips, and an ill-fitting faded housedress from another era hung loosely on her too-thin body.

"Would you like to see my baby's room, Miss Taylor?"

Gwen wanted to say no, that she'd spent more time with her than she'd originally planned, and that she wanted to meet her family for dinner before going home and reviewing her notes on the cold case that had become an obsession.

"Yes, I would, Mrs. Carruthers."

Rising from the chair at the kitchen table, she followed Janet out of the kitchen, down a narrow hallway and into a room at the rear of the house. Although neat and clean, the furnishings in the house were sorely outdated, the colors of olive green and orange predominating.

The cell phone attached to Gwen's waist vibrated. Reaching for it she flipped the top and read the number on the tiny screen. She had two missed calls: one from Shiloh and the other from her cousin Lauren. She would return the calls as soon as she finished her interview.

Janet opened the door, then stood aside for Gwen to precede her into a space that had become a shrine to Shelby. Black-and-white photographs, fading local and high school newspaper articles were taped to every wall surface.

The frilly cotton-candy pink canopy covering a white four-poster bed matched the bedspread. Everything in the room was either pink or white, which led Gwen to believe that pink had been Shelby's favorite color.

A collection of *Nancy Drew* mysteries lined a bookcase, along with other books and magazines. She read the spines of the magazines wrapped in clear plastic: *Screen Gems*, *Photoplay*, and *Seventeen*. Framed pictures from the movie magazines adorned one wall from ceiling to baseboard. She counted eight of Tab Hunter and six of Robert Wagner. There were too many of James Dean and Marlon Brando to count. There only a few Hollywood femme fatales: Marilyn Monroe, Elizabeth Taylor and Natalie Wood.

What drew her rapt attention were photographs of Shelby's classmates. In each of them Shelby was very conspicuous because of her slender, curvy figure, long, silver-blond ponytail, sparkling sapphire-blue eyes, and infectious dimpled smile. It was apparent because of her natural beauty and outgoing personality the cheerleader and straight-A student had been selected as her graduating class prom queen.

Gwen felt the hair stand up on the nape of her neck, followed by a rush of cold air. She shivered noticeably despite the heat. A sixth sense told her she was onto something, that intuitively the photographs either contained a clue or held the answer to the forty-two-year-old unsolved murder. She turned to find Janet staring at her with a strange expression on her face.

Her blue eyes caught and held her gaze. "Is there something wrong, Miss Taylor?"

"I don't know, but I have a strange feeling that what I'm looking for is tied to these photographs. Do you happen to have a copy of your daughter's yearbook?"

"Yes…yes, I do," she stammered as a rush of color swept over her pale face. "I kept all of my daughter's things. I even found some letters that boys had written to her."

"If you don't mind, I'll take those, too. I promise that no one will see them. If I find something in those letters that might give the police a clue to link someone to Shelby's murder, then I'll let you know before I disclose the contents."

"Shelby's gone and she's not coming back, so whatever is in those letters can't hurt her now. Losing my daughter destroyed my family. My husband started drinking when the police closed the case because of lack of evidence. He lost his job, and a month later he went out on his boat and put a bullet through his head. So, if you can find the bastard who killed my baby I know my Durant's soul will finally rest in peace."

"I can't promise you anything, but I'll do my best to bring you some closure."

"You're doing more than anyone has done in more than forty years."

Gwen wanted to tell the woman that she did not know why

she'd become so intrigued with the cold case, but now that she'd opened the door to the past she had to see it to its conclusion.

"I'm going to give you my cell phone number, so if you remember anything please call me. I don't care how insignificant it may seem, I still want you to call me."

Janet nodded as she gathered the St. Martin Parish High School 1964 yearbook off a shelf, running her hand over the dusty cover. She picked up a shoebox, handing both to Gwen.

"Thank you, Miss Taylor."

It was Gwen's turn to nod. She hadn't solved the case, but the fact that she had made an attempt was enough for the woman to feel a measure of gratitude.

Gwen pressed several buttons, activating her car's cruise control before she pressed a button on her cell phone. Lauren answered with a friendly greeting.

"I'm calling to tell you that I've changed my wedding date."

"Why, Gwen?"

"I decided I didn't want to wait until December to become Mrs. Shiloh Harper."

"Are you in the family way?"

"I don't know."

"When will you know?"

"In another week," Gwen admitted.

"You know there's a new home pregnancy kit that will tell you if you are even before you miss your period."

"Ease up, Lauren. I'm not in that much of a hurry to find out whether I'm pregnant."

"You don't sound too happy about this, cuz. What's up?"

"I had a heart-to-heart with my father last night, and I realize that I've stood in my own way when it came to personal happiness. I had a time for this and a time for that. And if what I planned didn't work out, then I revised my plans over and over until I didn't know what I wanted. I want to grow old with this man I find myself so in love with."

"I've never known you to talk like this, Gwendolyn."

"That's because I've never felt like this, Lauren. When are the kids finished with summer camp?"

"August 8. That's on a Wednesday."

"Can you and your family come down that Saturday for a wedding?"

"Of course we can. If you want I can take the kids out of camp early—"

"No, Lauren. Let them finish the season. I've already selected my dress. What I'll do is scan it and e-mail it to you. There's a store in Boston that carries the designer's gowns, so you should be able to find something similar to what I'm wearing. I'm going to ask Shiloh's sister-in-law to be in the wedding party, which means I want Caleb as a groomsman. I want Drew, Kayla and Royce included, too."

"What is your color scheme?"

"Pale pink and lime green." They were her sorority colors.

She told Lauren that Shiloh's brother Ian who was to be the best man had offered to prepare the food for the reception which would be held at the newly restored *Bon Temps*. The plantation shutters were in place, the walls repapered with the patterns she'd selected, moldings were scraped and painted, along with walls and ceilings. All that remained was scraping the floors and applying polyurethane and painting the mansion's exterior.

"I can't believe how much my life has changed since I've learned not to try and control what I can't control." Gwen glanced at the clock on the dashboard. "Look, cuz, I'm going to have to end this call. I'll call you either later tonight or tomorrow. And look for the dress whenever you go online."

She ended the call and pressed another button. "Hey you," she crooned when she heard Shiloh's voice.

"Where are you?"

The sparkle in her eyes faded as a frown creased her forehead. "Ex-cuse *me*." There was no mistaking the sarcasm in the two words.

There came a pregnant pause before Shiloh said, "Sorry about that. I called you more than two hours ago and left a message for you to call me."

"I'm calling you back, Shiloh."

There was another pause, only the sound of his heavy breathing in her ear. "Look, baby. I'm not checking up on you, but when I called the house and *Bon Temps* and didn't get an answer I sort of lost it."

"Who else did you call?"

"Nash. I thought that maybe you'd gone in even though it's not a day you're scheduled to work."

"Did you say anything to my folks?"

"No. I didn't want to alarm them in case something had happened to you."

"What's going to happen to me—" Her words trailed off when she heard a siren and saw a flash of lights in her rearview mirror. Her pulse accelerated when she realized she was being pulled over. "Shiloh, there's a cop behind me. I swear I wasn't speeding."

"Stop, then let me speak to him."

Signaling, she slowed, and pulled onto the shoulder. She'd lowered the driver-side window and had the cell phone out the window when the officer got out of his cruiser and approached her.

"Sheriff Harper wants to speak to you," she said, preempting whatever it was he wanted to say to her.

The deputy took the phone and put it to his ear. "Yes, I found her. She appears to be all right, sir. You've got it." He handed Gwen back her phone. "I want you to follow me, Miss Taylor."

"What for? Am I being arrested?"

The deputy smiled and shook his head. "No, ma'am. But Sheriff Harper wants me to bring you in. He said if you resist, then I should bring you in the cruiser. It's your choice, ma'am." He touched the brim of his wide straw hat.

"Mine!" she spat out like an impudent child.

"Please follow me."

She sat motionless, teeth clenched, her hands clutching the steering wheel in a death grip, seething. Shiloh had used the power of his office to put out an APB—an all points bulletin—for her car. He was nothing more than a tyrant, despot and a bully.

Waiting until the police cruiser drove around her, Gwen shifted into gear and followed him. She was grateful he'd turned off his lights. And for the second time in as many days she was given a personal police escort to her destination.

Deputy Caulfield moved closer to Gwen as the ferryboat pulled away from the pier. She sat, arms crossed under her breasts, as she stared out at the brown, brackish water. It was apparent the deputy didn't have much to do if his orders were to take her to his superior officer.

"What a waste of taxpayers' money, Deputy Caulfield," she whispered harshly. "Don't you have better things to do than escort me to your boss?"

The deputy stared straight ahead as he affected a stern expression. If he'd removed his sunglasses, then Sheriff Harper's fiancée would've seen the amusement in his eyes. Everyone at the station house was used to seeing Gwen when she came in on Tuesday mornings to gather information for her column with the *Tribune*. He'd found her to be wholly professional, because she never used her personal relationship with Shiloh to advance her position with the newspaper. Some of the deputies and those who made up the civilian staff had begun placing bets on the date she would eventually seek out the sheriff's office.

The ferryboat pulled alongside the wharf to the Outlaw. Gwen stood up and made her way down the gangplank, the deputy following. "Thank you for the personal escort," she said, smiling.

"Sorry, Miss Taylor, but I have orders to take you directly to Sheriff Harper." He cupped her elbow and led her up the wooden steps to the restaurant.

She lifted a shoulder. "Suit yourself."

Shiloh stared at Gwen as she entered the Outlaw with one of his deputies. A hint of a smile deepened the lines around his eyes when he noticed the stiffness in her back and the stubborn set of her jaw. She was not happy. Gwen was upset and he'd been scared stiff that something had happened to her.

He nodded to his deputy. "Thanks, Caulfield."

"No problem, boss."

Shiloh lifted an eyebrow at Gwen who'd folded her arms under her breasts while tapping the toe of one of her high-heeled patent leather sandals.

"We were waiting for you before…" His words trailed off when his cell phone rang at the same time a voice crackled through the two-way radio attached to the deputy's left shoulder. "Harper," he said, answering the phone.

Gwen heard "explosion" and "fire" and a chill shook her like a fragile leaf in a storm. Her annoyance with Shiloh evaporated, replaced by a fear that squeezed her heart. He'd survived one fiery explosion only to race off to confront another one.

She blinked back tears. *Come back to me, darling.*

Shiloh's eyes searched her face, reaching into her thoughts. "I'm coming back to you. Tell the others I have to answer a nine-eleven call."

He was there, then he was gone. Her gaze fixed on the space where he'd been. She closed her eyes and still his image lingered, the scent of his distinctive cologne, the breadth of his broad shoulders, the gold and green lights in his eyes, eyes that reminded her of pinpoints of sunlight coming through leaves and yards of Spanish moss.

The noise and activity in the restaurant pulled her from her private musings, and she opened her eyes to find Ian coming toward her. She affected a smile she didn't feel at that moment. Her gaze lingered on his grim expression. Instead of his customary tunic and black pinstriped chef's uniform, he wore a colorful Hawaiian print shirt and jeans.

Ian Harper saw fear in his future sister-in-law's eyes. He reached for her hand. "What's going on, Gwen?"

"Shiloh had a nine-eleven call."

Ian drew in a lungful of breath when he registered her flat, emotionless tone. "What is it?"

Gwen shook her head. "All I heard over a deputy's two-way radio was something about a fire and explosion."

Gritting his teeth, Ian muttered a savage expletive. His moss-green gaze swung back to Gwen. "Please don't say anything to my mother. Let's get back to the others."

They hadn't taken more than half a dozen steps when a young woman with raven-black hair, equally dark eyes and a rich olive complexion bore down on Ian.

"I have an emergency at home," she said in a French Creole dialect.

"Good luck," Ian replied in the same language.

The undercover agent had used an agreed upon code. He knew Inez's abrupt departure and Shiloh's nine-eleven call were drug-related, and that the explosion and fire had come from a meth lab.

Gwen smiled at her father when he stood up and pulled out

a chair for her at a round table in a corner of the crowded restaurant. "Thanks, Daddy." She stared at the six people staring at her, nodding to Augustine Leblanc, whom she hadn't seen since the night of the fund-raiser. "I'm sorry that I kept everyone waiting. Shiloh said to tell you that he had to answer a nine-eleven call."

Paulette Taylor stared across the table at her daughter. "Where were you, sweetheart? It's not like you to keep folks waiting."

Gwen picked up her menu, pretending interest. "I got tied up working on a story," she said in a quiet voice that belied her annoyance with her mother chastising her as if she were a child.

Her head came up and she waved away the carafe of wine as Millard attempted to fill her wineglass. She didn't intend to drink anything alcoholic until she verified her physical condition.

"Does everyone know what they want?"

Moriah smiled sweetly. "Yes. Just tell Ian what it is you want."

"I'll have the broiled seafood platter."

Paulette, waiting until Ian retreated to the kitchen to add Gwen's request to their party's order, laced her manicured fingers together. "What is it you're working on?"

Gwen wished she were sitting next to her mother so she could kick her under the table. "It has nothing to do with my column."

Natalee flashed her toothpaste-ad smile. "I hardly ever read the *Tribune,* but I read it now because I want to see if I can recognize any of the names of the people who are behaving badly."

Attractive lines fanned out around Augustine's dark eyes when he smiled. His graying straight black hair, brushed off a high forehead, lay in precise strands on the nape of his neck. His khaki-brown complexion, narrow face, high cheekbones and full sensual mouth were the result of a blending of races so indicative of the region.

"You've single-handedly done what our sheriff's department has been unable to do for years. And that is curtailing the proliferation of prostitution over near the Bienville waterfront."

Gwen smiled at the man who appeared completely enthralled with Moriah Harper. "No married man wants his wife or children to see his name in the paper because he was picked up for soliciting a prostitute."

"I don't know why a man would want to pay a woman to have sex with him when he has a wife at home," Moriah said, frowning. "Don't you agree, Mills?"

Millard picked up his glass of water and took a sip. "I'm going to pass on that one," he mumbled.

"What do you mean you pass, Millard Taylor?" Paulette practically shouted.

"Stop looking at me like that, Paul. I've never solicited a hooker. But I understand why men do it, and especially married men."

"Please pray tell me why?" Paulette drawled sarcastically.

"Because...because some wives don't...won't..." Millard did not finish his statement.

Gwen gave her father a sidelong glance. "You just put your foot in your mouth, Daddy."

"Won't do what?" Paulette asked.

Gwen glared at Paulette. "Let it go, Mama."

"I will not let it—"

"I said to please let it go," Gwen said between her teeth, interrupting her mother. "We're all adults and we know what Daddy wanted to say."

Paulette opened her mouth to argue with her daughter, then closed it as if realization had suddenly dawned.

Eyes downcast, she smoothed out the tablecloth next to her place setting. "All I'm going to say is that I've never given my husband a reason to pay for *sex*." She'd stressed the last word.

"Neither have I," Natalee intoned confidently.

Gwen exchanged a smile with Moriah. "Nor will I."

Ian came back, sat down next to Natalee, and draped an arm over the back of her chair. "What did I miss?"

Augustine raised his wineglass. "The ladies were talking about men paying women for sex."

Ian stared at his wife. "I've never had to pay for sex, because women usually pay me," he teased with a wide grin. Dropping his arm and pushing back his chair, he popped up like a jack-in-the box. "*Maudire!* I just forgot I left something in the kitchen."

Natalee's eyes nearly bulged from their sockets. "Oh, no he didn't just raise the hell up outta here after talking that *smack!*"

"Please, Natalee," Moriah said in a soft voice that challenged her daughter-in-law not to ignore her warning. She rounded on Augustine, green eyes flashing. "And don't you start, Augie, because you'll only wind up losing this round with me."

Augustine stared at Moriah under lowered lids. "You win because I let you win, *mon amie.*"

Moriah blushed to the roots of her curly hair. "I am not your girlfriend, Augustine."

He lowered his head and stared at Moriah as seconds ticked off. "Not yet."

Gwen realized she wasn't the only one holding her breath when there came a collection of sighs from around the table. It wasn't until Ian returned with a tray of fish, pork and chicken-filled appetizers and a cold antipasto that the tense moment ended.

Chapter 17

A week before she was to exchange vows with Shiloh Gwen moved back to *Bon Temps*. The temporary move served a twofold purpose: she could finish packing up her office before it was to be shipped to the home she would share with her new husband, and it would give her time to meet with the wedding consultant to finalize the plans for her wedding.

Her anxiety as to whether she was carrying Shiloh's baby was alleviated by the onset of her menses. It lasted two instead of the normal five days, but the show was enough to put her mind at ease.

She and Shiloh mailed out invitations to family members and close friends, welcoming them to the nuptials of Gwendolyn Paulette Taylor and Shiloh Ryker Harper in the small Roman Catholic church where he'd been baptized.

Her gaze shifted to the headlines of the latest issue of the *Teche Tribune*. It had been three weeks since the explosion and fire in an abandoned building near the waterfront, yet the incident was still on the minds of most parish residents.

The evidence collected by a team of bomb and arson experts revealed that the property had been used as a meth lab. The owner of the property denied knowledge of any illegal activity, which left local police and drug enforcement agents frustrated because they hadn't made an arrest.

Willis Raymond Benton's defense that he was an innocent victim when someone spiked his drink at a local club was strengthened because of the lab's existence, and his claim was subsequently corroborated by two of the six young men who'd been with him. They claimed their drinks were also spiked and that they'd passed out in the woods instead of attempting to drive home.

The D.A.'s office offered Willis Raymond Benton a plea bargain: ten years' probation, loss of his driver's license for five years, and an order to pay the relatives of the surviving infant two million dollars. When Gwen told Shiloh that the district attorney's office had caved under political pressure from Bram Benton, he cautioned her to leave the law to the lawyers, that he did not intend to discuss the case with her, and extracted a promise from her that they would never bring their work home.

The *Teche Tribune* sold out their weekly circulation with shocking headlines and Nash McGraw's op-ed columns were filled with innuendoes hinting of bribery and a coverup.

Keith Nichols' unannounced visit to the newspaper's office ended the impasse between his office and the publisher. Keith had threatened Nash with a lawsuit, citing libel and slander if he didn't cease and desist. Nash quickly acquiesced, saying that it was worth the threat because he'd increased the paper's circulation and revenue appreciably.

Gwen's gaze shifted from the newspaper to the stack of letters Janet Carruthers had given her. She'd read and reread them over and over and hadn't come up with a single clue. Most of them were innocent notes from boys who'd thanked Shelby for studying with them, while others complimented her because she'd changed her hairstyle or started a new trend when she wore a new outfit. None professed their love or hinted they wanted a sexual liaison. She wanted to discuss the case with Shiloh, but because of their promise to each other, she hadn't.

The doorbell rang, eliciting a smile from her. One of her first requests on the renovation list was to replace the doorbell. Rising to her feet, she went to the front door.

Peering through the security eye, she went completely still. She was expecting the wedding planner, not her cousin. She opened the door to find Lauren, Caleb and their three children grinning at her.

"Surprise!" the Samuels family shouted, as six-year-old Kayla showered her with a handful of colorful confetti.

Gwen looped her arms around Lauren's neck. "What are you guys doing here? You told me that you wouldn't be down until Thursday." A pair of eyes in a face so much like her own sparkled like polished onyx.

Lauren kissed her first cousin's cheek. "We changed our plans after I asked the kids if they wanted to wait and finish the camp season or come see their Aunt Gwennie and they opted for their aunt."

Pulling back, Gwen smiled at her cousin's husband. Amusement flickered in the amber eyes belonging to bestselling author C.B. Samuels as he ushered his two sons and daughter into the entryway. He'd recently celebrated his fortieth birthday and along with marriage and fatherhood he'd acquired a captivating presence that enhanced his stunning virility.

"You guys should've told me when you were coming, and I would've picked you up at the airport."

Dipping his head, he brushed a light kiss over Gwen's mouth. "We drove down," Caleb informed her. "Congratulations, cuz. I can't believe you're really getting married."

She patted his shoulder. "Believe it, cuz."

Extending her arms, she smiled at the younger Samuels. Ten-year-old Drew had grown at least an inch since she last saw him. Kayla had lost her baby fat, and four-year-old Royce, clinging to his father's leg, smiled shyly up at her.

"Come and give Aunt Gwennie a hug and kiss." Kayla raced into her embrace while her brothers were slower in responding.

"I didn't know you lived in a castle, Aunt Gwennie," Kayla whispered close to her ear.

Gwen smiled at the young girl. All of Lauren's children resembled Caleb. They'd inherited his slender lankiness, black curly hair, and citrine-colored eyes.

"Do you want to see it?" The three children nodded. Gwen winked at Lauren. "Come on up and I'll show you your rooms."

Lauren turned to her husband. "Cal, could you please bring in the bags?"

He bowed from the waist. "Yes, boss lady."

Lauren rolled her eyes at him, then followed Gwen across the highly polished living room floor and up the winding staircase to the second floor. "I have to agree with Kayla. This house is a showplace."

Gwen glanced over her shoulder. "And that's what it's going to stay—a showplace." She told Lauren that she didn't intend to make *Bon Temps* her permanent residence. "I'll open it for tours, and offer it for fund-raisers."

"Are you going to remove the furniture for the reception?"

Gwen shook her head. "No. The doors on the opposite side of the living room open out into a ballroom."

Kayla gasped when shown her bedroom, running to sit on a padded window seat. "It's for a princess."

Lauren ruffled her daughter's short curly hair. "That's because you are a princess."

The two boys were less effusive, especially Drew when told he had to share his bedroom with his younger brother who followed him around as if he were a rock star.

"And you're not sleeping in my bed," Drew said, glaring at Royce.

Royce crawled up on one of the twin beds. "I have my own bed," he countered proudly.

Gwen opened the door to a bedroom across the hall. "This one is for you and Caleb."

Lauren walked into a bedroom that was wholly Southern in nature. Creamy-white fabrics on dignified mahogany pieces and a pale sisal rug complemented off-white wallpaper dotted with delicate violets.

"Unbelievable," Lauren crooned. She ran her fingertips down the sheer fabric draping the decoratively carved posts on the four-poster bed. "I feel as if I've gone back a hundred years."

"I'll let you settle in, then once I finish meeting with the wedding planner I'll prepare lunch."

Lauren waved a hand. "Don't trouble yourself with lunch. We stopped and ate about an hour ago."

"I went food shopping yesterday because I knew I wouldn't have time later on in the week."

"As soon as Cal brings the bags in, I'm going to have the kids shower, then take a nap. They were so wired this morning that Cal pulled off the road and read them the riot act."

Gwen grimaced. It was not often that Caleb raised his voice to his children. "I'll call Shiloh and have him come over after his shift ends. We can all have dinner here tonight."

"You don't have to cook for us, Gwen. We can always order in."

"This is not Boston where you can order pizza or fried

chicken and have it delivered within an hour. The nearest takeout is ten miles away."

"*Damyum*," Lauren drawled. "You live in the country."

"Correction, cuz. I live in bayou country."

Lauren sat down on the edge of the bed. "You've done well, my sister. You have a beautiful home, you've fallen in love, and now you're going to marry your Prince Charming."

"Incredible, isn't it?"

Lauren angled her head, smiling. "Incredible no, mind-boggling yes, because it was only a couple of months ago that you said you didn't need a man, and were talking about having a test tube baby."

"I suppose I was talking smack."

"Wicked smack," Lauren countered, grinning.

The two women laughed hysterically. They were still laughing when Caleb entered the room carrying a bag. He put it down, shook his head, then left to check on his children.

Gwen threaded her gloved fingers through her father's as they lingered in the vestibule of the church waiting for the signal to begin their procession along the white carpet to the altar where Shiloh, Ian, Lauren, Caleb and Natalee waited with a priest.

Kayla, in a delicate white organza dress with a pale pink sash, and Royce in a white jacket, shirt with an Eton collar, short pants and knee socks with a pink bowtie and cummerbund, had strewn red, white and pink rose petals along the length of the carpet. Drew had carried a white silk pillow with the wedding bands tied to it with pink-and-green ribbon.

Millard stared at his daughter's strained profile as she took a deep breath, held it for several seconds before letting it out slowly. The strains of "The Wedding March" filled the church.

"Are you ready, princess?"

Gwen smiled and nodded. "Yes, Daddy."

She concentrated on putting one satin-covered foot in front of the other, her gaze fixed on one man. He was breathtakingly handsome in white jacket, shirt and tie. Her gaze dropped to the precise crease in his black dress trousers and shoes.

They'd gotten to see little of each other during the week; she'd spent all of her free time meeting with the consultant, who'd brought her up to date with the activities of the floral designer, photographer, musicians and pastry chef. The precise, organized woman had finalized the menu with Ian, while Gwen went to a bridal dress salon for a final fitting.

She met Shiloh at the church for a rehearsal, then later at Moriah's home for an elegant rehearsal buffet dinner Thursday evening.

Lauren in pale pink and Natalee in a darker hue looked like flowers as they held bouquets made of pink roses and blue-and-green hydrangeas with streamers of light green ribbons. Miniature rosebuds, in corresponding colors, were pinned in their dark hair.

Shiloh watched his bride as she came closer, his heart pounding painfully in his chest. This wedding day was so different from the one wherein he and Deandrea had exchanged vows in the office of the judge where he'd clerked after graduating law school.

He'd tried imagining what Gwen would look like as a bride, and failed miserably.

He'd also tried imagining what style of gown she'd choose, and again he'd failed.

The Elizabethan-inspired silk satin gown with a square neckline, Empire waist, capped sleeves, gold-and-platinum embroidered bodice and a sweep train was stunning. Her hair was swept off her face and fastened atop her head in a mass of black shiny curls. Her flyaway veil was a backpiece, attached to a jeweled barrette. A pair of magnificent pearl-and-diamonds earrings that had belonged to Gwendolyn Pickering hung from her pierced lobes. There was just a hint of a smile on her face, and for the first time since he awoke that morning, Shiloh smiled.

Time stood still for Gwen from the moment her father placed her hand in Shiloh's. She heard the words, repeated her responses, and it wasn't until she handed Lauren her all-white bouquet of roses, gardenias, tulips and peonies held together with yards of wide satin pink ribbon and her gloves so that Shiloh could slip a diamond eternity band on her finger that the significance and symbolic action hit her. His soft drawling voice, repeating his vows, jolted her like a quake's aftershocks. She repeated her vows, her voice sounding strangely loud in the eerie hush of the historic church. When she heard the priest tell Shiloh he could kiss his bride, she knew it was over.

More than twenty-five years of creating wish lists, making and breaking New Year's resolutions, and jotting down to-dos in her daily planner was over.

The tears filling her eyes blurred the face of the man who was now her husband when he cradled her chin and brushed her mouth with his.

"Hey you, Mrs. Harper," he whispered for her ears only.

A rush of heat singed her cheeks. "Hey, yourself, Mr. Harper."

Cradling her hand in the bend of his arm, Shiloh led his wife down the carpet and out of the church, smiling and ducking the shower of rice, bird seed and orange blossoms as a photographer captured their image for posterity.

They stood on the church steps smiling for those who snapped frame after frame of pictures. Bright sunlight glinted off the modern platinum band on his left hand as he once again held Gwen's face between his palms and kissed her.

He picked several grains of rice from her hair, smiling. "You take my breath away."

Leaning into her husband, her left hand resting on the shawl collar of his dinner jacket, Gwen pressed a kiss to the corner of his mouth. "And I love you, Shiloh Harper."

Shiloh held his wife to his heart, his thoughts echoing her words, his heart beating in unison with hers, and feeling what she felt. He'd waited a long time for someone like Gwendolyn Taylor-Harper to come into his life, and it was only now that he realized the wait had been worth it.

They returned to *Bon Temps* with the wedding party, posing for hundreds of frames on the manicured lawn, near the orchard under trees pregnant with their fruitful yield, inside the mansion along the winding staircase with the banister and newel posts festooned with pink flowers and light-green satin bows.

After the photo session ended, they stood in a receiving line thanking the one hundred invited guests who'd gathered under the shaded coolness of an immense white tent to dine on everything from caviar and exotic cheeses, to delicately prepared fish, savory chicken, lamb, *daube glace*—a cold spicy beef dish, and a plethora of Cajun and Creole dishes that had everyone reaching for anything liquid to counter the heat on a few sensitive taste buds. Bartenders mixed, stirred and popped bottle after bottle of quality French champagne. Ian Harper, as the wedding's chef and the groom's best man, had solidified his reputation as one of Louisiana's best chefs.

Gwen ate and drank sparingly as she accepted the good wishes from those who'd grown up and gone to school with Shiloh, and the personnel from the SMPD. The deputies who were scheduled to work stopped by during their meal break to offer their boss and his wife the best. Ian had provided takeout containers for those who were unable to remain long enough to sit and eat.

The afternoon became a blur as Gwen listened to the many toasts, cut the cake with Shiloh, and toasted each other with flutes of champagne. She was certain her father heard her sigh of relief when the wedding planner informed everyone that the frivolity would continue inside the house with dancing and a live band.

Shiloh's gaze narrowed when he noticed the sheen of moisture on his wife's flawless face. It was warm, but not so warm that she would perspire. "Are you feeling all right, darling?"

Gwen closed her eyes for several seconds. "I'm just a little dizzy."

He knew it wasn't the champagne because she hadn't taken more than three sips of the wine. "Do you want to go inside and lie down?"

Smiling at him, Gwen shook her head even though it was the only thing she wanted to do. She was exhausted and somewhat overwhelmed with being the center of attraction. Now she knew how Caleb felt whenever someone recognized him from his book jacket photo. C. B. Samuels had always managed to keep his private life private.

Would she, as the wife of a parish sheriff and soon-to-be-again district attorney be able to keep a low profile? She was certain as a member of the Genteel Magnolia Society she would be called upon to champion local civic causes, but they were just that—local.

She'd lost count of the number of judges in attendance, and she'd heard more than once that the governor had received recommendations from those in the judiciary that Shiloh Harper could soon become Judge Harper.

Shiloh dipped his head, pressing his mouth to her ear. "Are you certain you're not pregnant?"

Eyes wide, she stared at him. "You know that I got my period."

His expression did not change. "Did you take a test?"

"No! There's no reason why I should, Shiloh," she whispered. "If I'm not pregnant, then I'm certain I will be since we've decided not to use protection."

"I only asked because lately I notice that every time you drink something alcoholic you don't feel well. That never happened before we started sleeping together."

Gwen pondered his statement for a full minute. The first time she'd taken the Samuels family to the Outlaw she'd ordered a beer and managed to drink less than half of it because her stomach rebelled. The night of the rehearsal dinner she had not swallowed more than a sip of wine, and again she felt dizzy.

"You're right."

Reaching for her flute, Shiloh put it beyond her reach. "No more of that until you take a test."

The feasting, drinking and dancing went on for hours in the ballroom under the thousands of lights from a massive crystal chandelier. And as daylight gave way to dusk, those who were fortunate enough to garner an invitation to Gwendolyn Pickering's soirees so many years before felt as if they'd stepped back in time when elegantly attired men and women came to *Bon Temps* to indulge in parties where the races mixed without regard to the laws and mores that frowned upon these illicit liaisons.

Gwen shared two dances with Shiloh: her favorite, "You're My Everything," and his, "At Last." She danced with her father, then Ian, who reminded her of the man with the ill-fitting toupee at the fund-raiser. When she told her new brother-in-law that the little man should patent his hair as a backscratcher, the chef laughed so loud that heads turned in their direction.

After removing her headpiece, she joined everyone doing the electric and cha-cha slide, then she lost count of the number of men who asked her to dance. Deputy Sheriff Jameson came by, in uniform, to spin her around the floor before she was handed off to her uncle Roy, Caleb, Nash, and then Augustine.

Her face ached from smiling, and her back ached from being on her feet for hours. She managed to get Lauren's attention, motioning for her to meet her upstairs.

Gwen expelled a sigh as Lauren undid the many buttons on the back of her gown. "You can stay as long as you wish," she told her cousin. Her parents and Lauren's parents were also staying at *Bon Temps*.

"We'll stay the weekend, then head back Monday afternoon. Mom and Dad said they're going to hang out here with Aunt Paulette and Uncle Mills for a few days. They're all flying back together on Wednesday."

"Why don't you delay going back until they're ready to leave?"

"I don't think that's a good idea, because once the kids saw Cocoa they started complaining that they miss their dog. And you know my kids. Once they get onto something they don't know when to let up."

Gwen had brought Cocoa back to *Bon Temps* with her. "Shiloh never said he missed me, but went on about how he missed his dog until I had to remind him for the umpteenth time that Cocoa is *my* dog."

"Now she belongs to both of you."

"You're right, Lauren."

"Have you decided where you're going on your honeymoon once Shiloh gets his vacation?"

Turning, she stepped out of her gown. "I'm partial to Venice, and he wants Paris."

Lauren lifted her eyebrows. "Italy and France are close enough to visit both cities."

She nodded. "I'll think about it."

Shiloh had to complete his term as sheriff before they could plan anything definitive. They'd contemplated a to-do list, but she had quickly changed her mind. She knew it wouldn't be easy not to jot down notes in her daily planner or make a notation on slips of paper, and live an unencumbered life.

Lauren hugged Gwen and kissed her cheek. "That's your problem, Mrs. Gwendolyn Harper. You think too much. Let go and live. You just married the sexiest man in the parish, and here you are agonizing over something four months away. Think about what's going to happen between you and your man tonight."

Gwen returned her cousin's embrace. "On that note, I'll see you Monday morning."

"Have fun," Lauren called out over her shoulder as she walked out of the bedroom, closing the door softly behind her.

The door opened again twenty minutes later, and Shiloh walked into the room. He'd changed out of his formal attire and into a lightweight suit. Pushing off the chair, Gwen waited for him to approach her.

"I'm ready, Shiloh."

And she was. She was ready for her husband and for whatever they would offer each other.

He reached for her, pulling her to his chest. "Let's go home."

Holding her hand, Shiloh led her down a back staircase and out to where he'd parked his car. She was ready and he was ready, ready to live out the rest of his life with the woman he'd vowed to love, honor and protect at the risk of forfeiting his own life.

Chapter 18

Gwen closed her eyes and rested her head on Shiloh's shoulder as he carried her effortlessly up the staircase to their bedroom. They hadn't exchanged a single word since driving away from *Bon Temps* because there was no need to say anything. All they'd said or done before had led up to this moment when biblically they would become one with each other.

She opened her eyes and pressed her mouth to his warm brown throat. "Do you know what tonight is?"

"Yes. It's our wedding night."

"No, Shiloh. It's more than our wedding night."

Shiloh walked into their bedroom and placed her on the bed, his body following hers down. The light from a lamp on a table in the sitting room cast a warm glow throughout the expansive space. Supporting his greater weight on his forearms, he buried his face against the column of her neck. He pondered her cryptic statement, but came up blank.

"What is it?"

"I met you for the first time three months ago tonight."

He raised his head, his gaze searching her shadowy face. "It's only been three months?"

Gwen nodded. "Amazing, isn't it?"

Shiloh recalled the night he'd gotten the call that a woman who "talked funny" was stranded along the road. She didn't talk funny, but differently from those whose roots ran deep in Southern Louisiana. She talked different, looked different, and her attitude was different from the women he'd grown up with and known most of his life.

He didn't know Gwendolyn well, didn't think he would ever know her well, but that was her appeal, because every day with her was a surprise. He never knew what she would say or do, keeping him off balance and more in love with her. The only thing Shiloh was certain of was that his wife would never bore him.

"Yes, it is amazing. You're amazing."

"How, baby?" she crooned.

"I'll have to show you."

Shiloh lifted his eyebrows, his hands going to the pins in her hair. One by one he removed them before he combed his fingers through the tangled curls.

Gwen let her senses take over. This wasn't the first time she'd slept with Shiloh, but would become the first time she would share her body with her husband.

His touch was gossamer, fingertips grazing her flesh with each article of clothing he removed. There was only the sound of their measured breathing and the whisper of fabric against bared skin. Shiloh undressed her, and she returned the favor, divesting him of his clothes.

A soft gasp escaped her parted lips when he swept her off the bed and headed into the adjoining bathroom. A motion detector flooded the space with light. Shiloh touched the dimmer switch on a wall panel, and the bright yellow light faded to a soft, flattering pink glow.

Tightening her grip around his neck, Gwen inhaled the distinctive smell of the cologne clinging to Shiloh's body. She loved him, loved everything that made him who he was.

"I love you," she intoned close to his ear.

Bending slightly, Shiloh set her on her feet. He stared at her beneath lowered lids. She loved him, and he loved and adored her. He'd told her that more times than he could count, but whenever he was unable to say the words he showed her.

"Thank you." The two words were pregnant with a passion that came from a part of him no woman had ever touched.

He pulled her over to an area with a free-standing shower. Within seconds water pulsed from the many jets along the wall. The softly falling water fell over their head and bodies as they held each other, heart to heart.

Gwen felt Shiloh's strong heartbeat against her breasts, his sex, rising and hardening against her thighs. Time stood still for her when her husband shampooed her hair, then washed her body using his hands rather than her bath sponge. His fingers tempted, teased, taunted and tantalized her until she was closing to fainting.

Without warning, Shiloh became a cartographer, his mouth mapping every inch of her flesh, charting a course and claiming her as his. Their labored breathing overlapped the sound of falling water.

"Shiloh!" His name was torn from the back of her throat as the pulsing between her legs and heaviness in her breasts increased.

Hearing her strangled cry, feeling her trembling, and inhaling the rising scent of her desire mingling with the vanilla musk fragrance of Gwen's shampoo and body wash, Shiloh knew that his wife was close to climaxing. From the first time they'd shared a bed his mission was to know her body as well as he knew his own. It had taken every fiber of his self-control not to make love to her in the shower. Not tonight. Not on their wedding night.

He turned off the shower, while reaching for a bath sheet from the supply stacked on a table beyond the shower. He wrapped one around her body, blotting the water from her face and hair.

Not bothering to dry his body, Shiloh carried Gwen back to the bedroom and placed her on the bed. A knowing smile parted his lips when she extended her arm, welcoming him into her embrace.

He came to her before reversing their position. Shiloh lay on his back, smiling up at his wife. This night was to become hers, then his.

A low, guttural groan came from his constricted throat when she lowered herself over his erection. It was only the second time they'd made love without the barrier of latex, and he struggled not to release the passion straining for a quick escape.

Gwen closed her eyes rather than watch Shiloh staring up at her. She set the pace, sliding up and down, around and around, until she wasn't certain who she was or where she was. All she knew was that the man she straddled was the one she would love with her dying breath. His hands tightened on her waist, urging her to go faster, and she felt her breath inching up in her lungs—higher and higher as she fought against waves of ecstasy sucking her into an abyss from which there was no escape.

Shiloh's hands moved from his wife's waist to her breasts. A keening sound penetrated their harsh breathing as he increased the pressure until they swelled, the nipples pebbling. He felt the burning at the base of his spine as blood rushed to his sex and his head. Having Gwen straddle him hadn't drawn out the dizzying pleasure rushing headlong for escape. She gasped again, this time in shock when, still joined, he flipped her over on her back.

Shiloh loved Gwen, hard, long and deep until he felt his heart beating outside his chest. Gripping the pillow beneath her head, he quickened his thrusts until the dam broke and all and everything he felt for the woman who now bore his name erupted in a turbulent maelstrom of ecstasy deeper than any he'd ever experienced in his life at the same time Gwen cried out his name in a fevered whisper of awe.

He pressed his mouth to the base of her throat, feeling the runaway pulse beating there. He'd climaxed, but he hadn't had enough of his wife. Sliding along the length of her body, his tongue surveyed an expanse of silken flesh and tasted salt in his downward journey.

Pushing his face against the moist curls, Shiloh revived her passion at the same time he was aroused to a fervor that made him want to lie between her legs until hunger and thirst forced him from her bed.

Reversing his direction, his mouth retracing his journey, he covered Gwen's mouth, permitting her to taste their flesh, and joined their bodies, then began the dance of desire all over again.

Gwen welcomed him into her body and as the real world spun and careened on its axis she was transported to one where only she and the man in her embrace existed. And they found a rhythm that bound their bodies, hearts and minds in a coming together that lingered beyond their lovemaking.

Shiloh waited until his respiration slowed and his heart resumed its normal cadence, then gathered Gwen to his side, one leg holding her fast. He smiled when she melted against him like a trusting child.

She was perfect.

His world was perfect.

* * *

Gwen walked into the SMPD station house, smiling at the red-haired uniformed officer at the desk. "Good morning, Deputy Lincoln."

Frank Lincoln stood up when he recognized his boss's wife. "Good morning, Mrs. Harper. Are you here to see your husband?"

"No. I have an appointment with Deputy Jameson."

Frank caught the gaze of several officers and civilian employees before he took a quick glance at the telephone console. "Deputy Jameson is on a call, but if you want you can wait for him in your husband's office."

"That's okay. I'll wait here for Deputy Jameson." She sat on a wooden bench, unaware of the grumblings from those participating in the station-house pool. Each time she came in and didn't enter Shiloh's office they were forced to add to the pot.

"What's going on here?" asked a deep, drawling voice. Gwen and the others turned to find Shiloh standing outside his office, arms crossed over his chest. "Not everyone speak at the same time. Is there a problem, Deputy Lincoln?" he asked when the others resumed whatever it was they were doing before Gwen walked in.

"No, sir. Your wife...I mean Mrs. Harper is here to see Deputy Jameson."

"Does he know she's waiting?"

"Not yet, sir. As soon as he completes his call I'll let him know."

Shiloh smiled at his wife as he struggled to keep a straight face. He'd heard about the office pool and knew the police and civilian staff were taking bets on whether he would cross the line with his personal and professional relationship with her. The last thing he wanted was for Gwen to become the brunt of a station-house prank.

"Have a good day, *Ms. Taylor.*" She'd decided to keep her maiden name as her byline.

She returned his smile. "Thank you, Sheriff Harper."

Shiloh waited until Gwen sat back down on a wooden bench before returning to his office. Their honeymoon of one day was much too short. He'd surprised her Sunday morning with breakfast in bed when he made buttermilk pancakes, spicy sausage links, sliced melon and coffee. They'd spent the day listening to music, and talking about what they wanted for their futures.

He'd told her of his professional goal to attain a judgeship by his fortieth birthday, but since falling in love with her that wasn't as important as making her happy, while she confessed to shortening her wish list to one entry: to live happily ever after. Right now he was a happily married man for all of ten days.

Leaning back in his chair, Shiloh stared at the bound report on the corner of his desk. It was a list of initiatives drafted by the sheriffs of Southern Louisiana, of which he was one of three vice presidents, that would be submitted to the state's Police Jury Association.

He opened the cover, then went completely still when he heard loud voices, then a gunshot.

His stomach muscles contracted. Gwen was in the waiting area!

Pushing back his chair, he vaulted over the desk and flung open the door, heart pounding. The scene unfolding before his eyes made the blood run cold in his veins. Gwen lay facedown on the floor under the bench; the other civilians were also on the floor, and Frank, gun in a two-hand grip, trained it on a disheveled gray-haired man whose own gun was pressed to the head of a scantily dressed young woman. Both were on their knees.

"Gwen, baby," Shiloh whispered harshly, "are you all right?"

"Yes-s-s," came her strangled cry.

"Don't move."

Knowing she was unharmed made what he planned to do easier. Holding his arms away from his body, he approached the elderly man, motioning to Frank to holster his firearm.

"Put down the gun, Wesley."

Red-rimmed rheumy eyes shifted to Shiloh. Wesley Gibson had begun drinking heavily after his wife of more than forty years left the parish with his best friend.

"I'm going to kill this bitch for stealing my money."

Shiloh did not drop his gaze as he closed the distance between him and the retired fisherman. "If she took your money, then I'll arrest her. But, first you have to put the gun down."

A dozen pairs of eyes were trained on Shiloh, the crazed man with a loaded gun, and the trembling young woman who cried silently.

Wesley's lower lip quivered. "I can't, Shiloh. She took all my money."

Squatting so he wouldn't appear threatening, Shiloh stared directly at Wesley. "What did she do?"

It took several attempts before Wesley disclosed how the young woman had approached him and offered to show him a good time. But it was going to cost him.

"How much did she charge you?" Shiloh asked.

"She said I had to give her fifty dollars."

"Did you give it to her?"

"Yes."

"Did you have sex with her?" Wesley nodded. "I have to hear you say it, Wesley, so I can charge her with solicitation and prostitution."

Wesley blinked rapidly, trying to focus his gaze. "Yes, I gave her money for sex. I gave her the fifty, and she took all the money I had in a drawer next to the bed. And when I woke up this morning I went looking for her. When I asked her for my money she told me she didn't have it because she gave it to her boyfriend."

"How much did she steal from you?" Shiloh asked.

"Three hundred dollars. It was all I had left from my social security check."

"Give me the gun, Wesley, so I can arrest her."

"Are you really going to arrest her?"

Shiloh extended his hand. "Give me the gun. Butt first."

Wesley's hand shook as he lowered the automatic and handed it to Shiloh. A chorus of sighs filled the waiting room as the woman scrambled to her feet and headed toward the door.

Shiloh stood up. "Where do you think you're going, miss?" he shouted at her. Teetering on a pair of five-inch heels, she turned around. Smudges from her damp mascara left black streaks on her pale face.

"He told me to take the money," she said quickly.

Shiloh gestured to Frank Lincoln. "Read her her rights, book her, then find out who her pimp is."

Jimmie, who'd come out of his office to watch the tense interchange, ran a hand over his shaved head. "What do you want to do with Wesley?"

Shiloh expelled a breath. "Put him in a cell until he sobers up." He handed Jimmie Wesley's handgun. "Please put this away, too." He leaned closer to his deputy. "Get my wife out of here, and she's never to come back again. I want you to either fax or e-mail her whatever she needs for her column to the *Tribune*."

Jimmie Jameson stared at his superior officer. "I don't think that's going to sit too well with her. I've been helping her with a cold case and—"

"I just gave you a direct order, Deputy Jameson," Shiloh said between clenched teeth.

Jimmie nodded, dropping his gaze. "Yes, sir."

Turning on his heel, Shiloh went over to Gwen, helping her to her feet. "Jimmie's going to show you out." Dipping his head, he kissed her cheek. "I'll see you later on tonight."

Gwen's chest hurt. It felt as if she'd held her breath during the entire time Shiloh was negotiating with the man he'd called Wesley, not releasing it until the older man handed over his gun.

"I can't leave now, Shiloh."

He stiffened as though she had struck him. "It is not an option." He'd stressed each word. "Either you leave now, or I'll make a public announcement that you're never to come in here again."

Her jaw dropped. "You can't do that."

His grip tightened on her elbow. "I can and I will."

Gwen's temper flared. She'd been scared witless when Wesley fired the gun at the ceiling, but defiance and boldness had returned with her husband's impertinent directive.

"I'm a taxpayer in this parish…" She was never given the opportunity to finish whatever it was she intended to say when Shiloh's fingers, tightening like a vise around her wrist, led her toward his office. He closed the door so hard the vibration rattled windows.

Shiloh's anger with Gwen had become a red-hot scalding fury. Did she not know how much he loved her, that during the short time he'd negotiated with Wesley he prayed that Wesley wouldn't lose it, shoot the young woman, then shoot up the station house? He hadn't married Gwen only to bury her.

"Don't give me the speech about the freedom of information act, Gwendolyn, because right about now I don't give a damn about your column. I cooperated with Nash when he came to me about creating the Blotter because he wanted to hire you. But it ends today, *now*. I'm going to call Nash

McGraw and let him know that there will be no more information coming out of this department."

Shiloh's tone and words infuriated Gwen. "How dare you try and interfere with my career!"

"I dare, Gwendolyn Harper," he countered. "I dare because I love you and want to protect you. But I can't do that if you expose yourself to what just happened here today."

"And you think you're less vulnerable than I am? That old man could've shot and killed you like that kid killed your father."

"You're wrong. Wesley is harmless," Shiloh lied smoothly. Drunk, depressed, penniless, and threatening to shoot someone, Wesley Gibson had become a living, breathing time bomb primed to detonate with the slightest provocation. His hand moved to her upper arm. "Either you leave here with Jimmie, or I'll lock your ass up in the back until my shift is over. The choice is yours, Gwendolyn."

Gwen was so furious she could hardly speak. Her breath burned in her throat like an out-of-control fire. How dare he threaten her as if he were an avenging demigod. "Take your hand off me."

Shiloh released her, watching as she opened the door and closed it quietly behind her. He felt no victory in bullying or intimidating her the way he had, but what his obstinate, headstrong wife failed to understand was that he had to keep her safe, and that he would willingly sacrifice his own life to accomplish that pledge.

Chapter 19

Shiloh's directive that he would no longer provide the editor of the *Teche Tribune* with information from his office impacted readers, crime victims, perpetrators, and Gwendolyn Taylor-Harper's marriage to the sheriff of St. Martin Parish.

She hadn't been married a month and she and Shiloh had become polite strangers despite the fact that they still shared a bed. They hadn't made love since the incident at the station house. They went to bed, their backs to each other and woke with their limbs entangled. The first time Shiloh demonstrated an overture that he wanted to make love to her she gave him the excuse that she was too tired.

And Gwen hadn't lied to him. Waves of fatigue attacked her when she least expected it. She would've blamed it on working too hard, but the fact remained that she was hardly working. Nash had reassigned her to write copy and proof-read, and this arrangement suited her needs because she was in the office all the time, which left more time for her to work on the prom queen murder.

She'd also suspected that maybe she could've been pregnant, but dismissed that notion when her menses came on time. Again, it was scant, but it wasn't the first time her menstrual cycle went a little awry. She was due for her annual gyn exam at the end of October, and she planned to ask Natalee for a referral.

Gwen didn't get to see as much of her sister-in-law as she would've liked because of the jewelry designer's busy schedule. At a moment's notice she would fly off to Los Angeles, New York, Miami or Europe to confer with her select group of clients who'd commissioned her to design a new bauble. Her name had been touted as a designer on the move and one to watch when she collaborated with Danish jewelry house Georg Jensen.

"Aren't you ready to come to bed?"

Gwen's head came up and she turned to find Shiloh standing under the entrance to the room they'd set up as an office. Her gaze lingered on his face rather than his bare chest and the white drawstring pajama pants riding low on his hips. Cocoa, who'd fallen asleep next to her chair got up when she heard his voice, and trotted over to Shiloh.

"Not yet."

"What are you working on?"

"Nothing that would interest you."

Shiloh's expression did not change. It'd been three weeks since the incident at the station house, and it was apparent Gwen wasn't going to let go of her anger because he'd banished her.

Crossing his arms over his chest, he glared at her. "Why don't you let me be the judge of that."

Gwen turned back to the photographs in the yearbook. "Wasn't it you that said we would keep our personal life separate from our careers?"

His eyebrow lifted. "Yes, I did. But right now we don't have a personal life, Gwen."

She closed her eyes for several seconds. "And I don't have a career," she countered.

"You have a career. You're working for the *Tribune*."

She swiveled on the chair, her gaze filled with resentment. "That may be true, but I'm doing the work of an intern, not someone with their own byline. I may as well not be working."

"Why don't you quit?"

"And do what?" she spat out.

"Aren't you involved with the Genteel Magnolia Society and the book you're going to write for them?" Once she'd become a member of the group she'd told him about the book.

"We don't meet during the summer months."

The seconds ticked off as they stared at each other. Shiloh was the first to break the impasse. "I have to turn in now because I'm scheduled to work a four-to-noon tomorrow."

Gwen nodded, but as he turned to leave she said, "What year did your mother graduate from high school?"

Shiloh halted his retreat, but did not turn around. "1964. Why?"

"Did she go to St. Martin Parish High School?"

Lines furrowing his smooth forehead, Shiloh turned and stared at his wife. "No. She went to a parochial school. Why the interest in my mother?"

"I came across an article about a girl who was murdered a week before she was scheduled to graduate from the high school."

"What about her?"

"The Shelby Carruthers case was closed two months after her decomposing body was discovered in a shallow grave with a single gunshot to the back of her head. I read the coroner's report which stated she was shot with a .22. What bothers me is that no one in forty-two years has tried to find out who murdered her. And another thing that bothers me is that if a search had been conducted when she didn't come home or when her mother reported her missing, couldn't a search dog have found her body?"

Shiloh entered the room and sat down in an office chair near the antique desk where photocopied articles about the unsolved murder littered the surface.

"Let it go, darling."

She ignored the first endearment he'd uttered since the tense confrontation in the stationhouse. "Why is it everyone's telling me to let it go?"

"What do you mean everyone?"

"Nash McGraw told me the same thing. And now I'm beginning to wonder why."

"The answer is an easy one."

"Please, pray tell me why, Shiloh."

Shiloh stared at the curls that looked as if Gwen had combed them with her fingers. He curled his hands into tight fists to keep from touching her. He'd thought about reversing his decision just to have his wife back to the way it was before the Wesley Gibson incident. But whenever he recalled his reaction to hearing the gunshot and knowing that Gwen could possibly be in the line of fire he refused to relent.

"That was another time. People were in another place."

"What aren't you telling me, Shiloh?"

"You're going to have to talk to people who were alive back then."

"Like who?" she said softly, her eyes narrowing.

"My mother and a number of the Genteel Magnolias."

She wavered, trying to understand the man she'd married. In one breath he'd warned her not to get involved in the cold case, then his mood changed abruptly when he offered information that could possibly give her a lead in the decades-old murder.

A smile softened her mouth. "Thank you, Shiloh."

His gaze fixed on her mouth, he leaned over and kissed her. "You're welcome."

Gwen stared at the man she loved beyond description. She wanted to forget that as a newlywed she hadn't felt very married, that she'd missed the passion, the intimacy she'd experienced with her husband.

"Don't go up. Not yet," she urged softly.

The gold in Shiloh's eyes disappeared, leaving them a deep green brimming with tenderness, understanding and a gentle passion. He ran a forefinger down the length of her short nose. "Why?"

A mysterious smile lifted the corners of her lush mouth. "Give me a few minutes to put the desk in order, and I'll go with you."

Shiloh's laid-back body language belied the anxiety knotting his stomach muscles. He didn't want to get his hopes too high, but he prayed he would get his wife back. He wouldn't rush her, would follow her lead, but he'd missed her, missed her despite the fact they shared a bed. He watched intently as she placed a number of typed pages into a folder before slipping them into a monogrammed leather case.

Reaching over, he turned off a desk lamp, and swept her up in his arms as a soft gasp escaped her. "Have you weighed yourself lately?"

Gwen gasped again. "No, I haven't. Why are you asking?"

Shiloh climbed the staircase as Cocoa sat at the bottom, watching their retreat. The tiny puppy still hadn't learned to navigate the staircase.

"You're putting on weight."

She closed her eyes and rested her head on his shoulder. "I don't know why, because I'm not eating that much."

Burying his face in the scented strands brushing his cheek, Shiloh concentrated on placing one foot in front of the other. He entered their bedroom, placing Gwen on the bed. Slowly, methodically he removed her T-shirt and shorts, leaving her bikini panties. His gaze lingered on her breasts as he went through the motion of untying the drawstring to his pajama pants. He pushed them down his hips and stepped out of them. Less than a minute had elapsed when he slipped into bed, turned off the bedside lamp, and gently pulled his wife to him. She'd didn't struggle or protest, melting against his side.

It was a truce, a very fragile one, and an unspoken promise to return to the way it had been and would be again.

Two days after Shiloh suggested to Gwen that she talk to his mother she uncovered something that she'd gone over countless times. She'd compiled a listing of the names of the school's student body, then cross-referenced them with clubs that Shelby belonged to. There was one name that came up time and time again: Nash McGraw. The future publisher of the *Teche Tribune* had been a classmate of Shelby Carruthers and had joined every club of which Shelby was a member.

Positioning the desk lamp, she peered at the pictures featuring the various school clubs. Sure enough, Nash was in every photo with Shelby. There were only a few shots where he'd remained in the background, but in many he was in the foreground with Shelby.

There was one photograph that held her rapt attention, and because the yearbook pictures were grainy and in black-and-white, some of the images weren't as sharp then as they would've been with the current cutting-edge technology.

She flipped back to the group photograph of the graduating class for 1963, then to the upcoming class for 1965. There were only thirteen dark faces in 1963, twenty-six in 1964, and fifty-two in the class of 1965. It appeared as if Louisiana had lagged behind some other southern states in integrating their public schools. Gwen opened and closed the drawers in the desk, searching for a magnifying glass.

Reaching for the telephone, she dialed Shiloh's number at the station house. A clerk answered the call and put her through as soon as she identified herself.

"Hey, you."

She smiled. "Hey, yourself. I need to ask a favor of you."

"Ask away, beautiful."

"I need you to stop and pick up a magnifying glass."

"Why would you need a magnifying glass?"

"I can't explain on the phone. Please, darling, pick one up for me."

His laugh flowed through the earpiece. "You know I can't deny you anything. I'll bring it home on my dinner hour."

"Thanks, my love."

"You're welcome."

Gwen ended the call and let out an audible sigh. There were a few photographs she wanted to give a closer look.

But first she had to decide what she would prepare for dinner. She'd teased Lauren about settling into her role as mother and housewife as easily as a duckling took to water, but she'd confessed to her cousin that she also loved being married and looked forward to becoming a mother.

The pages of the 1964 St. Martin Parish High School yearbook were littered with yellow Post-its. One in particular held a red check. Gwen held the magnifying instrument over Nash's image, her heart thundering like the hooves of a racehorse.

She squinted, and then pulled back to get a better perspective of what she'd recognized as a handgun tucked into the waistband of Nash McGraw's slacks under a jacket. But on the other hand it was the expression on Nash's face, and not the gun, that caused her breath to catch in her throat.

Nash wasn't looking at the photographer, but at a black male student who'd captured the adoring gaze of no other than Shelby Carruthers.

"Shiloh?"

"Yes."

"Come look at this, please."

"Can't it wait until I finish typing?"

"I don't think so."

Shiloh saved what he'd typed into his computer, then crossed the room and leaned over Gwen's shoulder. "What do you have?"

She pointed to one photograph before handing him the glass. "Look at this one and tell me what you see."

Shiloh read the picture caption. "Nash McGraw, Shelby Carruthers and Jason Jefferson."

"No, Shiloh. Take a closer look at Nash."

His eyes narrowed. "He's carrying a gun."

"Can you tell the caliber?"

Shiloh angled his head. "No. Why?"

"Shelby Carruthers was shot with a small-caliber handgun. The ballistics report Jimmie gave me verified the bullet that killed her was a .22."

Hunkering next to her chair, Shiloh gave his wife a long, penetrating stare. "What are you *not* saying?"

"I think Nash McGraw murdered Shelby Carruthers."

Shiloh sat on the carpeted floor and eased Gwen down on his lap. He looped an arm around her waist. "You can't go around accusing someone of murder without evidence."

Gwen shifted until she faced her husband. "I don't have any evidence—at least not yet, but I do have a theory."

"Theories are for scientific experiments, darling."

"I went over every photograph in the yearbook, and he's in every photograph someone took of Shelby. If he'd done now what he did then it would've been called stalking."

"They were classmates, Gwen."

"True. But he joined every club she belonged to. I spoke to Dahlia Townsend this morning, and she told me that Nash used to follow Shelby around like a lovesick puppy. That confirms my theory about his stalking. Dahlia also told me that Nash and his father argued constantly. Nash wanted to go to UCLA because Shelby had applied to go there. The elder McGraw wanted Nash to attend Loyola, his alma mater, graduate, and eventually take over running the newspaper."

Pressing her forehead to Shiloh's, she kissed the end of his nose. "I need your help, Shiloh. I want you to get a warrant to search Nash's house for the gun. I'm certain he didn't throw it away because if it'd been found, then it might have been traced back to him."

Shiloh wrapped his arms around Gwen's body, holding her protectively to his heart. "You're getting ahead of yourself, Lois Lane. First of all, no judge will issue a warrant based on your theories. And secondly, Nash McGraw is a descendant of one of the parish's prominent families.

"He's been married to the same woman for more than thirty-five years. He's a father, grandfather, and despite his neutrality as a newspaper publisher he wields a lot of political clout. And I'm willing to bet that he if decides to run for public office he'd win."

Gwen shook her head. "I don't know what it is, but my woman's intuition tells me that Nash had something to do with that girl's death."

A low rumbling sound came from Shiloh's chest when he laughed. "Does your intuition tell you what your husband has planned for his wife for their day off together?"

"Tomorrow?"

"Yes, tomorrow."

She kissed his chin. "Whatever you have planned will have to wait because your girls have doctors' appointments. Cocoa has a vet appointment at ten and I'm going to the gynecologist at two." Gwen had decided not to wait until October for an annual exam.

Lines of consternation marred Shiloh's forehead. "Is something wrong?"

She expelled a sigh. "I don't know. My period isn't normal, and I'm tired all the time. I know I'm getting enough sleep, and I have to force myself not to take naps."

"I'll go with you."

"You don't have to, Shiloh."

"But I want to. Later on we'll go somewhere and have an intimate dinner."

"How intimate?" she asked.

"Very, very intimate."

"That sounds good to me, lover," she crooned seductively.

Shiloh kissed her forehead. "Why don't you go upstairs and turn in. I'll be up as soon as I finish typing my notes."

He stood up, bringing Gwen with him, and staring at her retreating figure until she disappeared from his line of vision. Moving over to the desk, he picked up her printed notes. He sat down, the shock of what he was reading hitting him full force. His wife's meticulous notations were as detailed and comprehensive as a law clerk's.

Her theories were more than that. They were facts, broad, concrete facts. After he'd read the report from the coroner's

office he knew Shelby's killer wasn't a she, but a he. There
was evidence that Shelby Carruthers had been *raped!*

Gwen glanced at the pet carrier on the rear seat before maneuvering out of the parking lot behind the small animal
hospital. Cocoa was still asleep.

The spirited canine had snarled and snapped at the veter-
inary assistant whenever she tried opening the puppy's mouth
to examine her teeth, and in order to complete the examination Cocoa Taylor had to be sedated.

Her cell phone rang. She glanced at the display. "Yes, Mrs.
Carruthers."

"You've got to come quick."

Gwen heard the panic in her voice. "What's the matter?"

"Please come and I'll show you."

Ending the call, Gwen executed a U-turn, heading in the
opposite direction. When she drove onto the property Gwen
saw a police cruiser and Shiloh leaning against a porch
column. What, she pondered, was her husband doing at
Janet's house on his day off? She got out of her car and made
her way up the three steps to the raised porch. She couldn't
pull her gaze away from his stoic expression.

"What happened? Why are you here?"

Shiloh grasped Gwen's hands. He saw his wife staring at
him with a look in her eyes he'd never seen before: fear.

"I got here just before you did. Mrs. Carruthers placed a
nine-one-one call when someone threw a brick through her
bedroom window."

Gwen blinked once. "Maybe it was a bunch of kids acting
out. But why were you called on your day off?" she asked for
a second time.

Shiloh shook his head, his gaze fusing with hers. "It wasn't a bunch of kids. And Jimmie called me when Mrs. Carruthers told him about the note wrapped around the brick."

"What did the note say?"

"Whoever typed the note warned Mrs. Carruthers that if she doesn't stop asking questions, she's going to end up like her daughter."

"I don't understand, Shiloh."

"What is there not to understand?" he spat out. "You've opened a Pandora's box, and in doing so you've spooked a murderer who thought that he'd committed the perfect crime."

"There's no doubt my asking questions has someone running scared, but who?"

"Who else knows you're trying to solve Shelby's murder?"

"I don't know."

"Think, Gwendolyn!"

"Don't yell at me, Shiloh."

"I'm not yelling, darling. I just need answers so I know how to deal with this depraved cretin."

"I've had contact with people at the D.A.'s, M.E. and St. Martin Police Department offices. You know I spoke with Dahlia and Nash. What I don't know is how many people Janet Carruthers told."

Shiloh nodded. "Let's go inside and ask her."

Chapter 20

Shiloh flipped the pages of a parenting magazine without reading any of the articles. The smiling faces of babies staring back at him drew a smile from him. He wondered what the children he'd have with Gwen would look like.

The thought of Gwen pregnant *unnerved* him. He didn't want it to become a reality, not now, not when she'd involved herself in solving the prom queen cold case. Janet Carruthers had admitted that she'd told a number of friends that Gwendolyn Taylor, a reporter for the *Tribune* had offered to help solve her daughter's cold case.

Shiloh had turned over the note to the crime lab for fingerprint analysis, but whoever had typed the note had used gloves. Even the paper was unremarkable—a common rag variety sold in most office supply chains.

He was aware that the only way two people could keep a secret was if one were dead. A murderer had struck forty-two years ago, and there was no doubt he would strike again if not apprehended. The one noteworthy aspect of the law was there was no statute of limitations on murder.

"Mr. Harper, would you please come in."

Shiloh's head came up and he rose slowly to his feet. A nurse wanted him to follow her. His heart pounding painfully in his chest, he made his way out of the waiting area and into a large sun-filled office. All of his trepidation dissipated when he saw Gwen's smile.

She stood up and looped her arms around his neck. "We're going to have a baby," she whispered close to his ear.

He went completely still. "Are you sure?"

"Very sure," her doctor confirmed. "Congratulations, Shiloh."

Doctor Stephan Honoree and Shiloh Harper had attended the same high school and graduated the same year. Stephan had gone to college to enroll in a premed program, while it'd been prelaw for Shiloh.

Shiloh smiled at Stephan. "Thanks."

He'd thanked his former classmate when he should've been thanking his wife. He'd suspected Gwen was pregnant, but she'd insisted she wasn't. She'd put on weight, tired easily, and her body rejected anything with a trace of alcohol. Everything had happened so quickly: falling in love, marriage, and now the news he was to become a father.

Gwen felt the runaway beating of Shiloh's heart against her breasts as he sagged against her. "Don't faint on me, Shiloh," she chided softly.

He forced himself to stand upright. "I'm okay. When?" he asked Stephan. "When...can we expect the baby?"

"I'm estimating late April, but it can be earlier, because right now I'm not able to pinpoint conception. However, as

Gwendolyn advances in her pregnancy the due date will become more apparent."

Shiloh's right hand made soothing motions over Gwen's back as he met Stephan's gaze. "Is there something I should know...do?"

"Just make certain she doesn't overtire herself."

Gwen wanted to tell the two men there was no need to talk about her as if she weren't there, but fatigue weighted her down like a lead blanket. And the fatigue returned the same time every day like clockwork—midafternoon.

"My nurse will give you a prescription for a supply of prenatal vitamins, some literature both of you should read, and an appointment for Gwendolyn to come back in a month."

Shiloh extended his right hand. "Thank you, Stephan."

"I'm honored that I'll have the privilege of delivering your firstborn."

Shiloh held Gwen's hand as he led her to the parking lot. He still could not believe they were going to be parents. When he'd asked Gwen to "make a baby" he hadn't thought it would happen so quickly.

She fell asleep as soon as he drove away from the doctor's office. She didn't wake when he stopped at the pharmacy to fill her prescription, or when he undressed her and put her to bed.

She woke hours later, and instead of dining out they grilled salmon, corn and vegetable kabobs on a gas grill. Gwen made several calls to Massachusetts to inform her family members that she was pregnant, while he made his own celebratory telephone calls.

Shiloh shifted to a more comfortable position on the bed. "I want you to stop working."

Gwen went still as she listened to the steady beating of Shiloh's heart under her cheek. "You're kidding, aren't you?"

"No."

Tilting her chin, she stared up at her husband. The light from a bedside table lamp slanting over his face flattered his even, masculine features. "Why?"

"Because you need to rest."

"I only work two days a week, which means I have five other days to rest." She felt the tensing in her hands. "What's really bothering you, Shiloh?"

"Nothing."

"You're not a very good liar, Shiloh Harper. Is this because of my suspicions about Nash?"

Resting his chin on the top of Gwen's head, Shiloh closed his eyes. "Yes. I want you to stay away from him."

"I'm not afraid of Nash McGraw."

"If he is who you believe he is, then you should be afraid. If he killed once, then he will kill again."

"Nash may be scared, but he's not crazy."

"I still don't want you working with him."

"He's going to spook if I show up tomorrow and resign my position."

"I really don't give a damn how Nash feels, but the fact remains I don't want you working for him."

Pulling out of his embrace, Gwen sat up. "If I hadn't read those back issues of the *Tribune,* if the cold case of the 1964 Prom Queen Murder hadn't piqued my curiosity you would have no qualms about me working for Nash McGraw." She glared at Shiloh, silently daring him to refute her.

He avoided her glare when he stared at a trio of black-and-white prints of magnolias, gardenias, and roses on a far wall. "You're right." His gaze swung back to hers. "But don't expect me to stand by and let you become a potential murder victim."

"What if I tell Nash that I have to work from home until my fatigue passes?"

A hint of a smile touched Shiloh's mouth. "That should work. At least it won't arouse his suspicions while…"

"While what, Shiloh?" she asked when he didn't complete his statement.

"I'm going to have someone keep an eye on your boss."

Her eyebrows lifted. "Who?"

Shiloh ran his forefinger down the length of her nose. "I can't tell you."

Gwen pressed her fist to his chest. "Shiloh!"

He caught her wrist. "Even if you beat me into a pulp I won't tell."

"I know a way of making you talk, Sheriff Harper," she crooned, sweeping back the sheet.

"No!" he bellowed as Gwen slid down the length of his body. Her interrogation ended when he reversed their position and loved her until both babbled incoherently.

Waiting until his respiration slowed, Shiloh reached over, turned off the lamp, and shifted Gwen over his chest until her legs were sandwiched between his. He loved her, loved her more than he believed he could love any woman.

And if it was Nash McGraw who'd sent the threatening note to Janet Carruthers, then the newspaperman would do well to get his business and personal affairs in order.

Gwen knocked softly on Nash's open door. "Good morning."

His head came up. He stared at her as if he'd never seen her before. "Good morning, Gwendolyn."

"Do you have a minute?"

He motioned to her. "Of course. Come in and sit down."

Gwen walked into the office and sat down next to Nash's desk. She didn't want to believe the benign-looking man she worked for was capable of murder. She'd found him patient, soft-spoken and polite, and she wondered what had Shelby done or said to Nash that pushed him over the edge, led him to rape and shoot her.

"I have good news and bad news."

He closed his eyes for several seconds. "Give me the bad news first."

"I'm going to need to work from home for a couple of months."

Nash's blue-gray gaze narrowed slightly. "What's the good news?"

"I'm pregnant."

He affected a bright smile. "Congratulations. What you ask is doable, Gwendolyn. I'll drop your work off at your house, and you can call me when you want me to pick it up."

"You don't have to come to my house. I'll come in and pick it up."

He angled his head, frowning. "But I thought you weren't feeling well."

"I didn't say I wasn't feeling well. I tire easily, but my doctor said that will pass after a few months."

"It's your call how you want to do your work." He reached over and picked up a small envelope. "I need you to transcribe this before five." He handed her the envelope.

"What is it?"

"Taped debates between Gregory Walters and Julius Riley. I'm putting out a special pre-election issue tomorrow."

Gwen stood up, tapping the envelope against her palm. "I guess I better go home and get started."

Nash rose to his feet. "I'm sorry about the rush job, Gwendolyn."

"Don't worry about it." Gwen didn't know what was on the tapes or how long they'd run, but she had to get home and transcribe them.

* * *

"Shiloh, I can't believe you did this to me!"

Gwen closed her eyes while gritting her teeth. She'd transcribed more than twelve pages of text, but couldn't print it because Shiloh hadn't replaced the cartridge. She glanced at the clock. She would have to print the disk at *Bon Temps*.

She reached for the telephone. "Hey you," she said when Shiloh answered his cell phone.

"Hey yourself. What's up?"

"I need you to stop and pick up a couple of ink cartridges on your way home."

"Damn! I forgot to you tell you that I used up the last one."

"I'll forgive you this time. I'm going to *Bon Temps* to print and edit something Nash needs by five. I…wait a minute, Shiloh, I have another call."

"I'll pick you up at *Bon Temps*."

"Okay." She heard a second beep. "Bye, Shiloh." She pressed the TALK button. "Hello."

"Gwendolyn, Nash. I'm sorry to rush you, but I just got a call from the printer. He has to have our copy by four."

She glanced at a clock on a side table. It was 2:50. "I'm going over to *Bon Temps* to print out the disk. Meet me there in half an hour."

"Thanks, Gwendolyn."

She put the cassettes in an envelope along with the disk, picked up her cell phone, and dropped them in her handbag. She walked out of the office, Cocoa right behind her. Since her visit to the vet, the dog followed her every move.

"Do you want to come with Mama?" Standing on her hind legs, the poodle barked excitedly. Gwen leaned over and scooped up her pet. "If you behave in the car I'll give you a little treat after we get back."

Gwen booted up her laptop and inserted the disk. She smiled as Cocoa raced in and out of rooms, reacquainting herself with her first home. Leaning back in her chair, she waited as what she'd spent three hours typing came out of the printer. She'd removed all of her books and photographs and her desktop computer from the office at *Bon Temps,* but left the laptop and printer. The ringing of the doorbell coincided with the last page settling into a tray. Smiling, she went to answer the door.

"Come in, Nash. I just have to proof what I typed, then pull out a clean copy."

Nash checked the time on his watch. "What if I proof while you edit?"

"That's a good idea. It'll go faster that way. Come on back to the office."

Nash smiled as Gwen closed the door. He followed her out of the entryway and across the living room. "I can't believe what you've done to this place in just a couple of months. I've known restorations to go on for years."

Gwen glanced over her shoulder at Nash. "*Bon Temps* had fallen into disrepair not dilapidation like some of the other antebellum mansions."

"Your aunt gave some grand parties here."

"Did you ever attend them?"

"No. But my daddy did. He was one of those Southern white men who didn't mind mixing socially with coloreds."

An invisible shiver snaked its way up Gwen's spine. The newspaperman had used a term that had gone the way of segregation. She stopped, turned and faced him. "We haven't been colored in more than fifty years, Nash."

A flush suffused his face. "Oh, I forgot. You people have been called so many things that I can't keep up with them: Negro, colored, black, and now African-American."

Shock rendered Gwen speechless before rage replaced it. "How dare you, you racist bastard!"

To her surprise he showed no reaction to her cursing at him; their gazes met. Nash McGraw seemed to change before her eyes like a reptile shedding its skin. His blue-gray eyes paled, leaving them a cold, frosty gray. He reached under his jacket and pulled out a small handgun.

They were standing in a hallway, the space about six feet wide, the nearest door more than three feet away, and Gwen knew her chances of making it into her office and locking the door behind were, on a scale of one to ten, a one.

Sheer fright paralyzed her. Nash McGraw had killed once, and there was no doubt he could kill again. Panic like she'd never known gripped her, but she forced herself to remain calm.

"Is that the same gun you used to shoot Shelby Carruthers?"

A feral grin pulled one side of Nash's mouth upward. "Still the reporter, Miss Taylor? My bad! I forgot that you're now Mrs. Harper. You should've left the police work to your husband, Mrs. Harper. I told you to let sleeping dogs lie, but you wouldn't listen."

"Why did you kill her?" Gwen asked, stalling for time.

She knew she couldn't outrun a bullet, and there wasn't anything she could use to defend herself. She refused to believe she would die before bringing her child into the world or celebrating her first wedding anniversary.

Nash stared without blinking. "I did everything for that bitch, and all I asked was for her to go to the senior prom with me, but she turned me down because she was going with Jason Jefferson."

"You killed her because she planned to go to the prom with a black boy?"

"I killed her because she laughed at me. She said although I was nice, she could never think of me as her boyfriend."

"But you could've asked another girl."

"There were no other girls. I loved Shelby. I wanted to marry her, buy her pretty clothes, and have her live in a nice house. I wouldn't listen to my daddy when he told me to forget her because she was nothing but swamp trash with a pretty face."

Nash's eyes filled with tears as Gwen's gaze shifted from his face to the gun in his right hand. "You did marry, Nash," she said softly. "You have a wife, children and grandchildren who love you. You are the publisher of—"

"Shut up!" he shouted, interrupting. "Shut the hell up! And don't move!"

Gwen did move, and it was to lean back against the wall, her palms pressing against the recently hung wallpaper. She closed her eyes and prayed, prayed that her life and the growing life in her wouldn't end like Shelby's.

She'd spent years making lists of what she wanted and planned for her life, and not once had she ever planned for her own death. She opened her eyes, her mind a dizzying mixture of hope and fear when she saw Shiloh standing under the entrance to the hallway, gun drawn.

Gwen had forgotten he told her he would meet her at *Bon Temps*. With a barely perceptible motion, he cautioned her not to move. She acknowledged him with a slow blink.

Nash took several steps and caught her wrist. "Let's go."

She pulled back, but couldn't break his grip. "I'm not going anywhere with you," she countered defiantly.

"It's your call. Either I shoot you here or out in the swamp."

"You wouldn't shoot me here, because it would be too easy for the police to trace the crime back to you."

"I don't care," he snarled between clenched teeth. Spittle had formed at the corners of his mouth.

"Yes, you do care," she continued recklessly as Shiloh inched closer. "You committed the perfect crime, Nash, and you would've gotten away with it if I hadn't seen that article about the unsolved murder of the 1964 Prom Queen."

"You…" Nash swallowed his voice when he found his throat caught in a death grip, felt the press of a gun barrel against the back of his neck.

"Drop it or I'll blow your head off."

Nash recognized Shiloh's voice; he tightened his grip on the butt of his revolver. He couldn't breathe, and his lungs felt as they were exploding from lack of oxygen.

Shiloh's arm tightened. "I'd hate to soil my wife's new wallpaper with your brains or soil her priceless rug with fecal matter, but I will kill you if you don't drop that gun."

Cocoa came running when she heard Shiloh's voice. She stopped, growling and snarling at Nash before her teeth sank into a spot above his ankle, causing him to drop his gun. The .22 hit the rug and Cocoa skidded out of the way to avoid being hit. Shiloh spun Nash around, his left fist connecting with his jaw. Nash crumpled to the floor like a rag doll, his head at an odd angle. Shiloh secured the automatic in the holster on his hip.

Gwen slid down to the floor, tears streaming down her face. She closed her eyes as she registered the familiar sound of tightening handcuffs. She opened her eyes when she heard voices and footsteps coming in their direction. A female deputy and Frank Lincoln crowded the narrow hallway.

Shiloh's gaze shifted to his wife, unaware that his hands were shaking uncontrollably. "Read him his rights, then take him out of here."

"What are you charging him with, Sheriff Harper?" Frank asked as he helped Nash to stand. Swelling was evident over his jaw where Shiloh had punched him.

"Start with the attempted murder of Gwendolyn Taylor-Harper, and then the 1964 first-degree murder of Shelby Carruthers."

Frank Lincoln held Nash upright while Deputy Genaya Williamson intoned, "You're under arrest for the attempted murder of Gwendolyn Taylor-Harper. You have the right to remain silent…"

Shiloh dropped to the floor beside Gwen, pulling her into his lap. "It's over, baby." Cocoa scrambled up his leg and settled down over his knee.

"He…he was going to kill me," Gwen sobbed against his neck.

"No, he wasn't. I never would've let that happen. Do you think I would marry you and then not be able to protect you?"

"I…I…don't know."

Shiloh smiled. "You're going to have to learn to trust me, darling. I had someone watching Nash. He couldn't have left his house or office without my knowing his whereabouts. It was just luck that I told you that I'd meet you here."

Pulling back, she stared at the smirk on her husband's face. She placed her hands over his uniform blouse, feeling the Kevlar vest under the tan fabric. "Why did you want to meet me here?"

"I wanted to give you something."

She nodded, her eyes filling with tears again. "When are you off duty?"

Shiloh glanced at his watch. "In less than an hour. Why?"

"I just want to go home."

Cradling the back of her head, Shiloh brushed a kiss over her trembling, parted lips. "I'll take you home."

"Now?"

"Yes, now."

He came to his feet, bringing Gwen with him. "It seems like you're putting on some weight, Mrs. Harper."

She smiled and kissed the end of his nose. "That's because I'm carrying your baby, Mr. Harper."

"No!" he teased, grinning. "How did that happen?"

Joy bubbled in her laugh as she kissed Shiloh with all of the love she could summon for one person. Together they locked up *Bon Temps,* activated the newly-installed security alarm, gathered Cocoa and drove back to the gated community and the Louisiana low-country house that was home.

Shiloh watched Gwen as she slipped a black velvet bow off the silver paper covering a small flat box. He couldn't pull his gaze away from the soft swell of brown flesh rising and falling above the décolletage of a platinum-hued silk nightgown. A knowing smile parted his lips when she opened the box and gasped.

Gwen removed a stack of gift certificates wrapped in a narrow white satin ribbon. Her husband had given her a gift of a year of services at an upscale spa for a full day of beauty for the next twelve months. The spa was noted for offering special services to pregnant women and new mothers.

Moving over and straddling his lap, she pressed her breasts to his bare chest. "How can I thank you for being so thoughtful?"

Combing his fingers through her hair, he held it off her face. "Just stay as beautiful as you are now."

She closed her eyes, smiling. "That's not going to be easy once I blow up."

"Wrong, darling. You'll be even more beautiful."

"You only say that because it's your baby I'm carrying."

"Sure, you're right," he drawled. He lowered his hands and cupped her hips.

Resting her head on his shoulder, Gwen closed her eyes. "Do you know what I want?"

"Tell me, baby."

"A po' boy."

Easing her up from his shoulder, Shiloh stared at her. "You're kidding, aren't you?"

She shook her head slowly. "No. I'm craving a po'boy."

His hands tightened around her waist and he lifted her off his body. "What's up with the po'boy?" he mumbled under his breath as he made his way toward the adjoining bath. "Whatever happened to pickles and ice cream?"

"Did you say something, darling?" Gwen called out to him.

"No, sweetheart."

She slipped off the bed. "Would you like company when you go for the po'boy?"

Turning on his heels, he closed the distance between them. Wrapping his arms around her waist, he pulled her to his body. "I thought you'd never ask."

Gwen curved her arms under his shoulders and kissed him with a passion she was never able to communicate—at least not with words.

She never knew that when she skidded off the road and into a ditch that she would meet and fall in love with the sexiest lawman in Southern Louisiana.

Epilogue

Gwen could feel her knees shake as she held the bible on which her husband had placed his right hand as he was sworn in as a judge for the Louisiana Supreme Court. Her eyes misted and she closed them briefly as photographers captured the moment for posterity. She felt a tugging on the hem of her skirt, but refused to look down at her three-year-old daughter.

Bianca had promised her mother and father that she wouldn't say anything during Daddy's swearing-in, but they were taking too long. "Mama," she whispered softly.

Gwen cut her eyes at her daughter, who recognized the gesture immediately. Standing up straight, she raised her right hand as she'd seen her father do, then repeated his oath to uphold the constitution of the State of Louisiana and the United States of America.

Those who'd gathered in the Baton Rouge courthouse

heard the childish voice repeating the oath verbatim and dissolved into fits of laughter. Gwen called her daughter a myna bird because she repeated everything she heard, but the teacher at her preschool said the precocious little girl had the gift of total recall.

Gwen turned her attention to her husband. Former D.A. and former Acting Sheriff Shiloh Harper was now Judge Harper. He'd realized his dream and so had she.

It seemed as if time stood still in bayou country, but not for Gwendolyn Taylor-Harper. She was wife and mother of a toddler daughter and infant son. She met with the ladies of the Genteel Magnolia Society whenever time permitted, hosted tours of *Bon Temps* for school groups, scheduled fund-raisers and social events in the historic antebellum mansion, and kept her journalistic instincts sharp when she wrote articles for the new editor and publisher of the *Teche Tribune*.

Nash McGraw, who took a plea rather than embarrass his family with a trial, would spend the rest of his life behind bars for the murder of Shelby Carruthers and the attempted murder of Gwendolyn Harper.

James Jameson was elected sheriff of the SMPD.

Ian and Natalee Harper were expecting their first— twins.

Augustine Leblanc had asked Moriah to marry him, but she told him she had to think about it. It had been a year since he'd proposed, and she was still thinking about it.

Gwen winked at her mother, who cradled her three-month-old grandson to her chest. A photographer motioned to her to move closer to her husband.

"Here come da judge," she whispered softly.

Shiloh lifted his eyebrow in his best Dwayne Johnson

imitation. He looped an arm over her shoulder, the sleeve of his black robe a startling contrast to her oyster-white silk dress.

"Can you *smell* what the judge is cooking?" he whispered before he anchored a finger under her chin and kissed her mouth. He deepened the kiss and cameras and flashbulbs captured the image that would appear in a major daily with the bold headline: ENTRAPMENT!

HAPPILY EVER AFTER

HAPPILY EVER AFTER

Prologue

The taxi pulled away from the long line of yellow vehicles parked at the curbside arrivals at Logan Airport, heading for the Boston suburbs while the two passengers in the back seat were oblivious to the softly falling snow, the raucous honking of car and bus horns and the surreptitious glance the driver gave them in his rearview mirror.

Lauren Taylor-Samuels inched closer to her husband, luxuriating in his warmth and the now-familiar fragrance of his after-shave.

Cal Samuels smiled, threading the fingers of his right hand through the thick black hair falling around the shoulders of his wife.

His wife! The two words were the most reverent ones he had ever uttered in his life. A feeling of indescribable peace welled in his chest as he lowered his head and pressed his mouth to Lauren's soft, moist lips. She moaned under her breath and Cal deepened the kiss, easing her lips apart with his searching tongue.

Shifting slightly, his mouth traveled to an ear, over a closed eyelid and up to her flower-scented hair. "I can't get enough of you," he whispered for her ears only.

A light tinkling laugh filled the darkened interior of the taxi. "That's because you're insatiable," Lauren replied, her soft, husky voice fueling his rising passion.

Lauren's left hand was as busy as Cal's mouth when it slipped under his sweater, moving with agonizing slowness over his solid chest and down to his flat belly.

Her searching fingers elicited a tortured groan from Cal and he crushed Lauren to his side. He held her captive until the driver turned down the street to a home filled with heart-warming memories from his often unpredictable and some-times turbulent childhood.

The taxi stopped in front of a three-story town house ablaze with golden light from the first and second floors. Lauren waited inside the taxi until the driver retrieved her luggage from the trunk and Cal paid him. Then anxiety, raw and un-controllable shook her and there was no way she could hide her trembling from Cal as he grasped her hand to help her out of the car.

His free arm curved around her waist. "There's nothing to be nervous about. My grandfather will love you as much as I do."

She managed a small tight smile and followed Cal up the stairs. He inserted a key in the lock and the door opened into an entry filled with the muted glow from a Tiffany lamp, highlighting an antique drop-leaf table, two pull-up chairs, and the staircase leading to the upper levels.

He dropped her bags to the floor and captured both of her hands. "I'll introduce you to my grandfather, then I'll give you a tour of our apartment." *Our apartment*. Suddenly she was jolted into reality, her breath rushing from parted lips. "Are you all right, Lauren?" he asked, giving her a questioning look.

Lauren nodded numbly, unable to believe all that had happened and was happening to her. It was only now—after returning to Boston did she realize what she had done.

She had married a stranger—a man she had known for a week!

"Let me take your coat, darling." Lauren moved, trance-like, as Cal helped her out of her coat and hung it in a closet with his. "Come with me," he urged, leading her through a spacious antique-filled living room. "Gramps is probably in his library."

Lauren missed the library's exquisite handwoven imported rug, the massive cherrywood furniture, the books packed tightly on floor-to-ceiling shelves and the framed artwork hanging on two facing walls, when the leonine head of the man seated on a blood-red brocade armchair came up slowly.

He rose to his feet and Lauren unconsciously took a backwards step. Cal's chest pressed against her back, not allowing her to move or escape.

"Gramps, this is Lauren—my wife. Lauren, my grandfather, Dr. Caleb Samuels."

Caleb Samuels' spare frame made him appear taller and more imposing than his six-foot height. A shock of pure white curling hair framed his angular dark-brown face, while his dark eyes glowing from that face rooted Lauren to the spot. He smiled a tight cold smile, inclining his head slightly.

Cal gave her a slight push and she was galvanized into action, remembering her manners. "I'm…I'm honored… Dr. Samuels."

The elder Caleb's smile widened, but it still lacked warmth.

"You may address me as Gramps," he stated, making it sound as if Gramps was a royal title he had inherited from his father.

"Have you and Lauren eaten?" Dr. Samuels asked his grandson.

"We had a snack on the plane," Cal said, escorting Lauren to a love seat. He sat, pulling her down beside him.

"I'll have Mrs. Austin prepare a special dinner to celebrate your…" His voice trailed off as he returned to the armchair and stared at Lauren. "Your hasty marriage," he continued, re-directing his attention to Cal.

Lauren half listened to the conversation between her new husband and his grandfather as she contemplated how she had taken leave of her senses.

Here she was sitting in the library of a world renowned geneticist and winner of a Nobel Prize for Medicine while he glared at her. There was no mistaking his disapproval.

Her throat grew dry as she realized Cal was wrong—his grandfather did not like her. Not liking her meant he would never love her.

She stared at the heavy gold signet ring which had adorned Cal's little finger and now graced her ring finger. The ring and the man sitting beside her were reminders of a week of madness. A madness in which she fell in love with, and married a stranger.

But did she love Cal? Did she love him enough to share her life with him? What had she done? The questions attacked her relentlessly as the realization of her impulsiveness clouded her face with uneasiness.

"Are you going to keep your maiden name, Lauren?"

Dr. Samuels' question startled her. "I think I'll use Taylor professionally," she replied. "It would probably be a little confusing for Summit Publishing to have two Samuelses on their payroll." This disclosure seemed to please the elder Samuels because he gave Lauren his first sincere smile.

Cal's hand curved around her neck, bringing her head to his hard shoulder. "I think Mrs. Lauren Taylor-Samuels should rest before dinner. She's been up before dawn."

Dr. Samuels rose again. "Please forgive me. We'll talk later over dinner. Cal, put your bride to bed while I let Mrs. Austin know that we'll have company for dinner."

Perhaps it was her own uneasiness but Lauren recoiled when she registered Dr. Samuels' reference to her being company. She was his grandson's wife and therefore family, not company.

Cal needed no further prompting as he led Lauren up a flight of stairs to the second floor. "Mrs. Austin has been Gramps's cook and housekeeper ever since my grandmother passed away fifteen years ago," he explained quietly. "They can't agree on anything, but Gramps won't fire her because he says he won't give her that satisfaction. He claims he's waiting for her to quit."

If Cal sought to lighten Lauren's mood, he failed. She stood in the middle of a large bedroom, staring up at him. "Your grandfather frightens me," she blurted out.

Cal wound his arms around her waist, pulling her close to his body. "I admit he's a little imposing when you first meet him but he's actually a pussycat, darling."

Cal's assessment of his grandfather did nothing to lessen Lauren's insecurity and she realized it wasn't the older man's disturbing presence as much as it was her own doubts and fear.

On Cay Verde it was all right for a twenty-two-year-old researcher to fall in love with best-selling writer C. B. Samuels and marry him after a week of passionate, unbridled lovemaking; but it seemed as if her sanity returned the moment she and Cal returned to a cold and snowy Boston, Massachusetts. The frigid wind cooled her passion, sweeping away the warm memories of the Caribbean island where she had lost herself in the lushness of the tropics and Caleb Samuels' expert seduction.

"Why don't you try to get some sleep," Cal suggested. He kissed the tip of her nose. "I don't want you to look as if I've kept you up all night when I get to meet your parents tomorrow."

Her parents. How was she to explain to her parents that she had married a stranger? She, Lauren Taylor, who had never done anything impulsive in her life had suddenly lost her heart and head to a sybaritic writer.

Lauren willed her mind to go blank before she dissolved into a paroxysm of tears. She undressed slowly and slipped into a nightgown after Cal returned with her luggage. She watched him watch her as she sat down on the edge of the bed she was to share with him. Could she pretend she loved him because at that moment she wasn't sure whether she truly did.

"Everything's going to be all right, darling," he said softly, as if reading her mind.

I hope you're right, she thought. Minutes later she lay in bed with Cal, staring up at the darkness. She ignored the hardness of his naked body pressing intimately to hers, feigning sleep. It was only when she heard his soft snores that she relaxed enough to find her own solace in sleep.

Lauren managed to finish her dinner without bolting from the table whenever she glanced up to find Dr. Caleb Samuels visually examining her. A shudder passed through her and somewhere she found the strength not to cry.

He hates me and I hate him.

How was she to live in a house with a man who hated her as much as he loved his grandson?

But he can't hate you, a little voice whispered in her head. He doesn't know you.

She drank two glasses of the rich red wine and it was enough to dull the misery pressing down on Lauren like a steel weight. She had made a mistake. She never should've married Cal. She didn't love him. She couldn't love him. She was too inexperienced to be a wife—especially to a man like Caleb Samuels.

Dr. Samuels touched a white linen napkin to his mouth. "I must excuse myself because I have a speaking engagement early tomorrow morning and I have to go over my notes before I turn in."

Leaning back in his chair, Cal nodded, smiling. "Good night, Gramps."

Lauren offered a small smile, mumbling, "Good night."

Cal waited until Dr. Samuels left the dining room, then reached across the table and refilled Lauren's glass. His golden-brown eyes lovingly caressed her delicate face. "I can't believe how lucky I am to have found you, Lauren." She rewarded him with a sensual smile.

Cal continued to stare at her as she sipped her wine. Could he see her fear, doubts? Did he know what she was thinking, feeling? He drained his glass, then rose to his feet and extended his hand across the table. "Let's go to bed."

Lauren did not protest when Cal gathered her in his arms and carried her up the staircase to their bedroom. She forgot about Dr. Samuels' censuring glares when she succumbed to the drugging effects of the wine, leaving Cal tossing restlessly until sleep overtook him.

Lauren lay staring up at the ceiling and waiting for dawn. She had reached a decision. What she was feeling now she felt when she first met him. She wanted away from him—out of his presence.

As Lauren Taylor the researcher, she had held her own with him, but as Lauren Taylor the woman he had overwhelmed her, and she knew she had to put as much distance between herself and Caleb Samuels or she would never survive his dynamic personality. She wasn't equipped to continue the farce she had helped create.

He had called her a child when she was introduced to him, and how right he was. She thought she was a full-grown woman, but her impulsiveness had proven the contrary.

Cal registered her change in breathing and turned over to find Lauren wide awake. His hand began a leisurely exploration of her exposed thighs.

"Don't!" Lauren commanded, her hand stopping his.

Moving quickly, Cal straddled her body, supporting his weight on his arms. "What's the matter, darling?"

Lauren pushed against his shoulders. "I don't want you to touch me."

A frown creased his forehead. "Don't touch you or don't make love to you?"

"Both." He released her and Lauren sat up, pressing her back against the headboard.

Cal inhaled deeply, closing his eyes. "What's up, Lauren?"

She combed her mussed hair away from her forehead with her fingers. "I can't be married to you," she blurted out.

He smiled. "That's too late because we are married."

"What I mean is that I can't *remain* married to you." Lauren closed her eyes, not seeing the blood darken Cal's tanned face as his eyes flamed with liquid gold fire.

"Say it, Lauren." His voice had a tone of lethal softness that frightened her more than if he had shouted at her.

"I'm leaving you," Lauren said without hesitating.

"Why?"

"Because...because I don't love you. I made a mistake to agree to marry you." She opened her eyes, registering his stoic expression, and at that moment he was a replica of his grandfather.

"I don't think I want to be married—not to you—not to anyone," she continued.

Cal stared at her, not moving or saying anything. If he had said something it would have made it easy—a lot easier for her.

Lauren panicked, tears filling her eyes and overflowing down her sable-brown cheeks. "Think of my happiness, Caleb!" she screamed.

Cal's gaze was cold, vacant and then he nodded. He hadn't said she could go, he just nodded.

Lauren never remembered dressing or packing her clothes or the taxi ride that took her home to her parents. She did remember walking into her mother's outstretched arms and collapsing with the pain and shame that shattered her into so many pieces that she wasn't certain whether she would ever be whole again.

Dr. Samuels returned in time to overhear the last of Cal's conversation before he replaced the telephone receiver on its cradle.

"Where are you going?"

Turning slowly, Cal stared at his grandfather. "Back to Spain."

"Where is she?"

Cal's jaw hardened as he slipped his hands into the pockets of his slacks. "She's gone."

"And you let her go?"

"Yes, Gramps. I let her go."

"Why?"

In spite of his pain Cal managed a brittle smile. "I want her happy. I love her just that much."

"And she wasn't happy with you?"

"No." His mouth thinned to a hard thin line before he turned on his heel and stalked out of the library.

Dr. Samuels' gaunt frame swayed slightly before he moved over to his desk. It had begun again. It was like it was nearly thirty years ago, and it was happening again with another generation. He was not able to change the past, but he was damned if he wouldn't do something this time.

Picking up the telephone, he dialed a number. "I need you to do some research for me," he said without preamble. "I want you to check out a Lauren Taylor. She lives in Boston and works as a researcher for Summit Publishing." The person on the other end of the telephone line needed no additional information. Her name was enough.

Dr. Samuels replaced the receiver and smiled. His dark eyes danced with sinister triumph, because he would make certain Lauren Taylor-Samuels would pay for her deceit.

Chapter 1

"When are you going to let Drew spend some time with me? You've lived here for nearly two months and in all of that time I've seen my grandson once. I can forgive you for everything else, but not that, Lauren Vernice Taylor."

Lauren peered calmly at her mother over the rim of a tall glass of iced tea. It was a familiar tirade. Even when she and Drew lived less than a mile from her parents, it was the same. Odessa Taylor complained bitterly that she did not see enough of her only grandchild.

"Drew has made new friends, Mama," Lauren replied in a quiet tone. "There're times when he doesn't want to come home to eat."

Odessa's delicate eyebrows formed an agonized frown. "You're not letting him eat with strangers, are you? Now, you know how I raised you, Lauren. Eat at your own table and sleep in your own bed."

Lauren gave Odessa a look that infuriated the older woman. "I can afford to feed my son and keep a roof over his head."

Deep color darkened Odessa's burnished-gold face and a sprinkling of freckles stood out in startling contrast across her nose and cheeks. At fifty-one she had given up trying to conceal them with makeup. Her clear brown eyes widened at Lauren's veiled retort.

"I know you can take care of your son, Lauren. You've proven that over the past four years."

Lauren placed her glass of tea on a table and moved closer to Odessa on the wicker love seat. Looping her arms around her neck, she pressed her lips to Odessa's stylishly coiffed short hair. "I'm sorry, Mama. I didn't mean to snap at you."

Odessa cradled Lauren to her shoulder. "Forgive me, baby. There are times when I can't stop being a mother."

Lauren's velvet black eyes caressed Odessa's exquisitely sculptured face. "No more than I can help being just like you, Mama. We may not look anything alike, but that doesn't change a thing. I *am* your daughter when I reprimand Drew that he doesn't need to sleep over at his friend's house because he has his own bed to sleep in."

Odessa and Lauren didn't look anything alike, but each woman had claimed her own beauty. At five foot three Lauren was delicate and fragile, her body softly curving and feminine. Her skin held the sensual deep browns of sable and mocha, reflecting a natural sheen of good health. Her large eyes sparkled like polished jet, mirroring her ebullient personality, and like Odessa's, Lauren's short hair was expertly coiffed and the overall result was a quiet, deceptive beauty.

Odessa patted Lauren's cheek. "You've done well by the boy, sweetheart."

Lauren pulled away from her mother, staring at the small bird perched on the railing of the wraparound porch. "He's my life."

"Will you ever make room for someone else, Lauren?"

Lauren ran a hand through her own hair, sighing. She wondered why her mother had waited this long to bring up the subject of her not dating or trying to secure a husband. Odessa usually began the moment she stepped out of her car, because there was nothing that the two women could not discuss openly with each other.

"Not now. I'm too busy."

"You're too busy, Lauren? When you go to bed at night—alone—are you too busy to feel lonely? You're only twenty-seven. Why have you elected to spend your life denying your femininity?"

Lauren stood up and walked over to the steps. She sat down on the top one, feeling Odessa's gaze boring into her back. "I don't deny I have physical urges," she confessed.

"But do you do anything about them?" Odessa questioned.

She propped her elbows on her knees, shaking her head. "No, I don't."

"Why not, Lauren?"

Confusion filled Lauren's dark eyes. Her expression was strained, somber. Flashes of an island, a week of frivolity, came back with sharp clarity as her lids fluttered. Images of a couple, a man and a woman, tawny-brown and sleek sable-hued limbs blending and writhing in unbridled passion on a large bed, washed over her.

"Why not?" Odessa repeated.

Lauren's shoulders slumped. "Because I'm not looking for a husband."

Odessa left the love seat and sat down beside Lauren, un-mindful that she wore raw silk slacks. "It doesn't have to be the way it was before, sweetheart. You were so young, so inexperienced."

"I was twenty-two and experienced enough, Mama."

Odessa's arms curved around Lauren's slim waist. "You may have been experienced, but certainly not worldly."

"That still doesn't change the fact that I should've never married Caleb Samuels."

"If that was the only way for me to get my grandson, then I'm glad you married Caleb Samuels," Odessa stated firmly. "But because you're a single mother it doesn't mean that you have to stop living. You're bright and you're gorgeous. Men should be wearing out the grass beating a path to this place."

Lauren managed a smile. "You're quite biased, Mama."

Odessa tilted her chin. "I have to be. You're a part of me. And you're my only child."

Lauren kissed Odessa's cheek. "I love you." Her eyes crinkled in laughter. "I'm going to make you a promise. As soon as Drew is in school I'm going to go out and get involved in some local organizations."

Odessa did not look convinced. "Does Andrew Monroe have anything to do with you not seeing other men?"

Shifting, Lauren stared at her mother. She knew Odessa always spoke her mind, but this was the first time she had ever mentioned the possibility that she thought Lauren was involved with Andrew.

"Andrew is my agent," Lauren stated in a voice laced with repressed annoyance.

Odessa ignored Lauren's indignant tone. "But does he want to be more than your agent, Lauren? Perhaps he wants to be your lover. Or better yet, your husband and a father to Drew?"

Lauren rose to her feet brushing off the seat of her shorts.

"Andrew will never be more to me than what he is now. And that is my agent and my friend."

Odessa stood up, towering above Lauren by four inches. "Don't misunderstand me. I like Andrew, Lauren."

"So do I, Mama. But not that way," she declared, waving at the mail carrier.

The mail carrier returned her wave, holding up a large envelope. An overnight envelope usually meant a check from Andrew. The last packet of research he had sold for her had earned him a sizeable commission.

"Good morning, Lauren," he called out as he made his way up the path to the house. "Wonderful weather we're having."

Bright sun glinted off Frank Burton's orange-red hair. Working outdoors and without a hat had turned his delicate skin the same fiery red as his hair.

Frank handed Lauren the envelope and a pen, nodding at Odessa. "Good morning, ma'am."

Odessa gave him her best smile. "Good morning."

Lauren glanced at the return address on the mailing label as she scrawled her signature across the receipt. She was surprised to see the letter was not from Andrew.

Frank took his copy of the receipt, flashing a toothy grin. "Have a good day, ladies."

"You too," Lauren and Odessa chorused in unison.

Odessa watched Lauren open the mail, then extract a smaller white envelope. "Who's it from?" she asked, noting Lauren's puzzled expression.

"It's from a Boston law firm."

Odessa looked over Lauren's shoulder. "Is someone suing you?"

Lauren slid a finger under the flap. "I hope not." No one

would ever sue her directly; she was a researcher and Andrew Monroe agented her work.

Her eyes quickly scanned the single sheet of type, rereading the words and not believing what she had read. Her legs were trembling as she sank down to the porch step, the paper fluttering to the ground.

Odessa caught her daughter's shoulders as she supported her head against a column. "What's the matter, baby?"

Lauren felt as if she had been transported back in time. It was mid-June, but then it could have been that brutally cold day in December when she and Caleb returned to Boston after a week-long stay on a private Caribbean island and she told him she no longer wanted to be married.

Icy fingers of fear had crept up her legs and lodged in her chest when she remembered Cal's expression. The fear had seized her heart, not permitting her to draw a normal breath. Now that same fear had returned.

"He knows, Mama," she mumbled. Her worst nightmare had surfaced.

"He who, Lauren?" Odessa could not disguise the hysteria in her voice.

"Cal knows."

"You're not making sense, Lauren."

Lauren paused to catch her breath. "There's going to be a reading of Dr. Caleb Samuels' will and I've been summoned to attend."

"What does that mean?"

Lauren closed her eyes, reliving the old man's face. Cal had brought her to meet his grandfather the day they returned to the States. She had spent one night under the elderly man's roof, seeing his censuring glares before she realized she had been too impulsive, that she shouldn't have married his grandson.

"It means that the late Dr. Caleb Samuels must have uncovered that I had given birth to his great-grandson."

Odessa put her hands on her hips. "How? And if so, why didn't he acknowledge Drew while he was still alive?"

Lauren opened her eyes. "I don't know. But I do know that Cal will be at the reading of the will."

"And you're going to attend. You have to, Lauren," Odessa insisted, seeing her daughter's impassive expression. "It's not for you, but Drew. You owe that to your little boy. He has a right to know who his father is."

"Let's not talk about rights." No one protected her right to choose when Cal took advantage of her vulnerability.

"But Caleb Samuels is Drew's father, and he has a right to know that he has a son."

"What will it all prove? Cal is as much a stranger to me as he'll be to Drew. There's no need to disrupt three lives: mine, Drew's and Cal's."

Odessa gave Lauren a long, penetrating look. "I think you're the only one who would be upset by all of this. It's going to come back to haunt you one of these days when Drew finds out that he could have had a relationship with his biological father but didn't because his mother didn't want to reopen an old wound. A wound too painful to bear."

"But Cal hates me, Mama. What if he wants Drew for himself? He hates me enough to fight for his son. I can't take that chance."

Odessa kissed Lauren's forehead. "I doubt that, sweetheart. Women don't lose their children that easily—even if the child's father is Caleb Samuels. And you can't take the chance that you won't lose Drew when he discovers years from now that you kept him from his father."

Lauren felt the tightness easing in her chest. "I know you're right. Deep down in my heart I know you're saying all of the right words."

"Don't listen to me. Think of Drew, then think of yourself. You've grown up with both of your parents. Isn't Drew entitled to that?"

"Cal lives in Spain," Lauren argued.

"Then perhaps Drew can spend his summers in Spain with his father."

"No!"

Odessa released Lauren and rose to her feet. She knew her daughter well enough not to press her. "Think about it, Lauren. I'll call you later."

Lauren sat on the porch step long after Odessa had driven away. She tried not thinking of the curve life had thrown her. One step forward, two steps backwards, and like it had happened one December day, Caleb Samuels would walk back into her life and change her forever. Only this time she would be prepared for him.

"Good morning. I'm Lauren Taylor. I have an appointment with Mr. Evans for ten."

The secretary offered Lauren a friendly smile. "Good morning, Miss Taylor. Mr. Evans will be with you shortly. You're to have a seat in the conference room. This way please."

Lauren followed the secretary up a flight of carpeted stairs in the elegantly appointed two-story building. She was shown into a spacious conference room with paneled walls and exquisite reproductions of pictures.

"Would you like a cup of coffee or tea, Miss Taylor?" the secretary asked.

"No—no thank you," Lauren replied, unable to pull her gaze away from the man seated at the oaken conference table.

Cal Samuels held back his surprise, rose to his feet, circled the table and pulled out a chair for Lauren in a show of civility, of politeness. It was as if nothing had happened; as if he had never met Lauren Taylor; as if they had never laughed, loved and married.

"Thank you," Lauren mumbled softly. He lingered over her head, inhaling the scent of her perfume, his warm breath increasing the heat in her face.

Cal straightened, moving away, and retook his own seat. An inner strength he never knew he possessed permitted him to affect his air of indifference while every nerve in his body screamed rage and frustration.

Seeing Lauren, being so close to her, threatened to break the fragile hold on his iron-willed control. He fixed his gaze on her small hands, recalling the heavy weight of his ring on her delicate finger.

His gaze returned to her face, and he was shocked by the full impact of her mature beauty. The little girl in a woman's body was gone; the naïveté in her large, expressive dark eyes was missing, and the waiflike slimness of her petite body had also vanished.

Everything he had remembered about her had disappeared and was replaced by a woman so hypnotically beautiful that for a brief second he was blind to her deceit.

He had loved her; he had offered her his life and his protection and she had thrown both back in his face.

I don't think I want to be married—not to you—not to anyone.

Her parting words were branded in his brain. He would carry them to his grave. Staring openly at her, Cal realized Lauren was alluring and much more composed than she had ever been five years before.

He hadn't thought he would ever see her again, and he

wondered why she had been summoned to the reading of his grandfather's will.

Lauren returned Cal's bold stare. He was graying prematurely. She wondered how old he was now—thirty-three or thirty-four? Staring at him, she saw more changes. He wore his hair closer-cut than he had when they married. His tawny skin was darker, bronzed by the Mediterranean wind and sun.

However, his eyes had not changed. They were still brilliant amber fires. But now they appeared more yellow than gold. She studied his face, feature by feature, noting that age had given Caleb Samuels a masculine sensuality not seen on many men.

She dropped her gaze. What unnerved her more than seeing Caleb Samuels again was the realization of how much Drew resembled his father. Drew had inherited Cal's angular face, black curling hair, high forehead and strong jaw. The little boy was an exact replica of Caleb Baldwin Samuels II.

The silence between them was smothering, deafening in its thickness. Cal's expression was grim as he watched her and Lauren was overwhelmed with the anguish stirring within her; she had lied to herself—over and over. Even when she knew it, she still lied. The knowledge twisted in her until she wanted to shout out that she loved him—had always loved him.

The door to the conference room opened and the cloying scent of an expensive perfume wafted through the space as a tall woman strode in. This time Cal was slower in rising to his feet when he glared at the woman dressed in black linen with a vibrant Valentino scarf draped casually over one shoulder. Her body was lush, her face a perfect oval, and she carried herself confidently, seemingly aware of the appreciative glances that followed her.

"Good morning, Caleb," she drawled. Her voice was low and hard, belying her curvaceous body and pampered face.

"Is it, Jacqueline?" he returned, his eyes blazing with an unnamed emotion.

Lauren watched Cal and the woman, feeling their tension. The woman was older than Cal, but not by much.

The woman Cal had addressed as Jacqueline gave him a sensual smile. "Of course it is, darling." She slid gracefully onto a chair. "After the reading of your grandfather's will we'll never have to see each other again." Cal sat down, his mouth tightening.

A pregnant silence ensued, Lauren staring at Cal, he staring at Lauren and Jacqueline throwing glares at Cal and Lauren. It was apparent there were bad feelings between Cal and Jacqueline and Lauren was certain Cal's hostility also extended to her because if his grandfather knew about Drew she was certain he also knew about his son, and she wondered why he hadn't asked her about the child.

She had tried to contact Cal after their marriage was annulled and she discovered herself pregnant—there was no way she was going to beg him to take her back because she was carrying his child; but if Cal had come after her asking that she give their marriage a chance she would've fallen into his arms and begged for forgiveness. But he did not come and she did not tell him that he had a son.

Nervously, Lauren crossed her legs under the table, smoothing out the slim skirt to her white silk dress. Unlike Cal and Jacqueline, she had selected pale colors: a white wrap dress with a shawl collar, white ostrich-skin pumps and matching shoulder bag. The color was the perfect foil for her clear sable-brown skin tones.

The door opened and closed a final time. A man entered,

cradling a folder under his arm. He took a chair at the head of the table.

His eyes were friendly behind the lenses of his glasses. His thinning hair was cut close, while he had compensated for his hair loss by affecting a neat beard.

"I'm John Evans," he began in a soothing, professional tone, "and I'm responsible for handling the legal work on Dr. Caleb Samuels' estate." He opened the file folder. "Miss Taylor?" Lauren nodded in acknowledgement. "Mrs. Samuels and Mr. Samuels."

Lauren's pulses raced and she wondered if Jacqueline was Cal's wife. She sucked in her breath slowly, then let it out, and for the first time since she'd received the letter from Barlow, Mann and Evans, she questioned her sanity. What was she doing here?

It's not for me; it's for Drew, she'd told herself and continued to do so. Her mind wandered when John Evans began reading from several typed pages in the file. She forced herself to concentrate on what he was saying.

"Dr. Samuels had our firm draw up what is considered a simple will," John continued. "His estate will be divided into three equal shares, the first going to his alma mater, Fisk University. A contribution of one million dollars has been designated to build the Dr. Caleb B. Samuels Academic Center from the proceeds of the sale of land of family holdings in Mississippi, Alabama and Georgia, originally deeded to Elias, Marcus and Jefferson Samuels, dated eighteen eighty-three, eighty-five and eighty-nine respectively. This contribution will be used to increase classroom space and house a research center dedicated to the study of African-American history.

"A gift of one million dollars from awards, including the Nobel Prize for Medicine, will be bestowed to St. Martin's

Hospital for their continuing research efforts in sickle cell anemia."

Three pairs of eyes were trained on the attorney. Lauren felt John Evans was saving the best for last. She glanced down at Jacqueline Samuels' clenched fingers. The band of diamonds on the third finger of her right hand glittered in contrast to her smooth umber coloring.

"Dr. Samuels has bequeathed the remainder of his estate to his great-grandson Drew Michael Taylor-Samuels."

"What!" Jacqueline screamed, bolting from her chair.

"Please, Mrs. Samuels," John pleaded.

Jacqueline recovered quickly, retaking her seat and smoothing back her straightened hair. "I'm sorry, Mr. Evans. It's just that it has come as a shock to hear that Dr. Samuels has a great-grandchild." She shot Cal a withering look then turned her wild-eyed gaze on Lauren.

"Just who the hell are you anyway? You don't look like *his* type," she said, frowning and marring her almost too-beautiful face.

Cal's eyes raked Lauren like fired citrines as his chest rose and fell heavily under the crisp front of his white shirt. Seeing Lauren again had robbed him of speech, and in its place was repressed rage. Now he knew why Lauren had been summoned to the law office. She had had his child. She had kept his son from him. She had compounded her deceit by not letting him know that he was a father.

"I'd like to continue, Mrs. Samuels," the attorney admonished in a velvet tone.

Jacqueline shifted her eyebrows. "Please do."

"There is proof that this child Drew Michael Taylor-Samuels is the issue of Dr. Samuels' grandson, Caleb Baldwin Samuels II, and Miss Lauren Vernice Taylor."

There was no doubt about Drew's paternity, Cal thought. Lauren was the only woman he had ever slept with, whom he deliberately wanted to get pregnant.

"What kind of stunt are you two trying to pull off?" Jacqueline gasped. She turned to Lauren. "You scheming little thief! You conspired with this piece of slime to cheat me out of what is due me."

Cal was galvanized into action. His open hand came down hard on the table, the sound resembling the crack of a rifle. "Watch your mouth, Jacqueline," he warned in a dangerously soft voice.

She half rose to her feet. "Or you'll what, Caleb?"

John Evans stood up. "Please, please. Try to restrain yourselves. I'd like to conclude this as soon as possible."

"Oh, there's more, Counselor," Jacqueline sneered.

John nodded. "Yes, Mrs. Samuels, there's more."

"Well, let's hear the rest of this bull," Jacqueline mumbled angrily.

John straightened his tie and sat down. "A trust fund will be set up in the name of Drew Michael Taylor-Samuels in the sum of one million dollars. Drew Michael Taylor-Samuels will be eligible to withdraw the sum total of one hundred thousand dollars each year, commencing with the anniversary of his twenty-first birthday.

"Drew Michael Taylor-Samuels will be entitled to this privilege with the proviso his parents Caleb Baldwin Samuels II and Lauren Vernice Taylor marry and share a common domicile within sixty days of the reading of this will, and shall remain married for a period of not less than one year. Failure to marry or to maintain a common domicile for the specified time stipulated by the terms of this document will nullify this clause and the proceeds are transferable to Jacqueline Harvell Samuels by default."

A smile played around the corners of Cal's mouth as he crossed his arms over his chest. Even though his mouth was smiling, his eyes were hard and cold.

"The sly old fox," Jacqueline mumbled softly, shaking her head. "He holds out the carrot, then snatches it back. I've always hated that heartless old bastard."

John Evans closed the folder. "Does everyone understand the terms of this will?"

Lauren understood it—too well, but that did not mean she would agree to the terms. There was no way she was going to let Dr. Samuels control her, not even from his grave.

A million dollars was a lot of money for Drew. More than she could ever hope to earn in her lifetime. She chewed her lower lip, frowning slightly. But what if Drew wanted to become a doctor like his great-grandfather? Would she be able to afford the cost of medical school without securing loans? Probably not, however she wasn't willing to tempt fate by permitting Cal in her life again. She had no intention of marrying Cal again just so that her son could inherit someone else's money.

Cal rose to his feet, resplendent in a lightweight navy blue summer suit. Lauren had almost forgotten his towering height and how well he wore his clothes. An even six-foot, Cal had managed to remain trim. She felt her face heat up when she realized she was quite familiar with his body—with and without his clothing, in and out of bed.

Jacqueline opened her purse and withdrew an enameled compact. She checked her face and snapped it shut. Running her tongue over her front teeth, she glanced up at Cal. "When's the wedding, Caleb?"

His gaze was fixed on Lauren's face. "Next month, Jacqueline," he replied, his eyes narrowing. Somehow Cal had forgotten Lauren's diminutive height, her petite body, the satiny feel of her flawless dark brown skin and the delicate feminine scent that was hers and hers alone. But he hadn't forgotten her passion. A passion so wild and so intense that he had not wanted to lose it once he found it. He would have given up everything he had, rather than give up Lauren Taylor-Samuels.

Jacqueline's expertly arched brows shifted as she watched Cal staring at Lauren, and for the first time since she had entered the room she visually assessed the mother of Cal's child. Lauren may not have been the type of woman Jacqueline had known Cal to consort with, but she did recognize something about Lauren Taylor most men would find irresistible: a little-girl innocence coupled with an overriding desire to protect her.

"Am I invited to the wedding...what is your name again, little girl?"

Lauren's head spun around. She did not know Jacqueline Samuels, and she did not want to, but there was something about the woman she disliked on sight. "It's Miss Taylor. And no you're not invited. It's going to be a private ceremony."

Jacqueline quickly assessed an obduracy in Lauren Taylor that wasn't apparent at first glance, and concluded the younger woman would not be an easy opponent. Gathering her purse, she said, "I don't mind not celebrating your wedding, but I'll sure enjoy its demise."

Jacqueline did not see the hateful glance Cal gave Lauren as she leaned over and patted Lauren's shoulder. "Good luck, little girl. You're going to need it to survive a year with the high and mighty Caleb Samuels. He's just a younger version of the heartless old bastard he was named for."

She walked out of the room and John Evans offered Lauren

a conciliatory smile. "If there's anything I can help you with, please let me know," he said.

Lauren stood up, extending a small slender hand. "Thank you very much. I have your card."

He grasped her hand, released her fingers, then turned to Cal. "You know where to find me."

Cal took the proffered hand. "Thanks again, John."

John winked at him. "Good luck," he returned softly.

Cal waited until John walked out of the conference room, then circled the table. He stood over Lauren like a messenger of death, his gaze drilling her to the spot. "You and I have to talk. Perhaps you can enlighten me on this child I'm supposed to have fathered." The fingers of his right hand closed around her upper arm.

Lauren had never denied her child, and she was not going to begin now. Not even to his father.

"You have a son," she replied through clenched teeth.

Cal's expression did not change. "So I've been told. Why did I have to wait until today to hear about it?"

Lauren's eyes widened as she stared at Cal in astonishment. "But...but didn't you know?"

His golden stare drilled into her. "No."

"But your grandfather knew."

"He knew and you knew. Everyone knew except me."

Her mind reeled in confusion. Why wouldn't Dr. Samuels tell Cal that he was a father?

Cal thrust his face close to her, so close she saw a light sheen of moisture on his upper lip. Close enough to note the tiny pores in his golden-brown skin. So close she could smell his after-shave mingling with his own personal masculine scent when she felt the heat of his breath and his rage.

"Who put you up to this? How did you con my grandfather?"

Lauren pulled her arm from his loose grip, snatching up her handbag. "Who are you angry with, Cal? It can't be me because I get nothing out of this deal. If you want or need the money that badly, why don't you seduce Jacqueline. She's still young enough to give you a son. That way you both can keep the money in the *family*." She turned and walked out of the conference room.

"Lauren!" Cal shouted after her.

She did not stop. She ignored the receptionist's smile, pushing open the front door and stepping out into the bright summer sun.

Lauren made it to her car in the parking lot, but could not escape. A large hand captured hers in an iron grip.

"I said we have to talk," Cal hissed closed to her ear.

Lauren stared at his hand holding her captive. "Let me go."

Cal loosened his grip, but he would not permit Lauren to escape him as he trapped her between her car and his body.

"I want to talk to you."

Lauren tilted her chin. "There's nothing to talk about."

He moved closer, pressing his chest against her shoulder. "That's where you're wrong, Lauren Taylor-Samuels. You and I have a great deal to discuss."

"It's Lauren Taylor. I'd stopped being Samuels years ago, you arrogant…"

Cal's frown vanished. "And you agreed to marry me and all of my arrogance," he countered with a hint of a smile.

Some of the defensiveness seemed to flow out of Lauren with his smile. He was right. She had agreed to marry him, aware of his celebrity status, the rumors surrounding his sybaritic lifestyle and his infuriating arrogance.

His lids lowered over the golden eyes with their dark brown centers. "I want to know about my son, Lauren."

Lauren's gaze went from his face to her hand. He released her, stepping back. "What is it you want to know, Cal?"

"Not here," he said.

A slight frown furrowed her forehead. "Where?"

"At my grandfather's house. You can follow in your car."

He left her, walking over to a sleek black sports car, not giving her the opportunity to protest. She waited until he had slipped behind the wheel and started up the motor before she opened the door to her own mid-size car.

Cal pulled alongside her, leaning over to the passenger side. "Try to keep up," he was shouting over the hum of the two engines.

"I don't speed, Cal."

Lauren could have been talking to herself as she watched the exhaust from Cal's car. She lost him at a light, forcing him to slow down and wait for her.

Unbidden, she remembered his high-speed driving along the narrow roads on Cay Verde. Sitting in the car with Cal, watching his long fingers shift gears, had given her a rush; a rush that matched the uncontrollable soaring she experienced when they had made love; a rush so indelibly engraved in her consciousness that she had not sought out another man to see if it could be duplicated.

Lauren slowed her car even more, and when Cal parked in front of the three-story town house she knew he was enraged.

He was out of his car, slamming the door violently before she shut off her engine. "Where did you buy your license?" he snapped, leaning into the open window.

Lauren rolled up the window and pushed open the door, forcing him to move quickly to avoid injury. "I said I don't speed. I'm used to driving with a child, and I intend to live long enough to raise that child."

Cal pushed his hands into the pockets of his trousers. He smiled broadly. "My son?"

"No, my son."

He sobered quickly, the smile fading. "Is he or is he not my son, Lauren?"

"You may have fathered him, but he is my son. Don't ever forget that, Caleb."

Cal studied Lauren, recognizing an inner strength he had missed at the law office. This petite woman—one he had loved and married—had carried and given birth to his son; the son he had prayed for; the son he had not known existed until today.

He extended a hand and pulled Lauren to her feet. "Let's go inside."

Chapter 2

Cal led Lauren through the entry and living room, then into the same library where she had first met the late Dr. Caleb Samuels in what now seemed so very long ago. Most of the furniture was covered with dust covers.

She felt as if she had stepped back in time where she could see the elderly man rising to his feet to greet his grandson with his new bride. The old man's dark eyes had blazed fire; a fire that seemed to pierce her stoic facade to see her fear when she realized how capricious she had been to marry Cal Samuels.

And that brief meeting with Dr. Samuels had been the catalyst to shock Lauren back to reality. She had made a mistake to marry—especially if that man was best-selling author C. B. Samuels.

Cal slipped out of his jacket, extracted the cuff links and rolled his shirt cuffs back over strong brown wrists.

"Please be seated." He waved a hand toward a chair. "Can I get you anything to drink?"

Lauren sat, crossing one leg over the other. "No thank you. I'd like to get this over so I can return home."

Cal studied her relaxed position. "Where's home?"

She waited until he removed a covering from a love seat and sat down before saying, "Grafton. North Grafton to be precise."

"How long have you lived there?"

"Two months."

"Do you like it?" Cal continued with his questioning.

"Very much. Look, Caleb. I…"

"About the child," he interrupted.

"Drew."

Cal nodded, closing his eyes. The sunlight pouring through heavy red damask drapes glinted off the silver in his hair, creating a halo effect.

Lauren felt a wave of uneasiness shake her. She did not think she would be so unnerved by seeing Caleb Samuels again, and she called on all of her reserves to deal with this flesh-and-blood man sitting three feet from her.

He was not a man a woman could forget easily. Meeting Caleb Samuels shocked and assaulted one's senses. Everything about him: his fluid walk, soft voice and his controlled personality. Lauren was surprised with his outburst at Jacqueline during the reading of the will.

"Drew," he repeated softly. He opened his eyes. "Why didn't you let me know about the child?"

"Why didn't your grandfather tell you?" Lauren retorted, answering his question with one of her own.

"It wasn't my grandfather's responsibility to tell me, Lauren."

"You know why I couldn't tell you."

Cal's jaw hardened as his eyes widened. "I don't know, Lauren. Perhaps you should tell me."

She chewed her lower lip, composing her thoughts. "I didn't find out that I was pregnant until after the annulment."

Cal leaned forward on his chair. "Not being married is not a factor when there is a child. I had a right to know there was a child."

Lauren knew he was right, and she floundered before his brilliant stare, huddling in her chair and offering no response.

Cal sucked in his breath, cursing to himself as he registered vulnerability in Lauren for the first time. He also shared the blame. He was equally guilty because he should have fought for her. He shouldn't have given in to her when she wanted to leave him. He still loved her; there was never a time since she had left him when he did not love her, and he realized now why his grandfather had not told him about the child. The elder Samuels thought if Cal didn't fight to hold on to his wife he would not have fought for his son.

"How old is he, Lauren?"

Lauren felt her throat tighten. There was no mistaking the pain in Cal's voice. This was not the Cal she remembered. When she'd told him she was leaving him, he showed no emotion. He merely nodded and she walked out on him.

"He'll turn four on September first."

"Does he know about me?"

"I've tried explaining that you don't live in this country."

Cal sat up straighter. "Does he know my name?"

"No."

"Why not?" he fired back.

"I didn't want to confuse him."

A sudden icy contempt flared in his eyes. "What were you

going to tell him five or ten years from now, Lauren? Would you be able to come up with an excuse good enough to make up for your forgetting to tell me that I had fathered a child, and that I wasn't allowed to be a father to that child?"

She wanted to refute his accusation, but could not. Her delicate jaw tightened as she glared at him. "It wouldn't have come to that."

"Why not?"

"Because I would've told Drew the truth."

"I'll tell him the truth when I see him."

Lauren was so enraged she could hardly speak. "You won't."

"That's where you're wrong, Lauren. I will see my son and we will marry—again."

Lauren felt as if Cal had caught her by the throat, not permitting her to escape. "Never," she croaked.

"I want my son, Lauren."

She felt her temper rise in response to his demand. "You'll get to see your son, but I…"

"I want my son and you," he insisted, cutting her off.

Lauren clenched her teeth. "I'm not going to marry you, Cal. I don't make the same mistake twice."

A tense silence enveloped the room as Cal lowered his chin and looked up at her from lowered lids. "I'd marry anyone to keep Jacqueline from getting another penny of my family's money. My stepmother destroyed my father and I'll be damned if she's going to make a mockery of his memory by inheriting my grandfather's legacy."

Lauren refused to relent. "Jacqueline Samuels is your problem, not mine."

"She's Drew's problem now."

"Leave Drew out of this."

"I won't, Lauren. Drew is the reason you're in Boston this morning. Drew is the reason we're having this conversation."

"I'm not going to let you use my son for your personal vendetta."

Cal shook his head, giving her a smug grin. "I thought he was *our* son."

She felt properly chastised. "Okay, Caleb, *our* son."

"I can't turn back the clock," Cal stated, crossing his arms over his chest. "Neither of us can, but I can make certain Drew will get what's rightfully his. His name may be Taylor, but he's also a Samuels."

After a long pause, Lauren asked, "What's this all about, Cal? Is it about money or is it about revenge?"

"It's about family. Whether you want to acknowledge it, Drew is family. The same way you were once family. My family."

"It's more like manipulation," she retorted angrily. "A dead man is manipulating our lives from his grave, and I want no part of it."

Cal concealed a smile. "If that's the case, why did you tell Jacqueline that she wasn't invited to our wedding?"

Lauren compressed her lips into a tight line. "I don't like people who call me a thief."

"Nothing you could say to Jacqueline could hurt her as much as your being Drew's mother."

Lauren's gaze was fixed on the toe of her shoe and she missed Cal's slow, seductive approval of her shapely legs in the heels. He had only glimpsed the natural grace and beauty waiting to flourish with her ripening womanhood when he first saw her on Cay Verde before he realized there was a mysterious spirit within Lauren that captured his heart.

He wanted his son, but he wanted Lauren more.

"When can I meet Drew?" he asked, startling her.

Lauren's head jerked up. She knew there was no way she could keep Cal from meeting Drew. No court of law would deny him his child, and it seemed as if she had waited years for this scenario.

"I'll call you," she replied calmly even though her heart was pounding and slamming against her ribs.

"When?" His voice was soft and gentle. Despite Lauren's deceit, Cal did not want to hurt her.

"Maybe tomorrow. I have to talk to Drew first."

"Where do you want to meet?"

"You can come out to the house."

They had reached a truce—an uneasy truce in spite of their very stubborn natures. Drew would meet his father, and even though Lauren still loved Cal she had no intention of ever remarrying him, regardless of the stipulations in Dr. Samuels' will.

Cal moved from the love seat and held out a hand to Lauren. He smiled when she placed her hand in his. "It's going to be all right, Lauren. I won't fight you for the child."

She gave him a tremulous smile. "Thank you, Cal."

His hands slipped up her arms, pulling her closer. He studied her face, feature by feature, trying to see if there were remnants of the woman-child he had married.

Her hair was different. What had been a simple pageboy was now stylishly cut short, the top full and curling and the sides tapered to frame her small face.

He gazed deeply into her large dark eyes, drowning in the

black pools. A familiar stirring flooded his body and he released her.

"I'll walk you to your car." There was an edge to his voice he could not control. He wanted her; he would always want her.

Lauren schooled her features not to reveal the desire pulsing throughout her body. She still had not gotten Caleb Samuels out of her system. It had been a long time—too long and yet she was powerless to resist him.

"You'll need my telephone number," Cal reminded her, walking over to a table. He wrote down a number on a pad near a telephone. Turning back to her, he handed her the sheet of paper. "I'll wait here for the call."

Lauren nodded and placed the paper in her handbag. Together they made their way to the front door.

Cal escorted her down the steps and took the keys from her hand. Unlocking her car door, he held it open until she slid behind the wheel. His gaze lingered on the expanse of silken leg and thigh when she sat down. Dropping the keys into her outstretched palm, he smiled.

"Don't drive too fast," he teased.

Lauren couldn't help laughing. The sound was natural and carefree, surprising both of them. "I won't."

Cal leaned in through the open window. "Call me," he ordered softly.

"I will," she confirmed.

Lauren's gaze was fixed on his mouth, her dark eyes caressing his full upper lip. It gave him the look of a petulant little boy. But she knew Caleb Samuels was anything but a little boy.

She turned on the ignition and Cal took several steps back to the sidewalk. Flipping her directional signal, Lauren glanced over her shoulder then pulled away from the curb with a scream of rubber hitting the roadway.

Peering up in the rearview mirror, she smiled. Cal's expression was one of mixed surprise and shock. She took the next corner slowly, turning down the street that would take her to her parents' house.

"How did it go?" Odessa asked after Lauren had kicked off her shoes and raised her stockinged feet to a chintz-covered ottoman on the sun porch.

Lauren's brow furrowed. "It was weird. Crazy. No, Mama, it was bizarre."

"How?"

A half-smile played at the corners of Lauren's mouth as she related the terms and conditions of the late Dr. Caleb B. Samuels' will. "All I have to do is marry Cal, live with him for a year and Drew will inherit in excess of one million dollars. That will include the interest it'll earn until Drew's twenty-one."

Now it was Odessa's turn to frown. "What I don't understand is how Dr. Samuels found out about Drew when you didn't tell him."

Lauren shook her head. "He must have had someone investigate me."

"And Cal didn't know?"

"He said he didn't know."

"Do you believe him, Lauren?"

Lauren remembered Cal's expression when John Evans revealed Drew's existence. There was no way Cal could've faked his reaction.

"Yes, I do."

"But why wouldn't Dr. Samuels tell Cal about Drew?"

Lauren pressed her head against the fluffy cushioned back of the rocker. "We'll never know. The dead don't tell tales." She pursed her lips. "I suspect Dr. Samuels wanted to pay me back for walking out on Cal."

"I take it Cal wants to meet his son?" Odessa continued with her questioning. Lauren nodded. "When and where will this take place?"

Lauren felt as if a weight had been lifted from her mind and body. Even though she had not thought it would ever happen, she had mentally prepared herself for the inevitable. Someday, sometime and somewhere Drew would meet his father.

"Probably tomorrow." She noted her mother's strained expression. "I'm going to talk to Drew tonight, then I'll call Cal tomorrow. I think it's best that Cal come to Drew rather than Drew go to him."

"I agree with you," Odessa concurred. "Now, how about you, sweetheart? How was it seeing Caleb Samuels again?"

Lauren had always maintained an open rapport with her mother, telling her things most daughters balked at disclosing; but how could she tell Odessa that what she had felt for Cal that wildly passionate week on Cay Verde was still alive. That she wanted to relive that week again—over and over.

"It went rather smoothly," she said instead. "Time has been kind to Cal even though he's a little more gray."

Odessa raised an eyebrow. "I asked about you, not Cal Samuels."

Lauren felt her face heat up. She had given away her feelings for Cal. "I'm still attracted to him, Mama," she confessed.

For once, Odessa decided not to press her daughter about her relationship with Caleb Samuels, recognizing Lauren's need to come to grips with the legal proceedings she had encountered earlier that morning.

"What about the money willed to Drew?" she asked.

"What about it, Mama? Someone mentions money and all of the sharks begin circling around the wounded prey, measuring for the final kill. Drew will not become that prey if I have anything to say about it."

Odessa rose to her feet, glaring down at Lauren. "Why is it always what *you* want?"

Turning her back, Lauren compressed her lips in a tight, angry line. Her mother was being pushy again. "Because he is my child, and I will always do what is best for my child."

Odessa reached for Lauren's arm, spinning her around. "It's time you started thinking of others, Lauren. You're not in this by yourself. Drew loves you, but you'd better get used to the possibility that once he meets his father he'll love him also." Her fingers grazed Lauren's cheek. "You're going to have to share your son with Caleb and whatever Caleb has to offer him.

"I want you to think of your son, darling," Odessa continued softly. She smiled seductively. "I'm also certain you can think of worse things than waking up in bed with Caleb Samuels."

Lauren laughed, her mouth softening. She felt desire sweep through her body when she thought about how it had been to share a bed with Cal.

"You're right about that, Mama."

"How much time do you have before Caleb's wicked stepmother can claim my grandson's legacy?"

"Sixty days," Lauren replied.

Odessa shrugged slender shoulders. "That's not too bad. The old despot could've said two weeks. That would've meant big trouble."

Lauren saw a mischievous glint in Odessa's clear brown

eyes. "Stay out of this," Lauren warned in a soft voice. "If you even think about interfering…"

"You'll what, dear?" Odessa asked with a saccharine grin.

"I'll think of something."

"You're dangerous when you think, Lauren."

"Don't test me, Mother."

"Don't call me Mother."

"Just don't interfere."

"But, baby…" Odessa threw up her hands. "Okay. I promise I won't interfere."

Lauren hugged and kissed Odessa. "Thank you."

"Are you and Drew staying for lunch?"

Lauren gave her mother a loving smile. "Of course."

"Sit and relax," Odessa suggested. "I'll call you when lunch is ready."

Closing her eyes, Lauren willed her mind and body to relax. The warm summer breeze filtering through the screened windows cooled her and reminded her of the warm trade winds rustling the fronds of palm trees on Cay Verde.

She smiled. She had passed the test. She hadn't fallen under Cal's sensual spell again, and he had no way of knowing how much she had loved him and still loved him.

There had been many times since Lauren left Cal that she tried remembering what he looked like, what he had smelled like, and the rapturous pleasure he evoked when he kissed, touched and tasted her body.

Lauren had fallen in love with Caleb Samuels on Cay Verde and she would love him forever.

Cay Verde—a lovers' paradise. That's where it all began.

Chapter 3

Lauren had never heard of Cay Verde until she was summoned to meet with the head of Summit Publishing's research department a snowy December morning five years ago.

"How would you like to spend seven days on a private island in the Caribbean, Lauren?" Bob Ferguson had asked once she was seated.

Lauren's gaze had shifted from Bob to the wide window behind his desk. A shield of gray obscured the sky. Snow had been falling steadily all morning.

"What do I give up in return?" she'd questioned, smiling.

"The most comprehensive research ever gathered on the Zulu nation."

Lauren knew the Zulus were African tribal people of Bantu stock, tall and powerfully built, but her knowledge was limited to those few facts.

Bob explained that a book packager had come up with a

series concept about the Zulu chieftain Shaka and his successors. He told Lauren the concept would be comparable in scope to the eight-book series of John Jakes' *The American Bicentennial Series,* and C. B. Samuels would be the major writer for the projected four-book series. Chiefs Shaka, Dingane, Mpande and Cetewayo would each have their stories, fusing historical facts with fictional accountings to produce what Summit predicted to be a potential blockbuster series.

Lauren was the newest and youngest researcher for Summit, but Bob Ferguson knew Lauren was also one of their best. Fortified with an excellent liberal arts background, she had been hired immediately after graduating from college and she'd been promoted several times within her first year. Her zeal and thoroughness in approaching each research project had caught his attention and every department head at Summit.

Lauren successfully controlled the torrent of excitement building within her. She was being offered a project most veteran researchers would gladly forfeit the many perks Summit offered its long-time employees.

Bob watched her impassive expression. "Before you make your decision, I think it's only fair to let you know that C. B. Samuels usually works very closely with his researcher, and he can be quite difficult when he doesn't get the facts he's requested."

Lauren had read about C. B. Samuels' volatile artistic temperament, but refused to let that thwart her. She was confident she would work well with the best-selling fiction writer.

"C.B. will live on Cay Verde until he completes the first book," Bob continued. "He'll then take a year off, return to Spain, then come back to Cay Verde to write the second book.

After that he's contracted to give us the third and fourth books within three years."

"What's the projected word count?" Lauren asked.

"Three-hundred to five-hundred thousand."

A slight frown appeared between her eyes. Big books meant extensive research. Buoyed by a burst of confidence, she said, "I'll accept it."

Bob let out his breath in an audible sigh. An unconscious voice had told him Lauren Taylor would accept the project, but somehow he couldn't bring himself to believe it until now. He was afraid that C. B. Samuels' reputation would prompt Lauren to reject the assignment as other researchers had done.

"Be ready to leave in two days. I'll have my secretary make the arrangements for your flight. You'll also get a generous check for expenses. There'll be more than enough to cover the cost of a new wardrobe. I hear the nightlife on the island is quite festive," he added, winking.

Lauren's smile was dazzling. "Thanks, Bob."

"Don't thank me, Lauren. You've earned this assignment."

"I'll do you proud." Her voice was low and filled with checked emotion.

Bob gave her a lingering look. "I know you will." He visually admired her tiny body as she stood up. "Call me once you get to Cay Verde," he said, also rising to his feet.

Lauren nodded and walked out of Robert Ferguson's office, her step light, her spirits soaring, ready for Cay Verde and C. B. Samuels.

Her flight to the Bahamas, then the connecting one in a small propeller plane to Cay Verde was uneventful and accomplished with a minimum of delay. Lauren arrived at noon, refreshed, ready to work and to enjoy the natural splendor of the island.

A driver, with a lilting island accent, acted as her tour guide, driving slowly along the major road and pointing out the sprawling residences belonging to the six families who had pooled their vast wealth and bought the island.

Lauren settled back against the aged leather seat in the vintage Mercedes convertible and reveled in the warm breezes caressing her face. Five hours earlier she had waited in Boston's Logan Airport, watching clouds race across a gunmetal-gray sky. Below-freezing temperatures had hinted of more snow.

"Here we are, missy," the driver announced.

He stopped in front of a large two-storied white stucco structure that was truly West Indian in character, with a red Spanish-tiled roof, veranda and Creole jalousie shutters. Exotic blooming flowers, banana trees and noisy, brightly colored birds added to the property's lushness.

Lauren was helped from the car and escorted into the house where she was greeted by a young woman barely out of her teens.

"Welcome, Miss Taylor. I am Judith," she said. "I am here to help you for your stay on Cay Verde. Please come with me." Her accent was the same as the driver's, lending a musical sound to familiar words.

Lauren smiled at Judith and followed her up a flight of stairs to the second level. Her bedroom was large and filled with bright sunlight. A massive four-poster canopy bed of Jamaican mahogany was the focus of attention, along with a matching armoire and rocker. These were the only pieces of furniture in the expansive space.

Judith closed the shutters and turned on a ceiling fan. "I'll draw your bath, then I will unpack everything for you. I will also bring a platter of refreshments."

Lauren wanted to tell Judith she did not want anything to eat, but decided against it. She did not know the customs on

Cay Verde and she didn't want to insult her absent host's hospitality or those in his employ.

An hour later, Lauren lay on the large bed, her head supported by fluffy pillows and fought to keep her eyes open. The flight, the heat, and the platter of broiled fish, fresh fruit and rum-spiked punch had taken its toll. Giving into the languidness weighing on her limbs, she slept, and it wasn't until later that afternoon she met Caleb Samuels for the first time.

"Have you lost your mind? She looks as if she's not old enough to drink and you want this...this child...to do the research for this project!"

He had not shouted the words, but Caleb Samuels did not have to. His intent was unmistakable. He did not want Lauren Taylor as his researcher.

"But Ferguson said she's the best," said a small, wiry man with glasses in a quiet voice.

"The best at what?" Caleb Samuels replied with a sneer, his eyes raking her body.

Lauren could not believe he would be that rude. Caleb Samuels had not bothered to hide his disdain.

"You don't have to like me," she countered, failing to control her quick temper and for the first time forgetting her position as a professional researcher. "But I am going to do the research on this project, Mr. Samuels. However if my youth offends you then I suggest we not communicate face to face. Modern technology has provided us with telephones and fax machines. Take your pick!" The blood pounded in her temples as she turned on her heel and walked away from the two men, not seeing the look of surprise on Caleb's face.

Lauren returned to her room and flopped across the bed, biting her lower lip and fighting back tears. She was angry at herself. She never should've allowed Caleb Samuels to bait her. She had fallen into his trap.

Inhaling, then letting out her breath slowly, Lauren vowed she would never lose her temper again—at least not with C. B. Samuels. She had to prove she was immune to his disparaging remarks, and conduct herself like the accomplished researcher she had become.

She left the bed, showered and changed her clothes for dinner. There was no way she was going to hide out in her room. Caleb Samuels would just have to get used to seeing her face.

Checking her watch, Lauren realized she had another hour before dinner was to be served. The dinner hour on Cay Verde usually began at nine and continued until eleven and sometimes as late as midnight. She decided to take a walk along the beach and she informed Judith she would be back in time for dinner.

Lauren made her way away from the house and down to the sea, carrying her sandals. The setting sun and cooler breezes refreshed her as she walked slowly along the beach, luxuriating in the beauty of the blue-green waters of the Caribbean quietly kissing the pure white sand.

Stopping, Lauren stared out at the large orange circle of the sun as it dipped lower and lower, meeting the uneven line of the sea, not seeing the figure of the man until he stood less than five feet from her.

The rays from the setting sun bathed him in flames, highlighting his tawny-brown skin and firing his golden eyes and turning his white attire a blazing red.

"I apologize for earlier today," he said in a voice so quiet Lauren had to strain to catch his words over the sound of the rustling sea. "It was rude of me..."

"It was arrogant of you," Lauren corrected. Cal smiled and

she sucked in her breath. Earlier that afternoon she had been too incensed to note that Caleb Samuels was more attractive in person than his photographs revealed.

He bowed slightly at the waist. "I'm sorry for my arrogance, Miss Lauren Taylor, and to prove that I'm truly sorry I ask that you forget our prior encounter. Think of this as our first meeting."

Lauren brushed several strands of wind-blown hair away from her cheek, unaware of the delicate, sensual vision she presented Cal. He had called her a child, but she was anything but a child. A pale pink sheer voile sundress, with a matching underslip, flattered her petite figure. On her, the deep-V neckline and bared back was innocent, yet on a woman with a more voluptuous body it would have been seductive.

She was different; so different from the other women he had met that for a moment he felt like a tongue-tied boy. Lauren Taylor was a sexy woman-child with exquisite dark-brown velvet skin, large mysterious eyes and a passionate, succulent mouth that cried out to be kissed. She had the sexiest mouth of any woman he had ever seen.

He extended his right hand. "Cal Samuels," he said, finding his voice.

Lauren hesitated, then grasped the proffered hand. "Lauren Taylor."

Cal held her fingers gently, then released them. "Will you have dinner with me, Lauren?"

She was caught off guard by his unexpected invitation, but recovered quickly. "I can't, Mr. Samuels. You're much too old for me," she answered with a saccharine grin.

Cal's jaw dropped slightly as he ran a hand over his curling hair. "I know I'm graying prematurely, but I'm only twenty-eight."

Lauren resumed her walk along the beach, Cal falling in step with her. "You're still too old."

He glanced at her profile, enchanted by her fragile beauty. Her delicate features, soft feminine fragrance and her wide-eyed look of innocence charmed him.

"How old are you?" he questioned.

She smiled, giving him a sidelong glance. "Old enough to drink. I'm twenty-two."

"But…but I'm only six years older than you," he sputtered. "I hardly think that constitutes 'too old.' I'll be on my best behavior," he continued almost pleadingly, moving in front of her and impeding her progress. "I promise."

Lauren smiled up at him, watching his smile grow wider as he leaned toward her, realizing she was past the point of his intimidation. "Not tonight."

"When?" The single word held a hint of desperation.

"Tomorrow," she answered.

"Good morning, Lauren."

The soft male voice prompted Lauren to open her eyes and she smiled up at the man looming over her, holding two cups of steaming coffee.

Bringing herself to a sitting position on the cushioned rattan lounge chair, she removed her sunglasses. She had awakened early and decided to sit under the sweeping leaves of a grove of banana trees to await breakfast.

"Good morning, Cal." Her smile was as dazzling as the bright sunshine.

Cal took a matching lounge chair, silently admiring Lauren's thick shiny hair, pulled off her face in a ponytail. She wore a body-hugging white tank top she had paired with a flowing white-gauze cotton skirt.

He handed her a cup of coffee. "Judith said you like your coffee light with one sugar."

She smiled at him, taking the cup. "Thank you."

Lauren concentrated on her coffee instead of staring openly at Caleb Samuels. The man was so compelling, his magnetism so powerful that a delicious shudder of desire swept over her. She wasn't very worldly and hadn't had a lot of experience with the opposite sex, but the man sitting beside her projected a virility so intoxicating that she was helpless to resist it.

Lauren had never been one to believe the sordid supermarket tabloids, but she wondered if some of the rumors surrounding C. B. Samuels' licentious social life were true. It was hard for any normal female to resist his slim, tanned, hard brown body, curling graying black hair, brilliant sunlit eyes and pouting mouth, and when she had gone to bed the night before she tried remembering everything about him, including the sensual timbre of his soft voice.

Leaning back in his chair, Cal closed his eyes. "What do you know about the Zulus, Lauren?"

Lauren glanced at his bold profile. His expression was closed, as if he guarded a secret. "Not much," she admitted.

His mouth curved into a smile. "I think you're going to have your work cut out for you with this project," he said and confirming that she would be his researcher.

"I want a lot of facts—detailed facts," he continued. "I want to know every historical event recorded about Shaka, his half-brother Dingane, Dingane's brother Mpande and Mpande's son Cetewayo. I need to know the political structure of each chieftain's regime, along with the customs and traditions. I want to know every facet of the nineteenth-century Zulus, including what they ate, drank and what kind of tribal society supported their existence.

"I need to know how they built their homes, their agriculture and the status of their women and children during each reign." Cal opened his eyes and stared at a smiling Lauren.

"Anything else, Cal?"

He returned her smile. "Yes, there is. The wars. I want to know who the Europeans were who challenged the Zulus for an empire that dominated southern Africa from the Zambezi River to Cape Colony. I need an accounting of any skirmish between the Zulus and the Europeans and a detailed description of a ferocious battle which rivals the battle of the Little Bighorn, where at Isandhlwana the British were nearly annihilated when they lost twelve hundred men on January 22, 1879. Another important battle resulted in a decisive British victory at Ulundi on July 4, 1879."

Lauren digested this information, knowing it would be months before she completed nearly one hundred years of Zulu history.

"How well do you know your Zulu chiefs?" she questioned.

"I know enough about them to write them as fully developed characters," he confessed. But at that moment Caleb Samuels wanted to know about Lauren Taylor. He wanted to know everything about her: what she liked, didn't like. What made her laugh, and what made her cry. He wanted to know whether she was sentimental, whether she had a sense of humor. Who was her favorite author? What kind of music did she enjoy? Whether she liked to dance or if she had been kissed—really kissed with the passion a man summoned deep within him; a passion he kept hidden until the right woman came into his life.

But was Lauren Taylor the right woman? He, Caleb Samuels who had met and known more women than he wanted to admit, wanted a little slip of a woman who was barely out of her teens. A woman whom he knew, instinctively, was all woman.

Cal caught a glimpse of Judith as she came out of the house. "It's time for breakfast," he informed Lauren.

Rising to his feet, he extended his hand to Lauren. He grasped her slender fingers, pulling her fluidly to her feet. He cradled her hand in the bend of his elbow and led her back to the house.

Walking beside her, holding her hand possessively, seemed so easy, so natural, as a slender thread of attraction bound them together.

Lauren shared the morning and afternoon with Cal, sharing meals and discussing the format of his book series. Cal's editor joined them after lunch, but the session was conducted with an undercurrent of tension; tension felt only by Lauren and Cal.

Cal waited for the other man to leave, then leaned across the small table and captured Lauren's hand, stopping her scrawling notes on a steno pad.

"Enough, Lauren," he ordered softly. "We've worked enough today. Remember, you owe me a dinner date. We both need to unwind."

She remembered Bob Ferguson's remark about the festive nightlife on Cay Verde, and while she had been on the island for two days she had not taken the opportunity to sample that festivity.

"That sounds wonderful."

Cal glanced down at his watch. "If it's all right with you we'll leave around eight."

Three hours later Lauren sat beside Cal in a vintage Mercedes, clutching the edge of her seat as the car sped over the unpaved back road. A warm breeze whipped her freshly shampooed curling hair around her face.

Swallowing painfully, she closed her eyes. "Cal…Caleb?"

"Yes, Lauren," he replied, not taking his gaze off the road.

Her heart pounded painfully in her chest. "Do you have to speed?"

Cal slowed the car. "Am I frightening you?"

"Just don't drive so fast," she insisted.

Cal smiled. The little girl in Lauren has surfaced. He covered her left hand with his right, holding it protectively on his hard thigh. "I'd never do anything to put you in danger," he crooned softly.

Lauren felt the flexing and unflexing of the muscles in Cal's thigh through the fabric of his slacks whenever he applied pressure to the gas or brake pedals. He had captured her fingers, not releasing them, and after a while she didn't want him to let her go. Sitting beside Caleb Samuels, having him hold her, offered her a sense of protection she had never felt with another man.

Cal parked outside a large structure that resembled a one-story thatched pagoda. Bright lights, live music and laughter spilled over and greeted them the moment the door opened.

Cal was greeted with a familiar fondness by many of the revelers, and for the first time Lauren felt the force of his celebrity status. He held her waist possessively when he introduced her to people Lauren had read about in *Town and County* or *Vanity Fair*. When asked about the release of his next book Cal mumbled something inane, which seemed to satisfy most of the curious partygoers.

Cal asked the maître d' for a table in a secluded corner and within minutes he and Lauren were seated. They sampled a platter of fried sweet bananas, codfish fritters, a savory rice with pigeon peas and spicy shredded cabbage.

Lauren took a swallow of her rum punch, her large dark eyes fixed on Cal's smiling face. "I don't think I'll ever get used to one-hundred-fifty-proof rum. Everything I eat or drink has rum in it."

Cal's eyes swept slowly over her wind-tossed curling hair, then down to her full lush mouth. "You'll get used to it."

Feeling the potent effects of the punch, Lauren shook her head, the curls dancing provocatively over her forehead. "I don't think I want to get used to it."

Cal held out his hand. "Are you steady enough to dance with me?"

"If I'm not, you'll have to hold me up."

"That shouldn't be too difficult. I doubt if you weigh a hundred pounds."

"A hundred and three," she confirmed.

"You're some heavyweight, aren't you?" he teased, coming around the table and helping her stand.

Cal led her onto the dance area and into the slow steps of a throbbing tune with a distinctive reggae beat. This dance was the first of Lauren's many dances with Cal as he led her expertly from one rhythm to another as the live band played on tirelessly.

Lauren pleaded thirst and Cal ordered another round of drinks. They sat at the bar, swaying to the beat of taped music coming through massive speakers. Like Cal and Lauren, the band had also taken a break.

Leaning over, Cal pulled a damp curl away from Lauren's cheek, and without a warning his mouth replaced his fingers against her moist face.

"Thank you," he mumbled.

Her eyes widened in surprise as she stared into the depths of his amber gaze. The flickering flames from a small candle on the bar highlighted the gold in his eyes and in his skin.

"For what?" she questioned.

"For being here with me, for being you and for being so beautiful, Lauren Taylor."

Everything disappeared around Lauren, except for the magnetic man beside her; she was aware of his warmth and strength, her own face growing warm under the heat of his gaze; their eyes locked as their chests rose and fell in unison.

His large hand took her face and held it gently, and even though Lauren wanted to, she couldn't pull away. His touch was hypnotic, spellbinding, and she leaned closer, wanting him to touch more than her face.

Lauren's forehead dropped to his shoulder as she tried bringing her fragile emotions under control. What was the matter with her? She hadn't known him—no, she didn't know this man, so why was she reacting so recklessly toward him. Was it possible that she could feel an immediate and a total attraction to Caleb Samuels?

Gazes were turned in their direction and when Cal looked up he noted them. He was conscious of Lauren pressed against his chest, but more than that he was aware of his reputation, and the need to protect her surfaced without warning. Malicious gossip had followed him most of his adult life but he didn't want that gossip linked to Lauren.

Curving a strong arm around her tiny waist, he assisted her from the tall stool. "Let's go home, darling."

Lauren nodded, winding her arms inside his jacket and around his back.

The floral fragrance from Lauren's hair and body tested the limits of Cal's self-control as he escorted her outside into the sultry night air. He helped her into the car before taking his seat behind the wheel. A low rumble of thunder shook the night and he pressed a button for the convertible top. Fat drops of rain splattered the windshield within minutes.

Lauren closed her eyes, pressing her head against the leather seat, unaware of the speedometer inching above the island's legal speed limit.

She tried sorting out her feelings for Caleb Samuels and failed miserably, and she was dismayed at the magnitude of her own desire for him. She had known of the strong passion within her even though she had denied the passion over and over.

The speed of the car, the low rumbling of thunder, the flash and crack of lightning and the pounding of rain on the canvas top echoed the blood rushing throughout Lauren's system.

She wanted Caleb Samuels—his maddening arrogance, literary brilliance, gentle touch, caressing voice and his over-whelming virility.

Her heart was pumping uncontrollably when he stopped the car at the house and came around to help her out. Within seconds his linen jacket, slacks and cotton shirt were soaked from the torrential downpour. Gathering Lauren in his arms, Cal raced toward the house and Lauren felt the rain pelting her hair and soaking her white organdy halter top and skirt. The moisture, heat and scent from their bodies lingered sensuously in her nostrils.

Once inside the entry, Cal lowered Lauren to her feet. "I think I'm lost in the Bermuda Triangle," she slurred, referring to the rum-laced drink she had consumed.

Cal smiled down at the dreamy expression on her face. "You won't drown, darling. I'll make certain..."

Lauren was too relaxed to register Cal's endearment, but she did notice his startled look when he didn't complete his statement. She followed his gaze, looking down. Her wet top was plastered to her chest like skin, the dark circle of her nipples showing through the finely woven white fabric.

Cal moved toward her without moving. He kissed her with his eyes, his tenderness and repressed desire.

"Caleb," she whispered as his lips brushed against hers.

His mouth covered hers, demanding a response. Lauren returned the kiss, exhibiting a hunger that belied her outward calm.

Cal felt her hunger, answering it with a deprivation he hadn't known he possessed. Without warning and for the second time that night Lauren was a captive in Cal's arms, as he took the stairs two at a time, his mouth still fixed to hers.

Lauren pulled her mouth away, gasping for much-needed air and pressed her face to his chest. His heart pumped strongly under her cheek.

She knew what was to come, but was helpless to stop it. She didn't want to stop it. She wanted to give in to the delicious desire dissolving her into a mass of quivering, pulsating ecstasy.

Cal carried Lauren into her bedroom, shutting the door behind them with his foot. He set her down on her bed, walking back to lock the door and light a fat, scented candle on the floor by the door. The flickering flame threw long and short shadows on the ceiling and walls, yet the flame wasn't bright enough to highlight the bed where Lauren lay. The window shutters were open and the rain-swept wind flowed into the room, giving the space a freshly washed fragrance.

Lauren blinked in the muted darkness, but could not see beyond her hand. She heard the whisper of fabric as Cal shed his clothes.

Closing her eyes, she let her senses take over as she felt the side of the bed dip. She opened her eyes, jerking when his fingers went to the waistband of her skirt.

"I won't hurt you, baby. Trust me," he said softly. Lauren

nodded her assent and he undressed her, gasping audibly once he had bared her body to his gaze.

Settling himself over her trembling limbs, he kissed her mouth and Lauren felt her insides warming, melting. His tongue caressed her lower lip, then the upper, and she began groaning once he took full possession of her mouth.

The heat began with the kiss and spread to her breasts and still further down to her belly.

Cal's mouth traced the heat, from her lips to her breasts, ribs, belly, staking its claim to her core.

Lauren trembled and moaned under his rapacious tongue. Caleb Samuels was doing things to her she did not know existed. He made her feel things she had never felt before— not with any man, and she wanted him the way she had never wanted any man.

Moving up her body, Cal took her hand and guided it to his thighs. "I want you, darling. But I have to know if you want me."

Her small hand closed around his flesh and she felt his heat, his fullness and his hardness.

"Love me, Caleb. Please," she moaned.

Cal positioned himself at the entrance to her femininity, pushing gently. Slowly, gently, he entered her tight, hot flesh, clenching his teeth to keep from crying out his own pleasure.

She took him inch by inch, until he was fully sheathed in her moist body.

Cal began a slow, stroking motion, withdrawing and plunging deeply into her womb. Lauren began moving in concert with him, keeping his rhythm before setting one of her own.

He felt her hot breath on his neck, the bite of her finger-nails on his buttocks and the soft whimpers rising from the back of her throat.

The pleasure began building, soaring and rushing until

Cal and Lauren were rendered mindless by the raw act of possession.

Everything exploded at once. Their primal screams merged, the moment ecstasy shattered them into fiery tongues of fire.

They lay together, a tangle of limbs in the flickering candlelight, waiting for their breathing to resume its normal rate.

Lauren snuggled closer to Cal's body and soon there was only the sound of her soft breathing blending with the now softer patter of falling rain.

Cal shifted, pulling a sheet up over their moist bodies. He smiled in the darkness. He would never have guessed that innocent-looking Lauren Taylor was capable of such passion. More passion than any other woman had ever offered him.

Lauren awoke the next morning and found Cal staring at her. "Good morning," she said shyly.

Tucking a finger under her chin, he pressed a light kiss to her lips. "Good morning, darling."

Lowering her head, she kissed his shoulder, her left arm sliding over his flat belly as Cal buried his face in her hair.

Cal could not believe he had spent the entire night with Lauren beside him. He usually made love to a woman, but never slept with them. He wanted no ties, no claims, no declarations of love and no commitments.

He wondered whether he didn't sleep with them because he was afraid of commitment—afraid that his life would mirror his parents' turbulent marriages.

But why hadn't he left Lauren Taylor's bed? What was so different about her?

Wasn't it time for him to put his fears to rest? Could he hope to capture the love and security eluding him for years?

He had to find out if Lauren was the one to exorcise his

ghosts. He turned to her, slowly and methodically preparing her to accept his passion, and after making love to her a second time he knew he loved Lauren with a love that was quiet, gentle and safe.

Lauren lay in bed on the fifth night of her stay on Cay Verde, her heart pounding wildly in her chest. "We don't have to get married," she protested.

"Yes, we do," Cal argued with a smile. "I will not sleep with you again unless we're married."

She bit down on her lower lip, frowning. She did not want to think of Cal not making love to her. Sharing her body with him opened up a world of passion she had not thought possible, and before she succumbed to the numbed sleep of a sated lover she prayed her time with him would never end.

Cal pulled her body over his, her legs nestled intimately between his. He kissed her tousled hair. "I love you, Lauren. I didn't think it would be possible for me to fall in love with you so quickly," he said incredulously, "but it happened."

What Cal didn't tell Lauren was that she was the first uncomplicated thing he had had in his life in a long time. He was tired of sleeping around, tired of making idle chitchat at social functions and he was tired of being alone despite a wide circle of acquaintances. Right at this moment, he realized he was ready to settle down and have children. He wanted Lauren to have his children; and for the first time since he began sleeping with a woman he hadn't taken measures to prevent contraception.

Lauren rested her chin on her arms folded on Cal's chest. "Do you propose to every woman you sleep with?"

His golden eyes moved slowly over her face. "No. And I've never proposed to a woman before."

Lauren shifted her eyebrows. "I'm the first?"

He nodded, smiling. "You're the first."

She was filled with a strange inner excitement with the knowledge that Cal loved her, because she believed she had fallen in love with him the first night she met him on the beach. He had overwhelmed her from the first time she shared his bed and he continued to overwhelm her, refusing to believe it was sex or his celebrity status.

"I'll be good to you, Lauren," he said, seeing her look of indecision. "I'll protect you, darling, and I'll always love you."

Lauren lowered her head, willing the tears behind her eyelids not to fall as his hands trailed over her back and hips.

"Please, darling," he pleaded.

"When do you want to marry?" she asked, her voice muffled in his neck.

"Tomorrow."

Her head came up quickly, revealing the tears staining her cheeks. "Why tomorrow? Why the rush?"

Cradling her face between his hands, Cal kissed the end of her nose. "I found you on Cay Verde and I want to make certain you belong to me before we leave Cay Verde." What he didn't tell her was that he was afraid of losing her.

"Caleb…"

"It's going to be all right, darling," he interrupted. "I'll make you happy."

Lauren floundered before the brilliance of his gaze, but not before she caught a glimpse of what Caleb Samuels had never exhibited to another human being—vulnerability.

You love him, her heart pounded rhythmically. At that moment she did love him—with all of her heart.

"Do you love me?" he asked.

"Yes," Lauren whispered, tears flowing unchecked down her face.

"Will you marry me?"

"Yes, Caleb."

The following afternoon found Lauren Vernice Taylor exchanging vows with Caleb Baldwin Samuels II in a private ceremony in a tiny white church with only the local island minister and his wife present.

Cal slipped the signet ring off his little finger and placed it on the ring finger of Lauren's left hand, kissing her passionately. They accepted the good wishes of the minister and his wife who showered them with a hail of rice.

He led her back to the car, leaning down to brush his lips over hers. "I'll buy you a ring when we return to Boston. Speaking of Boston," he continued excitedly, "we'll stay with my grandfather until we decide where we want to live."

Lauren stared up at the stranger she had just married. "Your grandfather?"

"He practically raised me," Cal informed her. "He's wonderful, darling. I carry his name."

Her brow furrowed in concentration. "Don't tell me your grandfather is the same Dr. Samuels who won the Nobel Prize for Medicine for his work in identifying gene abnormalities in fetuses?"

"He's the same," he admitted proudly.

She felt her first pang of doubt when she realized she had been a little too hasty in agreeing to marry a man she had known less than a week. She knew nothing about him or his family.

However, she pushed the thread of doubt to the farthest recesses of her mind when she lay in bed with Cal on their wedding night. Their lovemaking signaled a change in their lives. Being married had added a special quality to their coming together.

Cradled in Cal's arms and luxuriating in the aftermath of their passion Lauren knew she was in love with her husband.

But the fairy tale had ended when they returned to Boston. Lauren walked out on Cal and when she returned to Summit Publishing she asked to be relieved from her assignment. Bob Ferguson did not ask her why, but he had received word that Caleb Samuels decided not to write the series, saying personal business dictated he return to Barcelona.

Bob suspected all had not gone well between his researcher and C. B. Samuels, so he waited for Lauren to confide in him.

Three months later Lauren handed him her resignation, and he knew he would never uncover what had occurred on Cay Verde.

Chapter 4

Drew Taylor-Samuels lay on crisp clean sheets decorated with characters from a popular animated science-fiction series, and smiled up at his mother. "I want a story about the space invaders."

Lauren sat on a rocker beside her son's bed. This was a story-telling session that would not include Jamal, Space Warriors or Dr. Seuss. The story she planned to tell Drew was real even though it hadn't been written.

"I want to tell you about Caleb Samuels."

A frown formed between Drew's golden-brown eyes. "Who's that?"

"Caleb Samuels is your father," Lauren replied.

Drew's eyes widened as his mouth dropped slightly. "My daddy?"

Lauren nodded. "Yes, your daddy."

The young boy sat up, grinning. "I like stories about my daddy."

Lauren exhaled audibly, closing her eyes briefly. "This isn't a story, Drew," she began slowly. "What I'm trying to say is that your father is here."

"Here?" Drew leaned forward, pulling back the colorful sheets.

"No, darling, he's not here now." Vertical slashes marred the child's forehead. "He wants to see you."

The frown vanished quickly. "When, Mommy?"

"He's coming here to see you tomorrow."

"Where is he now?"

"In Boston."

"With grandma and grandpa?"

"No, Drew. He lives in his own house."

Drew pushed out his lower lip. "I thought you said he had a house in Spain."

"He does, but he's in the United States now."

"Is he going to stay in the United States?"

That was a question which Lauren couldn't answer and refused to try to answer. "I don't know, Drew," she said instead.

"When I see my daddy I'll ask him," Drew replied, puffing up his narrow chest. He stared at his mother, not seeing the tension tightening her facial muscles. "That was a good story, Mommy."

Lauren managed a tight smile. "Yes, Drew. Yes it was." Rising from the rocker, she kissed her son's forehead. "Don't forget to say your prayers before you go to sleep."

Drew lay down, closing his eyes and smiling. "I won't forget."

She turned off the bedside lamp and made her way out of Drew's bedroom to her bedroom where she fell weakly onto her bed. She had done it—told Drew his father's name, told him Cal was coming to meet him, and now all she had to do was wait.

The incessant ringing shattered the vestiges of Cal's sound sleep. Reaching for the telephone, he knocked it over. Mumbling a curse under his breath, he hung over the side of the bed, his fingers searching for the annoying instrument.

"Caleb?" came a husky female voice through the receiver.

"Yeah?"

"It's Lauren."

He sat up, all traces of sleep vanishing. "Yes, Lauren?"

"Drew wants to meet you."

Cal barely registered her words. His heart rate increased, pumping his blood, hot and wild, throughout his body.

"When?" Resting his head against the bed's headboard, he squeezed his eyes tightly. He had not met the boy, and already he was falling apart.

"If you can be here by eleven-thirty, we'll share lunch together."

"Give me the directions," Cal demanded. He listened intently, scribbling furiously on the pad on the bedside table. He repeated them into the receiver.

"I'll see you later," Lauren said quietly, then the line went dead.

Cal held the receiver to his ear, listening to the dial tone. He returned the receiver to its cradle and picked up his watch. North Grafton was about forty miles west of Boston and he had a little more than an hour to get there. Throwing the sheet off his naked body, he headed for the bathroom.

Shaving became a game of chance when his shaking hand cut the tender skin over his throat, not once but twice. He splashed cold water onto his face, then sucked in deep drafts of air. He had to slow down or he would never live to meet his son.

Cal straightened, looking at his reflection staring back at him in the mirror over the basin. "My son," he whispered to the reflection. "I have a son."

By some minor miracle Cal showered, dressed and managed not to wreck his car during his high-speed drive from Boston to North Grafton.

The countryside was awash with color with the advent of summer in all its glory. Trees, lawns and shrubs were resplendent in their verdant, lush dress. Cal caught sight of the small convenience store Lauren had mentioned, and turned down the narrow road leading to her house.

Downshifting, he slowed as a tiny furred creature scurried across the road, disappearing into the nearby woods.

Lauren had chosen well. Towering trees shading homes, light vehicular traffic and spacious lawns made North Grafton an ideal place to raise a child, and Cal was far enough from the noise and pollution of Boston to appreciate the town's sleepy quaintness and charm.

He spied Lauren's dark blue sedan and maneuvered into the driveway behind it. The screen door to the large white farmhouse opened and Lauren walked out. She rested a slender hip against the porch column, staring down at him.

Cal swallowed painfully as he unfolded his long legs from the low-slung sports car. Gone were the silk dress, sheer hose and heels. In their place were a pair of well-worn jeans, a T-shirt and bare feet. With her bare feet and unmade face Lauren looked more like seventeen than twenty-seven. She looked as young as she had when he first met her. Her eyes narrowed, her gaze going to the small white plastic bag he held in his left hand.

"I picked up a little something for Drew," he explained, walking up the steps. He stopped two steps below her and met her level gaze.

Lauren gave him a warm smile and Cal couldn't help but return it. "Thank you, Cal. Drew always gets excited when someone buys him something."

I'm not just someone, Cal thought. He was the boy's father. He peered over her head at the door. "I…I'd like to see him please."

Lauren turned, missing the anxiety thinning Cal's mouth. "Of course." She opened the door, waiting for Cal to precede her into the house.

Cal walked into a spacious living room, seeing only the young boy seated on a sofa in a colorful country French design. Ribbons of sunlight seeping through the lace curtains at the many windows confirmed that the child was truly an issue of his loins. Just looking at the boy was enough. Drew Michael Taylor-Samuels *was* his son.

They shared the same lean face, high cheekbones and forehead, eyes, lean jaw and dimpled chin. Cal moved closer, smiling. Drew also had a tiny mole near the left eye that gave his young face a distinctive quality. He was so filled with emotion that he wanted to shout out his joy, but decided not to startle or frighten the child.

Lauren sat down beside Drew, cradling him to her breasts. "Drew, this is your father," she explained softly. She watched Drew staring up at the tall man who looked so much like him. "He's waited a long time to meet you." Glancing up at Cal, she said, "Cal, this is Drew."

Cal hunkered down in front of Drew, extending his right hand. "I'm pleased to meet you." His eyes were shining like polished citrines.

Drew crossed and uncrossed his sneakered feet, staring down at the scuffed toes, his hands sandwiched between his jean-covered knees. Slowly, reluctantly he extended his right hand. "Hi."

Lauren released Drew, nodded at Cal, then walked out of the living room.

Cal sat down next to Drew, smiling. The child was perfect. "How are you?" he asked, not knowing what else to say to a child.

Drew would not look at Cal. "Good. Mommy said you lived far away in Spain and that you don't know me."

Cal caught Drew's chin and raised his face. "That's true, Drew. If I had known that I had a son I would've come back a long time ago to find you."

Drew's amber-colored eyes widened. "Really?"

Cal shifted his arching eyebrows. "Really."

Bright color flushed Drew's sun-browned tawny cheeks. "Do you have another boy?"

Cal's laugh was full and rich when he threw back his head. "No," he finally answered. "You're my only child." He extended his hand with the small plastic shopping bag. "I didn't know what to bring you, but I hope you'll like this."

Drew gave him a tentative glance before reaching for the bag. Cal knew immediately that he had chosen well.

"Wow! Oh, wow," Drew exclaimed breathlessly. He slipped the dark blue baseball cap, emblazoned with a red *B*, on his head. "Thank you," he got out in a shy voice, offering Cal a hint of a smile.

The tightness in Cal's chest eased. He dropped an arm around Drew's shoulders, then suddenly without warning the child was in his arms as he cradled his son to his chest.

Pressing his lips to Drew's soft, curling black hair, Cal

closed his eyes. "I'll never leave you." His composure faltered when Drew wound his arms around his neck, holding him tightly. "No matter what happens between me and your mother I'll never leave you," he whispered against his son's ear.

"I don't want you to go away, Daddy."

Cal experienced a riot of emotions. He didn't know whether to laugh or cry. Drew had called him "Daddy."

Burying his face against Drew's neck, Cal did not see Lauren reenter the living room and observe them. She bit down hard on her lower lip and slipped quietly to the kitchen.

Tears Lauren had not permitted to fall years before fell now. She had always prided herself on being strong, facing adversity head-on. But this time she could not help the soft sobs draining her as she buried her face in her hands and released the guilt she had carried for so long that it had become a part of her everyday existence.

She had made a mistake not telling Cal about her pregnancy, and only now could she admit that to herself.

She had cheated Cal, she had cheated Drew, and she had cheated herself out of the love the three of them could've shared.

She made it to the half-bath off the kitchen and bathed her swollen eyes with cold water. She dried her face, reliving the scene with Cal holding Drew. Man and child, father and son. They had found each other.

The realization of what had happened pierced her like a knife. Drew had found his father and Cal his son. But where would that leave her?

Cal said he wouldn't fight her for Drew, but his claim did not have to be physical. Just by virtue of being who he was, a male figure to a male child, would that be enough for Drew to switch loyalties?

She had not had to share Drew with anyone for almost four

years. He was hers and hers alone. Even her mother complained that she had become too possessive with the child. But Cal had as much a right to his son as she. Lauren wondered if she would be selfless enough to give up a little of Drew to his father.

She left the bathroom and returned to the kitchen, turning on a burner under a large pot of water, then busied herself setting the table in a dining nook. She added spaghetti to the boiling water and heated a casserole dish filled with a fragrant marinara sauce and meatballs in the microwave oven.

Drew pulled Cal into the kitchen. "You can wash up in here, Daddy. Mommy gets really, really mad if I don't wash my hands when it's time to eat," he whispered softly.

Cal's brilliant gaze impaled Lauren as he stared at her, visually examining her face. He knew she had been crying.

"Mommy is very special, Drew," he said almost reverently. "And we must always make certain she's happy."

Drew steered Cal toward the small bathroom. "Mommy's always happy. She laughs and sings all the time."

Cal glanced back over his shoulder at Lauren. A slight smile crinkled her puffy eyes. "That's good to know."

Drew and Cal made a big show of washing their hands. Drew squealed when Cal flicked the water off his hands and it sprayed his face.

Drew put his hands under the running water and shook them out wildly.

"I give up," Cal pleaded. He glanced up at the mirror over the basin, pointing. Droplets of water dotted the glass.

"Uh-oh," they both chorused, then dissolved into a paroxysm of giggles.

Cal tore a sheet of paper toweling from a rack. "I think we'd better clean this up," he whispered conspiratorially.

Drew was still giggling when he slipped into his place on the bench at the table. "Sit next to me, Daddy."

Cal complied obediently, watching Lauren fill a glass at Drew's place setting with milk. He had spent a restless night trying to sort out his feelings after seeing her again, shaken because he realized he still loved her and loved her with the same intensity he had felt on Cay Verde.

After her betrayal, after her deceit, he had continued to love her.

He was amazed that after five years he had changed, yet his feelings for Lauren hadn't changed. Five years before he had been twenty-eight—a very jaded twenty-eight, and Lauren had not been wrong when she told him he was too old for her. By that time he had lived on two continents, socialized with a hedonistic group and had written four best sellers.

He had blamed his behavior and lifestyle on his being the offspring of a tempestuous relationship between a dancer and a noted Boston entertainment attorney who married, divorced, remarried only to divorce a second and final time.

Cal had also spent half of his childhood crossing the Atlantic Ocean between Boston and Barcelona, and when he met Lauren Taylor she offered him what he had sought for a long time—peace, a respite.

Lauren sat down, bowing her head. Drew did the same. Cal lowered his head, feeling somewhat sheepish that it had been a long time, too long, since he had offered thanks for the food placed before him.

"Will you please say grace, Cal?" Lauren asked in a quiet voice.

Cal racked his memory, coming up with one he had learned as a child in Barcelona. The words flowed, fluidly and musically. Both Lauren and Drew raised their head, staring at him.

Lauren blinked slowly, studying his smiling face. "Don't you know one in English?"

He shifted his eyebrows, the gesture reminding her of Drew's. "No."

Drew gave his father a sidelong glance. "What did you say?"

Cal stared down at Drew. "It's Spanish. I thanked God for the food, the hands that prepared it…"

"That's Mommy," Drew interrupted.

Cal glanced over at Lauren. "Yes, that's Mommy. And I also thanked the farmers who grew the food."

Drew puffed up his narrow chest. "Say some more Spanish, Daddy."

Cal ruffled Drew's hair. "Would you like to learn to speak Spanish?"

"Oh yes! Yes, yes, yes!" Drew squealed.

Cal smiled at his animated expression. "We'll begin tomorrow. If that's all right with your mother," he added, noting a slight frown from Lauren.

"Can we, Mommy?"

Her frown vanished as quickly as it had formed. "It's 'may we,' Drew." Her large dark eyes shifted to Cal. "Maybe you should go slowly. Not too much too soon."

Cal knew exactly what she meant, and his mouth tightened. Lauren wasn't going to let him back in her life.

Lauren was quiet during the meal, electing to let Cal and Drew interact with each other. It wasn't easy, but she had to let them have their time together.

Cal and Drew reached for the last slice of crisp Italian bread at the same time. "Let's choose for it, Daddy."

"Two out of three gets it," Cal announced.

"Odds, even, odds," Drew shrieked. "I win!"

Cal turned down his mouth, pouting, and Lauren couldn't stop her laughter from bubbling up and out. He glared at her.

"What's so funny?"

Lauren smothered her laughter. "You. I thought you were going to cry."

Drew broke the slice in half. "Here, Daddy. I don't want you to cry."

A high-pitched yelp and barking filtered through the open windows and Lauren stared across the table at Drew. It was what they had been expecting for days.

"Missy's having her puppies," Drew whispered, his eyes wide and glittering with excitement and anticipation.

Lauren slid off the bench, stopping to slip her bare feet into a pair of worn espadrilles. Drew urged Cal off the bench and followed his mother to the garage.

"Don't get too close," Lauren warned Drew as he and Cal joined her in the coolness of the garage. A large Old English sheepdog lay on a pile of blankets in a corner.

Cal moved closer and hunkered down, laying a hand on the bitch's head. Missy's dark eyes opened and closed as she labored to bring forth the life writhing within her distended abdomen.

"Don't touch her, Daddy!" Drew shouted. "She bites."

Cal went to his knees and pressed his ear against Missy's heaving side. "This little lady's in too much pain to bite. All she wants is to have her babies and rest."

Lauren and Drew could not believe that Missy hadn't snapped at or bitten Cal. They had found the abandoned dog two weeks after moving into the large farmhouse.

Lauren had not been ready to assume the responsibility of caring for a dog when she had to care for a preschooler and make her home habitable for the coming winter. Somehow she managed to get close enough to the snarling animal to wash away the dirt and grime to see the abject abuse the dog had endured. The deep, raw gashes under the thick coat of black-and-white fur sickened her.

She pushed the dog into the back of her car and drove like someone possessed to Tufts University School of Veterinarian Medicine. Missy underwent surgery and spent three days at the school recovering from the surgery and her infected wounds. Lauren was handed a bill and the news that Missy was pregnant.

Not only had she been saddled with a house that needed numerous minor repairs, but also a pregnant dog who snapped and growled at anyone who came within five feet of her.

"How's she doing, Daddy?"

Cal continued stroking Missy's side. "She's doing just fine."

Lauren went to her knees beside Cal. "I can't believe she likes you," she said in awe. "I feed her, but that doesn't stop her from trying to bite me."

"An animal can sense your fear or anxiety," Cal replied. "Missy knows I'm not going to hurt her."

"Somebody hurt Missy real bad before Mommy and I found her," Drew stated proudly.

Cal extended a hand to Drew. "Come pet her."

Drew took a few steps backwards, shaking his head. "Oh no. She'll bite me."

Cal glanced up, noting Drew's anguished expression. "Try it, Drew. She won't bite you."

"Don't force him, Cal," Lauren said, recognizing Drew's reluctance and fear.

Cal looked at Lauren, seeing her tender expression as she stared at Drew. "How's he to overcome his fear if he doesn't face it, darling?"

Lauren did not visibly react to the endearment that seemed to slip fluidly from Cal. Her gaze narrowed. "He's only four, Caleb."

"And he's old enough to have a pet he's not afraid of, Lauren. What's the use of having the dog around if neither of you are going to interact with it?" he countered.

"Missy is a watchdog," Lauren shot back.

Cal grunted under his breath. "Some damn watchdog," he mumbled low enough so that Drew couldn't hear him. "Not only does she frighten the neighbors, but also her master."

Lauren stared at the attractive cleft in his strong chin, then pulled her gaze back to his luminous eyes. "Mind your own business, Caleb Samuels," she replied softly.

He flashed a maddening grin. "It's too late, Lauren Samuels. Drew's my business. And you're also my business."

Lauren felt a shock of annoyance. He had continued to refer to her as a Samuels. "Wrong. And stop calling me Lauren Samuels."

Cal leaned closer. "I didn't give you up, Lauren. You walked out on me because you were a coward, and I don't acknowledge the actions of a coward." She opened her mouth to defend herself, but he stopped her, stating, "We'll talk about it later."

Her jaw snapped loudly and she gritted her teeth. Lauren knew she was not going to have it easy with Caleb Samuels. She had only spent a week with him—a glorious week, but Drew had permitted her a glimpse of what it would be like to live with the man. Not only had he inherited his father's looks but also his stubbornness. Lauren realized stubbornness flawed her own personality, but to recognize and meet it head-on in someone else was exasperating.

It was nearly an hour before Missy whelped her first puppy.

Cal sat on the concrete floor, cradling Drew on his lap as the boy stroked the silky fur on Missy's massive head.

"She likes me," Drew replied in an awed tone. It was difficult for him to contain his excitement as he witnessed the miracle of birth when Missy birthed her second puppy.

There was complete silence as instinct took over. Missy took care of the membrane covering the minute, shivering puppies, cleaning them with her large pink tongue.

Lauren felt the tightness in her own chest ease as Missy nudged her tiny wet babies under her belly. The puppies managed, after several attempts, to locate the swollen nipples to begin nursing.

"Why don't they open their eyes, Daddy?"

Cal rested his chin on the top of Drew's head. "All babies are born with their eyes closed."

Drew glanced up at his father. "Even me?"

Cal glared at Lauren, his eyes saying what she knew his lips wouldn't. "Yes, Drew. Even you," he finally said.

Drew pointed at the nursing puppies. "Did you do that to me, Mommy?"

The heat in Lauren's face had nothing to do with the warmth of the summer afternoon as she watched Cal's gaze move to her breasts.

"Did you, Mommy?" Drew asked, repeating his question.

"Did you, Lauren?" Cal echoed with a sinister grin.

"Yes, I did," she replied, lifting her chin. "It's nature's way of feeding a baby," she explained to Drew.

Cal gave Lauren a nod and an approving smile. "I'm sorry I missed that experience, darling."

For a long moment Lauren stared at him. He was serious. Cal had missed so much and so had she. She had missed not sharing the news of her pregnancy with him, missed his watching her belly swell with his child, missed his soothing away her fears in the labor room, and she'd missed his expression when he could have witnessed the birth of his son; a son who was completely and undeniably his son—their son.

Cal eased Drew off his lap, rising to his feet. His tan slacks were streaked with dirt. Lauren noticed the dark smudges on his knees.

"Jeans are the norm when hanging out around here," she stated.

Cal glanced down at his slacks. "I'll remember that next time."

Drew had not moved from his kneeling position beside Missy. All of his attention was directed on the nursing puppies. "Can I stay and watch, Mommy?"

"Yes. But don't touch the puppies," she warned.

"I won't," Drew complied, not turning away from the whelping corner.

Lauren turned and went back into the house. She washed her hands, then began clearing the table of their half-eaten lunch.

Turning, she bumped into Cal. He took the plates from her hands. "I'll help you."

"No!" she shouted before she could stop herself.

"What's the matter?" There was an expression of genuine concern on his face.

"Just go, Caleb."

His jaw hardened. "Why?"

"I don't want your help."

"What do you want, Lauren?"

"I want you to leave *me* alone. You wanted to see your son and I've agreed to that, but that's where it ends. I don't want to have anything to do with you."

"I, I, I! That's all I hear from you, Lauren. It's always you and no one else. How about me, Lauren? How about Drew? What about Drew inheriting what is rightfully his?"

Lauren's temper flared, matching Cal's. "Let's clear the air about your grandfather's will. I do not and will not concede to his antiquated scheme of forcing us to stay together. This is not the Middle Ages."

Cal tried bringing his turbulent emotions under control. Losing his temper only fueled Lauren's. "He didn't put us together five years ago, Lauren. We married because we loved each other, not because anyone forced us to live together."

"That doesn't change the fact that a dead man is manipulating our lives."

"But he left us a way out."

Her gaze narrowed. "How's that?"

"We only have to remain married for a year, Lauren. That's only three hundred sixty-three more days than we had five years ago."

"But we have to live together."

"People who are married generally do live together."

"No, Cal," she replied, shaking her head for emphasis. "I can't."

He took a step closer, his breath washing over her face. "My grandfather let you off a lot easier than I would've done if I had discovered you had my child and not told me. In other words, he saved your butt, Lauren."

"What are you talking about?"

Cal prayed he would not explode. He still loved Lauren, still loved her passionately yet she would not let him come to her with love.

"I would've sued you for joint custody of my son." His eyes were cold, forbidding. "You were my wife when Drew was conceived, and as your husband I had a right to know that you were carrying my baby. No court of law would've denied me *that* right, Mrs. Samuels, while you willfully and deliberately kept me ignorant of that fact."

Lauren felt her composure break. "Then do it, Caleb! If you want revenge that badly—then sue me!" Her hands curled into tight fists.

"It's not about revenge, Lauren. It's about Drew and his future."

Lauren had thought about the money Dr. Samuels had bequeathed his great-grandson. She knew Drew probably would not need the money because she was certain Cal would provide for the child's future, but the fact remained that she wasn't given a choice in whether she wanted to be with Cal. The decision was taken out of her hands—their hands.

There was a pulse beat of silence before she asked, "If it's not revenge, then is it about not wanting Jacqueline to have the money?"

The tense lines around his mouth relaxed. "It's about not wanting Jacqueline to have the money," he admitted quietly. "But it's also about my son."

Lauren turned away from Cal, trying to sort out all that had happened in the past twenty-four hours. Why was it every time she encountered Caleb Samuels her life whirled out of orbit. What was there about him that unbalanced her?

"Please go," she ordered.

Cal stared at her straight back. "I'll leave, but I'll be back at six. We'll eat dinner out."

She bristled at his unexpected demand. "I…"

"Just be ready, Lauren," he snapped, turning on his heel and walking out of the kitchen and back to the garage, leaving Lauren glaring at his retreating figure.

Lauren evoked rage in him that stripped him of every shred

of control he had over himself or his emotions. She had pushed and challenged him to new limits. She had unwittingly seduced him, married him, then walked out of his life, leaving a void that still lingered, and she had kept his son from him. But all of the deceit would end. This time Lauren would not be the only winner.

Chapter 5

Drew propped an elbow up on the table, supporting his chin on the heel of his right hand. "I thought we were going to McDonald's," he grumbled under his breath.

"Take your elbow off the table, Drew," Lauren chastised softly.

Cal laid aside the menu he had been reading. "What is it you want?" he asked the pouting child.

"A hamburger," Drew mumbled.

Cal smiled, placing a hand on his son's head. "I'm certain the chef can grind a sirloin steak into a burger."

Drew dropped his arm, the vertical slashes between his eyes vanishing quickly. "Can he make it fast?"

Cal glanced over at Lauren, noting the smile softening her moist, lush mouth. He arched a questioning brow and lifted broad shoulders under his cream-colored linen jacket.

Lauren leaned closer to Cal. "Drew wants to eat fast food so that he can get back home to the puppies," she explained.

"Yeah! The puppies," Drew shrieked.

Cal was at a loss for words. How could he explain to a four-year-old that he had to pull strings to garner a reservation at one of Boston's most elegant and popular restaurants to celebrate his newly discovered fatherhood?

Lauren came to his rescue, explaining, "The puppies are like new babies, Drew. They'll sleep most of the time. The only thing they're going to do for the next week is eat and sleep."

Drew looked distressed. "When can they play with me?"

"Give them a couple of months."

The child did not look convinced as he looked at his mother under lowered lids. "How long is a couple of months?"

"Sixty days," Cal answered, his gaze fixed on Lauren's face, burning her with its brilliant intensity.

"I can count to a hundred and I know sixty is a lot," Drew said, frowning again.

"Sixty days will come very quickly, Drew," Lauren remarked, staring back at Cal.

"Too quickly," Cal retorted.

Sixty days was not a lot to Lauren. She couldn't wait for it to come because ever since she walked into the law offices of Barlow, Mann and Evans her life and her future were no longer her own to plan or control, because for the second time in her life she had lost control of herself. Why, she thought, was it always because of Caleb Samuels?

When she thought about it, her situation was more like something from a script for a TV soap than real life. How could Dr. Caleb B. Samuels being of sound mind and body formulate such a preposterous scheme? But had John Evans said that Dr. Samuels was of sound mind and body when he wrote his will?

She remembered the attorney stating that it was a simple will, then she ignored the rest of the legal language until he mentioned the equal distribution of the late doctor's estate.

"Mommy, there's Uncle Andy," Drew said in a hushed voice, temporarily forgetting about the puppies.

Turning, Lauren glanced over her shoulder. Andrew Monroe was heading for their table, grinning broadly.

Andrew's friendly smile did not falter when he recognized the man sitting between Lauren and Drew. Cal rose slightly and pulled back Lauren's chair as she stood up.

Lauren extended both hands, returning Andrew's appealing smile. "Who are you entertaining tonight?"

Andrew caught her fingers and pressed a light kiss to her lips. "Tonight I'm wining and dining."

Lauren cocked her head at an angle. "Who is she?"

Andrew's dark green eyes sparkled. "I don't know. She's a blind date."

Lauren looped her arm through the expensive fabric covering her agent's arm. "Andrew, I'd like you to meet Caleb Samuels." Cal was slow in rising to his feet. "Cal, Andrew Monroe, my agent." She felt the muscles bunch up under her hand and extracted her arm from Andrew's.

The two men gave each other predatory glares, then shook hands. Lauren let out her breath, unaware that she had been holding it in. The tension eased when Andrew hunkered down beside Drew's chair and dropped an arm around the boy's shoulders.

"What have you been up to, Drew?" Andrew asked.

"I have a daddy and Missy got new puppies," Drew managed to explain in one breath.

Andrew affected an expression of surprise. "Now, that's what I call headline news." He managed a smile for Drew. "You know you promised me a puppy, Champ."

Drew nodded. "Yup. But you can't have it for sixty days."

"I'll wait." Andrew stood, nodding at Cal. "My pleasure, Caleb." He winked at Lauren, leaning over and kissing her cheek. "I'll call you tomorrow," he told her quietly.

Cal seated Lauren before retaking his own place. He studied the menu without seeing the printed words. It was obvious Lauren and Andrew Monroe shared more than an agent-client relationship, and he did not have to have the intelligence quotient of a rocket scientist to know that Drew had been named for Andrew.

He stared at Andrew seated at a nearby table. Andrew's thick waving blond hair, electric green eyes and deep tropical tan made him a very attractive man; a man Cal was certain Lauren found attractive.

The sommelier's presence redirected Cal's attention. The man uncorked a bottle of wine and filled two glasses with the pale rosé Lauren had selected earlier to accompany their meal. Drew's glass was filled with a mixture of ginger ale and cherry syrup.

Cal's gaze caught and held Lauren's as she stared at him across the table. The light from the small lamp on the table reflected off her satiny dark skin. The scene was so natural yet so unnatural. They appeared the normal family dining out at the end of the week. But they were not a normal family. They were a family of strangers.

He raised his glass, smiling. "May I make the toast?"

"Please," Lauren conceded, raising her glass.

Drew, watching his parents, did the same.

The harder Cal tried to ignore the truth the more it persisted when he realized he had been waiting and holding out for Lauren. No woman he had ever met could duplicate or replace her. Knowing this he said solemnly, "A toast to the weddings, births, graduations and our grandchildren as we pass through this life together as a family."

It was another ten seconds before Lauren reacted to the toast. He had deceived her; he wanted more than a year of her life—he wanted a lifetime.

Her hand was steady, her voice low and controlled as she made her own toast. "To Caleb and Drew and a lifetime of love between father and son."

"Now me," Drew said, not wanting to be left out. "To my Mommy and Daddy and Missy and her puppies."

Lauren laughed, dispelling the strained mood created by Andrew's appearance and Cal's toast.

While dining, she caught a glimpse of Andrew's blind date, a young woman with curling red-gold hair. The angle of Andrew's head indicated he was quite enthralled with her.

Cal saw the direction of Lauren's gaze. "How long has Andrew been your agent?"

Lauren gave him a demure smile. "About four years."

Lowering his chin, Cal's lips twisted into a cynical smile. "You met him before you *met* me?"

"No. I met him after I'd met you. He became my agent and a good friend. I named Drew for him."

Cal put down his fork, placing both hands, palms down, on the pale pink tablecloth. The muscle in his jaw throbbed as he compressed his lips. "I take it you're close friends?"

Lauren heard the censure in his voice. "Very close." Her eyes met his, not wavering. "And we'll continue to be," she added quietly.

Cal blinked once. "I see."

She raised her chin. "Do you, Caleb?"

He refused to answer because what he wanted to say was better left unsaid. Andrew Monroe was not Drew's father yet he had secured a place of importance not only in his life, but also in Lauren's.

However, he could not blame Andrew if he was attracted to Lauren. There was something about her Cal had not been able to resist when he first met her. She was captivating. Whether she was stylishly dressed, as she was now in a polished cotton pumpkin-orange slip dress and matching collarless cropped jacket, or in a pair of jeans, Lauren Taylor-Samuels was alluring and incredibly feminine.

The soft light from the lamp shimmered on her smooth velvet-brown face, highlighting the darkness of her eyes, the delicate sweep of her high cheekbones and the sensual curve of her full, sexy mouth.

Her mouth. It fascinated him. The sweet fullness of her lower lip he had tasted over and over until he was more intoxicated by the pliant flesh than the potent drinks he had consumed on Cay Verde.

Her voice. Even the sound of her voice, low and husky, had turned him on. He had lain in bed, eyes closed, listening to the sound of it as it filtered over his naked flesh like a luxurious fur pelt.

Bits and pieces of the days and nights he had made love to Lauren floated about him like the silent whisper of a snowflake. He could see it, feel it, but then it disappeared in the heat, leaving only a damp trace of its existence.

There had been times when he thought he had imagined her. She was in his life, and then she was gone.

Drew was nodding over his plate before he finished his hamburger and Cal signaled for the waiter and the check.

Drew had forgone his regularly scheduled afternoon nap with the appearance of his father and the birth of the puppies.

Cal carried Drew out to the parking lot, placing him on the back seat of the car.

Lauren caught Cal's arm as he held the passenger door open for her. "No speeding, Caleb."

He frowned at her. "I wasn't speeding."

"Yes, you were," she argued.

"I was only doing seventy," he retorted.

"Then you were speeding."

Cal dangled a set of keys under her nose. "Do you want to drive?"

She took the keys from his fingers. Her heels rapped sharply on the asphalt as she walked around the car and slipped behind the wheel. She started up the engine, waiting for Cal to get into the car.

Leaning over, she stared up at him. "Are you getting in?"

Cal folded his long frame into her small car. "I didn't expect you to take me up on the offer."

"One thing you'll learn about me, Caleb Samuels, and that is I accept all dares. Buckle your seat belt," she ordered when he crossed his arms over his chest.

His chuckle was low and confident. "I dare you to marry me again," he said quickly.

Her fingers tightened on the gearshift. "Marriage is excluded."

"Don't try to weasel out of it, Lauren."

"I'm not trying to weasel out of anything, Caleb."

"You're angry because you're caught in your own trap," he taunted.

Lauren shifted into first and maneuvered out of the parking space. "No, I'm not."

"Not trying to weasel out of your dare, or you're not angry?"

She concentrated on her driving. "The answer is no to both questions."

"Then why did you call me Caleb?"

"It's your name, isn't it?"

He arched his eyebrows, smiling. "Yes. But you only call me Caleb when you're angry or whenever we made love." He ignored her withering glare. "I used to love the little sounds you made in bed, Lauren."

Lauren stopped for a red light, catching a glimpse of his straight white teeth out of the corner of her eye.

"You're a pig."

"Why? Because I'm honest, darling."

"And I'm not?"

"No!" All traces of his teasing vanished quickly. "I'm going to ask you one question," he stated in a gentler tone, "and I want you to give me an honest answer. If you can't or won't, then don't say anything. But please, please, Lauren, don't lie to me again."

Lauren was angry; angry with herself and that she had permitted Cal to bait her. She did not have to look at him to feel his tension. She felt it radiating all around her.

"What is it you want to know?"

"Why did you leave me?"

Lauren stared out through the windshield. She was stiff; stiff and brittle enough to shatter into a million pieces if he touched her, and she could not look at Cal or she would lose control.

"I was afraid," she whispered.

Cal moved as close as his seat belt would permit him. "You were what?"

Lauren blinked back tears. "I...I was so afraid, Caleb."

"Pull over and stop," Cal ordered. Lauren signaled, maneuvered out of traffic and parked. "I'll drive," he informed her when he noted her deathlike grip on the steering wheel.

Lauren pressed her head back against the headrest, trying valiantly to bring her emotions under control. Unbuckling her seat belt, she slipped out of the car, exchanging seats with Cal.

Cal started the car, savagely shifting into gear. The sound of Lauren's voice telling him that she had been afraid unnerved and angered him.

He had wasted almost five years—*they* had wasted five years. If he had insisted that she give him a reason other than the one she had they would not have lost those years.

There was complete silence on the return drive to North Grafton, neither Lauren nor Cal initiating conversation.

Cal pulled into the driveway, turning off the engine. "I'll carry Drew," he said, and Lauren nodded.

She unlocked the front door and led the way through the living room and up the stairs to the second floor. Flipping on a wall switch, Lauren looked down before stepping into Drew's bedroom. It was a habit she had acquired once Drew began walking. She had fallen and sprained her wrist when she slipped on the small toys he usually left scattered about the floor.

Cal laid the child on his bed, removing his shoes, socks and outer clothing while Lauren went into an adjoining bath. She returned with a damp cloth and towel, washing away the traces of catsup from his face and hands. Drew stirred, mumbling unintelligibly about the puppies, then settled back to sleep once he was covered with a lightweight cotton blanket.

Lauren turned off the bedside lamp and a night-light glowed, bathing the bedroom in a soft pink glow. She left the room, leaving Cal standing beside the bed.

She walked into her bedroom across the hall and kicked off her pumps. Sitting down on a bentwood rocker, she crossed her legs and waited for Cal. Minutes later he stood in the doorway, hands thrust into the pockets of his trousers.

Lauren sensed his disquiet. "Thank you for dinner."

"It was a bit brief," he said stiffly.

She managed a slight smile. "It was still nice."

He returned her smile. "Do you mind if I come back tomorrow?"

"No, I don't mind, Cal." She gave him a direct stare. "I won't stop you from seeing your son, but I'd prefer you not plan outings that include me. The only thing I ask is that you let me know in advance where you're taking Drew and when you expect to bring him back."

Cal straightened from his leaning position, hands tightening into fists. "Is that all, Lauren?"

She nodded. "That's all."

He walked into her bedroom and sat down on a window seat. He ran a hand over the mauve and gray quilt-patterned cushion.

"Well, I have a few things to say." His expression was a mask of stone. "Right now Drew is too young to understand what divorce is all about, but there are wounds and scars associated with broken marriages that some children never recover from. Besides too many children are growing up not knowing who their fathers are."

Lauren had had more than enough time to plan her rebuttal when she had replayed this scenario after she discovered she was carrying Caleb Samuels' child.

"It was never my intention to keep Drew from you. If that was my original intent I never would have named you as the father on his birth certificate, and your grandfather wouldn't have been able to prove that Drew was his great-grandson. I'm not that selfish."

"But you're unreasonable," he countered, running all ten

fingers through his graying curls, lacing them together at the back of his head.

"Why do you say that?" she asked.

"Because you won't marry me."

Lauren let out her breath in a loud sigh. "Why can't you let it go?" she whispered.

"Damn it, I can't!" His hands came down and curled into tight fists. "I can't, Lauren."

Lauren left the rocker and walked over to stand in front of Cal. For a second, she glimpsed pain. He was hurting.

Sitting down on the window seat, she curbed the urge to hug him. "Why can't you understand…"

"I don't want to understand, Lauren," he interrupted. "I married you because I wanted to spend the rest of my life with you."

"Why me and not some other woman?" Lauren questioned, realizing she should've asked Cal the same question when he asked her to marry him on Cay Verde.

He stared down at her upturned face. "Because you were not like any other woman I'd known up to that time. The women I'd…" He let his words trail off.

"The women you'd slept with," she finished for him.

"The women I used to see," he insisted. "I never knew if they were with me because they enjoyed my company or whether it was because of who I was.

"It was different with you, Lauren." He reached for her hand and cradled it gently in his larger one. "Do you remember what you said to me the first time we met?"

Her lashes shadowed her eyes. "Yes." Cal pulled her hand to his chest and she felt the steady, strong pumping of his heart. "I said you didn't have to like me."

"Oh, but I did, Lauren," he confessed. "You were so

innocent yet so seductive. And you scared the hell out of me," he also admitted with a wide grin.

Lauren's head came up quickly. "What are you talking about? I was the frightened one. When you asked me to marry you I was too frightened to say no because I didn't want to stop sleeping with you. But you said you wouldn't sleep with me again unless we were married."

He brought her hand to his lips and kissed her fingers. "That's true. And if you hadn't agreed to marry me I would not have slept with you again."

"Why not?"

"Because I didn't want to hurt you. And eventually I would have. You would've returned to Boston and I probably would've continued doing what I had been doing, but it would've always been in the back of my mind that I had taken advantage of you."

What Cal didn't say was that the week he had spent on Cay Verde was magical; she was the magic, and he wasn't willing to let go of the magic. He had thought of her as a beautiful, mythical spirit that had captured him and refused to let him go.

Unconsciously, Lauren laid her cheek against his hard shoulder. "I thought of my stay on Cay Verde in terms of a trip to a fantasy island. I was overwhelmed with the enchantment of the blue skies, turquoise waters, palm trees, exotic flowers, warm trade winds and potent rum drinks. I'd escaped from my humdrum life as a researcher to discover paradise. And in that paradise I encountered the worldly, sybaritic Caleb Samuels. However, that Caleb Samuels was nothing like the rumors I'd heard or the stories I'd read."

Cal felt the electric static of her touch and her warmth. "Don't tell me a woman of your intelligence reads those supermarket rags?" he teased.

Lauren chuckled, pulling away and Cal felt her loss immediately. "Only if I'm on a very long checkout line." She sobered, folding her hands together in her lap. "But the fantasy faded when we came back to the States. It was then that I questioned my sanity. Boston was not Cay Verde and your grandfather did not welcome me with open arms."

Every muscle in Cal's body tensed. He stared down at her. "What did my grandfather say to you?"

"Nothing."

A frown creased Cal's forehead. "Are you certain?"

"He didn't have to say anything to me, Cal. His not saying anything said it all. He did not approve of your choice in a wife."

Cal relaxed again, pulling Lauren into the circle of his embrace. He felt her stiffen, then relax. "My grandfather was a strange man. He never approved of my father's marriages. And I suppose my mother and Jacqueline gave him reason enough to disapprove of them."

Lauren realized she knew nothing about the private Caleb Samuels. The man she knew was the best-selling author, the jet-setter, the celebrity, the literary genius who had written four bestsellers before he was twenty-eight; he was the man who dated beautiful women, whose photograph had appeared on the cover of *Ebony* and who had been voted in as one of the beautiful and sexy people for *People* magazine. She had known only one side of Caleb Samuels, and that side she had known intimately.

"What happened to your mother?" she asked softly.

"She's still alive. We share a house in Spain." Cal pulled back, giving her a hopeful smile. "I'd like to take Drew to Spain with me during a holiday."

Lauren's fingers curled into a tight fist against his chest. "I don't know."

He covered her hand with his. "You don't have to give me an answer now." He gave her a sad smile. "There is something I have to tell you, Lauren. Perhaps it'll help you to understand why my grandfather put Drew in his will and why he's forcing us to live together.

"My mother waited until I was seven before she married my father," he began, shocking Lauren with his disclosure. "Even after she married him she refused to live with him. If she was feeling generous, she permitted my father to see me for a weekend or for a few weeks of the summer. There were times when I saw my tutor and the housekeeper more than my parents."

Cal lowered his head and an unnamed emotion flowed from his penetrating eyes. Lauren felt as if he were X-raying her head and her heart, willing her to feel what he was feeling.

"My parents were divorced for the first time when I was ten. Two years later they remarried. This union changed all of us when we lived together as a family for the first time. I experienced erratic sleep patterns because I was afraid to go to sleep then wake up to find that I'd been dreaming. It became a dream because three years later it all ended. They divorced for a last and final time and I returned to Barcelona with my mother. The divorce destroyed my father, and he changed, becoming a detached cold stranger to me. I knew he loved me, but he loved my mother more.

"I turned sixteen and my grandfather became the dominant male figure in my life. The times I returned to the States he and I shared fishing trips, baseball and football games and long walks in the snow. Gramps saved me, Lauren. He helped me through the most critical time in my life—adolescence. What I shared with my grandfather I want to share with my son. I want him to come to me when he has a problem he doesn't feel comfortable discussing with you, and I want to help you to help him become the very best that he can be. And because my grandfather didn't want Drew to mirror my life he's forcing us to be together. David Samuels never fought for the right to be my father, but my grandfather wants to make certain I will. Even if he has to do it from his grave."

"You can't accomplish everything in a year," Lauren said, trying to ease the tight fist around her heart.

"We'll begin with a year," he replied quietly. "A year was a lot more than what I was given at Drew's age. If we remarry it won't be for you or me, but for Drew."

Lauren felt attacked by her emotions; twin emotions of desire and fear. She wanted Cal. She wanted his presence and his reminder that she was a woman; a woman who had experienced the full range of her femininity, and she was filled with a fear; a fear that Drew would become a defenseless, hapless victim when she and Cal separated.

She bit down hard on her lower lip. If she gave Cal a year of her life, Lauren knew it would end with one casualty— Lauren Taylor. She couldn't marry him again, then go through the pain of another separation.

"Think about it, Lauren," Cal said, breaking into her thoughts. "We still have fifty-nine days."

She nodded slowly. "I'll think about it," she promised.

"Do you mind if I take Drew out tomorrow?"

"No...no I don't mind." Her head was reeling from Cal's confession.

They sat, side by side, silent, each lost in their private musings. Without warning, Cal stood and glanced down at Lauren. "Good night."

She didn't look up at him. "Good night, Cal." She sat on the window seat until she heard him drive away, then made her way to her attic retreat where she entered her thoughts in a journal. Her small, neat script filled more than four pages. The ink had not dried on the last page when she printed in bold letters what she had printed every day since she began her journal the day after Drew was born: I LOVE CALEB B. SAMUELS II, AND I WILL LOVE HIM FOREVER!

Chapter 6

Lauren had weeded and watered her vegetable garden, fed Missy and put up several loads of wash by the time Cal arrived at eight.

He stood in front of her, holding his arms away from his body. "Better?" He was dressed in a pair of navy chinos, a blue and white striped rugby shirt and a pair of navy blue deck shoes.

Lauren opened the screen door, nodding and admiring his casual attire. "Much better."

His gaze lingered on her shorts, tank top and sandaled feet. "Am I too early?"

"You're just in time for breakfast."

Drew raced across the living room, arms outstretched. "Hi, Daddy."

Cal swung Drew high in the air, then cradled him to his chest. "Hi, partner. What do you have planned for today?"

"I have no plans," Drew whispered in Cal's ear.

"How about a baseball game? The Yankees are in town and perhaps we can see someone blast a few over the Green Monster."

Drew affected a serious expression. "I don't know a Green Monster, Daddy."

Cal pressed his forehead to Drew's. "The Green Monster is the wall at Fenway Park where the Red Sox play baseball."

Drew laughed. "I want to catch a ball, Daddy."

"Drew had better pick up the toys in his room or Drew is going to catch some trouble," Lauren said quietly, watching the interchange between her son and his father.

"Aw, Mommy. Do I have to? I'm only a little kid."

Cal lowered Drew to the floor. "Being a little kid has nothing to do with you not obeying your mother."

Drew pushed out his lower lip, pouting. "I don't know how to put them away," he mumbled.

Cal crossed his arms over his chest. "Do you know how to play with them?"

"They just jump out and play with me," Drew explained, swinging his arms above his head.

"Tell them to jump back into place," Lauren retorted, struggling not to laugh. "You have five minutes, Drew."

Drew gave his father a pleading look. "Daddy, I can't."

"Do it, Drew," Cal ordered in a stern tone.

Lauren and Cal went into the kitchen while Drew stomped up the staircase to his room.

"Is he always this obstinate?" Cal asked.

"Always," Lauren confirmed.

Cal sat down on a tall stool, smiling at Lauren. "He must have inherited his stubbornness from you."

Lauren gripped the handle to a griddle and stared at him. "I suggest you quit while you're still ahead, Caleb."

He held up his hands in a gesture of surrender. "Sorry, ma'am."

Cal watched Lauren as she busied herself preparing breakfast. He had spent the night sorting out all that had happened since seeing her again, and had come to the conclusion that he could not intimidate Lauren. Intimidation fueled her quick temper and she came back at him with everything she could muster and knowing this he decided to romance her; romance her the way he had done on Cay Verde.

His tension eased and a rush of desire, a peaceful, soothing desire swept over him. He would win Lauren's love. She said she had loved him on Cay Verde and he wouldn't stop until she said so again.

Lauren cooked dozens of silver dollar-sized blueberry pancakes, Cal and Drew devouring them as soon as they came off the griddle. She slipped four on a plate for herself and joined them at the table.

"These are the best, Mommy," Drew got out between bites.

Cal nodded in agreement, his mouth full. "You're a fabulous cook, Lauren," he said after swallowing.

"She's the best, Daddy. Mommy makes funny cookies."

Cal raised an eyebrow at Lauren. "What are funny cookies?"

"They are cookies cut into different shapes," she explained. "I usually make them for special occasions."

"My birthday is a special occasion," Drew announced.

Cal smiled, wiggling his eyebrows at Drew. "You're right about that." He drained his second cup of coffee. "Let's clean the kitchen, partner, then we'll head out to the mall before we go to the ballpark."

Drew's jaw dropped as he gasped loudly. "But Mommy cleans the kitchen, Daddy."

"If Mommy cooks, then the men clean."

"But cleaning is for girls," Drew protested.

"Who told you cleaning is for girls?" Cal questioned.

"Tommy's daddy said that only girls clean up."

"Who's Tommy, Lauren?" Cal asked, scowling.

"He lives next door." She glanced across the table at Drew, affecting an expression he was familiar with.

"Let's clean up, Daddy," he said quickly.

Lauren eased off the bench and leaned over Cal. "You shouldn't have to negotiate, Caleb," she whispered in his ear.

Cal caught her hand, pulling her down to sit beside him. "What do you do?" he whispered back, circling her waist with his right arm.

Lauren felt his hot breath on her neck. The sensual aura that was Caleb Samuels swept over her, battering down her defenses.

"You give him the *look*."

Cal lowered his head, his mouth brushing over her ear. "What's the *look?*"

Her head came up slowly, her mouth only inches from his. Time stood still, then spun out of control, transporting them back to an island where they had escaped party revelers to find their own private sanctuary; a sanctuary filled with primal desire and love.

They had made love in its rawest form: mating.

Cal was hypnotized by the dark fires in Lauren's eyes and the lush moistness of her lips, calling him to taste her succulent fruit over and over.

"It's going to be a while before he can interpret that look," Cal said with a knowing smile. "And that won't be until his hormones start running amuck."

Lauren dropped her gaze, charming Cal with the demure gesture. "I'm going to leave you *men* to your chores." He released her and she slid off the bench and walked out of the kitchen.

Moisture had formed between her breasts and her heart was beating rapidly. Inhaling deeply, she made her way up the staircase to her attic retreat. She opened a set of double windows and a light breeze swept into the large space, cooling her fevered flesh.

She wanted Cal and he knew it. There had been no way she could hide it from him.

She flopped down on a daybed, cradling her arms under her head. Maybe if she had slept with another man, any man, after her brief marriage to Caleb Samuels she would have purged him from her system. Perhaps then she would not have the erotic memories that haunted her relentlessly without warning.

Time and time again she relived his breath washing over her moist face, his fingers searching and finding the secret, hidden parts of her body and wringing spasms of desire from her.

Closing her eyes, Lauren could still feel his teeth on her sensitive breasts, biting and suckling them until she thought she was going to lose her mind. She remembered his softly spoken words that calmed her; the soothing voice whose commands she obeyed blindly when he told her to open her mouth and her legs to him.

She opened her eyes, staring up at the pale wallpaper on the ceiling. One year. First it had been one week and now it was one year. Could she afford to give Cal and Drew their year together? Could she afford not to think about what she would gain or lose?

"Lauren?"

She sat up at the sound of the male voice. "I'm over here."

Cal stepped into the attic, glancing around the yawning space. He smiled at her. "Drew said I'd find you up here."

She returned his smile. "This is my inner sanctum."

Cal walked over to a wall of shelves filled from floor to ceiling with books and sheaves of magazines. "When do you work?" he asked, examining the spine of one book.

"Usually at night." Lauren moved off the daybed and joined him at the built-in shelves. "Once Drew's in school I'll change my schedule."

"How many hours do you usually put in each night?"

She shrugged slender shoulders. "It depends on the subject matter and how quickly the material is needed."

Opening a book with a tattered cover, Cal stared at the copyright date. "Will you work for me?"

She remembered the Zulu project. "You don't want me, Cal."

His head snapped up and he stared at her. "Yes I do. I recall being told that you were the best."

"I am good," she replied confidently. "But we don't work well professionally."

"It'll be different this time."

"Why?"

"Both of us are older, more mature, and I don't think we would allow our personal feelings to affect our professionalism."

Lauren knew Cal had spoken the truth. She was older, mature and much more experienced. She wouldn't be so easy to seduce this time.

She nodded. "What do you have in mind?"

A slight smile tilted the corners of his mouth. "I've been toying with a story line ever since Summit offered me the Zulu project. How much do you know about ancient African kingdoms and their religions?"

"North or south of the Sahara?"

"North and south," Cal replied.

Lauren raised her chin, giving him a saucy grin. "Enough."

His eyes brightened in excitement. "Will you do it?"

"Have you put anything down on paper?" she asked, not committing herself. Cal shook his head and Lauren took his arm and directed him across the room. "Come with me."

She led him to a section of the attic where she had set up her computer. She sat down, switching on the screen. Patting the chair beside hers, she smiled up at Cal. "Please sit down." He sat while she booted up the program.

"Talk to me, Cal."

He met her steady gaze. "What about?"

"Your story line."

Cal began, hesitantly at first, then all of the thoughts and ideas he had buried away in the deep recesses of his mind flowed. Lauren typed as quickly as she spoke, his words coming to life as amber letters covered the screen.

Drew entered the attic silently, taking a small stool near the desk. He had learned to sit and wait for his mother to acknowledge him whenever she worked at her computer. He fidgeted, crossing and uncrossing his legs. Patience waning quickly, he left the stool and crawled onto Cal's lap.

Cal held Drew, his plot unraveling slowly but smoothly. As his story unfolded, the tension and uneasiness he had felt whenever he tried writing this novel slipped away. Words he had tried putting into a tape recorder rushed out like a swollen stream.

His voice finally faded and he felt a combination of exhilaration and relief. It was over; his story was out.

Lauren pressed a key, storing the material. Excitement shone from her large, dark eyes. "It's fabulous, Cal."

"I like it too, Daddy," Drew chimed in.

Cal hugged Drew, kissing his forehead. "And I like you, too." He tightened his grip on his son, staring over his head at Lauren. Something intense flowed from his entrancement, his gaze slowly appraising her face and body. What he had tried to deny shocked him like a bolt of electricity.

All he had to offer Lauren was a reminder of a week of shared passions on a private tropical island. A week that had changed her life forever.

He had been drawn to Lauren because she was able to touch him the way no woman had been able to do before that time. She continued to touch him, for he had been unable to replace her with other women even after she left him.

He needed her. She was comforting. With her he felt only peace, a peace even when she stubbornly refused to give in to his demands, and guilt nagged his conscience. He needed her, he needed Drew; but did Lauren need him? Her life appeared uncomplicated and filled with predictability. She had a new house to decorate, a young child who looked to her for love and nurturing, and a profession that provided her with security for a comfortable way of life.

Taking a glance at the clock on her desk, Lauren said, "It's after ten. You guys should leave now if you want to go to the mall, then make it to your baseball game."

"Are you coming to Boston with us, Mommy?"

Lauren winked at Drew, trailing her fingers over his smooth cheek. "Not this time, sweetheart."

"Are we going to see Grandma and Grandpa?"

"Grandma and Grandpa are coming over Sunday because Sunday is Father's..." Her words trailed off as she realized it would be Cal's first Father's Day celebration.

"I'd like you to share dinner with us tomorrow," she said to Cal. "You'll get to meet my parents."

"Good," he replied without hesitating. "I'm looking forward to meeting them."

Drew jumped off Cal's lap. "I'm going to get my baseball cap," he shouted, running out of the attic.

Cal laughed, shaking his head. "Does he ever walk?"

"Never." There was also a trace of laughter in Lauren's voice.

Cal sobered quickly. "I'm very serious about you being the researcher for my book, Lauren. And I prefer not to go through Andrew Monroe."

Lauren knew she had not imagined Cal's resentment of Andrew. "He's my agent, Cal."

He may be your agent but I was your husband, Cal told himself. "I don't want Andrew Monroe involved in this, Lauren, and if you insist on involving him I won't write the book."

Lauren registered the look of implacable determination on his face. "You have to write it." It had been more than five years since C. B. Samuels had released a new book, and the story line for this book was worthy of a Pulitzer. She noted the thinning of Cal's mouth and she knew it was useless to argue with him.

"Okay, Cal. No Andrew," she conceded.

Leaning over, he cradled her face between his hands and kissed her mouth tenderly. "Thank you, darling."

Lauren felt the explosive heat from his mouth and body. It was still alive. The passion had not cooled.

Cal pulled back and stared down into her startled eyes. "You don't realize how special you are, darling. You've given me Drew, so I owe you a gift, Lauren."

She couldn't talk as she nodded numbly. All Caleb Samuels had to do was touch her, kiss her and she was lost. She hadn't matured that much. The man had captured her heart and refused to let it go.

"I'll see you later," Cal said quietly, releasing her and rising to his feet.

"Have a good time." Lauren couldn't control the breathless timbre of her voice.

She sat, wondering if she could take the risk. Could she risk marrying Cal again and come out of the final separation unscathed?

But Lauren knew even if she didn't marry Cal again he would always be in her life. There was no way he was not going to be involved with Drew. He and Drew had bonded quickly and no matter what happened between his parents Drew would have his father.

The phone rang and Lauren answered the call. It was Andrew Monroe, telling her he had received her latest packet of material. Andrew did not mention Caleb Samuels and neither did Lauren before he hung up. Andrew Monroe was the only person, aside from her family, who knew who Drew's father was.

Intuition told Lauren that Cal did not like Andrew and the feeling was mutual, and she was caught in the middle. Her love for Andrew was a special love. He was a friend, a confidant she loved, but she was not in love with him. He had become a protector—for her and Drew and the love that had developed between the three of them was one of closeness and family.

Thinking of family, she called her mother, informing Odessa that Cal would join them for their Father's Day celebration. She hung up, sighing audibly. She had to find something suitable for a Father's Day gift for her son's father.

Chapter 7

Drew arrived home asleep in Cal's arms, and Lauren overrode the child's feeble protests when she gave him a bath, washing away the distinctive odor of mustard and popcorn.

Dressed in cotton pajamas, Drew groped for his bed and was sound asleep before Lauren turned off the light and joined Cal in the kitchen.

Cal sat at the table, drinking a cup of freshly brewed coffee. Lauren gave him a warm smile. "Drew's one tired little boy."

"Make that one tired little boy and one very tired daddy," Cal admitted, returning her smile with a strained one of his own.

Lauren filled a cup with coffee and added a splash of milk. "It's going to take a while before you adjust to parenting," she said, using her hip to close the refrigerator door. She walked over to the dining nook and sat down opposite Cal. "But for you the worst is over. Feedings at 3:00 a.m., and teething can test the limits of one's sanity."

Cal stared at her from under heavy eyelids. "I missed everything that was important, Lauren. I missed you telling me that I was going to be a father. I missed seeing my son's birth, and because of you I missed all of the important milestones."

His voice was void of emotion and it chilled Lauren, and at that moment she felt as if he could hate her. His gaze shifted to his cup, searching its black depths for answers she could not give him.

"I'm sorry, Cal," she apologized in a quiet voice. "But I can't spend the rest of my life atoning for doing what I thought was the right thing to do at that time.",

Cal raised his head, peering intently at her strained expression. "You'll make it up to me," he stated flatly. "I'll make certain of that," he added, rising to his feet.

Lauren watched him walk to the sink and empty the remains of his coffee into it. He rinsed the cup and placed it in the dishwasher. There was a pregnant silence, the absence of sound oppressive.

She knew she had wounded him, and he was angry because she walked out on him. She had trampled Caleb Samuels' male pride because she had left him after being married for only two days. It was only now, after two days, that she saw a man who was very different from the one she had met on Cay Verde.

Which man was the real Caleb Samuels? This one was more of a stranger than the one she'd met on Cay Verde. She had married him, borne his child, and still he was a stranger.

"What time is dinner tomorrow?" he questioned, managing to display a polite smile.

Lauren's composure was as fragile as an eggshell and she exhibited a calm she did not feel. "Three. It's very informal. Weather permitting we'll eat outdoors."

Cal nodded, running a hand over his hair. His fingers

lingered on his neck, massaging the tight muscles. "Do you need my help with anything?"

"No thank you." She wanted him away from her, out of her house. His presence had become too unsettling and disturbing.

"Good night, Cal," she said, dismissing him.

Cal's fatigue vanished quickly when he realized Lauren had again unceremoniously asked him to leave. The frustration he had experienced when he sat in John Evans' office and saw his ex-wife again threatened to swallow him whole.

He loved her; he hated her; then he loved her again, and he wanted her; he wanted to take her in his arms, take her to his bed and bury himself in her moist heat.

Lauren was frustrating and an enigma. She wasn't as worldly or sophisticated as the other women he had known yet she was more uninhibited and generous than all of the others combined, and with her innocence she had given him the chance for a rebirth, a renewal of his spirit and his flesh.

With the renewal she had given him a child—his son.

"Good night, Lauren." Without another word he turned, walking out of the kitchen and out of the house.

Lauren waited before making her way to the front door. She stared out at the shadowy twilight, trying to belay her quiet anxiety; an anxiety that indicated she wanted Caleb Samuels back in her life; she wanted to live with Caleb Samuels—as husband and wife.

Sitting down on the cushioned softness of the white wicker love seat, she pulled her legs up under her body.

Cal's passionate confession came to mind. *My mother waited until I was seven before she married my father. Even after she married him she refused to live with him.*

"Why?" Lauren asked the encroaching nightfall. Why did Cal's mother wait so long to marry his father? Why had she refused to live with David Samuels? Why was Drew's life mirroring that of his father's? She had so many questions and no answers to those questions.

She shifted her legs, and a small object fell to the porch. "Drew," she mumbled. It was probably another one of his numerous little trucks. Leaning over, Lauren picked up a gaily wrapped square package.

There was still enough light to read the tiny tag attached to a streamer of white ribbon: HAPPY MOTHER'S DAY.

Her hands were steady as she stripped the pale blue paper from a navy blue velvet box. The gift was from Tiffany's. Lauren recalled Cal's *I owe you a gift*.

She opened the box, staring numbly at a bracelet. Now her hands were shaking as she retreated to the living room and examined the heavy bangle under the light of a floor lamp. His gift to her was a three-tiered gold circle of precious stones.

She snapped the bracelet of ruby baguettes, banded by twin rows of round diamonds, around her wrist. Blood-red sensual rubies and brilliant blue-white diamonds winked back at her.

Lauren removed the bracelet, replacing it in the box and holding it to her chest.

He didn't owe her anything. Cal had given her love, joy and Drew. Nothing he could ever buy for her could equal the love, joy and Drew.

"Oh, I love him," Lauren whispered. Her hands shook slightly as she bit down hard on her lower lip.

Her mind burned with the memories of Cay Verde and she wanted to relive the week over and over again—with Cal. But, she pondered, could they relive the experience if they remarried? Had the separation changed them so much that they wouldn't be able to recapture the tenderness and trust to survive the year they were forced to remain together?

Lauren was aware that Cal loved and trusted her on Cay Verde, but she was not so naive to believe that he still loved her after she deceived him. She knew he wanted her—he had always wanted her the way she had wanted him and continued to want him.

I want him in my life *now!* There, she had admitted it to herself. She hadn't thought that Drew needed his father for at that moment she thought only of herself.

She felt a bottomless peace, knowing she needed to share her joy with someone. Within minutes she made a call, then waited for the one person who had taunted her for years to release the demons who had tormented her since she returned from Cay Verde bearing Caleb Baldwin Samuels' name while unknowingly carrying his child in her womb.

Gwendolyn Taylor sat on the daybed, her legs tucked under her body, eyes wide in surprise. "If you're asking me to be your maid of honor, then you must be getting married. But to whom? Where *is* he, cuz? I've never seen you with a man since you've come back from that Caribbean island or—wait—don't tell me you and Andrew..." Her words trailed off as Lauren shook her head.

"It's not Andrew, Gwen."

Gwen's large dark eyes grew rounder as her mouth formed a perfect O. "Who?"

"Caleb Samuels." Lauren couldn't believe she could sound so calm while her heart pounded uncontrollably.

Gwen screamed and the first cousins fell into each other's arms, hugging and crying at the same time.

Lauren and Gwendolyn were first cousins, born within

weeks of each other and closer than sisters. The resemblance between them was striking, and many people thought they were siblings. Gwen was an inch taller and her body slightly fuller than Lauren's, and both of them wore their hair short and curling.

Gwen patted her chest with a manicured hand, exhaling heavily. "Now that's what I call headline news."

"Don't you dare print a word of this until I make it official." Gwen's "People, Home, and Style" column was a popular feature of the *Boston Gazette*. The *Gazette* offered a refreshing change from the *Boston Globe* and *Boston Herald* reporting. It featured news on a hometown scale, focusing on local personalities and places of interest.

Gwen frowned. "Why isn't it official?"

Lauren rested her elbows on her knees crossed in a yoga position. "I haven't told Cal that I would marry him again."

"And why not?"

Lauren revealed everything that had happened since she'd received the letter requesting her presence at the reading of Dr. Caleb Samuels' will. "All I have to do is marry Cal, live with him for a year and Drew will inherit his share of his great-grandfather's estate."

"And if you don't, Jackie Samuels will get it," Gwen stated, an expression of astonishment still apparent in her eyes.

"That is the stipulation," Lauren confirmed.

"What do you know about Jackie Samuels, cuz?"

Lauren shrugged her shoulders. "Nothing, except that Cal doesn't want her to get a penny from his grandfather's estate."

"I've never met your C. B. Samuels, but I have to agree with him, Lauren," she said soberly. "I've heard that Jackie Samuels is a first-class b-i-t-c-h. I remember reading about her when she broke up a liaison David Samuels was having with a woman he'd been seeing for years. He and the woman were engaged to be married, but once Jackie arrived on the scene the woman was history—ancient history."

Closing her eyes, Lauren knew she had to act and act fast. She had to protect Drew's inheritance. Opening her eyes, she stared at Gwen, and the other woman recognized the stubborn streak in Lauren by the set of her delicate jaw.

"Can you do me a favor, Gwen?"

"Sure, cuz, anything."

"Find out everything you can about Jacqueline Samuels."

Gwen patted Lauren's hand. "Give me a few days to check the morgue at the *Gazette*. If I can't find anything there, then I'll call someone at the *Globe* or *Herald*. Now, how about we toast this most wonderful news?" she suggested, lightening the mood.

Lauren sprang to her feet, smiling. "Excellent idea."

"Do you love him?" Gwen asked as Lauren made her way across the room.

Turning slowly, Lauren gave her cousin an incredulous look. "Of course I love him, Gwen. Why do you think I'm re-marrying him?"

It was Gwen's turn to shrug her shoulders. "I don't know. I thought maybe you were doing it because of Drew."

"No, Gwen. It's not because of Drew. I'm doing it for the same reason I married Cal in the first place—love. There was a time when I thought I'd married him because I was caught up in an idealistic romanticism and a physical attraction so strong that I thought it was infatuation—one set of glands calling to another. I went through periods of insecurity, feeling excited and eager, but not genuinely happy. I had nagging doubts, unanswered questions and there were things about Cal I should've known but never knew. All I knew was that he was this incredibly gentle, passionate stranger who swept me off my feet the moment I met him.

"But the separation changed me, Gwen, because now I'm calmer, patient and willing to give our marriage a chance to work. My life is going the way I want it to go. I have a career I love, the house I've always wanted and a wonderful son, and marrying Cal will complete the circle."

Gwen arched her eyebrows. "So you're ready to settle and play house, cuz?"

Lauren rested her hands on her hips. "You just watch me work it, cuz!"

"What I want to watch is C. B. Samuels in the flesh," Gwen countered.

"You'll get to meet him, Gwen."

"When?"

"Next week."

Gwen pushed out her lower lip in a pout. "Do you think he'll give me an interview?"

"Cal doesn't grant interviews." This was something Lauren *did* know about the man she was going to remarry.

Gwen nodded in resignation. "Go get the champagne so we can toast your upcoming nuptials."

Lauren and Gwen spent the next two hours talking and sipping champagne, laughing uncontrollably when they recounted the pranks they'd played on unsuspecting friends growing up.

It was past midnight and Gwen turned down Lauren's offer to spend the night, explaining she had scheduled an interview with a local musician over Sunday brunch.

"Who knows," Gwen threw over her shoulder as she stood on the porch with Lauren, "Maybe I'll be lucky enough to see the sex muffin again. The next time it won't be because I'm on assignment."

Lauren hugged her cousin. "Thanks for being my maid of honor."

"I'm honored you asked. I'll call if I get any information on Jackie Samuels."

Lauren waited until her cousin drove away, then returned to the house. She had made her decision. She would remarry Caleb Samuels, live with him a year and fulfill the terms of Dr. Samuels' will.

Gramps had won the first round.

"Mommy! Mommy! Daddy's here."

Lauren heard Drew's strident voice coming through the open windows. He's early, she thought, glancing up at the clock over the sink. It was only two-thirty.

Cal walked into the kitchen with a grace not seen on most men, except dancers. Head erect, shoulders thrown back and his slim hips rolling in a sensually fluid motion, he always managed to turn heads wherever he went.

His walk was something she recognized immediately when she first met him on Cay Verde.

Everything about Caleb Samuels was measured and unhurried. Each word he spoke and each motion he made. She remembered that even his lovemaking had been slow, methodical and unhurried, sending her beyond herself and spewing a flood-tide of explosive pleasure.

The muscles in her stomach contracted when she thought about making love to him; seeing him, touching him, had brought back the vivid memories. Each time he touched her she was certain he could feel her trembling hunger.

His gaze went to her bare wrists, then moved slowly up to her face. He handed her two decorative shopping bags.

"I didn't know what you were serving so I brought red and white wine."

Lauren wiped her hands on a towel, smiling. "Both are appropriate. I'm serving red meat and poultry." She took the bags from him, her fingers brushing his, and Cal pulled away as if he had been burned.

The air was radiating with tension—sexual and emotional as she concealed a mysterious smile. "I've decided to marry you," Lauren announced softly.

Cal stood motionless in the middle of the kitchen, breathing heavily through parted lips. She had given in. It was so easy, too easy to digest all at once.

"Why, Lauren?" Cal chided himself as soon as the words were out. She had accepted; why did he want to know why?

Lauren turned back to cutting up the vegetables for a garden salad, unable to look at Cal. "I'm doing it for Drew," she lied.

At that moment Cal didn't care why she had decided to marry him again—all that mattered was that she had agreed to do it. He reached for her, cradling her gently in the circle of his embrace. She stiffened slightly before she melted against the solid hardness of his body.

Lauren curved her arms around Cal's waist, resting her cheek against his chest. It felt good, so natural to be in his arms. She had not realized how much she had missed his touch, his warmth.

She raised her face, smiling up at him. "You're going to have to let me go so I can finish cooking."

Cal caught her chin between his thumb and forefinger. His gaze lingered longingly on her face, focusing on her mouth. His head descended slowly and he staked his claim in a slow, drugging kiss.

Lauren rose on tiptoe, her arms going around his neck. She moaned softly as his tongue traced the outline of her mouth seconds before his teeth sank tenderly into her lower lip.

Cal devoured her mouth, and an explosive heat swept through Lauren; a sexual heat she had not felt in years.

It wasn't for Drew. She had consented to remarry Caleb Samuels because she still was in love with him—she had never stopped loving him.

Lauren pushed against his chest and he released her. Both of them were breathing heavily.

Cheeks flaming, she glanced away. "I have to finish the salad," she mumbled, not recognizing the sound of her own voice.

"I'll see about Drew," Cal offered as an excuse before walking out of the kitchen.

Lauren prepared all of the fixings for her salad, then re-treated to her bedroom to change her clothes. She took a quick shower and pulled a white sundress with narrow straps, a loose waistline and a swingy skirt over her perfumed, scented body. She slipped her bare feet into a pair of white leather sandals at the same time she heard her parents' car pull into the driveway.

Skipping lightly down the staircase, Lauren met her mother and father as they were coming up the porch. She hugged her father, kissing his cheek and pushing an envelope with a gift certificate to a sporting-goods store into his hand. "Happy Father's Day, Daddy."

Roy Taylor curved an arm around his daughter's waist. "Thank you, princess." He stared down at the envelope. "You didn't have to give me anything, Lauren."

Lauren smiled up at Roy. "I know I didn't, but I wanted to." She kissed her mother, looping an arm through Odessa's. "Cal's here," she informed her.

Odessa looked over Lauren's shoulder. "Where is he?"

"Probably around the back with Drew."

Lauren led her parents along the path to the rear of the large house. She spied Cal and Drew on a webbed lounge chair, the child sitting between his father's outstretched legs as Cal read the colorful Sunday comics.

Cal saw Lauren and her parents approaching, and he eased Drew off the chair and stood up. He noted that Lauren had not inherited her mother's looks. However, the two women shared the same graceful body.

He stared at Lauren as if seeing her for the first time. Seeing her in the sundress brought back the vivid reminder of the evening he had met her on the beach on Cay Verde and had apologized for insulting her because of her youthful-looking appearance. Even though her hair was shorter and the dress a different color, Lauren had an aura of feminine sensuality that still aroused him.

Lauren stood beside Cal, looping a bare arm through his. "Cal, I'd you to meet my parents. Odessa and Roy. Mama, Daddy, this is Caleb Samuels."

Cal extended his right hand to Roy Taylor. "My pleasure, Mr. Taylor."

Roy pumped his hand vigorously. "Roy will be enough, Caleb."

Cal turned to Odessa, lowering his head slightly and giving her a sensual smile. "I'm honored, Mrs. Taylor."

Odessa's cheeks colored under the heat of his golden-eyed gaze. "Odessa," she said breathlessly.

Taking a step forward, Cal leaned down and kissed her smooth, scented cheek. "Odessa," he repeated.

Lauren exhaled, her heart thumping uncomfortably. She didn't know what to expect from her parents.

Odessa gave Cal her winning smile, but there was a look in her eyes that Lauren recognized immediately and she tensed.

"I hope you're not returning to Spain at the end of the summer, because I'd hate for my grandson to get used to you, then have to miss you."

Lauren bit down on her lower lip, shaking her head. Her mother was notorious for being facetious, however, Cal seemed amused by her statement.

"I'm not going anywhere for a long time," he stated solemnly, staring down at Lauren.

Odessa arched her eyebrows. She was stopped from interrogating Cal further when Drew caught her hand. "Grandma, come see the puppies. Missy had puppies. You too, Grandpa."

The elder Taylors followed Drew to the garage to view the puppies while Lauren and Cal stared at each other.

His eyes crinkled in a smile. "I see where you get your incredible beauty from. Your mother is stunning."

Lauren laughed. "You lie so nicely, Cal. I look nothing like my mother."

He sobered quickly. "Beauty is not about looks, Lauren. It's one's inner spirit that radiates beauty, not one's face. A perfect example is Jacqueline. She's as wicked inwardly as she is beautiful facially."

"Wicked stepmothers only exist in fairy tales, Cal."

"Well, this one lives and breathes. And with Jacqueline, your first line of defense is never to underestimate her as your opponent."

"Jacqueline Samuels is not my opponent," Lauren argued.

Cal let out a sigh of exasperation, his lips compressed in a grim, tight line. "Just watch yourself, Lauren." He stared at her intently.

Lauren digested his warning, not wanting to believe she

had anything to fear from Jacqueline Samuels, but something nagged at her despite her confidence.

Remembering Cal's gift, she pulled a small velvet pouch from the large pocket in her dress. "Happy Father's Day, Caleb."

He took the pouch and shook out the contents. The heavy gold ring he had given Lauren was cradled in the palm of his large hand. She had returned the ring he had given her when they married. Lauren took the ring from his palm and slipped it on the little finger of his left hand.

He captured her eyes with his, seemingly undressing her. He was remembering the time he had slipped the ring on her finger.

Gathering her in his arms, he held her gently, rocking her back and forth. "Thank you, darling," he whispered in her hair.

Lauren felt her breasts tighten and swell against his chest. Cradled in his embrace she mentally relived making love with Cal.

Closing her eyes, she inhaled his masculine scent, felt the whisper of his breath over the planes and curves of her stomach and thighs; she felt the moistness of his tongue as it trailed along her inner thigh and over the dark, moist mound concealing her womanhood; she relived his strong fingers cupping her breasts gently, thumbs stroking her distended nipples, and she relived his tongue plunging deeply into her mouth over and over, drinking the sweet ambrosia she willingly offered him.

Her husband; her patient, sensual husband.

But he was not her husband—not yet.

Lauren was smiling when she opened her eyes. She was to become Mrs. Caleb Samuels for the second time in less than five years. How many women were fortunate enough to marry the man they loved, not once but twice?

Chapter 8

The mood was relaxed and lively for the Father's Day dinner; savory strips of butterfly lamb and split Cornish hens were cooked to perfection on the gas grill. The accompanying side dishes included egg noodles with a mustard-sage sauce, a garden salad and another salad of lobster and artichoke hearts with a lemon dressing.

Drew's excitement was endless. He reveled in the praise from both his grandparents as he ate everything on his plate.

Lauren stared at Cal over the rim of her wineglass, feeling as if she had known him for years rather than a sum total of ten days. He appeared so at ease with her parents, while the elder Taylors seemed comfortable and friendly with the stranger who had once been married to their daughter.

Lauren caught Odessa's eye, smiling. Her gaze shifted to

Cal and he returned her smile. They had decided to wait until dinner was completed to announce their marriage.

"Mama, Daddy, Cal and I have decided to get married."

Odessa's mouth dropped, snapped closed, then dropped again. "When?"

"Next month," Cal replied.

"When next month?" Odessa asked, placing a hand to her throat.

"Either the last Saturday in July or the first Saturday in August," Lauren stated. She and Cal would have a month to become acquainted before living together.

Odessa crossed her arms under her breasts. "You're not giving me much time. I have to send out invitations, mail announcements to the newspapers, order flowers, food and arrange for the church."

"No, Mother!"

Odessa's eyes suddenly filled with tears. "Indulge me, Lauren. Please, baby. Just this one time. I didn't get to see you married the first time. You cheated me out of seeing my only child married," she wailed, her chin trembling.

Roy pulled Odessa to his body and kissed her forehead. His wife sniffled dramatically against his shoulder as he murmured softly in her ear.

Lauren felt as if her composure were under attack. She couldn't deal with all of the emotions bombarding her. She was unable to shake off Cal's warning about Jacqueline, her mother resorting to tears to get her way, and her father glaring at her as if she were an enemy for upsetting his wife.

She glanced over at Cal and saw him watching her, his forehead furrowed in concern. He nodded and she knew what she had to do.

"Okay, Mama. But I want it small and very private."

Odessa's crying stopped immediately. Turning, she smiled at Lauren and Cal. "Small and private," she repeated.

Sighing heavily, Lauren returned Odessa's smile. "We'll talk about it tomorrow."

Drew helped Cal and Roy clear the table while Lauren and Odessa brewed coffee and sliced a freshly prepared strawberry shortcake for dessert.

Odessa noted Lauren's impassive expression. "It's going to work out, darling," she whispered softly, then turned and retreated to the patio, carrying the carafe of steaming coffee.

Closing her eyes, Lauren gripped the edge of the counter tightly. She felt like a hypocrite. She was to take the vows of matrimony yet knowing every word she'd utter would be false; false and empty.

Love and cherish, in sickness and in heath.

But she did love Caleb Samuels. Opening her eyes, she stared at him as he stood with Roy loading the dishwasher.

Lauren had always been honest with herself and she knew her feelings for Cal were changing, intensifying. She looked forward to seeing him, hearing his voice and having him touch her.

He turned and caught her staring and his golden gaze held her captive. Could he see beneath her controlled exterior to feel her apprehension? Could he see her hope that after she married him his feelings towards her would change? Could she hope that he wanted to marry her again for the same reason he had married her on Cay Verde? Could he see her hope that this marriage did not have to end after a year?

Cal mumbled an apology to Roy and crossed the kitchen. He didn't know how or why, but he knew Lauren was uneasy about something. It was as if her inner spirit called out to him to help her.

Reaching for her hands, he held them firmly, tightening his grip when he felt her tremble. "Are you all right?"

Lauren nodded, not meeting his gaze, and tried unsuccessfully to extract her fingers. "I'm fine," she managed in a husky voice.

Cal lowered his head. "You don't look okay."

Lauren felt her apprehension spiral. Could he also sense what she was feeling? Did he know that she wanted him? Wanted him the way a woman wanted a man? The way a wife would want her husband?

"I'm just a little tired," she admitted, and she was. She had pushed herself relentlessly the past two months. Decorating the house, taking care of Drew and compiling research had left her exhausted.

Cal's arms went around her shoulders, holding her protectively against his body. He pressed a light kiss to her forehead.

"I think we should consider a honeymoon."

"Honeymoon!" Lauren practically shouted.

He gave her a warm smile. "Yes, honeymoon."

Odessa reentered the kitchen from the patio. She watched Cal cradle Lauren's face between his palms and drop a kiss on her pouting lips.

"It's settled," he stated in a firm tone. "We'll take a week off and relax."

Lauren's fingers curled around his strong wrists. "But I can't afford to take a week off. I have a project to complete for Andrew. Who's going to watch Drew? And there's Missy and the puppies."

"Your mother can take care of Drew. When my mother comes for the wedding she can extend her stay for a week and take care of Missy and the dogs if you don't want the animals in a kennel."

Lauren squinted up at Cal, not seeing her parents watching the tense interchange. She shook her head. "No, Caleb."

His hands held her head firmly, not permitting her movement. "Yes, Lauren." His eyes darkened and grew cold. "I need you healthy and sane for the next year. I lost you once. And I swear it will not happen a second time," he said so quietly that only Lauren heard the veiled promise.

She felt an icy chill grip her. "Take your hands off me," she ordered in a soft voice.

Cal released her, but not before he kissed her for the second time that day, leaving her mouth burning with a fire that ignited her whole body.

Odessa and Roy exchanged knowing glances. Both of them turned and made their way to the patio, Odessa holding Drew's hand and pulling him with her. There were a lot of things his mother and father had to work out, and it was better that they were left alone to do it.

Lauren pulled the back of her hand across her mouth as if to wipe away any trace of the taste of Cal's lips on hers.

The gesture amused him. He leaned forward to kiss her again and she ducked under his arm.

"Stop, Caleb!" Her protest sounded weak even to her own ears.

Cal caught her arm, spinning her around to face him. "Stop running from me."

"I'm not running from you," she protested.

He pulled her up close to his chest, frowning as she closed her eyes. "Are you afraid of me, Lauren?"

Opening her eyes, Lauren prayed he would not feel her slight trembling. She wasn't afraid of him; she was afraid of herself and what she felt whenever he looked at her or touched her.

Raising her chin, she managed a sensual smile. "No, Cal.

I'm not afraid of you." At that moment she wasn't. Not with her parents less than fifty feet away.

What he didn't know was that she was afraid of herself; afraid of what she felt whenever he touched her; afraid she would blurt out her love for him; afraid that he would reject her love the way she had rejected his love.

Cal smiled and released her. "If what you say is true, then I'd like you to have your parents babysit Drew tomorrow night."

"Why?" His request gnawed at Lauren's newfound confidence.

"We haven't spent any time together—alone."

Nervously, she bit her lower lip. "There's no need to be alone."

A look of implacable determination filled Cal's eyes. "I beg to differ with you, Lauren. There are a lot of things we must discuss before we remarry."

Lauren knew he was right. There were a lot of things to discuss and a lot of questions to be answered. "Okay, Cal. I'll ask my mother if she'll take care of Drew."

Cal lingered in the kitchen after Lauren retreated to the patio. He needed time alone to regain his composure.

The more he saw of Lauren the more he wanted to see her. He couldn't help himself when he kissed her; he wanted to kiss her again and again—all over her body.

Be careful, he warned himself. It would be disastrous if he found himself so much in love with his beautiful little wife that he wouldn't let her go after a year, because he was enough of a realist not to think beyond the year with Lauren. She was marrying him for Drew, not because she loved him, a fact he could not afford to forget.

Cal made his way out of the house, joining the Taylors and devouring the strawberry shortcake Lauren had made earlier that morning.

* * *

For once, Odessa was speechless when Lauren asked her if she would look after Drew Monday night. She quickly agreed and cradled Drew on her lap where they both made plans about what they intended to do together.

Roy gathered Lauren to his side, pressing a kiss to her forehead. "Thanks for the gift certificate and for the lamb, baby girl."

Lauren wound her arms around her father's thickening waist. "Anytime, Daddy." She patted his slightly protruding belly. "You're putting on weight," she told her college-administrator father. "Sitting at a desk is telling on you."

"I'll have to walk three miles tomorrow just to offset those two slices of shortcake."

Rising on tiptoe, Lauren kissed his cheek. "Get Mama to walk with you."

Roy Taylor's black eyes swept over his wife's willowy figure. Odessa, a retired school librarian, was as slim as she was when he first married her thirty years ago. "There's nothing wrong with Dessa's body. She's perfect."

Lauren was surprised to see the obvious flames of desire in her father's eyes as he stared at her mother. It was something she would never experience with Cal at her parents' age.

"Cardiovascular, Dad."

"And there's nothing wrong with Dessa's heart," he said softly.

"Case closed," Lauren conceded with a smile.

Lauren, Drew, and Cal walked the elder Taylors to their car and watched until it disappeared from view.

"Drew! Drew! Can I see the puppies?" shouted a high-pitched childish voice from the neighboring house.

Drew grasped Lauren's hand. "Mommy, can I show Tommy the puppies?"

She smiled at the excitement flickering in his gold-brown eyes. "Yes. But the two of you stay in the garage, and remind Tommy not to get too close to Missy."

"Thanks, Mommy. See you later, Daddy…" Drew was already racing around to the side of the house.

Lauren stood beside Cal, staring out at the verdant lushness of the thick green grass sloping down to the road. Ribbons of sunlight filtered through towering trees throwing lengthening shadows on every light surface. In another two hours dusk would begin its quiet, soothing descent on North Grafton.

Cal threaded his fingers through Lauren's, leading her back to the porch. He seated her on the wicker swing, sitting down next to her and winding an arm around her shoulders.

Lauren melted against his chest, savoring his warmth and masculine strength. Her lids fluttered closed when he brushed her forehead with a light kiss.

A low chuckle filled Cal's chest. "Be careful, love. We're beginning to act like an old married couple rocking on the porch after dinner."

"You're old, Caleb," Lauren teased in a drowsy voice, opening her eyes. "You're the one with the white hair."

His fingers tightened around the slender column of her neck. "It's silver," he corrected softly.

"And that makes you old."

He smiled. "How old?"

"Just too old."

"Too old for what?" he asked against her hair. When she didn't answer, he curved a hand under her chin and raised her face to his. "Too old for what, darling?"

A delicious shudder heated Lauren's body under his penetrating gaze. She wanted so much for their upcoming marriage to be a normal one. But it was not to be.

"Nothing," she finally replied.

Cal settled her cheek on his chest and stared up at the differing shades streaking the sky. A satisfied smile touched his mobile mouth. He certainly wasn't too old to make love to a woman; especially if that woman was Lauren.

Cradling her soft body, inhaling her sweet feminine scent and tasting her velvety lush lips was like an aphrodisiac.

At twenty-seven Lauren Taylor was all woman and he tried remembering if she had been that alluring at twenty-two. Had he been able to sense the essence of her womanliness because he lived so jaded an existence?

Caleb B. Samuels II always took responsibility for his mistakes, and he had made a mistake to let Lauren go five years ago. It would not happen again. He would marry her again, but he would not let her go so easily a second time.

Lauren slipped off her sandals, pulling her legs up under her body. Relaxing, she gave in to the gentle swaying of the porch swing. Aside from her attic retreat, the porch was her favorite place in the large, airy farmhouse. Its wide proportions were perfect for the all-weather white wicker love seat, chaise, tea cart and swing. Brilliant flowering fuchsia, hanging from clay pots and two large window boxes filled with colorful impatiens blended with the pale blue seat cushions and pillows dotted with a delicate pink and white floral print.

She was content to sit with Cal and rock in silence, savoring the quiet of the early Sunday evening, the cool breezes sweeping the countryside, and the comfortable peace Caleb Samuels offered her.

It was a scene she had dreamt of as a girl: a husband, wife and child sharing their love and enjoying their home.

Get real, Lauren, she told herself. She had the child, the house and she was going to gain a husband who was a stranger; a man she had slept with; a man she had married; a man who had stirred the passions she hadn't known she possessed, and a man she would marry and lose again within a year.

There was so much she wanted to know about him. There were so many questions that needed answers. "Cal."

"Yeah?"

"Your mother."

"What about her?" he asked drowsily.

"Why did she wait so long to marry your father?" Cal laughed and the sound startled Lauren. "What's so funny?"

"My parents. They were the most mismatched couple that ever existed. My mother was a brilliant, temperamental dancer and my father was a rigid, controlling attorney whose specialty was the entertainment business—the stage and recordings. They were complete opposites yet they couldn't stay away from each other. There was so much passion between them that to be in the same room with them was tiring. It wasn't until I was older that I realized some people can love to an excess. My father loved me, Lauren, but he loved my mother so much more. And his love smothered her and she fought him. They fought without uttering a word by hurling smoldering glares at each other and these were the times when I wanted to run away and hide. I retreated to a world of books and by the time I was nineteen I knew I wanted to be a writer. My first book was published at twenty-one, and every time I began a new book it was like retreating all over again."

Lauren stared up at his stoic expression. "It's been a long time between books, C.B."

Cal kissed the end of her nose. "This one is going to be different, Lauren."

"Why?"

Cal didn't get the chance to answer as the sound of a car's engine shattered the quietness of the evening. Lauren sat up when she felt tension tighten Cal's body. Andrew was out of his car and striding up the walk before she extracted herself from Cal's embrace.

Andrew whistled off-key as he bounded up the steps, smiling broadly. Lauren returned his smile, not seeing the scowl Cal shot her agent.

Andrew extended his hand to Cal. "Hello."

Cal rose slowly to his feet and shook the proffered hand. He resented Andrew; he resented his unannounced intrusion and he resented his close relationship with Lauren.

"Good evening, Monroe," Cal returned in a stilted tone. He couldn't address him as Andrew. The name was too close to his son's, and that only reminded him that Andrew Monroe had solidified his influence not only in Lauren's life but also Drew's.

Lauren looped her arm through Andrew's after he released Cal's hand. The smile she offered him mirrored her deep affection for the man who was her agent and friend.

Leaning over, Andrew brushed a light kiss on her cheek. "I'm sorry I didn't call, but…"

"You didn't call because you hate telephones," Lauren teased, placing a small manicured hand on his chest. "Please sit down." She gestured toward the love seat.

She retook her seat on the swing but Cal did not sit. The fingers of his right hand curled possessively around her neck and she shivered in spite of the warmth from his hand. Staring up at Cal, she smiled and covered his fingers with her own.

"I'm going to check on Drew," Cal said, tactfully dismissing himself.

Lauren nodded, feeling somewhat bereft after he had removed his hand. Her dark gaze followed his retreat as he walked down the steps and disappeared from view.

"Is he back to stay?"

Her gaze swung back to Andrew's, and for the first time since Lauren had known Andrew his eyes were not bright with laughter. The green orbs resembled cold, hard, uncut frosted emeralds.

She felt a prickle of annoyance. What she had felt in the restaurant when she introduced Cal to Andrew had not been her imagination. The two men did not like each other.

"And what's that supposed to mean, Andrew?"

Andrew crossed an ankle over a knee, running his thumb and forefinger down the crease in his tan slacks. His head came up slowly and he impaled her with his angry glare.

"I won't mince words, Lauren."

"Then don't," she retorted stiffly.

"He's going to hurt you."

Lauren smiled a sad smile. "He can't hurt me."

"And why not?"

She inhaled deeply, then let out her breath in a soft shudder. "Because I don't love him," she lied smoothly. "I've never loved him," she added.

Andrew steepled his fingers, bringing them to his mouth. "I don't believe you, Lauren. You married the man, had his child and you don't feel anything for him?"

Lauren tilted her chin in a defiant gesture. "I don't believe you drove out here to discuss Caleb Samuels. Or did you?"

Andrew studied Lauren for a long moment. She looked the same yet something about her was different.

His familiar smile was back in place. "You're right. I didn't. The movie right to option Lloyd Caldwell's book on the

Negro baseball leagues has been finalized. Filming is scheduled to begin in Vancouver in two weeks. Caldwell wants you as the technical advisor for the film. The entire project should take about six months. Two to three to shoot and another two to go through production and editing."

The shock of Andrew's disclosure hit Lauren full force. The excitement of working on a movie set paled quickly when she remembered the turn her life had taken—the change based on her decision to remarry Caleb Samuels.

"I can't do it." Her refusal was quiet and final.

Andrew gritted his teeth. "Why not?" he hissed.

"I'm registering Drew for preschool."

"Get him a tutor," Andrew insisted.

Lauren gave him a level look. "Drew needs children his own age, not a tutor."

Bracing his elbows on his knees, Andrew leaned forward. "It's not only Drew, is it?" His voice was soft and coaxing.

She arched an eyebrow and smiled. Very few things escaped Andrew Monroe's quick mind. "I'm getting married."

Andrew arched his own golden eyebrows. "You're going to remarry a man you don't love?"

"I'm doing it for Drew."

"And what does Lauren Taylor expect from this marriage to her son's father?"

"Nothing, Andrew. Nothing."

"You deserve more than nothing, Lauren. You deserve love, trust and fidelity. And judging from what I've read about C. B. Samuels you can't expect…" His voice faded when he noted her expression. He had overstepped the boundaries of their friendship.

Andrew was right and Lauren knew it. Both of them knew it. She did not deserve to be hurt a second time. But if she was careful there would be no hurt, no pain. As long as she did not lose her heart to Cal she would be successful and a winner.

"I'm sorry about the film, Andrew."

Andrew sat back on the love seat, shrugging wide shoulders. "It's all right. I'd hoped that you would consider getting into film work."

"Maybe in the future when Drew's older."

Andrew appeared deep in thought as he steepled his fingers. "You're the best researcher I've ever agented."

"That's because I'm the only researcher you've ever agented," Lauren teased.

Andrew's low laugh dispelled the somber mood. "You're right about that. When's the big day?"

"Late July or early August."

"Aren't you rushing it?"

Lauren shook her head. She and Cal had to marry before August twentieth or Drew would forfeit his inheritance to Jacqueline Samuels.

"Am I invited?"

Lauren moved over to the love seat and looped her arm around Andrew's waist. "Of course you are."

Andrew cradled her cheek against his shoulder, pressing his lips to her curling hair. "You've broken my heart, Lauren Taylor."

Pulling back, Lauren glanced up at his crestfallen expression. "If I didn't know you so well I'd believe you, Andrew Monroe."

"You're special to me, Lauren. Very special."

Lauren sobered, seeing his green eyes darken with an unnamed emotion. She and Andrew were a good team. He agented nonfiction authors and the research she compiled for them added to the authenticity of their work.

"And you're very special to me," she replied. "Would you

like to see the latest additions to the Taylor menagerie?" Lauren hoped to lighten the mood with talk of Missy's puppies.

Andrew stood, pulling her up to him. "Well, since I can't convince you to marry me and have my children I suppose I'll have to settle with being godfather to your children and providing a home for the offspring of your pets."

She glanced up at Andrew. "You never asked me to marry you."

Andrew followed Lauren into the house. "I was going to, Lauren Taylor."

"Liar," she threw over her shoulder.

"I'm not lying," he protested, staring at the smooth flesh of her bared shoulders and back.

"I would never marry my boss."

Andrew caught up with Lauren in the kitchen. "You're right about that. Because I would never fire you."

Turning, Lauren gave him a long, penetrating look. "Wish me luck, Andrew. I need you to be happy for me."

He leaned closer. "I'll always be happy for you. You deserve the best that life has to offer."

Winding her arms around his waist, she rested her head on his chest. "Thank you, Andrew. Thank you."

Cal stood in the doorway leading from the garage, watching the intimate interchange between Lauren and Andrew. He managed to quell the rage racing headlong throughout his body. Rage and jealousy. He wanted from Lauren what she so freely offered Andrew Monroe, and at that moment he wanted Lauren. He didn't just want to give her his name again, but all he could offer a woman: his protection, his love and his passion.

Shock after shock rocked him to the core with the rush of possessive waves taunting him.

She's mine, he thought. Lauren was his woman and he wouldn't share her—not with Andrew Monroe and not with any man.

Lauren extracted herself from Andrew's loose embrace and discovered Cal staring at her. He had been so quiet she thought she and Andrew were alone in the kitchen.

But that was something she was beginning to notice about Cal. He entered a room so quietly that when she glanced up he usually startled her with his presence.

Yet his presence was anything but quiet. It screamed and radiated his virility and his brilliance.

"Andrew is going to see the puppies," she explained in an even tone.

Cal nodded and stepped aside. He waited until Andrew disappeared into the garage with Drew and Tommy, then moved toward Lauren.

"I will not put up with my wife being pawed by another man." His voice was like velvet while his eyes flashed fire.

Lauren felt her temper rise. "I'm not your wife."

"You were before and you'll be again."

"Then don't accuse me of anything until I do become your wife again."

Cal captured her upper arms, his thumbs moving sensuously over her bared flesh. "You like him touching you?"

"Stop it, Caleb."

He pulled her closer to his body. "You like him kissing you?"

She couldn't respond as his head came down and he covered her mouth with his. His fingers were like manacles of steel while his lips stroked hers like heated honey. Her fists against his chest eased and unclenched, fingers spreading out and moving up to his broad shoulders.

His tongue swept over her lips, questing and seeking entrance to the moist heat of her mouth. Moaning, she inhaled and her lips parted, giving him the access he sought.

Cal tasted her lips, her tongue, the ridge of her teeth, then the ridged roof of her mouth. The little sounds coming from Lauren made him tremble with desire.

All of his senses were heightened from the crush of her firm breasts against his chest, the heat of her body, the silken feel of her skin and the floral fragrance clinging to her hair and flesh.

Holding her, tasting her—now he knew why he had taken Lauren Taylor to his bed and married her. In her innocence and naïveté, she held nothing back. She was passion, a fire burning out of control.

His hands moved frantically over her back and slid down to her hips. A tortured groan filled the kitchen and it was several seconds before Cal realized it had been his.

He pressed her hips to his middle, permitting her to feel what he was unable to control. His maleness searched through layers of fabric, making her more than aware of his hardness.

Lauren felt as if she were drowning; she was drowning and she didn't want to be rescued. Feelings she had tried to repress surfaced like an explosion, scorching her with fire. The fullness in her breasts spread lower, bringing with it a throbbing dampness.

"Caleb," she moaned, throwing back her head and baring her neck. "Ah-h, Caleb."

He heard his name through the haze of desire and buried his face in her throat. Gulping for much-needed air, he closed his eyes, trying to regain a measure of control.

His pulses slowed, the ache in his groin eased and he pulled back. What he saw in the depths of Lauren's jet-black eyes shocked him. She wasn't afraid of him. She wanted him. A slight smile softened his mouth.

Registering his smile, Lauren squared her shoulders and tilted her chin. "I suggest you try to exercise more self-control, Caleb Samuels."

"I don't have the willpower, darling," Cal drawled, grinning.

He released her and Lauren turned her back. She wasn't reprimanding Cal but herself. She should've resisted him. She was hopelessly and completely helpless when it came to Caleb Samuels. It was as if her reason for being born female was to exist solely for this man.

Cal took a step, leaning forward and pressing a kiss to the back of her neck. "I'll see you tomorrow," he said softly.

This time when Caleb Samuels left Lauren's house he was grinning broadly. It all had come together. He was one step closer to making Lauren his—forever.

Chapter 9

Lauren did not know why, but she missed sharing breakfast with Cal. He had called to inform her that he had an early morning meeting with John Evans to draw up his will, and as she replaced the receiver on its cradle she felt numbed. It was about to begin. Her life was going to change—forever.

After feeding Drew, she sat down with a calendar selecting alternative dates for her wedding.

She decided on a number she needed for invitations, doubling the number in case Cal wanted to invite his relatives and friends.

Lauren also made a note to call Gwen so that they could go and look at dresses. Thinking of Gwen made her wonder how much information she had uncovered on Jacqueline Samuels, and even though Cal had warned her about Jacqueline, Lauren could not bring herself to believe his stepmother would try to sabotage their marriage.

* * *

Odessa arrived in time to join Lauren and Drew for lunch. She kissed her grandson with a loud flourish, whispering in his ear the plans she made for their time together.

"Have you set the date?" she asked Lauren, slipping onto the bench beside Drew.

Lauren sat down and passed her mother a bowl of shrimp salad. "The first Saturday in August. That'll give us an extra week."

Odessa nodded. "Have you called Reverend Lewis?"

Lauren paused, shaking her head. "I'm not having a religious ceremony." She watched the natural color drain from Odessa's face, the sprinkling of freckles across her nose and cheeks standing out in vivid contrast.

"Why not, Lauren?"

She bit down hard on her lower lip, inhaling. "I can't be a hypocrite, Mama. I can't get married in church, knowing it's not for the right reasons."

Odessa recovered, taking a sip of lemonade. "What are you planning to do?" Her voice was a raspy whisper.

"Have Uncle Odell marry us at your house."

"Is that what you really want?"

"Yes, Mama. That's what I want."

"What about Caleb? Do you think he'll go along with what you propose?"

Lauren smiled at her mother. "I don't think he'll object."

Not only did Cal object to her decision not to marry in a church, but he was extremely vocal in his objection. He paced the length of the porch, clenched fists thrust in the pockets of his trousers.

"You're selfish, Lauren." He stopped long enough to glare

at her. "Not only are you selfish, but you're also spoiled beyond belief.

"How can you raise a child when you're acting like a child?" he continued, not giving Lauren an opportunity to defend herself. "Why is it so difficult for you to compromise?"

Lauren smiled, the gesture further incensing him. She had revealed that she wanted a civil ceremony at her parents' home with her mother's brother, a state supreme court justice, officiating.

"Are you finished, Caleb?" she asked in a saccharine tone.

Cal barely nodded. He was angry enough to shake Lauren until she was too weak to fight him, and she had been fighting him as much as he was fighting his own feelings for her.

He never thought she would get under his skin like an invisible itch, shattering the shield he had put up to resist her. She had wounded him once; it would not happen again.

Lauren rose from the porch swing and moved over to stand in front of Cal, fighting tension as well as frustration.

"Don't talk to me about compromise, Caleb." Her voice was low and calm despite her rising anger. "For the past week I've compromised my life, my very existence. And if your grandfather had died a week later, we would not be having this conversation right now."

His eyes narrowed. "What are you talking about?"

"Andrew came here yesterday to offer me an opportunity to work as a technical advisor on a film about the Negro baseball leagues. I spent more than six months researching the facts for Lloyd Caldwell, feeling what those talented men felt when they walked out on the playing fields in those dusty, hot towns and cities throughout the country. I lived and breathed through the lives of the players, on and off the baseball diamond, knowing many of them prayed every night that they would eventually make it to the major leagues despite the color of their skin. I wanted more than anything else to relive that experience on a movie set.

"I wanted it, Caleb. I wanted it almost as much as I wanted my baby." Turning her back, she closed her eyes. She had not planned to tell Caleb about Andrew's offer but it was out and she couldn't retract it.

"I had to turn it down, Caleb, because the next year of my life doesn't belong to me. It belongs to you and Drew so how selfish can I be?"

Cal walked over to Lauren, his hands going to her shoulders. He encountered his own personal anguish as he noted her pain-filled gaze.

Neither of them would come out of their marriage of convenience unscathed. Lauren would give up her independence for a year while he was willing to give her a lifetime of trying to right the wrongs, unaware that all he wanted from her was love. An emotion that could not be bought or bartered.

"Darling." His voice was low and quiet.

Lauren jerked out of his embrace, taking a backward step; she couldn't stand for him to touch her—not now, not when she hated herself for loving this man as much as she did.

Why couldn't she forget the week on Cay Verde? Why couldn't her mind erase the feel of his hands, the taste of his mouth, the way her body responded to his. How could this man, a stranger, know her better than she knew herself?

She walked with stiff dignity down the porch and around to the back of the house. She wanted to run, but where could she run to escape Cal? Even if she had crossed an ocean he still would continue to haunt her; haunt her like he'd been doing for years.

Lauren flopped down on the colorful hammock strung

between two sturdy maple trees. With one leg trailing out of the hammock, she swayed gently in a slow, hypnotic motion.

Closing her eyes, she wondered how her life could change so abruptly. Whenever Caleb Samuels appeared, her world tilted on its axis, not permitting her a modicum of control.

Pulling her leg up into the hammock, she listened to the sounds floating around her. The few moments of solitude she'd managed to capture in the past when she lay in the hammock would become a memory. Cal, who had been a part of her past was now her present and her future.

The crush of a solid male body startled Lauren, and her eyes opened. "What are you doing?" she gasped. Cal quietly and unexpectedly had joined her on the hammock. Either he had to make some noise when he approached or she was certain to experience cardiac arrest.

There wasn't enough room for them to lie side-by-side in the hammock, so Cal shifted and settled her over his body, her breasts flattened against his hard chest and her legs cradled between his.

Lauren's heart pounded wildly as she tried escaping the arm of steel around her waist. "Let me go, Cal."

He lowered his chin and veiled his face in her thick black curly hair. "I can't do that, Lauren." He tightened his hold on her body. "I let you go a long time ago. That will not happen again."

Lauren decided on another plan of defense. "This hammock is going to fall. It's not designed to hold our weight."

Cal smiled, closing his eyes. He did not want to move. The feel of Lauren's body was much too pleasurable.

"We're not overweight, Lauren. It'll hold at least three hundred pounds," he added confidently.

She buried her face in his throat. There was no way she

could ignore the swelling hardness pressing intimately against her bare thighs not covered by her shorts.

"Please, Caleb." Now her voice was a throaty whisper.

Cal's hands cupped her hips, holding her captive to his rising desire.

"Please what, *querida?*" he crooned. "Please don't let me go? Or please love me?"

"Please," she repeated weakly.

"I haven't come to you a stranger, Lauren," Cal continued hotly against her ear. "And I haven't come to break up your home and harm our child. I've come to be your husband and your lover." He felt her stiffen. "And I do want to be your lover," he confirmed in a tone filled with quiet conviction.

"You want free sex, Cal," she said against his chest.

He went rigid. "I don't need 'free sex' as you call it, Lauren. Sex is not the same as desire."

"It is to me," Lauren countered.

"I must teach you the difference," he said, laughing.

"I don't want to learn."

"I know you'd be a quick study, *querida.*"

Lauren tried freeing herself from his embrace and failed. He was too strong.

"Stop wiggling, *querida,* before we fall."

"Stop calling me that."

"What? Darling? But you are my darling," Cal crooned.

Lauren lay still, then when Cal relaxed his grip on her body she scrambled from the hammock. Cal, reaching out, grabbed her shirt and they tumbled heavily to the ground.

Cal cradled her body when they landed, his taking the full force of the fall and all of Lauren's weight.

Lauren gritted her teeth against the shock. Cal's arms fell

away and she rolled off his prone form. It took a few seconds to note he hadn't moved.

She felt a rush of blood in her head as she crawled back to Cal. His head rested at a grotesque angle as a sensation of dread washed over her. He was so quiet, so still.

Trembling fingers touched his jaw. Lauren was too upset to register the length of his lashes as they lay on sculpted cheekbones or the exquisite outline of his sensual mouth. She stared at him, feeling the icy fingers of fear replace the heat in her body.

Her fingers trailed down to his neck and she discovered a strongly beating pulse. Lauren whispered a prayer of thanks. He was alive, even though she wasn't certain whether he was conscious.

"Caleb," she said close to his mouth. "Caleb, can you hear me?" Her slender hands cradled his face. "Please, Caleb…" Her voice broke.

"I can't lose you a second time," she continued, trying to gather enough courage to leave him to call for emergency medical assistance.

She felt him shudder, then draw in a deep breath. "Come on, darling," she coaxed softly. "Wake up. Please wake up." Cal moaned, but did not open his eyes. "Don't try to move. I'm going for help." He moaned again. "It's all right, Love. I'll be right back." Leaning over, Lauren pressed a tender kiss to his lips.

In less than a heartbeat Lauren found herself on the ground, Cal pressing her down to the thick carpet of grass. His golden eyes impaled her.

"Darling—love," he drawled, leering at her expression of surprise. "I don't want to lose you a second time," he taunted.

Lauren shook with impotent rage as Cal made her his

prisoner. "You…you low-life. You liar!" she screamed in his face.

Cal settled his full weight on her slight frame. "Liar," he rasped against her moist face. "You're the liar, Lauren Samuels. You're lying to yourself and you've been lying to me."

"I hate you, Caleb," she snapped, as much from anger as from humiliation.

He lowered his head. "No you don't, darling. No more than I can hate you."

Lauren glanced away from the golden orbs that probed beneath the surface to see what she had vainly tried to conceal.

"You can't hide, darling, no more than I can continue to lie to you or myself," Cal continued. Her lids fluttered then came up and he smiled a tender smile. "I want to make love to you."

Lauren buried her forehead against his shoulder. How could she tell him that she would give herself to him, there on the grass at that moment, if only he told her that he loved her? That she would offer him all she could as his former and future wife.

Cal shifted and reversed their positions, holding her protectively. "If I could, I would put you inside of me, Lauren. I need you just that much."

She registered his words and her heart wept. Cal had openly shown her his vulnerability for the first time. He was hurting and she was watching him bleed.

Winding her arms around his neck, she breathed deeply against his throat. "We'll make it, Cal," she said quietly.

He smiled, burying his face in her hair. He was certain they would make it. They would make it because Lauren possessed what he had sought all of his life. To him she embodied a family unit: mother, father, child and home, and becoming a part of a family unit was as precious to him as taking his next breath.

"Are we going out tonight?" he questioned softly.

"I have to think about going out with you," she replied.

Pulling back, Cal stared down at her impassive face, unable to conceal his disappointment. "Why?"

Lauren felt her stomach muscles tighten. Cal looked so much like Drew did whenever she turned down the child's request to do something he truly wanted to do.

"Because you gave me a wicked scare, Caleb Samuels."

Cal's gaze drank up her beautiful delicate features. Cradling her face between his hands, he leaned over and touched her mouth with his. "I'll never do that again, darling. Never," he promised, taking full possession of her sweet, hot mouth.

Lauren gave herself up to the magic of the man and the moment; a man she loved; a man she would love as long as she lived.

Cal waited for Lauren to change clothes before suggesting they return to Boston where he could also change. Their unexpected romp on the grass had left noticeable stains on his pristine white shirt, and it was after five o'clock by the time he maneuvered his Porsche into a spacious parking lot along the waterfront area in Newburyport.

Historic Newburyport's downtown area, a National Historic Landmark, had been remodeled in its original Federalist style. Newburyport was Lauren's favorite city in the Commonwealth of Massachusetts.

Lauren walked alongside Cal, a light breeze lifting the flap of a hip-fitting cotton sarong-style skirt in an orange and black jungle print over her smooth, shapely legs while the warm summer sun beat down on her exposed arms under a bright orange silk tank top. A pair of black patent-leather slip-on sandals completed her winning, attractive attire.

"Slow down, Cal," she protested, trying to keep pace with his leisurely long-legged stride.

He tucked her hand into the bend of his elbow, slowing his pace. "I'm sorry," he apologized, smiling down at her.

Lauren felt her breath catch in her throat as she returned his smile. Caleb Samuels was breathtakingly attractive in his cambric shirt and slacks. The thin white linen fabric was a startling contrast against his deeply tanned golden-brown skin.

"Are you hungry?" he asked, taking furtive glances at her soft passionate mouth.

"A little. Do you mind if I suggest the restaurant?"

"Of course not."

Cal was pleased when Lauren said that the restaurant served excellent food while catering to casual dining and attire, for he wanted to relive the casual, relaxed atmosphere they had experienced during their stay on Cay Verde.

However, in contrast to the solitude of Cay Verde, the narrow streets of Newburyport were crowded with pedestrians. Tourists, with cameras hanging from necks and shoulders, stopped to peer into windows at every novelty shop and Lauren was as amused at Cal when he lingered on the boardwalk along the Waterfront Park and Promenade to watch the boats bobbing weightlessly on the Merrimack River. It was with much reluctance that he left and she steered him in the direction of The Grog.

The sounds of live music and laughter greeted their entrance. It was the dinner hour and the restaurant was alive with tantalizing smells and high spirits.

They were shown a table after a short wait and given menus. The smiling young waitress gave Cal an eyeful of thick fluttering lashes and straight sparkling teeth.

"Would you like a cocktail?" she asked, addressing Cal.

He arched an eyebrow at Lauren. She nodded. "Please give us a moment to decide."

The waitress did not move. She continued to stare at Cal. "Aren't you C. B. Samuels?" she questioned in a nervous, breathless twitter. "My father has all of your books," she continued in the same twittering tone. "Wait until I tell him that I served you," she gushed.

Lauren smiled at Cal's bemused expression after the young woman finally walked away. He hadn't confirmed or denied that he was C. B. Samuels.

"Your public hasn't forgotten you, C.B.," she teased.

Cal grimaced. "Very funny, Lauren." He took a glance at the menu, his burnished-gold eyes moving slowly over the printed words. "What do you say we share a bottle of champagne?"

Lauren thought about the two glasses of champagne she had shared with Gwen. Resting her chin on the heel of her hand, she gave him a sensual smile. "What are we celebrating?"

His gaze met hers, his eyes crinkling in laughter. "Why, our engagement, of course."

"Okay." Her voice, dropping an octave, contained a breathless quality. She was caught in a snare of Cal's making, unable to free herself from his powerful, magical aura. She noted the attractive cleft in his chin and the sensual curve of his full upper lip. She surveyed his face, committing it to memory, for she would need the memories—all of them—after their year of marriage ended.

"What would you like to eat?" Cal reluctantly pulled his gaze away from her beautiful face.

Lauren knew what she wanted, without looking at the menu. "I'd like a cup of clam chowder and the chicken fajitas."

Cal perused the menu further, then signaled the staring waitress, giving her their order.

Over glasses of champagne, chowder and their entrées, Lauren and Cal discussed the plans for their upcoming wedding. Cal agreed on the first Saturday in August, promising he would call his mother so she could reserve her flight from Barcelona.

"Is there anyone else you'd like to invite?" she asked him. "Cousins, uncles or aunts?"

He shook his head. "You, Drew and my mother are all the family that I claim."

She was curious about whether he actually had other relatives, but decided against asking. "Will it bother you if we don't get married in a church?"

Again Cal shook his head, his eyes fixed on her face. "No, Lauren, I don't mind."

"Where are we going for our honeymoon?" He had conceded to a civil ceremony, and it was only fair that she concede to a honeymoon.

"To the Berkshires," Cal replied with a wide grin.

"I'm not much for roughing it, Caleb," she retorted.

"It's quite civilized, love. The house has indoor plumbing and electricity."

She studied his smirking expression. "Is it your house?"

"Yes. I bought it after the sale of my first book," he admitted. "I use it for a writing retreat."

Lauren swirled a small amount of the pale bubbling wine around in her glass, staring at the gold liquid. "When was the last time you used it?"

Cal stared down at his outstretched fingers on the tabletop. The overhead light glinted off the signet ring on his left hand. "About three months ago."

Lauren felt her heart leap. She had no idea Cal had been in the States. "How often had you come to the States?"

"Two, maybe three times a year." His gaze caught and held hers. "And my grandfather never once hinted that I had fathered a child."

Lauren shook her head in amazement. "Dr. Samuels knew the living couldn't argue with the dead, so he waited to die to become the master puppeteer, pulling the strings and manipulating lives."

"He was quite a character," Cal stated, smiling.

"I have a feeling you like all of this."

Cal's eyes roved leisurely over her face and down to her revealing neckline. His gaze and laugh was lecherous.

"I couldn't have thought of a better plot if my life depended on it," he confessed.

Lauren managed to look insulted. "You have a dirty laugh, Caleb."

That's not all that's dirty, Cal thought. His mind conjured up the sensual image of Lauren naked—hot and moaning in his arms.

"There's nothing dirty about what I want to do with you," he stated solemnly.

Lauren sobered when she saw the liquid fire ignite the golden flames in his eyes. Her insides swirled, skidded, her body warming and growing heavy. The heat in her face flamed under his entrancing examination. Her hand shook slightly as she raised her glass to her lips and swallowed the dry, bubbling wine.

"It's going to happen, Lauren, whether we want it or not," he predicted.

The invisible web of attraction that had been so apparent years before was stronger, nearly out of control. Lauren's mind told her to resist, but her body refused to follow the dictates of her brain.

"Sleeping together will change everything," she said.

"It will only change us," Cal argued softly.

That was what Lauren feared; she didn't want to change; she wanted to hold onto the memory of Caleb Samuels without experiencing the pain of losing him twice.

She straightened in her chair, pulling her shoulders back. The motion stretched the silk fabric of her top taut over her breasts, drawing Cal's fevered gaze to the firm mounds of flesh. She hadn't worn a bra under the bright orange garment.

Cal closed his eyes, still seeing the outline of her nipples thrusting against the silk top. More images came rushing back. He remembered Lauren's breasts. They were small and firm, with disproportionately large dark nipples. Even before he had tasted her breasts the nipples were hard and distended. Fire shot through his groin and he groaned.

Lauren peered closely at Cal. "Are you all right?"

No, he wanted to scream. He wasn't all right. He was in pain; a hot, throbbing, excruciating pain that could only be relieved by her.

"I'm fine," he lied, opening his eyes. He hated lying to her, but how could he tell Lauren that he hurt and that his pain was emotional and physical.

"Do you want dessert?" he asked through clenched teeth.

"No, darling," she crooned.

Cal shifted uncomfortably, knowing he couldn't stand up without Lauren noting his arousal. "I think I'll have something," he said quickly. Sitting and eating would give him the time needed to bring his raw passion under control.

Half an hour later Lauren and Cal walked out of The Grog and onto Middle Street. His large hand closed possessively over her fingers, pulling her to his side.

"I think we need to walk off a few calories," she suggested. They had shared the generous slice of apple pie à la mode.

"Where do you want to go?"

"Market Square. There's a sweetshop that sells homemade fudge and assorted truffles that my mother can't resist."

Cal followed Lauren's lead, his arm going around her waist. "Your mother isn't the only one who can't resist candy. There're times when I have an uncontrollable craving for something sweet."

Lauren's right arm curved around his slim solid body. "I thought you were more controlled than that," she teased.

"There are certain passions I never want to control," he countered, kissing her ear.

She had no problem interpreting his double meaning, knowing what particular passion he was referring to. Making love to Cal conjured up unbidden memories and the blood roared hotly in her face and body.

They turned down Market Square and Cal stopped in front of a jewelry shop. The showcase displayed a large selection of antique pieces.

"You need a ring, Lauren," he stated, then steered her into the beautifully appointed shop.

A woman with short gleaming silver hair and a rich gold tan smiled at Cal. "May I help you with something?"

"I need an engagement ring for my fiancée and bands for both of us."

Lauren was too surprised to respond until the salesclerk reached for her left hand to measure her third finger.

"Caleb," she warned quietly, but a scowl from him preempted any further protest.

"A five," the woman murmured. "You have very slim fingers." She glanced down into the display case. "What's your preference? Antique? Contemporary?"

"Contemporary."

"Antique."

Cal and Lauren had spoken in unison.

"Antique," Lauren insisted, giving Cal the *look*.

"I think I have something you'd like," the woman said, reaching into the case for a ring with a large oval diamond.

Lauren shook her head. "Not that one." If she was going to have an engagement ring she wanted one that suited her personal taste. "I'd like to try that one."

Cal leaned closer, his chest pressing against her back. A slow smile parted his lips. Lauren had chosen one with an exquisite emerald-cut diamond, flanked by square-cut baguettes.

"I like it," he stated. Taking the ring from the woman's hand, he slipped it onto Lauren's finger. It fit perfectly. "It was made for you, darling." His voice was as soft and soothing as a caress.

Lauren held her hand out in front of her, her heart pounding uncontrollably. The ring was magnificent.

"Do you want it?" Cal questioned, smiling at her dazed expression.

"Yes." The single word was barely audible.

The salesclerk smiled at the young entranced couple. She touched Cal's hand to garner his attention. "I'd like to measure your finger to fit you for a band. I suppose you'd want matching bands?"

"Yes," Lauren and Cal chorused.

It took longer to select bands which suited both of their tastes. They finally decided on an unadorned style that was in keeping with the elegant simplicity of Lauren's engagement ring.

Cal extracted a credit card from his wallet and gave it to the salesclerk. His expression did not change as he signed for the purchase. Lauren was worth every penny he would ever spend on her, for she represented something money could not buy. She was his security, his ultimate success.

"Thank you, Cal," Lauren said softly, giving him a demure smile, "for the ring and the bracelet."

His face creased into a sudden smile. "Oh, so you did find the bracelet?"

She basked in the shared moment of their bliss. "Yes, and I intend to wear it on special occasions like weddings, birthdays, graduations and for the birth of our many grand-children," she stated, repeating the toast he had made the week before.

Your forgot our children, Cal thought, for he knew as surely as his encompassing love for Lauren that she would bear another child—his child.

They made their way across the street and into Something Sweet and purchased an assortment of fudge, brittle and truffles for Odessa. Lauren beamed with pride when a sales-woman complimented her on her ring. She thanked the woman and looped her arm through Cal's as they left the shop.

So this is the way it feels to be promised to someone, she mused. She had to admit it was comforting and gave her a sense of protection.

Lauren then realized that Cal wanted all of the traditions that went along with a man and woman planning a life to-gether—engagement, rings and wedding ceremony, and she wondered if he was being traditional because of his parents' unorthodox marriages.

I'll make it work, she thought, her fingers biting into the flesh on Cal's arm. *I'll make him fall in love with me again so he won't leave after the year is over.*

"A nickel for your thoughts, *querida,*" he said, watching her expression change.

Lauren stopped and stared up at him. The thick lashes framing her large dark eyes were like a fringe of black velvet.

Her mouth softened in a smile. "I feel so wonderfully happy, Cal," she confessed without guile.

He cradled her chin in one hand, his thumb tracing the delicate curve of her jaw. Lauren's sable-brown skin felt like satin to his touch. He had stopped questioning why fate had led him to her, and he opened himself to receive everything she had to offer.

"Making you happy makes me happy, darling." There was a slight hint of wonder in his voice, as if he hadn't expected her to be truthful with him.

But what Cal wanted to hear most from Lauren she withheld. He wanted to hear that she loved him.

"Where do you want to go now, *querida?*"

"Let's go home," she suggested in a low inviting tone.

Cal needed no further prompting. Lauren was feeling what he felt. They wanted to be alone—with each other.

Chapter 10

Lauren stared through the windshield as Cal maneuvered his sports car into the driveway to her house. She moved her left hand and a shaft of fading sunlight caught the precious stones on her finger. Within a month she was to become Mrs. Caleb Samuels for the second time, and, as before, he was still a stranger—a stranger she had married, a stranger whose child she had borne, and a stranger she loved without question.

She tried weighing all that had culminated since the reading of the late Dr. Caleb Samuels' will. Events occurred so quickly that she found it difficult to sort out what was real and what was not an ongoing dream where she would wake up in a cold sweat.

But this Caleb Samuels was real—a hot, breathing, flesh-and-blood man, and she was also alive. The part of her Lauren thought had died when she walked out on Cal was also alive—hot and breathing, and she wanted nothing more than to lie in Cal's arms and experience again what it meant to be a fulfilled woman.

At that moment Lauren knew she had to stop hiding, running and lying. She wanted Caleb Samuels. There was never a time when she didn't want him.

"I have to see after Missy, then throw a few things in an overnight bag," she said quietly.

Cal merely nodded. He did not move as Lauren slipped out of the car and made her way up the steps to the porch. He sat, shaken, amazed and overwhelmed with the emotions gripping his mind and body. Lauren was ready to come to him willingly, without fear, and offering all that he had sought since he first slept with her.

Lauren checked her answering machine for messages, finding one from her cousin. Gwen had reported that Jacqueline Samuels was in partnership with a record producer specializing in new talent.

Gwen also said that it had been rumored that Jacqueline was instrumental in breaking up her partner's marriage when his wife returned unexpectedly from a business trip and found her husband and Jacqueline in bed together at their vacation bungalow on Martha's Vineyard.

"Nice lady," Lauren mumbled under her breath.

She did not want to think about Jacqueline. She had enough to think about when she realized what was to happen.

Methodically she packed what she needed for her overnight stay at Cal's house, turning and making her way downstairs before she could change her mind.

Lauren found Cal in the garage with Missy and her puppies. The large canine was standing with her front paws on Cal's chest while the two tiny gray pups sniffed at his feet. She smiled, unable to believe Missy could be that playful.

"I changed her water and gave her enough food until we get back tomorrow," Cal said around Missy's shaggy head. He pushed her gently until she regained her footing.

Missy ambled toward Lauren, sniffing her cautiously. She held out a tentative hand, patting her pet. "Take care of your babies, little mother." Missy responded with a loud bark.

Cal took Lauren's tapestry overnight bag from her loose grip. He smiled at her and she returned it, successfully masking the glint of uneasiness in her eyes.

"Let's go, *querida*."

Lauren wasn't able to draw a normal breath until Cal parked the racy sports car in front of the town house that had belonged to four generations of Samuelses.

"I hope you don't drive that fast with Drew," she admonished with a frown. Cal smiled sheepishly, giving her a sidelong glance. "Caleb, no," Lauren wailed.

His right hand caught the back of her head—incredibly strong fingers holding her captive. "I'm careful, sweetheart."

Lauren pounded his chest with a small fist. "Don't you dare sweetheart me, Caleb Samuels. Careful isn't enough. If you hurt my child I'll..."

Cal caught her hand in an iron grip. "Drew is also my child, Lauren." He thrust his face close to hers. "You have to stop thinking of him as *your* child. He's *ours*."

She rested her forehead on his shoulder, closing her eyes and inhaling his distinctive masculine scent.

"I know he's ours. It's just that he's been mine for so long."

Cal smiled in the shadowy darkness of the car. Drew was

his and Lauren was his. Curving a hand under her chin, he lowered his head, brushing his lips over hers.

"Let's not fight, Lauren." She nodded. "Are you ready to go in?" She nodded again.

Lauren undid her seat belt while Cal climbed out of the car and came around to help her out. He picked up her overnight bag and the decorative shopping bag with Odessa's fudge and truffles.

Cal felt Lauren hesitate as he took her arm to lead her into the town house. "What's the matter, darling?"

She stared up at the building's facade. "I was just remembering the first time I came here with you. I was so frightened. And I'll never forget the way your grandfather glared at me. He hated me, Cal."

Cal tightened his grip. "No, he didn't, Lauren. He was more angry with me than he could've ever been with you. He claimed I gave you up too easily."

"I didn't leave you a choice."

A cold, hard expression settled across his features. "But I did have a choice, Lauren. I could've refused to let you go. I could've fought you and not agreed to the annulment. But I didn't because I saw what it did to Mother when she wanted out of her marriage. She cried that she felt trapped and there were times she was so depressed that I feared for her sanity.

"So I didn't fight you because I wanted you happy, darling. That's all I've ever wanted for you, and that was for you to be happy with me."

Lauren offered him a small, shy smile. "But I am happy with you, Cal."

His dark expression did not change. "But you weren't..."

She cut his words off by placing her fingers over his mouth. "I am now, *querido*."

Her attempt to speak Spanish amused Cal as the corners of his mouth tilted in laughter. "What other words do you know?"

"All of the curses," Lauren confessed, laughing.

He laughed harder. "You would."

They were still laughing when they walked into the living room. Cal sobered and he watched Lauren's reaction as she visually examined her surroundings. He hadn't known she was apprehensive about coming to the place that had been home to a countless number of Samuelses. There was so much he did not know about Lauren Taylor, and there was so much he wanted to know about her and it bothered him that he had only known her physically.

"What would you like, Lauren? What do you want me to give you?" he asked in a quiet voice.

Lauren, surprised by his request, wanted to say, *your love,* but said instead, "Just you, Caleb Samuels. Just you."

Cal pulled her close, holding her gently, protectively. "You have me, baby. All of me."

She wound her arms around his waist, pressing her cheek to his chest. Tears of joy filled her eyes and she blinked them back before they fell. "Thank you, Caleb."

A deep chuckle filled his chest. "If I'd known that all you wanted was me, then I could've saved a few dollars by not going into jewelry stores." He caught her right hand, placing light kisses on her fingers when he felt them curled into a fist. "Just teasing, love. You're worth every penny I'll ever spend on you."

Lauren pulled back and smiled up him. "I'd better call my mother and let her know where I am."

She walked over to the telephone, and dialed her parents' number. Odessa answered after the second ring. "Hi, Mama. I just wanted to call and let you know where to find me if something comes up."

"What on earth can come up, Lauren Vernice Taylor? And if it did, don't you think I'd know where to find you," Odessa grumbled.

Lauren watched Cal watching her and she turned her back. "Mama, I'm not at home," she continued softly. "I'm here in Boston—at Cal's house."

There was a stark, pregnant silence. "You...you're spending the night with...Caleb?" Odessa's voice had dropped to a whisper.

"Yes, I'm spending the night with Caleb," Lauren replied firmly, and without giving Odessa an opportunity to say anything else, she read off the number on the telephone. "Cal and I will pick Drew up after breakfast."

"Make it after dinner," Odessa shot back. "It appears that you're going to be busy and so am I. My grandson and I have plans to take in a matinee. We also have a few other things to do before dinner."

"Mother!"

"Good night, Lauren. Now you and Caleb have fun."

Lauren held the receiver to her ear, listening to a droning dial tone. She replaced the receiver, shaking her head.

"What did she say?" Cal had noted her blank expression.

"She said we can't pick Drew up until after dinner. They've made plans to do a few things."

Cal came closer to Lauren, a devastatingly irresistible smile parting his lips. "Aside from her beauty, I knew there was something about your mother I couldn't resist."

Lauren took a step backwards. "What's that?" Her eyes were wide, her breathing shallow.

"Her perception," he said, reaching for her when a wall blocked further retreat.

"Caleb!" Lauren whispered in desperation.

"Too late," Cal countered. "You're my captive for the next twenty-four hours, darling. Screaming, begging or praying won't help."

"No, please…" The rest was lost as Cal swept her up in his arms, kissing her deeply. Her world spun as he carried her out of the living room and up the stairs to the bedroom where they had slept years ago.

He lowered her gently to his bed, his body following, cradling her with his warmth, strength and masculinity.

Cal rained kisses all over her face and neck, and the small fists pressed against his chest unclenched, then her hands moved sensuously up and down his back. He felt her heat, inhaled her fragrance and tasted the sweet ambrosia of her mouth.

His hands slipped to her waist, pulling her top from the confines of her skirt. He was touching her, tasting her, but Cal wanted to see Lauren—all of her.

Reaching out, he flicked on a bedside lamp, flooding the room with a soft yellow glow.

Lauren closed her eyes and tried to turn over but Cal was too quick. His hands held her captive, and even though she struggled against his loose grip she couldn't free herself. He held her captive—her heart and her body.

Cal rested one arm over Lauren's upraised ones, while his free hand inched her tank top up her midriff over her breasts until he freed her of the silk garment.

She heard his breathing deepen as it exploded from him. Opening her eyes, she stared up into the amber eyes burning her naked breasts.

Cal felt the blood pool in his groin, the swelling hard and heavy between his thighs. Having Lauren like this, in his bed, in his life, was something he had prayed for over and over once he'd lost her; finding her again, possessing her again had unlocked his heart and his soul.

Slowly, painfully, methodically, he rediscovered her body kissing every inch of bared skin he caressed. "Beautiful," Cal whispered reverently. "You are so very beautiful, *querida.*"

Lauren felt beautiful; beautiful, adored and loved. She had made the right decision to share herself with Cal. With him she felt alive, a complete woman.

As Cal placed tiny kisses along the sloping curve of her rib cage, Lauren wound her fingers in his hair, around his ears, then her fingers grazed the smoothness of his clean-shaven jaw.

"Caleb," she gasped as the heat from his mouth seared the junction at her thighs.

Quickly, smoothly, Cal reversed their position, his strong hands cupping the fullness of her bottom. "Don't move, darling. Please, don't move."

His passions were raging out of control and Cal didn't want to spill out his own pleasure before giving Lauren hers.

But Lauren did move as she unbuttoned Cal's shirt, baring his broad chest to her heated gaze, discovering his chest was darker than his face—a deeper, richer tawny brown.

Bending lower, she placed small kisses along the strong column of his throat, then down over the muscles of his smooth chest. Her fingers clutched wide shoulders as she leaned closer, rotating her hips against his.

The heat rising from Cal's skin was clean and masculine and Lauren savored the erotic sensation as her exploration grew bolder. Lowering her head, her tongue flicked over the flat circle of his breast, bringing the nipple to a hard, pebbly beading.

Cal's hands tightened into fists and he struggled valiantly not to toss Lauren onto her back and finish what he had begun.

Closing his eyes, he swallowed back a groan. Her hot

mouth went from one breast to the other as Lauren suckled him like a starving infant seeking succor. His groans became strangled gasps and he threw back his head in supplication.

Lauren lay flat on Cal's prone figure, pressing her bare chest to his. She was aware of all of the changes taking place in his body and the unrestrained sounds of sexual pleasure erupting from the back of his throat.

The runaway pounding of his heart filled her with a strange feeling of power. She did excite Cal; she could please him. A hot ache rose within her own body and she prayed she could continue to play out her role as seducer before begging him to take her.

His large hands cradled the back of her head as she kissed him, hard and deep. Deprivation, longings, desires and all of the love Lauren felt for Caleb Samuels poured from her hungry mouth.

He shuddered violently. It was not from passion as much as it was from fear; the fear that Lauren possessed the power to control him—totally. Her hands, her mouth, her body took him beyond himself where he could not recognize the person he had become. She held her present, his future and his very life within her grasp and she did not know it. All he needed from Lauren was a word, a gesture of rejection and he would cease to exist.

Lauren's fingertips feathered over Cal's ribs to the waistband of his slacks. Her breath was coming faster but she couldn't stop. She had to finish what she had begun.

Rising slightly, her mouth still hungrily devouring her lover's, she unzipped his slacks. The heat from Cal's lower body escaped like tongues of fire from a roaring furnace. Her hands slipped lower, over low-cut briefs, closing on the solid bulge straining for escape.

Cal's control was shattered. "No!" It was too much.

Lauren ignored his protest, gently increasing the pressure and the pleasure on his swollen, throbbing maleness. "Yes, Caleb," she whispered.

"No," he repeated. Quickly reversing their positions and their roles, he held her effortlessly as his captive, his eyes glittering wildly like those of a cornered animal. The muted light from the lamp shadowed his face, but not the brilliant golden eyes with the dark brown centers that stood out like beacons.

Cal shrugged out of his shirt and his raw sensuality sucked Lauren in whole. The muscles rippling in his upper body under skin layered with pigments of ocher and alizarin brown, the film of moisture bathing his flesh and the natural musky male scent of his body and aftershave assaulted all of her senses. Caleb B. Samuels II was beautiful; he was perfect; he was so unequivocally and undeniably male that it screamed out its very essence.

"Thank you, darling," he crooned, having regained control of his runaway passions. Now it was his turn to return the pleasure. He would love Lauren unselfishly as she had loved him.

He removed her skirt, bikini panties and her sandals, stroking her like a master violinist caressing a priceless Stradivarius. He became a sculptor, his fingers moving and lingering over every curve, every plane. "Now it's time I give you something back."

Something in his tone should have warned Lauren, but she was totally unprepared as he slid down the length of the bed and knelt at her feet, moving up and tasting naked flesh in his journey to stake his claim not only on her body but also her heart.

Lauren rediscovered all of her erogenous zones: the soles of her feet, behind her knees, the inside of her thighs and even her armpits.

Cal left a moist trail over the fullness of her buttocks, ignoring her soft pleas that he stop. He had no intention of stopping; not until he loved every sweet, smooth inch of her silken body.

His head dipped between her thighs. "Caleb! Oh, Cal…" she cried out, gasping uncontrollably.

Stop, Caleb, her head screamed. Her protests echoed loudly in her brain until her throbbing flesh responded to his methodical ministration.

"I…" The rest was lost in the gasps and sobs of ecstasy escaping her constricted throat. She couldn't disguise her body's reaction, arching against his thrusting tongue, her hips undulating in a wild, unrestrained rhythm.

Emotions welled up in Lauren and she did not understand nor could she explain them. Tears formed behind her eyelids and flowed down her cheeks. The pleasure had shattered her into tiny pieces, stripping her bare where she lay naked and vulnerable for the pain only Cal could inflict.

Cal felt her trembling. He also registered her sighs of repletion as he inhaled her feminine muskiness, his tongue catching the droplets clinging to the tangled curls between her silken thighs. He moaned, taking a deep breath.

"You're a joy, darling," he crooned, nibbling at the moist mound. "Beautiful, loving and so wonderful."

He slipped out of his slacks and underwear, then moved over Lauren's limp form. Moisture coated her body, shimmering on her sable skin like dappled sunlight.

She wound her arms around his neck, crying softly. "Shhh, baby. Don't cry." His touch was gentle, his voice comforting, but Lauren couldn't stop her tears.

He held her until she quieted. She loved him so much she hurt. She thought she would find love satisfying and peaceful, but she was wrong. Knowing she would lose Cal after a year stabbed at Lauren, making her bleed.

After a long silence, Cal asked, "Are you all right, sweetheart?"

Lauren sniffed loudly. "Yes, Caleb."

He kissed her forehead, brushing back damp curls. "Did I hurt you?"

"No," she answered with a soft laugh.

Cal pulled back and stared down at her spikey wet lashes. "Then, baby, why the tears?"

Lauren buried her face in the hollow between his shoulder and neck. "Because it was so good, so magical," she confessed softly.

"That was only the beginning," he promised, dropping a kiss on the top of her head.

Raising her chin, Lauren stared up at Cal. "Really?"

"Really," he repeated, kissing the end of her nose. He found it hard to believe that Lauren was so womanly, yet at times reacted so innocently. He smiled and she returned his smile, and Cal felt a stirring in his loins. Groaning, he closed his eyes.

Catching her lower lip between her teeth, Lauren inhaled sharply. Cal's hardness searched between her thighs, seeking possession.

"Ah-h," she gasped.

"Oh, yeah," he countered, his lips brushing her as he reached over to the bedside table to secure the foil packets secreted in the drawer.

In less than a minute he was buried deep in her burning body, their breaths mingling and fusing.

Cal moved slowly, deliberately, savoring the moist heat of her tightness. Gritting his teeth, he called on all of his control not to end the exquisite pleasure hurtling through his lower body. He wanted to prolong the poised explosion just a bit longer; long enough to offer Lauren all he had: his love.

Gripping the pillows cradling her head, Cal pulled back, then plunged deeply. He increased his rhythm, and Lauren began moving in concert with him, faster and faster, harder and deeper. A wild, primal cry erupted from the back of his throat and he released the explosive, rushing obsession that had been building, ever since the moment he was reunited with Lauren Taylor.

The first time he had taken Lauren to his bed it had been in lust and passion. This time it was in love and passion.

He loved her; he loved her with everything he had to give another human being.

A quiet, soothing feeling swept over him as his passions ebbed with a comforting pulsing. He had come home. The woman cradled in his arms was his safe harbor.

Fulfilled, they lay together, limbs tangled in exhausted pleasure. Cal shifted and Lauren snuggled against his length. A satisfied smile touched her thoroughly kissed mouth as she fell asleep.

It was later, much later, that Cal joined her in sleep.

Lauren heard the distant ringing through the thick fog of sated slumber. She stretched, her leg encountering an immovable object. She came awake immediately, sitting up.

"Stop wiggling, Lauren," a drowsy male voice ordered.

Turning to her right, she tried making out Cal's face in the darkened bedroom. There was only the sound of his soft breathing.

"Caleb," she whispered loudly.

Cal turned over quickly and flicked on the lamp, his amber gaze encountering her wide stare.

"What is it?" His voice was gruff, but he couldn't help it. It had taken hours before he found solace in the comforting arms of sleep. Making love to Lauren had disturbed him and he knew he could not and would not let her go after the time limit expired on their arranged marriage.

Lauren pulled the edge of the sheet up over her naked breasts. "I thought I heard the phone ringing."

Cal inched closer to Lauren, pulling the sheet out of her grasp, his gaze lingering on her breasts. They were perfect, even though they were small. He reveled in their firmness and the ripe succulence of her large dark nipples.

"You could've come up with a better excuse to wake me if you wanted me to make love to you, *querida,*" he crooned, winking at her.

She felt her face and body heat up under his accusation when Cal pointed to the silent telephone on the bedside table.

"But I did hear the telephone," she insisted. She met his burning golden eyes, her pride surfacing. "If I wanted you to make love to me I'd just come out and say it."

He moved over her body. "Say it," he challenged, his breath hot and searing against her throat.

"No," Lauren retorted, closing her eyes when his fingers inched up her inner thigh.

"Say it," Cal repeated in the heat of her moist mouth, his hand finding her feminine garden of secret pleasures.

She arched against his questing finger, taking all that he offered and countering his challenge with, "If you want me you'll have to take me."

He took her, much like the first time they'd shared a bed. Holding nothing back, they offered each other unbridled, primitive mating.

It ended with Cal bracing his back against the headboard,

gasping for breath while Lauren lay trembling from the ecstasy that lingered long after Cal had withdrawn from her body.

Both of them were frightened; frightened as to where their passions would lead and what they would become if they ever parted.

Chapter 11

Lauren snapped the ruby and diamond bracelet around her right wrist, fingers lingering over the circle of gold and precious stones. She had promised Cal she would wear his gift for their wedding.

Sucking in her breath, she closed her eyes. Their wedding; she and Caleb Samuels were to become husband and wife for the second time.

Events of the past month had begun like a whirlwind, then escalated. All of the responses were acknowledged from invited guests, the caterers had finalized the menu, she and Cal had picked up their marriage license and Cal had moved most of his clothes and personal items into her house in North Grafton.

Still experiencing the effects of differing time zones, Joelle Samuels helped a frantic Odessa pull together all of the loose ends for their children's wedding.

Opening her eyes, Lauren stared back at her reflection in

a full-length mirror. Her wedding attire was not the traditional white lace and satin gown but a floor-length, long-
sleeve white satin and Alençon-lace fitted sheath with a side
drape and high slit. Beaded pearls banded the low-décolleté
oversized collar, sleeves and the seductive scalloped slit and
hem, and two large satin roses were nestled along the soft
folds of the draped fabric. Her headpiece, a small pillbox hat
with a veil of pearl sprays and beading complemented her
thoroughly modern dress.

Odessa, Joelle and Gwen stared in silence when Lauren
turned to face them. She managed a nervous smile. "I'm ready."

"Caleb has chosen well," Joelle stated proudly in a soft
voice that still carried a trace of a Louisiana drawl.

"Thank you," Lauren replied, her smile widening.

Joelle nodded, smiling. Tall, reed-thin and exotic-looking
in appearance, fifty-five-year-old Joelle Samuels turned heads
everywhere she went.

"You're beautiful, baby," Odessa mumbled, sniffling
back tears.

Lauren's hands curled into tight fists. "Oh, Mama, if you
start crying I won't be able to walk out of this room."

Gwen Taylor knew if her aunt cried so would Lauren.
"Aunt Dessa, please." Her mind churning quickly, she walked
to the bedroom door and opened it. "Uncle Roy!"

Roy Taylor rushed into the bedroom, staring at the four
women. "What's the matter?" His jet-black eyes shifted frantically over the feminine forms covered in silk and satin.

"Mama's going to start crying," Lauren whispered.

Roy took charge. "Joelle, you take Dessa downstairs while
Gwendolyn and I will take care of Laurie." In his own rush
of nerves he had reverted back to the name he had called
Lauren when she was a child.

Roy placed both hands on his daughter's shoulders and pulled her to his body. "You have to forgive your mother, Laurie. She hasn't been herself lately."

Lauren nodded. No one had been themselves lately. It seemed as if she and Cal managed to argue over nothing and everything. The one time he raised his voice to her she threw a pillow against the wall after he stalked out of the house and drove away.

Tilting her chin, Lauren stared up at her father. "I just want it over, Daddy."

Roy heard his daughter's desperate plea. Lauren had undergone a lot of strain since Caleb Samuels walked back into her life. He kissed her forehead, smiling. "Let's go downstairs and get it over."

Cal stared at Lauren's profile throughout the brief civil ceremony. He was spellbound, unable to pull his gaze away from her face.

She was enchanting. His bride was like a summer rose, slowly opening and coming forth in a full flowering fragrant fragility.

"The ring, Caleb."

Judge Odell Parker's sonorous voice shattered Cal's entrancement with his lovely bride. He extended his hand to Drew and the child slipped the circle of gold off his thumb and placed it in his father's outstretched palm.

Drew, dressed in white short pants, knee socks and shoes, a crisp white shirt with an Eton collar and white tie had the honor of being his father's best man. He found it difficult to control his childish excitement as the time neared for his parents' wedding.

Cal slipped the ring on Lauren's finger, grinning proudly.

Lauren repeated the action as she slipped a matching band on Cal's long, tapered finger.

"By the power given me by the Commonwealth of Massachusetts, I pronounce you husband and wife. Caleb, you may kiss your bride," the judge concluded.

Lauren missed her mother sobbing silently against her father's chest, the unshed tears glittering in Gwen's eyes and the triumphant gleam in Joelle Samuels' golden gaze when Cal lowered his head and covered her mouth with firm lips.

Cal gathered Lauren tightly, seemingly trying to absorb her into himself. Now he was complete, whole, and for that he had to thank Lauren.

"Thank you, darling," he whispered against her pliant mouth. "Thank you for my son and for giving him his legacy."

Lauren stiffened his embrace, her head spinning and making her faint. Cal had said nothing about loving her. *He could've lied,* she thought. At that moment even a lie would've been better than saying nothing, and she began to suspect what Cal felt for her was only passion. They were perfect in bed—their lust for each other evenly matched.

Cal covered the small hand resting on the lapel of his tuxedo jacket with his larger one, unaware of Lauren's uneasiness. He squeezed her fingers gently only relinquishing his claim when Roy held out his arms to his daughter.

Roy gathered Lauren to his chest, kissing her cheek. "You're no longer my baby, Laurie. You now belong to your husband as he belongs to you."

Lauren recovered, smiling up at her father, seeing sadness in his dark eyes. "I may be a married woman, but I'll always be your baby, Daddy."

She pulled out of her father's arms, stepping back and looping an arm through Cal's. She stood in the shadowed coolness of a large black and white striped tent ready to receive the good wishes of her family members and guests.

Odessa wanted an outdoor celebration and the weather had cooperated. The day was awash with bright sunlight, a clear sky and warm summer breezes, and Odessa's black and white silk dress emphasized the color scheme for her daughter's special day.

Lauren felt the muscles tense under Cal's arm with Andrew's approach. The attractive red-haired woman who had been Andrew's blind date clung possessively to his hand.

Andrew flashed Lauren a lopsided grin. "I knew you'd be a beautiful bride." Leaning over, he kissed her cheek. "Even though you're married, I'll still be here for you if you need me," he whispered in her ear, green eyes twinkling. He extended a hand to Cal. "My best, Caleb. I'd like you and Lauren to meet Danelle. Danelle, Caleb and Lauren Samuels."

Cal shook Andrew's hand and nodded to Danelle. "Thank you for coming."

His polite facade did not slip. He had overheard Andrew's statement to Lauren, but he didn't want to spoil his wedding day by confronting the agent about his relationship with Mrs. Caleb Samuels, and one thing Andrew Monroe would come to know was that Caleb Samuels was a selfish man, and not for any reason would he share what he considered to be his and his solely.

Lauren couldn't bring herself to eat any of the expertly prepared food. After two bites, the succulently tender filet mignon seemed to stick in her throat. She caught Cal's raised eyebrows as she reached for a glass of champagne.

Cal forced his gaze away from her revealing neckline, staring down into the velvety blackness of her large eyes.

"Are you all right?"

Lauren took a swallow of the sparkling dry wine. "Yes." Her voice was low and breathless.

Cal ignored the other guests seated under the striped tent. Everyone was eating and drinking while silent waiters stood by each table.

"You're drinking and not eating," he stated flatly.

Lauren's glass was poised in midair. It was only her first glass of champagne. "Do I need your permission to drink?"

"No. But..."

"Then don't monitor my actions," she shot back in a quiet voice. "You have your son and your wife, Caleb. Shouldn't that be enough for you?"

Cal's features hardened. "No, it's not enough."

Her gaze raced over her husband's face. Cal was exquisite in formal dress. He had worn a black and white striped silk tie and cummerbund with his tuxedo and his graying hair appeared a gleaming silver against the loose curling black strands. Spending time outdoors with Drew had darkened his face to a healthy glowing chestnut brown.

"What do you want?" She enunciated each word.

Cal could not believe the sharpness in her tone. Her voice was low yet cutting. What had he said? What had he done to set her on edge?

Gripping her elbow tightly, he eased her up from her chair. "We need to talk."

Ignoring the inquisitive stares of their guests, Cal led Lauren out of the tent toward the house. Once inside the spacious Colonial structure he closed the front door behind them.

Pulling Lauren to his chest, Cal cupped her face in his hands. He lowered his head, tasting her mouth. "To answer your question, I want you Lauren Samuels," he murmured between nibbling kisses. "I want you and only you," he continued, then took full possession of her mouth.

Lauren pushed against the solid wall of his chest. "No, Caleb."

His hold slipped down to her tiny waist. Raising his head he stared at her. "Yes, Lauren. Drew isn't the only one I want in my life."

"You needed me to fulfill the conditions of your grandfather's will."

"I want you for you, Lauren," he refuted.

She wanted so much to believe him. She wanted to believe that he loved her and he wanted her because he loved her.

"I'll always want you, sweetheart. Even when you don't want me." He ran a finger down her throat and over her chest to the soft swell of breasts rising above the revealing décolleté.

Lauren sagged weakly against his body, closing her eyes. "What have we gotten into?" she sighed, realizing the enormity of their situation for the first time. "We've allowed someone else—a dead man—to dictate our destiny."

"My grandfather was a very wise man, darling. I have a feeling he knew exactly what he was doing when he rewrote his will."

"But we don't love each other, Cal. People who marry one another usually do it because of love and commitment," she argued softly. "Not only have we married once, but twice and it has been for all the wrong reasons."

Cal leaned back, noting the distress marring the loveliness of her delicate face. Lauren was strong, yet whenever her vulnerability surfaced it was impossible for her to conceal it from him.

A sad smile touched his mouth and he shifted a dark eyebrow. "Who knows, Lauren. Perhaps one day we'll fall in love."

"I doubt that, Caleb," she replied with a heaviness in her

chest. How much more could she love him, and how was she to spend a year with him, sharing her life and offering him her body and knowing he wouldn't return her love?

"A lot can happen in a year or less." He pressed a tender kiss on her lips.

Lauren wished she could feel as confident as he did. "Perhaps you're right," she replied, inhaling. The gesture caused her breasts to rise above the beaded neckline and it was Cal's turn to inhale sharply. "I think we'd better get back to our guests or they'll think we couldn't wait to begin our honeymoon."

Cal nodded, smiling. "I don't think the honeymoon could get any better than what we've already shared," he teased.

Lauren felt her face heat up and she stared down at the toes of her white satin pumps showing through the provocative slit.

Cal laughed openly, adding to her discomfort. Even though she had shared her bed and body with Cal, Lauren still did not feel as comfortable as she should've been whenever he teased her about their passionate lovemaking.

His arm curved possessively on her waist as he directed her out of the house and into the bright afternoon sunlight.

Lauren and Cal returned to the tent to an expressive silence, all gazes directed at them. Cal's arm tightened noticeably on her body, and he displayed a wide grin.

"Post-marital jitters," he stated, smiling down at his wife.

Lauren nodded her confirmation. "I'm okay."

The cacophony of voices started up again when Cal seated Lauren. He retook his own chair, draping a proprietary arm over the back of hers. He signaled the waiter at their table with a slight motion of his free hand.

"Mrs. Samuels needs another plate," he ordered quietly.

Within minutes a plate appears with filet mignon, a green vegetable salad with an orange-hazelnut dressing and a zesty corn salad in a cilantro dressing.

Lauren ate most of the food, her spirits lifting. All that mattered was that she was in love with her husband, and she would spend the next year of her life with the man she loved.

After everyone had eaten their fill, the festivities moved inside. The caterers had set up long tables filled with sweet pastries and liquid refreshment. The arrival of a small combo signaled a night filled with music and dancing.

Soft light from a massive overhead chandelier in the living room shimmered off the highly waxed pale oak flooring and played off the silver in Cal's hair as he led Lauren in the first dance of the evening.

Lauren, having removed her headpiece, felt Cal's mouth on her temple as he swung her expertly into his arms. She melted against him, remembering the many dances they had shared on Cay Verde.

She felt he held her too close for propriety, but she followed his strong lead without tripping or stepping on his patent-leather dress slippers.

"Did I ever tell you that you dance very well, Mr. Samuels?" she said, smiling up at Cal the moment he relaxed his grip.

His thick dark lashes shadowed his eyes when he stared at her smiling mouth. "My mother insisted that I learn to dance. Dancing was her life and anyone in her life was swept along with it."

"I think my Uncle Odell is quite taken with your mother." Lauren peered around Cal's shoulder to find her uncle engrossed in conversation with Joelle. "His wife died two years ago," she added, noting the surprise lifting Cal's eyebrows.

"Mother has mellowed these past few years. Perhaps she won't be too hard on him."

"I've sat in my uncle's court. He can hold his own." Lauren countered with a knowing grin.

"Matchmaking, darling?" Cal queried, lowering his voice and his head.

"Of course not," she replied innocently.

"Good. Now, let's hope your agent and his red-haired girl-friend can amuse each other long enough to contemplate a legal liaison so that he can leave my wife the hell alone."

Lauren's jaw dropped, but she wasn't given the chance to reply to Cal's caustic dig at Andrew, when her father cut in to claim his dance.

The frivolity continued for hours, long after Lauren and Cal toasted each other with champagne, cut the artfully decorated three-tier wedding cake and Lauren had thrown her bouquet of cream-colored roses, tulips and orchids. Cal flashed a Cheshire-cat grin when Danelle caught the flowers and waved them in front of Andrew.

Gwen nodded to Lauren and the two women slipped away to the small guest bedroom on the second floor.

Gwen sat down on the bed, watching Lauren remove the bracelet circling her wrist. "I must say that Caleb Samuels has fab taste in jewelry." She sighed, falling back on the bed. "I'm going to enjoy writing up this wedding for my column. Especially since the bride wore an original Scaasi gown."

Lauren undid the many satin-covered buttons along the beaded sleeves. She hadn't been able to resist the stunning garment once she saw it in a Boston bridal shop.

"At first my mother thought it was a little too risqué, but I reminded her that I wasn't having a church wedding."

"I never knew Aunt Dessa was that conservative," Gwen complained. "Her own yellow dress was equally risqué with a revealing neckline and side slit." She sat up. "But could you imagine stuffy old Reverend Lewis salivating over your chest and dress. He probably would've had apoplexy before he finished the ceremony."

Lauren laughed and stepped out of the dress, changing quickly into a pair of lightweight gabardine slacks and a cotton and silk blend sweater. Gwen hugged and kissed Lauren, whispering ribald suggestions in her ear that she should consider making her honeymoon an exciting and memorable one.

Lauren's face was still burning when Cal knocked on the door and stepped into the room.

"I don't want to rush you but we do have to cover more than a hundred miles tonight."

"And you intend to make it in an hour," she teased.

"I've stopped speeding." His expression was stoic.

"Since when?" Lauren picked up a shoulder bag, making her way to the door.

He caught her arm, taking the bag. His gaze lingered on her mouth. "Since this afternoon, Lauren. It suddenly hit me that as a husband and father I have to be more responsible. I have to take care of you and Drew, therefore I can no longer afford to take the risks I used to take before."

"You don't have to take care of me," she replied.

He leaned over her. "Don't tell me what to do, Lauren." The softly spoken words were layered with steel.

Lauren felt a flicker of annoyance. They hadn't been married a day and already Cal wanted to control her, and she wondered if he was more like David Samuels than he realized.

"I am not your responsibility. Therefore, you will not have to take care of me," she stated flatly.

His mouth tightened and thinned. "Let's not argue about it."

Her large dark eyes narrowed. "Yes. Let's not."

Turning, she made her way down the hall to the staircase leading to the back of the house. Lauren didn't know why but she felt the need to argue with her husband. She wanted to release the frustrations torturing her night and day.

She wanted to tell Caleb Samuels that she loved him; she wanted to tell him that she wanted to spend not a year but the rest of her life with him, and she wanted another child.

The yearning for another baby had surfaced unexpectedly. It happened after a tender session of lovemaking when she and Cal seemed content to make the pleasure last as long as possible.

They both had tempered their passions, holding back, until fulfillment was a sweet, soaring warm release of sated ecstasy. She lay awake for hours afterwards, remembering the soft flutters in her womb whenever her unborn son moved, and she wanted to experience those sensations again.

However, Lauren knew it had to be different if she ever found herself pregnant again. This time she wanted to plan for a child, and the child had to be wanted both by her and by Cal.

They slipped out of the house unseen by anyone. Lauren thought it best they not make their departure known to Drew. She had suggested it as much for herself as for her son. The thought of leaving him for a week had gnawed at her conscience. It would be the first time she would be without him for more than two days.

Cal settled her into the sports car, closing the door with a solid slam. It was apparent that his own temper was still smarting from her statement that she was not his responsibility.

He started up the car, shifted into gear and began the westward journey across the State of Massachusetts.

"Odell has offered to escort my mother around," he stated after a lengthy silence.

Lauren's head came around and she stared at the smirk on his face. "Then I wasn't wrong. I knew he liked her."

"What else do you know?" Cal asked in the quiet tone that always sent a ripple of longing throughout her.

She frowned. "What are you talking about?"

"It appears as if you're quite perceptive about a lot of things. What else have you picked up?"

"About what?"

"Not about what, about who?"

"About who, Cal?"

"About me, Mrs. Samuels."

Lauren pulled her gaze away from the shadowy outline of his features. Night had fallen and the only light came from the glow of the dials on the dashboard and from the headlights of oncoming traffic.

She searched her memory for changes in Cal since the day they had met again at the attorney's office, but came up blank. He was usually even-tempered and relaxed, and she knew he didn't like Andrew.

"I don't know, Cal," she admitted. "You tell me."

Cal let out his breath slowly, shaking his head. "No, Lauren. I won't tell you. If you don't know by now, then you'll never know."

His fingers gripped the steering wheel savagely. Didn't she know? How could she not know that he loved her? When he made love to her he not only gave her his body but also his spirit. He gave her everything he had, leaving himself naked and vulnerable to the pain that Lauren and only Lauren could inflict.

Both of them wrestled with their private demons as the

sleek Porsche ate up the highway, Cal concentrating on his driving while Lauren closed her eyes.

"Wake up, darling. We're here."

Lauren woke immediately. "I'm sorry I wasn't much company," she apologized with a delicate yawn.

Cal smiled, noting her heavy lids. "You needed the rest. You've been through a lot."

Lauren placed her hand in Cal's and he pulled her gently from the car. She leaned against his chest and he cradled her body to his, offering his warmth. The air in the mountains was cool at night.

"We've both been through a lot, Cal," she mumbled, snuggling in the crisp cotton of his pale blue denim shirt.

"And now it's time we think about offering each other a measure of happiness, *querida*." He rested his chin on the top of her head. "My grandfather may have forced us back into each other's lives but that doesn't mean we can't make this marriage of convenience work."

Pulling back, Lauren stared up at him. She registered his plea, but the darkness would not permit her to see his features clearly. She wanted so much to see the tenderness emanating from the smoldering depths of his fire-lit eyes.

Lauren opened her mouth to blurt out her love for him, then at the last moment bit down on her lower lip to swallow back her confession. She would not tell him; not yet.

Rising on tiptoe, she kissed his mouth. Her lips told him what her tongue wouldn't as she kissed him with all the emotion she could summon for her husband.

Cal's heart thudded wildly against her breasts, and Lauren knew by the obvious changes in his body that he desired her.

"Let's go inside," he gasped, breathing heavily in her ear.

Chapter 12

This wedding night was different from the one they had shared on Cay Verde. Lauren came to Cal with a passion that was strong, uncomplicated and boundless in its intensity.

Five years ago she had been innocent and ignorant—innocent in that she wasn't very experienced or worldly, and ignorant of her very passionate nature.

No man had ever been able to reach inside of her to erase the inhibition she wore like a shield of honor. No man but Caleb Samuels.

Lauren had stopped asking herself why she couldn't resist Cal. Each time they came together she felt as if she renewed her life cycle.

Hands, mouths, tongues caressed and tasted nakedness until Cal and Lauren grew impatient to sample the oneness that transported them to a private sphere where they ceased to exist as separate entities.

Lauren's decision to use an oral contraceptive provided both of them with a maximum pleasure they hadn't thought possible.

Gritting his teeth, Cal called on all of his control not to give into the rush of ecstasy spiraling wildly with each thrust into his wife's tight, hot body.

Lauren wrapped her legs around his waist and gave herself up to the hysteria of delight ravaging her mind and body. If she couldn't tell Cal that she loved him, then her body would. Each and every time she lay with him she whispered silently over and over that she loved him.

She surrendered completely to the sensations straining for release and she gasped in the shattering, explosive pleasure, clinging to Cal when she felt him also surrender to the forces dissolving their captive hearts.

Smiling, Lauren gloried in the light kisses raining on her face and mouth, then feathering over the rapidly beating pulse along the column of her neck.

An aching tingling lingered in her breasts and between her thighs. Moving slightly she felt Cal stir within her body and she moaned sensually.

"Are you all right?" he asked breathlessly.

Lauren moaned again. "I'm fine, darling."

She was better than fine. A soothing, comforting feeling of banked fires, passion and love swept over her as she drifted off to sleep.

Lauren descended the staircase, following the distinctive aroma of brewing coffee. She had discovered upon waking that the house in the mountains was anything but rustic. Constructed of glass, wood and stone, it sat on a rise overlooking a small lake. It was the perfect retreat for a writer or artist who craved solitude.

Her bare feet did not warn Cal of her approach as she made her way into a spacious sun-filled kitchen.

Cal sat at a bleached pine table, feet anchored on a chair while his fingers raced quickly over a laptop computer. She moved into his line of vision and he glanced up, a tender smile softening his mouth and smoothing out the lines of concentration in his forehead.

"Good morning, Mrs. Samuels. I can say that now, without you going for my throat," he teased.

Lauren floated to his side, winding her arms around his neck. "Good morning, Mr. Samuels." Her mint-flavored breath whispered over his awaiting lips.

Cal placed the laptop on the table, pulling Lauren down to his lap. "Are you ready for breakfast?"

She glanced up at the clock over the sink. It was past noon. She had slept away all of the morning. "I think brunch would be more like it."

The fingers of Cal's right hand were splayed over her flat belly while his left played in the thick glossy curls around her ears that Lauren had managed to control with the assistance of a curling iron.

He remembered the tousled curls scattered over her head in sensual disarray when he awoke earlier that morning. He lay beside her, watching her as she slept and wondering what dark secrets she kept from him. He found it hard to believe that Lauren could come to him so willingly, offering her body in total abandon while withholding any hint of deeper feelings for him; he pondered whether their relationship was destined always to be one-dimensional. Would they share only Drew and their passions?

"I'd much prefer dessert," he replied with a teasing grin.

Lauren laughed lightly. "Brunch first, Caleb Samuels."

He stuck out his lower lip, pouting. "But I want dessert." Lauren pulled out of his embrace, standing up with hands on her hips. She gave him the *look*. He rose with her. "All right, warden, brunch first."

They ate brunch at a restaurant that catered to family-style dining. Most of the patrons were dressed in jeans, sweats or jogging attire.

After dining, Cal gave Lauren a tour of the square block of the business area that featured a mini-market, gift shop, bank, post office and service station. They bought staples to stock the refrigerator and pantry and returned to the house for an afternoon of boating.

"Don't rock the boat, Lauren," Cal warned as he dipped the canoe paddle in the clear lake water.

Lauren anchored her hands on the sides of the canoe and swayed. "What's the matter, Caleb?" she taunted. "Can't you swim?"

Cal pulled the paddle into the boat. "Of course I can swim. Can you, darling?"

She was never given the opportunity to reply. Cal tipped the canoe, spilling both of them into the cold water. Lauren sputtered and splashed water while trying to hold onto the overturned boat.

"Caleb!"

Cal was beside her in seconds, holding her up. "I won't let you drown."

Lauren pushed against his chest. "I won't drown. I can swim," she rasped, treading water.

Cal righted the canoe, flipping agilely into it. He extended a hand and pulled Lauren after him.

"You ruined my hair," she wailed, patting the water-soaked strands.

He gave her a baleful glance. "You look beautiful."

Lauren sniffed loudly. "If I looked like a toad you'd say that I look beautiful," she grumbled.

Cal's expression changed. "Damn right." His grin slipped away when he noticed the outlined of her bare breasts under her wet T-shirt. He hadn't lied to her. She was beautiful. With or without her clothes—wet or dry, and he suspected she didn't know just how beautiful and sexy she was without even trying.

He loved the rich dark brown of her skin, the thick blackness of her hair and the velvety serenity of her dark eyes. He admired her feminine fragility and her grace. He welcomed her calming spirit and respected her intellect.

"Thank you, Gramps," he mumbled under his breath.

"Did you say something?"

Cal shook his head and continued paddling, unaware that Lauren's fingers trailed in the water, skimming over large floating lilies. Without warning, she scooped up a handful of water, splashing his face.

"You're going to pay for that stunt," he threatened softly, blinking through droplets. Cal jumped out of the canoe as soon as it touched shallow water, pulling it up on the soggy bank.

He reached for Lauren, but she had slipped from the boat with the quickness of a wood nymph, running toward the house.

Cal's longer legs caught up with her and he wrestled her to the grassy lawn. The heat from his body burned through their wet clothes.

His weight held her captive as he lowered his head to claim her mouth in a kiss that was more of a reward than punishment.

"I want you, baby," he confessed, pressing his lips to her

closed eyelids. "I want you so much it frightens me." His tongue traced the length of her nose before he took her mouth again.

Lauren, relishing the sweetness of his mouth, arched, making him aware that she was ready to accept him.

The waning rays of the late afternoon sun warmed her limbs as he removed her wet clothing, exposing her to the quiet, private beauty of the countryside.

Cal did not protest as Lauren helped him out of his wet shirt and shorts, then straddled him.

There on the grass, in full view of nature's majesty, they made love. It was slow, unhurried and profoundly satisfying.

They waited until their breathing resumed its normal rate before returning to the house, both of them changed by the uninhibited act.

Lauren did not want Cal to leave her, and she waited for the right time to tell him.

The time never seemed right and Lauren decided to enjoy her husband and all that he offered her. The seclusion of the large house afforded them the privacy she sought, and when the weather proved hot enough she and Cal swam with a minimum of clothing, then made love under the sun or the stars.

She and Cal prepared sumptuous dishes under the summer skies, broiling steaks, lobster tails or freshly caught trout on an outdoor grill. The days and nights blurred and with the passing of time Lauren fell more and more in love with Cal.

A tiny voice whispered incessantly that Cal loved her, but somehow Lauren couldn't bring herself to believe it.

Lauren pulled a lightweight blanket up to Drew's chin. "Go to sleep, darling," she urged in a low, soothing tone. "You'll be able to ride your bike again in the morning."

"Okay," Drew said around a yawn.

She kissed his forehead. "God bless. I love you."

Drew's eyes closed. "Love you, too," he slurred before sleep claimed his exhausted body.

Lauren sighed in relief. She and Cal had only been back two days, but it had taken every minute to undo the haphazard schedule Odessa had afforded her grandson.

She wanted to reprimand her mother for permitting Drew to stay up hours beyond his scheduled nap and bedtime. Then there were the forbidden foods: potato chips, jelly apples, bubble gum, French fries and soda. Odessa had given her a sheepish grin, saying it had been a special week.

Lauren adjusted Drew's night-light and made her way down the staircase where Cal sat talking with his mother on the front porch.

Pushing open the screen door, she stepped out into the magical darkness of the hot summer night. Cal rose and seated her on the swing. The golden light from porch lamps was flattering to her delicate features.

"How about something cold to drink, darling?" he asked, leaning over and inhaling her floral scent.

Lauren ran a hand over her moist cheek. "Yes, please," she replied with a warm smile.

Cal straightened. "What would you like, Mother?"

"Just water thank you, Caleb."

Joelle had closely observed her son with his new bride since their return. She recognized something about him that had never been apparent before: a calming spirit. Gone was the self-imposed control that never seemed to slip, and the cold remoteness in his sun-lit eyes had also disappeared.

"Don't hurt him, Lauren," Joelle said quietly after Cal disappeared into the house.

Lauren stared at Joelle. The older woman was sprawled gracefully on the chaise. "Why would I do that, Joelle?"

"I don't think you would deliberately hurt my son, but it could happen because he loves you," Joelle explained. "He may not have loved you the first time you married but it's different now. And knowing that he's a father has also changed him."

Lauren couldn't help notice the tingle of excitement within her at her mother-in-law's statement; but she knew better than anyone that Cal did not love her.

"I won't hurt my husband," she declared adamantly, adding silently, how could they not help but hurt each other when their year ended. Neither of them would escape unscathed.

"Thank you, Lauren." Joelle appeared deep in thought before she spoke again. "I caused David more pain than he deserved. He loved me, Lauren," she confessed. "He loved me so much that he never had anything left for his son. And that's all Caleb ever wanted from him—his love."

"Why did you move to Spain?" Lauren questioned.

"Vanity," Joelle answered as honestly as she could. "The principal dancer in my dance troupe became ill one night and as her understudy I filled in for her as Carmen. The next morning I was touted as the Josephine Baker of Barcelona. It all went to my head and when the troupe left Spain for France, I stayed.

"I was twenty when I met David Samuels for the first time. I'd returned to the States for a tour and he had come to see me dance. He followed me from state to state, begging me to marry him. I laughed and told him I was too young but he wouldn't give up. I returned to Europe four months later, hoping I could forget him but it wasn't that easy. My concentration was off and my performances suffered. The director of the company sent me back home to recuperate, but instead of going to Baton Rouge I went to Boston.

"I barged into a meeting that David was chairing and crooked my finger at him. I thought he was going to faint when he saw me and he politely excused himself. I told him I was prepared to dance for him—every night if he would marry me."

"Why did you wait so long to marry him?"

Joelle managed a small smile. "I see you know the story." Lauren nodded. "I felt I had to have total and complete control of my life, but that wasn't easy with David. He was unyielding—all or nothing. He was dogmatic that we name our son after his father. I only gave in because I was too depressed after having the baby to fight him."

"Knowing this you married him twice," Lauren said in awe.

"I had to get him out of my system. And when I left him the second time I knew it was finally over."

Cal returned with a tray of lemonade and sparkling water and the conversation came to an abrupt end.

Lauren, Cal and Joelle sat on the porch laughing and talking until the older woman pleaded fatigue. She said she had to be up early because she and Odell had planned to visit Cape Cod before she returned to Spain.

Neither Cal nor Lauren mentioned a possible liaison between Joelle and the widowed judge. Both of them were too concerned with their own futures.

Chapter 13

Lauren focused her attention on Drew. The child was shoveling food into his mouth as quickly as he could chew and swallow each forkful.

"Don't eat so fast, Drew," she warned.

Drew mumbled something unintelligible, his mouth filled with rice and snow peas.

"Swallow your food, then talk," Cal suggested.

Drew chewed, his gaze darting from his mother's to his father's smiling face. "I have to eat fast and go to bed." The words rushed out after he had swallowed the remains of his dinner. "Daddy says I have to get up early to go fishing or the fish don't bite when it's late. I told Missy to have Bandit go to bed early so he won't be tired when we're ready to leave."

"If Bandit's sleepy I'm certain he'll sleep in the van," Lauren replied, hoping to reassure her son that the frisky puppy would survive his first outing away from the house.

Drew wiped his mouth with a napkin, then assumed the posture of resting his elbows on the table and cradling his chin on the heels of his hands. He waited for his parents to dismiss him from the table.

Lauren thought the gesture was one Drew was comfortable with until she realized Cal also rested his chin on his hands whenever he was deep in thought. It always amazed her how much the two of them were alike—in looks and gestures.

Cal made an expressive flourish of wiping his mouth with his napkin, placing it alongside his plate. He glanced down at his watch.

"I think it's time we home boys turn in so we can get up early for our trip." He punctuated his words with a yawn. "Can you take care of the dishes, darling?" Only Lauren saw him wink.

Drew mimicked his father, stretching and yawning. "Little homey sure is tired."

Lauren smothered a smile when Drew referred to himself as "little homey." Father and son had become the Grafton Home Boys and Cal differentiated between the home boys by calling Drew little homey.

She waved a delicate hand at her husband and son. "I think I'll be able to manage."

Drew scrambled from his chair, circling the table to pull back Lauren's chair. He had seen Cal do it, and lately he'd imitated his father's every gesture.

"Daddy and I will help you with the dishes when we come back. Promise," he added, his large eyes brimming with excitement.

Lauren leaned down and kissed Drew's cheek. "Thank you, sweetheart."

Drew's arms curved and tightened around her neck. He placed a noisy kiss on her cheek. "Good night, Mommy."

"I'll see you later," Cal whispered to Lauren.

She blew him a kiss before clearing the table. A small smile played around her mouth. Cal and Drew were about to embark on their first fishing trip while she had made her own plans to spend the weekend in Boston. Cal had agreed to take Missy and Bandit, thereby permitting her complete freedom.

Humming to herself, Lauren quickly cleaned the kitchen. She and Cal had been married for two months and it appeared as if their hunger for each other would never abate.

They made love at night, early in the morning, and there were times when they both took time away from their work to seek the other out during the day whenever Drew was at school. Lauren continued to do her research in her attic retreat while Cal elected to use the sun porch at the rear of the house for his writing.

Cal did not talk to her about his writing except to solicit her input on a historical fact. The times he joined her in bed, hours after she had retired, he came with repressed tensions that carried over to his lovemaking; only after he'd spilled out his passion did reason and sanity reign for the two of them.

The kitchen cleaned, Lauren made her way upstairs. She heard Cal's and Drew's voices in the child's bedroom, and she smiled. Cal was readying Drew for bed.

Their sharing the responsibility of looking after Drew allowed Lauren more free time for herself than she had had in the past, and she knew even after their year together ended Cal was certain to continue his involvement with his son.

Lauren entered her bedroom and headed to the adjoining bath. This was one night when she'd be able to enjoy a leisurely bath.

Filling the tub with warm water, she added scented bath crystals, then brushed her teeth and cleansed her face before slipping off her clothes and stepping into the bathtub. Sliding down into the silken bubbles, she sighed.

Lauren closed her eyes and lay in the bathtub until the water cooled and the bubbles disappeared. She opened her eyes and discovered Cal leaning against the door, arms crossed over his chest.

She sank down deeper in the water, heat stealing into her cheeks. "How long have you been standing there?"

His smile was sardonic. "Long enough to see *enough.*" He reached for a thick, thirsty bath sheet, and held it out to her. "I put Drew to bed and now it's time for his mother."

Moving closer, Cal waited for Lauren to stand, and draped the bath sheet around her water-slicked body. He lifted her from the tub and carried her into the bedroom.

"You're wetting the bed," Lauren protested as he laid her on the crisp sheets.

Cal stripped away the towel and covered her body with his. "It doesn't matter, baby. One way or the other it still will get wet," he breathed into her mouth.

Lauren moaned softly when his hands began a gentle exploration of her naked body. She began her own exploration, helping to relieve him of his clothing.

"You started this," she hissed between clenched teeth, "and I intend to finish it."

Cal pulled her over his body, smiling up at her. "You won't get a fight from me."

Straddling his thighs, Lauren settled herself over his rigid flesh. The swift, smooth motion elicited a moan from the both of them.

"Cal…oh, Caleb," she gasped, her desire spiraling out of control. The fires were now fever-pitched and Lauren knew there would be no prolonged bout of lovemaking this night.

Cal watched the play of differing emotions on his wife's face. There was never a need for her to fake her responses. He felt every fiber of her as if they shared the same body.

He cupped her breasts, thumbs sweeping over her distended nipples. Closing his eyes, Cal let his senses take over. He felt her soft, wet flesh sheathing his, heard her quickly rising labored breathing, inhaled her distinctive feminine fragrance and tasted her silky flesh.

"Lauren," he groaned aloud when she pressed her breasts to his chest, her hips moving rhythmically against his. "Please, baby. Don't torture me!" he gasped.

Lauren buried her face between his neck and shoulder, quickening her rhythm. "Let it go, Caleb. Please!"

Cal's arms tightened around her body. "No!" He wanted it to last—forever if that was possible.

"Please, darling," she pleaded.

He thought their lovemaking couldn't get any better but it had. Each time Lauren offered herself to him he treasured the joining as a gift and a reward; a reward for his loving her.

But he had to let it go. Either that or he would go crazy.

His release was strong, hot and wildly exciting, as was Lauren's, and he bit down on his lower lip to keep from embarrassing himself.

He loved her; he loved Lauren enough to give up his life for her, and at that moment he did because for a few seconds he experienced what the French call *le petit mort*.

Cal's hands cradled the soft fullness of her bottom as he placed light kisses on her moist temple. *"Te amo, querida,"* he whispered against her ear. "I love you, darling," he translated into English.

Lauren lay motionless, only the beating of her heart indicating she was still alive. Total satisfaction and fulfillment vibrated throughout her entire being.

His declaration of love was lost to her for she had retreated into a cocoon of a sated, dreamless sleep.

Cal eased Lauren's form down beside him and covered her with the sheet. His gaze caressed her lovingly as he examined the woman who had been fated to him.

Reaching up, he flicked off the lamp and turned to Lauren, pulling her gently to his side.

"I love you, Lauren Samuels."

Knowing he could say it aloud lifted his spirits to soaring heights, and he couldn't wait to tell her.

Cal slipped quietly from the bed, hours before threads of light lined the dark sky. He listened to Lauren's soft even breathing, deciding not to wake her and curbing his desire to kiss her. He would kiss her and tell her how much he loved her when he and Drew returned from their weekend fishing outing.

He used the guest bedroom to wash and dress, then woke Drew, whispering softly to the child not to make any noise that would wake his mother.

It was four-thirty by the time Cal urged Missy into a minivan. He picked up the whining, wiggling puppy and placed it in the large space behind the fold-down rear seats.

Drew adjusted his shoulder harness and seat belt, unable to quell his excitement as he was to embark on what he considered to be the best event of his young life thus far. He'd predicted that it was going to be better than celebrating his fourth birthday.

Cal slipped into the van, turned on the engine, then secured his seat belt. Glancing quickly at Drew, he smiled. He was about to share with his son what David Samuels had never shared with him, and he was grateful that he had been given a second chance at life—a chance to have a meaningful relationship with his son and a chance to discover love and happiness with a woman he wanted to share the rest of his life with.

"Ready, little homey?"

"Yeah!" Drew replied in a loud whisper.

"Well, let's go."

Cal backed out of the garage, with Drew acting as navigator so they wouldn't bump or scrape Lauren's car. He winked at Drew, giving him a thumbs-up sign before they gave each other high-fives.

Lauren rolled over to the opposite side of her bed and woke up. His body was missing, his heat had evaporated, however his scent remained. Reaching over, she hugged the cold pillow. Cal had left without waking her.

Stretching languidly, Lauren arched her feet, extending her arms above her head. The weekend was hers and hers alone. She had planned a shopping outing along Boston's Newbury Street; then she was to meet Gwen and their friends at a popular upscale supper club for an informal gathering.

She noted the time on the bedside clock and practically jumped from the bed. She had wanted to be on the road by ten to avoid the crush of Saturday morning traffic.

Lauren complimented herself when she showered, dressed and backed her car out of the driveway within forty-five minutes. Cal's Porsche was parked in a corner of the garage. The two-seat vehicle was a constant reminder of his former bachelor days for he now referred to himself as a family man, and within two months they had become a stable nuclear family: father, mother and child.

Concentrating on her driving, Lauren refused to think of when it would all end. She had promised herself that she would not think about what was to happen the following August because she was too in love with Cal to permit a thread of apprehension or disappointment to shatter her world of enchanted contentment.

Lauren wound her way through the throng standing shoulder-to-shoulder at the bar in Off the Beaten Path. The club's name was totally incongruent to its location. It was in the heart of downtown Boston and had become a favorite hangout for anyone in publishing.

An attractive man with a modified fade and luminous dark eyes blocked Lauren's path. His gaze swept appreciably over her face and body.

"Looking for me?" he asked, displaying a sexy smile.

She couldn't help but return his smile. "I don't think so." She tried stepping around him, but he wouldn't move.

"You here alone?"

Lauren sighed heavily, running a hand through her hair. He caught the flash of bright lights from her rings, nodding. "So the pretty young honey is taken," he crooned. "You should tell your old man not to let you walk around looking this sweet unless he's attached to some part of your fine little body." He made a big show of stepping aside to let her pass.

Lauren spied Gwen and waved to her. Her cousin was sitting at a table with two other women.

Gwen stood up, hands braced on her hips. "I see you still have it, girl."

Lauren hugged and kissed her cousin. "I hope you're not talking about Don Juan." She crooked her thumb in the direction of her spurned admirer.

"The brother truly has the gift for gab. I think of him as a walking greeting card," Gwen whispered in her ear.

"I think I'll stick with Caleb Samuels," Lauren admitted with a wide grin.

"Who wouldn't prefer C. B. Samuels?" a youthful-looking reporter from the *Boston Gazette* crooned, hugging Lauren when she sat down.

Lauren greeted the book editor from Summit with a wave and a warm smile. "How's life at the top?"

The woman's face brightened. "I'm breathing rarefied air. I'm still not used to being associate editor of the textbook division."

The conversation turned to publishing news and Lauren felt as if she had never left Summit when she was brought up-to-date on the events at the book company. It had been a long time—too long since she had been out with the "girls."

Over drinks and an assortment of entrées and appetizers the conversation shifted to boyfriends, husbands and failed relationships.

The noise level escalated as loudspeakers blared the latest hits, and Lauren found she had to shout to be heard even by those seated nearest her.

"Now, there's one sex muffin I'd like to take a bite out of," Gwen mumbled to Lauren.

Following the direction of Gwen's gaze, Lauren went still. She recognized Jacqueline Samuels with the object of Gwen's admiration, missing the breadth of the man's wide shoulders, deep copper-brown complexion, perfect white teeth as he smiled, a mobile male mouth, strong chin and the tilting slant of coal black eyes when her eyes locked with those of the woman clinging possessively to his arm.

"Something wrong, cuz?" Gwen asked, registering the stillness in Lauren.

"That's Jackie Samuels," she replied quietly.

"He looks a little young for her," Gwen mused aloud as Jacqueline directed her escort toward their table.

"I don't think many things bother the lady if she's out to get a man," Lauren remarked.

Jacqueline stopped at their table, tightening her hold on the massive upper arm covered in creamy cashmere. Her gaze darted quickly over Lauren's expertly coiffed hair, tasteful makeup that complemented a shocking pink silk skirt she had paired with a short slim forest-green suede skirt and matching green suede shoes.

"Isn't it nice that Caleb let his little wife out for the night," Jacqueline sneered. She glanced around. "Or is he here babysitting you?"

Lauren stood, facing the woman and curbing her impulse to slap her blind, swallowing back the words threatening to spill from her tongue. She did not want to stoop to Jacqueline's level by trading vicious barbs.

Lauren's anger faded quickly when she saw a male figure move behind Jacqueline. "I'm here with *him*." She motioned with her chin.

On cue, Andrew Monroe strolled over to Lauren, resting both hands on her shoulders. Jacqueline licked her vermilion-colored lips, wrinkling her nose, and concluded with, "What a naughty, naughty little girl you are." She patted her escort's thick shoulder. "Let's go, lovey. We must circulate."

Letting out her breath, Lauren turned to Andrew. She found his brilliant dark green eyes crinkling in amusement.

"Thanks."

Andrew dropped an arm over her shoulders, kissing her cheek. "You're quite welcome."

Everyone at the table stared at Lauren and Andrew. "Aren't

you going to introduce us to your friend, Lauren?" the Summit book editor asked, giving Andrew an admiring look.

Lauren held Andrew's hand, smiling. "Nikki, Kai, and, of course, Gwen. Ladies, my agent Andrew Monroe."

"Hello, Andrew," the three women chorused as one. Andrew laughed and blushed attractively under his tan.

"What are you doing here on a Saturday night without a date?" Lauren questioned after Andrew pulled up a chair and seated himself next to her.

"I'm waiting for Danelle. She had to fill in for a nurse who called in sick. I told her I'd meet her here," he explained, visually admiring Lauren's smiling face. "Marriage agrees with you, my friend," he added in a quiet tone.

Raising her chin, Lauren sighed, smiling. "Thank you. I recommend you try it."

"Slow down, Lauren. I haven't known Dani that long."

She affected a moue, peering at him from under her lashes. "Who mentioned Danelle?"

Andrew blushed again, lowering her head, then without warning he stood up. "You owe me a dance, Mrs. Samuels," he said quickly, hoping to make up for his faux pas. "I never got the chance to dance with you at your wedding."

Lauren wasn't given the chance to protest as Andrew pulled her from the chair and steered her to the dance floor. The throbbing sound of a slow dance number flowed through speakers hidden in the walls as couples swayed intimately to the hypnotic composition.

Lauren enjoyed dancing with Andrew, but at that moment she wished Cal were there instead. She was as familiar with every line of her husband's body as she was with her own.

Closing her eyes, she pretended she was back on Cay Verde in Cal's arms and loving him unselfishly, and unknowingly her look of love was captured by those who were not able to see what lay buried deep within her heart.

The number ended and Andrew escorted Lauren back to the table, then took turns dancing with each woman in their party, charming them until Danelle's bright hair caught his attention. He introduced Danelle and hurriedly escorted her out of the club for their own private party.

Lauren left Off the Beaten Path after midnight and drove back to the town house. She was grateful for the Boston residence, having grown very attached to the spacious rooms and furnishings.

A slender figure jumped at her from the shadows as she placed her key in the front-door lock. "I was hoping you'd show up here."

Lauren gasped, recognizing the hard, raspy feminine voice. Anger replaced her shock as she stared at Jacqueline Samuels. "What do you want?"

Jacqueline moved under the stream of the outdoor light. Seeing her this close, under the unflattering light, Lauren did not find Jacqueline as beautiful as she originally thought. There was a hardness around her eyes and mouth that may have indicated too many late nights and perhaps too many men.

"I need to talk to you, Lauren."

"I think not," Lauren replied.

"I think I do," Jacqueline shot back, her voice hardening even more. When she knew she had Lauren's attention, she continued, "I think you ought to know something about your husband that could possibly save you from future heartache."

Lauren removed the key from the lock, slipping it into her jacket pocket. "Why should you concern yourself with my well-being?"

Jacqueline licked her lips, reminding Lauren of a cat who had just eaten her fill. "We sisters must stick together."

"You're not my sister."

"Well, not in the literal sense. I just want you to be careful with Caleb Samuels."

Lauren was tempted to unlock the door and leave Jacqueline where she stood. But on the other hand she wanted—no, needed—to hear what Jacqueline wanted to warn her about.

"Say what you have to say, then get out of here."

"Caleb slept with me when I was married to his father."

Lauren brushed past Jacqueline. "Good night."

"Ask him, little girl," Jacqueline called out to her back. "Ask him whose baby I was carrying when I married his father. Ask him if I had carried to term whether the baby would've been his son or his brother. Ask him, little girl!" she screamed.

Lauren managed to fit the key in the lock and turn it with trembling fingers. She opened and closed the door, groping through a fog of anguish, as pain lodged in her chest, threatening to make her sick.

"Liar," she whispered, closing her eyes. "She's lying." She had to be lying, Lauren thought.

But what if Jacqueline wasn't lying?

Lauren held her head with both hands, pressing the heels against her temples. She didn't want to think—couldn't think. Not now.

But she would take Jacqueline's suggestion and ask Cal. All she had to do was wait.

"Mommy, look what we got for you!"

Lauren held out her arms to her son, accepting his noisy, moist kiss on her cheek. She ran a hand over his curling hair. "Fish?"

Drew's cheeks were flushed with high color. "No...I mean yes. We got fish and something else." He disappeared into the house, the screen door slapping loudly against the frame.

Lauren crossed her arms over her chest, watching Cal unload the minivan. Don't let it be true, she pleaded to herself.

Missy jumped from the van, barking for her puppy to follow her lead. The rounded ball of black and white fur rolled out of the van, landing on Cal's feet.

Cal reached into the van and carefully withdrew a small bundle. He made his way toward Lauren, one hand hidden behind his back.

She moved off the porch in a short, jerky motion, resembling a marionette being pulled by different strings. A little cry escaped her parted lips when Cal thrust a kitten at her.

"No! Caleb, you didn't."

He pulled back, cradling the kitten to his chest. "Drew wanted it."

Lauren felt like crying. "Drew?"

"Well, the both of us," he admitted.

"Caleb." She struggled not to lose her temper. "My home is beginning to resemble a zoo. I get rid of one puppy and you bring home a kitten. We have one very big dog and one puppy who'll soon grow up and also be a very big dog. I don't need another animal."

Cal's free hand went to her waist, pulling her to him. "I'm away from you for two days and I don't get a kiss or an 'I miss you.'" He pressed his unshaven cheek to her silken jaw, searching for her mouth.

"Stop it!" She pushed against his chest. "You're hurting me. Besides, you smell like fish."

Cal released her, his eyes wide in surprise. "I suppose I would smell like fish if I've been fishing."

She studied his face unhurriedly, wanting to see what it was that made her fall in love with him, and she wanted to see if she could identify the evil that would permit him to sleep with his father's wife.

Without saying another word, Lauren turned on her heel and headed back to the house.

"Can Drew keep the cat?" Cal called out to her back.

Lauren stopped, fists clenched tightly. "I don't care, Caleb. I don't care about anything you do." She walked into the house, closing the door behind her.

Cal stared at the door, lines of concern creasing his forehead. Something was wrong with Lauren. He had noticed the strain in her voice and the stiffness in her body. What had happened to her in his absence?

He decided to shave and shower before seeking her out. If something was wrong he had to right it. He loved her and it was time he told her.

Chapter 14

Cal slipped into the bed next to Lauren, smiling. Her eyes were closed, her breathing deep and even, but he knew she wasn't asleep.

He had waited as long as he could before coming to bed, hoping to give her a chance to work through whatever was bothering her.

Tonight she wore an ethereal white cotton nightgown with full flowing sleeves and a scooped neckline edged with delicate white lace. She had brushed her hair until it was smooth and shiny, while her face glistened with a fresh, clean innocence.

Leaning over, Cal turned off the lamp. "Are you still angry about the kitten?"

There was silence.

"Are you angry because Drew and I went off without you?" More silence.

Cal sat up and flicked on the lamp. "Damn it, Lauren!
What the hell is going on?"

Lauren rolled over and sat up. Her black eyes were burning
like polished onyx. "It's you, Caleb," she rasped. "I need to
know if you slept with Jacqueline while she was married to
your father."

"What!" The single word exploded from Cal's mouth as
his luminous eyes widened in astonishment.

"Answer my question, Caleb," she demanded.

"I will not," Cal countered.

"Then it's true." Lauren fought back tears.

"Hell no, it's not true."

Lauren pounded the bed with both fists. "Then tell me, Cal.
Tell me you didn't sleep with her." Her eyes, filling with tears,
overflowed.

Pulling her to his chest, Cal kissed her cheeks. "I never
slept with Jacqueline, darling." His hands made soothing
motions on her back. "I wouldn't sleep with that woman if she
was the only one left on the planet."

"She said she slept with you and you got her pregnant,"
Lauren half cried and half laughed against his bare chest.

"Jacqueline would never permit herself to get pregnant,
Lauren. She hates children."

"How do you know that?" Lauren eased back and stared
up at her husband.

"She's the oldest of seven children and she always had to
look out for her younger brothers and sisters. She listed
children as her pet peeve in her high-school yearbook."

"How do you know this?"

He sighed heavily before continuing. "She told me this one
night when she was drunk. In fact she told me her life story.
The sad thing is that she woke up the next morning unaware

that she had disclosed some very intimate details about her childhood."

"You dated Jacqueline?"

"Of course not, Lauren. I met her at a party and she sort of latched onto me for the night. She was a singer trying to make it in the recording field. I told her that I'd introduce her to my father who could possibly put her in touch with a few producers and that was that. The next thing I heard was that my father had married her."

"She told me you had slept with her."

"When?"

"Last night."

Cal grasped Lauren's upper arms, holding her tightly. "She came here?"

"No. She was waiting for me at the house in Boston."

"What else did she say?"

"Nothing else. Just that you had slept with her."

Cal mumbled a savage curse under his breath, then crushed Lauren to his body, not permitting her to draw a normal breath.

"Cal, you're hurting me," Lauren gasped.

He loosened his grip. "I'm sorry, darling. It's just that I don't trust Jacqueline, and I love you too much to have anything happen to you."

"You what?" She could hardly lift her voice above a whisper. Had he said what she thought he said.

"I love you, Lauren Samuels."

This time the tears that filled her eyes were tears of joy. "Say it again, Caleb Samuels."

Cal eased her down to the pillow, his smiling face looming above hers. "I love you, Lauren Taylor-Samuels."

She returned his smile. "And I love you, my husband."

Reaching over, Cal turned off the lamp and he demonstrated wordlessly how much he truly did love her.

"Caleb," Lauren cried out as she rushed into the enclosed sun porch. "Bandit chased Scrap up a tree."

Cal pushed a key, storing what he had put into his laptop and followed Lauren.

The kitten and puppy who usually got along well had begun to cause havoc. The large puppy couldn't resist teasing the kitten whenever it wanted to sleep, resulting in the cat inflicting numerous scratches on the dog's sensitive nose.

"I'm going to get rid of both of them," Cal mumbled angrily under his breath when he saw the frightened kitten on an upper branch of the tree. "Either they learn to get along or they're going to…"

"To what, Caleb?" Lauren crooned, pushing the sleeves to her sweater up to her elbows. "They're beasts, animals, not children," she snapped. "You can't reason with them like you do with Drew."

"Damn the beasts," he grumbled, measuring up the tree.

"Get a ladder, Cal," she warned when she realized what he intended to do.

"The ladder will only reach so far, Lauren."

Bending slightly, he jumped up and caught hold of a lower branch and pulled himself up, his legs curving around the limb.

"Don't move, Scrap. Daddy's coming." The kitten responded, moving further away from Cal, his back arched in fear. "Stay put!" Cal shouted.

"Don't yell at him," Lauren admonished ten feet below Cal.

"Here kitty, kitty." His teeth were clenched as he inched

higher and higher, praying the branches would support his weight.

Cal cursed to himself. Lauren was right, but he was loath to admit it. The puppy and kitten had become twin packages of trouble. Unlike Missy, Bandit did not want to stay outdoors. He whined until he was allowed into the house, and once in he chased and teased Scrap relentlessly. Most times Lauren enjoyed their antics, but then there were times when even Drew complained that they made too much noise.

"Be careful, Cal," Lauren called out softly, lines of worry creasing her forehead.

"Stay, Scrap. Stay, Scrap," Cal repeated over and over. It seemed like hours instead of minutes as he made his way gingerly up the tree. One branch dipped dangerously and the kitten fell, landing agilely on its feet. But Cal was not as fortunate as the feline. He fell to the ground, landing with a solid thump as Scrap scampered toward the house.

Lauren was beside Cal in seconds, swallowing back her fear. Her fingers raced frantically over his face.

"Caleb?" She hardly recognized her own weak, trembling voice.

Cal's eyelids fluttered and he managed a small smile. "Hello, precious." Lauren's fingers grazed the swelling lump over his left eye and he sucked in his breath. "Don't touch it," he warned, closing his eyes.

Lauren jerked her fingers away. "Don't move, Caleb," she ordered when he tried pushing himself into a sitting position, the motion bringing a wave of pain and nausea.

"Lauren," he moaned, falling back to the leaf-littered ground. "I'll always love you," he whispered before darkness blanketed him in a comforting cocoon of painless respite.

He was still, too still. It was like it had been only months before, but this time Cal was not feigning an injury. His shallow breathing and the moisture bathing his face indicated he was going into shock, and this time Lauren didn't hesitate to leave him, racing to the house to call for emergency medical assistance.

She completed the call, grabbed a blanket from a closet, then returned to Cal. Scrap had also come back, settling down on his master's middle.

Lauren shooed the cat away and covered Cal with the blanket. She then sat down beside him and prayed.

"Your husband has suffered a concussion, Mrs. Samuels."

"No broken bones?" Lauren asked the tall, imposing physician.

"His X-rays are negative."

"When can I take him home?"

The doctor ran a hand through a shock of thick graying hair. "We'd like to keep him in a quiet, darkened environment for at least two days. He's young and in excellent health, therefore I don't expect any complications."

Lauren nodded, chewing his lower lip. "May I see him?"

The doctor registered her apprehension. "Of course, Mrs. Samuels." He led her down a corridor and into Cal's room.

She stepped into the darkened room, barely making out the still form on the bed. She moved closer to the bed and reached for Cal's hand. He did not respond to the slight pressure of her fingers. Raising his limp hand, Lauren kissed his long, beautifully tapered fingers.

"I love you, Caleb Samuels," she murmured against his palm.

Cal heard the softly spoken words yet he could not bring himself to respond. The pain—dull, throbbing and relentless—detached his brain from his body.

"I'll be back later, sweetheart," she crooned in the low, soothing voice Cal treasured.

She released his hand and suddenly he felt cold; cold and alone with his private pain.

"When are you going to get some sleep, Lauren?" Odessa asked her daughter.

"Tonight. Cal's home and now I can relax."

Odessa stared at Lauren, noting the deep hollows in her cheeks and the circles under her large eyes. It appeared as if Lauren had taken her role as wife seriously: in sickness and in health.

"You love him, don't you?" Odessa questioned directly.

Lauren's head swung around and she returned her direct stare. At another time she would have denied the truth, but now she knew it was hopeless and useless to do so.

"Yes," she answered after a quiet moment. "I love Cal very, very much."

Odessa's face brightened with a beautiful smile. "Does this mean that you two don't plan to divorce or annul your marriage after a year?"

"Yes."

Odessa crossed her arms under her breasts, grinning. "When can I expect another grandchild?"

Lauren felt a ripple of excitement throughout her body. Cal's accident had disrupted her normal routine and she hadn't thought about taking her contraceptives. As it was, she had to call her doctor for an appointment before he wrote another prescription.

"As soon as I discuss it with your son-in-law," Lauren stated with a smile that matched Odessa's wide grin.

"Don't wait too long, Lauren."

"I won't, Mama." She had told her mother the truth—she wouldn't wait too long.

Cal had been home for more than a week yet he hadn't resumed writing. Most times he lay in bed hours after Lauren rose, gritting his teeth against the bright light inching through the drawn drapes.

He hadn't complained about the dull pain racking his head but he knew he couldn't continue to hide it from Lauren.

Cal heard a soft meow and turned his head slowly. Scrap crept into the bedroom and stood by the bed. Lifting a hand he motioned to the kitten.

Scrap sprang to the bed and settled himself at the foot, burrowing down into a comfortable position on the thick comforter. In the past Lauren had screamed about having animals in her house and, in particular, on her bed but lately nothing seemed to upset her.

Last night she had broached the subject of their having another child and if he hadn't been in so much pain they would have started immediately.

Cal wanted another child. The thought wrung a wry smile from him; this time he and Lauren would have a glorious time making a baby.

"Mail call," came Lauren's throaty voice, breaking into his reverie.

Cal pushed himself up against a mound of pillows and extended his hand. He noted Lauren's slight scowl at the small mound of fur at the foot of the bed, but it vanished quickly.

She handed Cal a stack of envelopes and magazines, that floated down beside him. Scrap stirred, opened one gold-green eye, yawned, then settled back to sleep.

"You know I can't abide animals on my bed," she mumbled, adjusting the pillows for Cal.

"Me or the cat?" he teased, tossing the thick stack of mail in his lap.

Lauren kissed his ear. "Not you. I'm talking about your furry friend who has hired himself out as your foot warmer."

"Do you care to replace him?" He gave her a pained, lecherous grin.

"Don't rush it, tiger. You're still not one hundred percent. I see you grimace when you don't think I'm looking."

"What else do you see, all-knowing wife?"

"It's not what I see, Caleb, but what I know. And I know you're not up to a wrestling match." Leaning over, she kissed his forehead. "I'll be back later."

Cal's right hand captured her chin and he held her gently while pressing his lips to hers. "I'll join you for lunch."

Lauren smiled, running a forefinger down the length of his nose. "I thought you enjoyed having your meals in bed."

He released her. "I enjoy having only you in my bed."

"Me and Scrap." Lauren blew him a kiss and walked out of the bedroom.

Cal smiled and settled back against the pillows. Lauren was right. Somehow he couldn't resist the friendly, cuddly little kitten. It followed him around and meowed to be held. Scrap had become more his pet than Drew's.

He stared down at the stack of envelopes on his lap, recognizing the return address of his agent. He had completed a detailed outline and the first five chapters of his new novel.

Opening the envelope, Cal scanned the one-page letter quickly. A wide smile creased his face. Three major publishers were interested in his work and the agent was scheduled to auction it the following month.

I still have it, he thought. The five-year drought of not writin
or completing anything was over. He had not depleted hi
creative reservoir, and *Cross of Deception* would become
bestseller. He was certain of that, and only now would he sho
Lauren what he had written. They would celebrate together.

Cal slipped a letter opener under the flap of a kra
envelope, shaking out its contents. As the glossy photo
spilled out on the comforter, the breath was sucked from hi
lungs. The pain in his temples intensified as he gritted his teet
and groaned audibly.

"No!" His intense pain bounced off the bedroom walls a
he flung the envelope and its contents off the bed.

All of his joy vanished with the images on the slick pape
Pain he thought he would never feel again slashed at him r
lentlessly, coming in waves.

"Not again," he hissed through clenched teeth. "Not again!

Lauren retreated to her study and opened her own mai
Opening envelopes, she stacked pamphlets and sheaths o
pages in differing piles. She had received the information sh
sought on the beginning and spread of Islam throughou
northern Africa. It was what she needed to complete he
research for Cal.

She opened a kraft envelope similar to the one Cal ha
received. The photos slid out and she felt the floor come
at her.

How could she explain? The photos were too real, to
damaging to refute. The image of her in Andrew's arms, ey
closed, her head against his chest and his chin resting on h
head said it all. She looked like a sated woman in the arms
her lover.

Someone had taken a photograph of her and Andrew wh

they shared the dance at Off the Beaten Path the weekend Cal had gone fishing with Drew.

Jacqueline Samuels!

It had to be her or she had put someone up to do it.

The phone rang and Lauren snatched up the receiver. "Hello." Her voice was breathless, as if she had run a grueling race.

"Did you see this morning's *Globe*?" came Gwen Taylor's hushed voice.

Lauren bit down hard on her lower lip to stop its trembling. "I think I know what's in it."

"Oh, cuz, I'm so sorry. Usually I'd get wind that something like this is going to blow. But this time it was very hush-hush." There was a pause before Gwen said, "Does Caleb know?"

"I don't know," Lauren replied, still stunned, "but I'm certain he'll find out soon enough. Which means I'm going to have to explain everything before it blows up into something neither of us will be able to control."

"Good luck, cuz. After I hang up I'm going to find out who took those pictures and sent them in. There's one sex biscuit at the *Globe* who has been after me for more than a year to go out with him. I think I'll call him up and interrogate the sweet, sticky honey bun. Bye!"

Lauren replaced the receiver, gathering the damaging photographs. With a heavy heart and a heavy step she walked out of her study and down the stairs.

Yes, he knows, she thought, the moment she saw the photographs strewn over the bedroom carpet. The glossy black and white photos in Lauren's hands fluttered to the floor when she saw Cal hold his arms out to her.

Relief girded her limbs as she raced across the room and flung herself against her husband. His warmth, his strength and his love flowed through her.

"Caleb, Caleb," she whispered over and over, as much from relief as from shame. "I only danced with him."

Cal captured her chin between his thumb and forefinger, raising her face. He surveyed her trembling mouth and the profound pain in her midnight eyes.

"I know that and you know that," he stated with a smile.

"But—but it's in this morning's *Globe*. Gwen just called and told me."

Cal ran a hand through the thick curls of her hair. "It's all right." He nodded when her eyes widened.

"But don't you care, Caleb?"

"Of course I care, darling." There was a lethal calmness in his eyes. "And I'm going to find out who took those pictures and who sent them to the *Globe*." He didn't tell her that he suspected Jacqueline.

The phone rang, preempting what Lauren had to tell Cal. He picked it up after the first ring. "Hello."

"This is Andrew. May I speak to Lauren?"

"I think it's better that you speak to me, Monroe. Lauren's rather upset right now."

"I'm more than upset," Andrew shouted. "Right now I'm about as mean as cat piss."

Cal stared at the cat at the foot of his bed. He didn't think Scrap would appreciate Andrew's reference to cats.

"I think we should discuss this without losing our heads," Cal suggested.

"I'm on my way," came Andrew's reply.

Lauren watched Cal hang up the telephone, his features settling into a stern loathing.

"Jacqueline was at Off the Beaten Path the night I was there," she informed Cal.

His expression did not change. "But she didn't take the

photos. They were taken by a professional. This is not the first time she has done something like this and I want to catch both Jacqueline and her flunky in the same trap."

Lauren frowned. "What are you talking about?"

"Jacqueline sent my father damaging photographs of her kissing me."

"But how did you come to kiss her if you didn't date her?"

"She had someone take the picture when I congratulated her after she'd been signed to a record deal. It was the only time I'd ever kissed her, because even though I never liked my father's wife I was happy for her at that moment. Of course it caused a rift between me and my father that never healed. He died of a massive heart attack a month later."

Lauren digested this, unable to believe that someone would go through such lengths to destroy lives. "What are you going to do?"

"Beat Jacqueline Samuels at her own game."

"That's telling me exactly nothing, Caleb Samuels." Lauren felt her own temper rise.

He threw off the sheet and blanket. "Excuse me, Lauren, but I must get dressed." He headed for the bathroom, leaving her staring at his magnificent naked male body.

Lauren sank down to the bed and lay staring up at the ceiling. She refused to think about what was to come. But she knew Jacqueline had to be stopped. Stopped before she harmed Drew.

Right now Drew was too young to read headline captions in tabloid gossip columns, but he wasn't too young not to understand virulent gossip repeated by adults and older children.

Closing her eyes, Lauren waited for her husband.

Chapter 15

Lauren, Cal and Andrew sat at the kitchen table, analyzing Jacqueline Samuels.

"Do you think she'll try something like this again?" Andrew questioned.

"Not if we don't give her an opportunity," Lauren replied. "My meeting you at the club and dancing with you was a stroke of luck for Jacqueline." She glanced over at a frowning Cal. "It will not happen again."

"That may be true, however I don't intend to spend my life looking over my shoulder, hoping someone isn't lurking in the background with a camera ready to take incriminating pictures of my family," Cal stated, his frown deepening. He slid off the bench. "Excuse me. I have to take something for this headache."

Lauren stood with him, placing a hand on his arm. "How bad is it?"

He tried smiling but it was more a grimace than a smile.

"Not too bad," he lied. Lauren dropped her hand and he walked out of the kitchen.

He's lying, she thought. Touching his arm revealed a rigidness associated with intense pain and/or tension. It was enough that Cal had to deal with recovering from a concussion, but having to deal with Jacqueline Samuels' treachery was another matter.

It was then that Lauren decided to take control of her life and her marriage. "I'd like you to leave, Andrew. Cal's tired and in pain. Dealing with Jacqueline will have to wait."

"But he wanted..."

"He can't, Andrew," she interrupted.

Andrew rose to his feet and stared down at Lauren, complete surprise on his face. "Are you certain this is what you want?"

"It is," she replied in a firm tone.

"Jacqueline Samuels can't hurt me, Lauren," Andrew insisted. "It's you and Caleb she wants..."

"We'll discuss this some other time," Lauren cut in. Rising on tiptoe, she kissed his smooth cheek. "Thank you for coming."

Andrew shrugged his shoulders, nodding. "Let me know when you and Caleb are ready to tar and feather our nemesis."

Lauren saw Andrew to the door and watched him drive away. What Andrew did not know was that Jacqueline did not want to hurt her or Cal. She wanted Drew's money; money she felt belonged to her; money Dr. Caleb Samuels denied her; money she needed. But for what?

Cal had disclosed that his father provided generously for Jacqueline in his will. She had been left with property, bonds and cash, and David Samuels had not been dead that long for Jacqueline to have exhausted her resources—or had she?

"Where's Monroe?"

Lauren turned at the sound of Cal's voice and she gave him a warm smile. "He had to leave."

Cal massaged his temples with his forefingers. "It's just as well. I've had enough of Jacqueline for one day."

She moved to his side and wound an arm around his waist. "What do you say we go for a walk, eat lunch out, then come back here and relax before Drew gets home from school?"

Cal cradled her head to his shoulder. "That sounds like a wonderful idea."

Lauren flashed a tender, open smile. "I'll be right back. I need a jacket."

"I'll wait on the porch for you," he replied, opening the front door.

He stepped out onto the porch, inhaling the crisp autumn air. The trees were a riot of color: yellow, orange, red and varying shades of gold against towering evergreens.

Cal felt the band of tightness around his forehead easing. The medication was working quickly, and for the first time in a week he was pain-free.

He was pain-free and gloriously happy, and he had Lauren and his grandfather to thank for that.

Lauren was perfect—perfect in every way—in or out of bed.

No one, and that included Jacqueline, could do anything that would disrupt his marriage to Lauren.

The storm door slammed and Cal turned, finding Lauren dressed in a pair of jeans, sweater, lightweight jacket and a pair of wool gloves. So much for a jacket.

He threw back his head and laughed, the sound floating upward and startling several birds perched on trees near the house. They screeched, flew several feet, then settled back to warming themselves in the bright fall sun.

Cal held Lauren's hands firmly between his own. "I don't think you're going to need these, precious. It's not freezing."

"It's forty-two degrees and that's cold enough for me."

"I'll keep you warm," he crooned, pulling the gloves from her hands and slipping them into the pockets of his beige cords. He pulled her right hand into the curve of his arm over thick cotton sweater.

"What about this one?" She held up a small, well-groomed hand.

"Put it in your jacket pocket."

Lauren shifted, pushing her hand up under his sweater. Her fingers caressed bare skin. "I prefer this kind of warmth, Caleb Samuels," she sighed, resting her head on his chest.

His insides melted in sensual excitement. The feel of Lauren's fingertips floating over his chest was unbearable and his body reacted violently.

Without warning, she was lifted into the cradle of his arms. "I think the walk is out this morning," he stated hoarsely, his warm breath fanning Lauren's upturned face.

She lowered her gaze in a demure gesture. "What do you want to do instead?"

Cal turned back to the front door. "Let's see if we can't go about increasing our family. I never liked being an only child."

"Neither did I," she replied, burying her face against his hard shoulder.

Cal opened the door, stepped inside the house, then kicked closed with his foot. "Boy or girl?"

"It doesn't matter," Lauren murmured, closing her eyes as Cal carried her across the living room and up the staircase to the second floor. "As long as it is healthy."

"I'm partial to a girl," he replied, walking into the bedroom and lowering Lauren on the bed. "A little girl who looks exactly like her mother."

"I'm willing to bet it will probably look exactly like…"

Her words were stopped when Cal's mouth covered her possessively.

Everything stopped and was forgotten—even Jacqueline Samuels' attempt to destroy their marriage—when Lauren and Cal abandoned themselves to the fires engulfing them with the erotic passion that had eluded them for weeks.

Two days later Gwen's source came through with the information Lauren and Cal needed to unravel Jacqueline's plot to secure Drew's money.

Jacqueline had paid the photographer with a check drawn on her recording company's account, but it had bounced. The photographer was more than willing to disclose that Jacqueline had not made good on the check.

"So you see, cuz, it appears as if the lady has money problems. What I don't understand is why. It's been rumored that her company is raking in the dough."

Gwen leaned closer to be heard over the incessant babble of voices at the Harvard Book Store Café. Lunch at the popular dining establishment was always like a family reunion. You never knew who you would meet and everyone appeared to talk at once.

"Maybe Jacqueline's company needs an audit," Lauren mused aloud.

"I know a sex muffin at the IRS who just might like to look into a certain record company's books, if you know what I mean," Gwen suggested.

If the situation hadn't been so serious Lauren would've laughed. Gwen Taylor knew more sex muffins and biscuits in more places than she had fingers and toes.

Lauren opened her mouth, but Gwen held up her hand. "Say no more, cousin. Consider this a done deal."

"How can I thank you, Gwen?"

Gwen leaned over and hugged her cousin. "Get me an interview with Caleb Samuels."

Lauren hugged her back. "Done."

Gwen's smile faltered. "Are you certain he'll agree to it? You know he's never agreed to be interviewed. That's why there's always been so much made-up gossip about him."

"I'll get him to change his mind," Lauren promised.

"It's like *that?*" Gwen retorted, shifting her eyebrows.

"Yes, it is, cuz," Lauren said smugly.

"Well, girl, I must say you really have it going on if you can accomplish this feat." Gwen glanced down at her watch and gasped. "If I don't hurry I'm going to be late for a departmental meeting."

"I'll drop you off," Lauren offered.

"Thanks." Gwen gathered her handbag and leather-bound notebook.

Lauren drove Gwen back to the *Boston Gazette* building, thanking her again for all of her help. Gwen shrugged it off with a wave and a smile.

"Don't worry, cuz. It's just about over."

The four words echoed in Lauren's head as she turned her car in the direction of North Grafton. It had to be over so that she and Cal could live their lives without the invisible fears threatening to drive them apart, and she prayed it would be soon.

"Lauren! Lauren! Darling, look at the headlines!"

Lauren scrambled from the bed, not bothering to put on a robe or slippers. She met Cal as he bounced up the staircase.

He eased her down to the top step and sat beside her. Flicking open the *Boston Herald* he showed her the blaring headline: RECORDING EXEC INDICTED IN PIRATE SCAM.

It was enough. Lauren did not have to read further. The photograph of Jacqueline Harvell Samuels, handcuffed and head lowered was victory enough.

She stared at the photo of the defeated woman. "I feel sorry for her, Cal."

Cal raised her chin. "Don't, baby. Jacqueline brought all of this on herself. She just rolled the dice once too often and they came up craps."

He gathered Lauren in his arms, stood up and made his way back to the bedroom. She nuzzled her nose to his warm throat, inhaling the smell of the early morning air still lingering on his skin.

Cal dropped the newspaper on the floor by the door, then settled Lauren on the bed. Stripping off his robe, he melted into her outstretched arms, naked and wanting.

"Now, we're truly free," Lauren breathed into his mouth.

Cal moaned and entered her willing body. Yes, they were free; just like the characters in his book, they had shattered their bonds to find the freedom to live and love for future generations of proud African descendants.

Epilogue

"Mr. Samuels, can you hold your daughter so that we can get a family shot?"

Cal reached for the squirming eleven-month-old child. Kayla had just learned to walk and she did not like sitting still for more than thirty seconds.

"Drew, please stand next to your mother," the photographer directed softly.

Drew leaned against Lauren's shoulder as she sat on the wicker love seat.

Cal managed to catch and hold onto Kayla, although the child protested loudly against his firm hold on her body.

He tossed her high in the air, then whispered in her ear. The petite, golden-eyed girl giggled uncontrollably.

"Let's do it now," Cal called to the photographer as he sat down beside Lauren.

The photographer got off three frames before Kayla's giggles vanished. "Wonderful. Thank you very much."

Drew fidgeted with his white bow tie. "Can I change now?"

"Yes," Lauren and Cal replied in unison.

"Da-da, Da-da," Kayla repeated in a rhythmic singsong, patting Cal's face with her tiny hands.

He kissed her forehead. "You want to change, too?" They all moved inside the house.

"Ma-ma, Ma-ma," Kayla cried, holding her arms out to her mother.

Lauren took her daughter from Cal, smiling. "I know what kind of changing she needs."

"She never wants me to change her," Cal said, taking off his jacket and tie.

"That's because you don't sing to her," Lauren said over her shoulder as she started up the staircase.

Cal stood at the foot of the staircase, watching Lauren ascend slowly with their daughter cradled gently in her arms.

Their home was filled with family and friends—well-wishers who had come to help him celebrate the success of his latest book. It had made it to first place on all of the major bestseller lists.

Cal had dedicated this book to Lauren and their own captive hearts, knowing when he sat down to write it that she had already captured his heart many years before on a private island in the Caribbean.

"Caleb."

He glanced up at Lauren standing at the top of the staircase. "Yes?"

She offered him a shy smile. "The next one is going to look like me."

She walked away, leaving him with his mouth gaping in

shock. He sank down to a step, laughing. Lauren always thought of the most unorthodox ways of telling him that he was going to be a father.

He was still laughing when Roy Taylor came to tell him that everyone was waiting for him to say a few words.

Cal stood up, whispered the latest news in Roy's ear and the two men shook hands and pounded each other's backs.

"I must say that you turn out some beautiful children," Roy complimented.

Cal patted his father-in-law's back again. "Why thank you, Roy."

"Don't give him all of the credit, Daddy. He couldn't do it without my help."

Both men turned at the sound of the throaty feminine voice. They were not aware that she had silently come down the stairs.

"And don't you ever forget that, *precious*," she added, flashing Cal a sensual smile.

"I won't, *precious*," he replied, taking Kayla from her mother's arms and setting her on her feet.

Lauren and Cal lingered before going out to the patio to join their guests.

"Did I show you how much I loved you today?" Cal crooned against her ear.

"I don't think so," Lauren answered gently. "But I'm not opposed to a demonstration. Later, that is."

"Then later it will be."

Lauren and Cal had many more times and many more years to prove their love to each other—again and again, over and over.

ROCHELLE ALERS

Rochelle Alers has been hailed by readers and booksellers alike as one of today's most popular African-American authors of women's fiction. With nearly two million copies of her novels in print, Ms. Alers is a regular on the Waldenbooks, Borders and *Essence* bestseller lists, and has been a recipient of numerous awards, including a Golden Pen Award, an Emma Award, a Vivian Stephens Award for Excellence in Romance Writing, a *Romantic Times BOOKclub* Career Achievement Award and a Zora Neale Hurston Literary Award. A native New Yorker, Ms. Alers currently lives on Long Island. Visit her Web site www.rochellealers.com.

KIMANI
ROMANCE

Bestselling author
Brenda Jackson
introduces
the Steele Brothers
in a brand-new
three-book miniseries

Solid Soul

by **Brenda Jackson**

COMING IN JULY 2006
FROM KIMANI™ ROMANCE

Love's Ultimate Destination

Visit Kimani Romance at www.kimanipress.com

KRBJSS

KIMANI
ROMANCE

Take a trip inside the exclusive world of gentleman's clubs, where a cocktail waitress is more than what she seems...

The patrons of a swanky gentleman's club know her as Jackie Parks, but can local mogul, Warren Holcomb, see past the legendary long legs to see what lies beneath?

her secret life

by Gwynne Forster

COMING IN JULY 2006
FROM KIMANI™ ROMANCE

Love's Ultimate Destination

Visit Kimani Romance at www.kimanipress.com

KRGFHSL

KIMANI
ROMANCE™

"PLAY WITH BAD BOYS, BUT DON'T TAKE THEM HOME."

Jen St. George has always
lived by this one simple rule.
Will fast-moving bad-boy,
Tre Monroe, prove her wrong?
Is true love possible in…

FLAMINGO PLACE
by Marcia King-Gamble

COMING IN JULY 2006
FROM KIMANI™ ROMANCE

Love's Ultimate Destination

Visit Kimani Romance at www.kimanipress.com

KRMKGFP

KIMANI
ROMANCE

SEX, LIES, BETRAYAL...

To hide his growing attraction to his
new employee, Carlton Harrington, III
makes Latonya Stevens work long,
hard hours. But late nights spent at
the office together make denying their
mutual attraction impossible.

DOES THEIR LOVE
STAND A CHANCE?

If Only You Knew
by Gwyneth Bolton

COMING IN JULY 2006
FROM KIMANI™ ROMANCE

Love's Ultimate Destination

Visit Kimani Romance at www.kimanipress.com

KRGBYK